Born in Ireland, the land of the storytellers, JP Fox began writing as a personal challenge more than anything else. Inspired by his daughter's idea for a children's book with illustrations, he wondered if he could write a story. After three months, he had 100,000 words. From then on, manuscripts piled up in a bottom drawer. He gave little thought that his stories might end up on someone else's bookshelf.

In his leisure time John enjoys woodcraft, watching snooker on YouTube, and loves a good courtroom drama.

JP Fox

Endless Winter

AUSTIN MACAULEY PUBLISHERS™
LONDON * CAMBRIDGE * NEW YORK * SHARJAH

Copyright © JP Fox 2023

The right of JP Fox to be identified as author of this work has been asserted by the author in accordance with sections 77 and 78 of the Copyright, Designs and Patents Act 1988.

All rights reserved. No part of this publication may be reproduced, stored in a retrieval system, or transmitted in any form or by any means, electronic, mechanical, photocopying, recording, or otherwise, without the prior permission of the publishers.

Any person who commits any unauthorised act in relation to this publication may be liable to criminal prosecution and civil claims for damages.

This is a work of fiction. Names, characters, businesses, places, events, locales, and incidents are either the products of the author's imagination or used in a fictitious manner. Any resemblance to actual persons, living or dead, or actual events is purely coincidental.

A CIP catalogue record for this title is available from the British Library.

ISBN 9781398425521 (Paperback)
ISBN 9781398425538 (ePub e-book)

www.austinmacauley.com

First Published 2023
Austin Macauley Publishers Ltd®
1 Canada Square
Canary Wharf
London
E14 5AA

Winter seemed endless.

And just as the first daffodils of the new spring showed their vibrant yellows to the surrounding landscape, the winter gave out a final, selfish display of its power and struck the flowers with a chill frost as if to prove that it still held dominance over the other seasons.

One

Ordinarily, Ben's thinking leaned towards the opinion that wintertime was the season when sensible people stayed indoors and built huge log fires and watched television or read of new bridges or the latest concept in skyscrapers or, as Elizabeth had encouraged him, to be more daring in his reading choices, to travel across the world's oceans and terrains via atlases and biographies, follow the footsteps of famous explorers Jacques-Yves Cousteau or Burke and Wills.

When Elizabeth became sick, he would often join her on the veranda during his days off and on weekends. For reasons he couldn't figure out, Elizabeth took to the outdoors more often, despite the weather. He didn't delve into her rationale; he assumed it was down to her illness that gave her a different slant on life and living. Unless it was pouring the heavens down, she would—as often as her homely duties, or her well-being, allowed—aim for the back porch or the garden as her preferred place to be.

She wasn't a great gardener, more of a learner, but she loved what she did. It was *not* Ben's personal choice to sit in near-arctic conditions, as he viewed winter, but out of love for her he joined her; only after donning several jumpers and a parka. He remembered how she swapped anecdotes with him about his inferior metabolism and thin blood, and how he needed to build himself up for a *real* cold snap.

As he ventured into the frigid air, the best the veranda could offer, he reflected on Elizabeth's humorous digs at him and despite the warm memory of her laughing face, his lips could muster up the thinnest of smiles. A robin appeared on the paint-worn wooden rail barely six feet away and eyed the man wrapped up in layers of garments that helped to ward off the thick, frost-laden, creeping air. The only parts of his body uncovered were his eyes, nose and the upper part of his mouth, showing a thick black moustache from razor neglect. The rest of his body was resolutely wrapped in winter woollens. He looked to the wrought-iron table beside him for a piece of bread. Elizabeth *always* had a morsel for the birds.

The table was empty save for a half-filled bowl of ice. Not even a drop of water to offer the little fellow, he thought. Elizabeth would not have been so remiss! The little creature hopped back and forth on the rail, unperturbed by the absence of crumbs. Ben thought the robin showed no signs of offence whatever; rather the bird's merrily hopping about was a sign of gratitude for all the times Elizabeth *had* made provisions for it and the rest of his avian friends.

Ben purposely sat in the chair she used to occupy. He shifted and nestled into the shape of the chair. The memory of a sweet aroma filled his nostrils, the unique scent that belonged to Elizabeth. More memories flooded back. He felt he could reach his hand out and find her fingers caressing his; he closed his eyes and savoured the moment. Reality made it only a fleeting glimpse before salty water welled up in his pained, dark-ringed and sleep-deprived eyes. In the short-lived mental recall, he saw her clean eyes and infectious grin: the eyes that were fresh and gentle, the smile that reached out to others and invited them to share hers. Especially did he love the frequently-made symmetrical hollows her smile created on her soft cheeks. How often he had kissed them.

He sprung his eyes open and aimed them where he expected her to be; standing before him and holding their infant girl on her hip. Instead, he found a hazy sun striving to climb above the young hawthorn bush they planted four years earlier, before Stephie came along. The tears flowed easily at first when he recalled the excitement she showed on seeing the tree produce its brand-new petals of pink-red among a sea of tri-fingered dark-green leaves.

Tears flowed fast and hard knowing that she would not see the colours of the spring again, nor would he have the pleasure of soaking up her joy. He wept out loud, his chest heaving in sympathy with his aching heart, his tears meeting up with the flow of the incoming tide in the distance. He felt they would not abate until ebb tide, or maybe not at all, so overwhelmed was he with the loss of his first and only love. How he hated that cruel ocean!

The robin flew away.

Was the sociable bird responding to his tears and couldn't bear the sorrow, couldn't share the grief? Ben was sure that's how Elizabeth would have reasoned, anyway, although the birds didn't fly away when *she* tended their daily needs. *She* didn't stir up sadness in any person nor any creature. It was not in her nature.

His thoughts transferred voluntarily to a happy time he spent with her, in the cool of late autumn, on the veranda overlooking the sea. Elizabeth used to sit and watch the many subtle movements of frothed waves drifting towards the shore, sometimes dying before they reached any size at all. She wondered where they came from to reach their final destination. And while she pensively raised the question, she really was pondering her deeper thoughts aloud, as if querying the whys and wherefores of life.

She would ask quietly: Had these little waves explored the world's oceans, enjoyed the whole experience, left a little ripple in oceanic history and then died an unobserved death in a small obscure cove? Like a salmon ends its existence after an unforgiving voyage from universal waters to a familiar stream in the mountains, finally shedding the next generation of eggs before surrendering to nonentity?

Ben remembered the occasion when he left to make a hot cup of tea, and butter the scones Elizabeth made the previous evening; he noted a worrisome frown spread across her face. Taking no particular notice of it at the time, he put it down to part of her on-going musings on the reasons for life, especially a life shortened by tragedy fatale. He wished he had shown more interest, wished she had invited him into her thoughts.

How could he have known what the next day would bring?

Stephie's chubby face flashed before him for the millionth time during the last few months. He could see her eyes skipping about under her eyelids when he checked on her while the kettle boiled and the scones warmed in the microwave. Fast asleep and clearly in childhood dreamland, the two-year-old sorted out experiences and knowledge gained in the previous twenty-four hours, slotting into memory cells that make sense only to infantile order. Under his breath, he heard his own words repeat how beautiful she looked, just lying there, so innocent and perfect. His mind played back her lovely eyes, a near copy of her mother's; her round face, a reproduction of her grandfather's cheery features.

His daughter got all her looks from Elizabeth's side of the family, he almost regretted, but in retrospect, he thought, with a father's pride, Stephie would have grown up with his quick brain and partiality for mathematics. He wept again for his child. She would never see the inside of a school nor learn of how numbers relate to the world around her or where Kenya or Peru is; she would never know why the wind blows or the need for forests on hillsides. Nor would she go through puberty or give her parents trouble as a teenager; nor fall in love nor marry nor produce grandchildren for her parents to be proud of and visit often.

Again, Ben became agitated by the negativity his reclusive thoughts punished him with. His mother had lovingly warned him about isolation, that it wasn't good for him. And through his mother his doctor encouraged him to connect with his family and friends during his awful term of grief and loss; that time *would* come to his rescue, that he *would* feel better, that he was strong enough to cope with the deep hurt. Ben doubted all their opinions.

'What do they know of my pain?' he convinced himself on a daily basis, that he alone understood the gnawing, grinding ache that mercilessly invaded all his organs and spilled over into abject anger at all segments of society that offered no reprieve, no solace. There were days he hated himself for being so angry, especially towards his mother. She did *not* deserve such treatment from a son who owed her so much. No, not for a mother who put her own grief to one side while she guided her only son, her only child, through the painful aftermath of his father's tragic death.

In his teenage years, the time of life when a boy needs the manly, fatherly role model for reassurance, for comparisons, for ease into manhood, Ben's father took no part. A wild youth with a learner's permit, too much alcohol and a few of his pals urging him to test the car for speed, made sure of that. His father survived in an unconscious state for several hours before succumbing to 'too much damage to his insides', as the surgeon tactfully explained, or tried to, at least.

Ben recalled the emptiness, the numbness that swept through his body in the taxi home from the hospital. Even the normally warm, maternal hug his mother gripped him with offered him no amnesty from the void that filled his chest cavity. He felt angry with his father for being in the wrong place at the wrong time. At night in his bed, he poured out voluminous hatred on the boy who took a fearsome weapon in the shape of a small car and stampeded the life out of his dad. The same boy was released from a correction centre, having paid for his foolishness at the expense of taxpayer's money, and then got straight behind the wheel of a new car, courtesy of his parents.

They were thrilled to have their son released earlier than anticipated and rewarded him with another weapon of destruction, believing incarceration had taught him a valuable lesson: that he would *never* drive drunk again. Due to overcrowding in the prison, but not given as a reason, the warden scrawled his

Parker-driven moniker across a document that suggested a pattern of 'good behaviour', the warden's way of finding spaces for the next intake of juvenile criminals. What his parents *did not* see, mainly because their favourite son had not shown it or felt it, was a sign of sorrow for his youthful error.

Nor did Ben or his mother ever receive an apology from the convicted teenage drunk or his parents, neither before, during or any time after the trial. For years, Ben tried to get his head around the fairness in sending a person to prison for six months for taking the life of another person. Even now, nearly twenty years later, the judgment handed down remained a thorny impasse, one that remained difficult to deal with. And now with Elizabeth and Stephie gone, and with no one to take the blame for their deaths, the persistent impasse, the absence of justice, cut a deeper groove in his sensibilities.

He got up suddenly and frightened a thrush. The bird had landed on the table in search of a bite and had not discerned the camouflaged figure in winter greys. The young bird startled him as he startled the bird; he questioned why he stood up so abruptly. Somewhere in the coldness, a rhythmic hammering banged inside his brain. The noise could have come from anywhere, so dislocated was he from the world beyond his sadness. He listened consciously. He gave more attention to the tap-tapping and having identified that it came from the metal gate at the side entrance—until it morphed into his mother's voice calling out his name.

'Ben! Benjamin! Are you there?' Rosa Tavistock called out sharply, her voice teetering on the border of agitation. Ben turned his attention in the direction of the shrill sounds. His mother, his ever-faithful mother, had come to cheer him up. Sucking in a deep breath, he resigned himself to letting her in. What he didn't want was more encouragement to mix with people and 'heal' among friends and family instead of remaining isolated and morose. But it was also hard for him to ignore his mother as though she didn't matter, as though her tender concern had no merit whatever.

He couldn't deny the support she had been to him in his growing up years without his father. Imagining that suffering such pain was unique to him and him alone, one day his mother spoke sharply to him that *she* had lost the man she loved as well. It was a turning point in his sorrow; it gave him a new perspective on pain and he began to reciprocate the hurt with her. Their relationship entered a new level when feelings aired and shared brought them closer.

In his early twenties, when he brought girls home to meet his mother, Rosa was able to direct and advise him accordingly. The last girl he brought home was

Elizabeth. Instantly, the two women had liked each other. Elizabeth was the only girl he brought home after that. She and Ben were married twelve months later.

Unlocking the gate, he did just enough to acknowledge his mother's existence and led her back to the porch and through the French doors. No words were exchanged. In the kitchen, Rosa gave him a warm and tender look and a strong hug; it replaced the words she wanted to say to him. She went straight to the kettle and filled it, then took a plastic container of homemade vegetable soup from a shopping bag and loaded it into the microwave. Ben removed some of his clothing and put a few logs on a neglected fire. He loved a roaring fire at any time, even though the radiators oozed sufficient heat to keep most people comfortable.

He obeyed his mother's order to sit down. She placed the steaming soup before him and a hot cuppa for her. In between the gaps she remarked how thin he looked; how he needed to keep eating well; that a shave would cheer him up. What she really felt was it would cheer her up to see him coming to terms with losing Elizabeth and Stephie. He made an acknowledgement of her concern. It came out as a grunt.

'I rang you several times this morning, Ben.'

He played with the spoon, moving it back and forward in the bowl, shifting a circle of soft carrot from one side to the other.

'You really must try to answer the phone, if only to let me know you are…alright! I worry so much about you, son.' She glanced towards the telephone and saw the receiver dangling over the edge of the table; the distinct beep-beep-beep singing its monotonous song confirmed Ben had removed it purposely; she decided to make no further comment.

'Carla asked me to visit her soon. Your uncle Simon is not getting better; his heart is starting to push against his ribs.' Ben responded with the barest glance at his mother's face. He raised the spoon to his lips and blew indifferently on the hot food. She shook her head when he put it back in the bowl uneaten, untasted. She tried to coax him to eat, but her words only irritated him. He wanted to bark at her for her interfering in his personal loss and for trying to dictate to him when and how he should get over it. He knew he was exaggerating her well-meant mother-concern; that she wasn't really the domineering type, and deep down he knew she was truly distressed over his ordeal. He cushioned his annoyance with the pretext that he wasn't hungry right now.

'I had a piece of toast earlier, Mum. Really, I'll heat this up again… later, when I feel like it.'

Rosa resigned herself to the stalemate once again. It was clear that her son was spiralling downhill in his depression. She asked him between sips was he taking the tablets Dr Ames prescribed for him, and did he need a prescription filled. Ben snapped at her.

'Please, Mum! Stop! I'm not depressed! I'm *hurting*! Can't you see that? I've lost the two people that gave me reason for getting up in the morning. The loves of my life that made me whistle on my way to work; to sing and skip about with so much happiness that it made others jealous…' He stopped and bit his lip in a vain attempt to control the emotion that swept over him as an overwhelming wave swamps a little boat.

He sobbed uncontrollably, his arms flailing left and right as though searching for a place to settle, a rope to cling to for safety, a lifebuoy to hang onto in his emotional storm. Covering his face with his hands, he wept bitterly on the tablecloth. He tried to speak but his sobbing blocked his air pipe; partial words came out. Had his mother been able to decipher his anguish she would have heard him gibber about saving his wife and child from the malicious waters that first sapped their energy and then saturated their lungs; stole their lives like a kidnapper steals for a ransom. But instead of money, the sea wanted his happiness snuffed out, as a downpour extinguishes a warm fire. That was the price he paid, whether the demand was real or imagined. He would rather have given his life for theirs.

If only someone had asked him.

Rosa Tavistock bore the pain, not just for her personal loss of Elizabeth and Stephie, but also for her son's loss. She stretched across the table and stroked his hair with both her hands, trying to inject some comfort into her boy, but the moment was too much for her; she felt useless as a mother to soothe his pain as she once was able to in his early childhood. His sobbing groans vibrated in her fingertips and quivered all the way to her heart. She joined him in his tears.

Ben continued to struggle in the turbulent waters of his anguish. Somehow he had managed to grab hold of a tiny hand and haul her little body out and drag himself and her onto the ocean's edge. The water burnt his eyes; his nostrils filled with salt; the spicy tickle in the back of his throat stung his tongue and gums, and made him gag. He raised his head from his mother's caress and wiped the tears that leaked past his lips.

Rosa watched him stiffen and gaze straight ahead. She thought he was about to say something profound, something that he had discovered about himself and was ready to move on from his grief. But he disclosed nothing of his thoughts. His lips remained tightly closed while he trembled. That horrible afternoon Stephie's little body was found on the beach was like a dream to him; no matter how many times he recalled the scene, it continued to be surreal. He remembered pushing his way through the crowd that had gathered and feeling they were deliberately blocking his approach to his little girl to prevent him from seeing her white face, her lifeless two-year-old innocent personality laid out on a bed of sand next to a slimy frond of green-black, tangled seaweed.

Rosa silently urged him to speak. More than once she begged him to let out his feelings, good or bad, angry or subdued; she would listen without disparagement or blame. He told her, often, *if only* he had been at home that day, things would have been different, likely they would have been together, then this whole grim reaper scenario would have not happened.

'Do you know, Mum, that Stephie still had red paint on her toes? Her shoes and socks were gone, but the nail polish Elizabeth painted on her tiny toenails a few nights before was still there. Bright red, scarlet.'

Ben spoke calmly, as though he was relating a personality trait Stephie had displayed to him just yesterday. His voice was tender in telling the anecdote, with the hint of a proud smile for his daughter's development. Rosa was afraid to comment in case he started bawling again. The doctor told her it was good for him to cry; it was a release of his tensions, of his anger, of his torment. Or, she was slow to speak because *she* didn't want to feel the pain of it all through his distress. She had her own suffering to bear.

At least she was able to talk to her friends, her doctor, others, and as hard as that was, it brought huge relief to her spirit. It also took the emphasis away from her distress, allowing her to sympathise with her son's. He had lost more than she had, but sometimes, yes sometimes, it was difficult for her to evenly divide or compare her personal loss with his.

'I loved Stephie so much, Ben, I…loved…them so much…I…I know I'm going to need help…to bear the loss. I can only imagine the emotional hammering you are going through. I…think we…we need each other, Ben?'

Ben managed a weak, counterfeit smile and rested his hand on his mother's, an acknowledgement of her request, but whether he could deliver was another matter. A week or so after the accident, he had agreed to stay at his mother's house, for her sake really. Preferring his own company, where no one could preach their brand of 'cure' for his pain, he returned to 'his place of grief', where the scent of Elizabeth and Stephie persisted. Staying at his mother's only lasted a few days. That was when he discovered the broken window in the bathroom.

The skin on his face, he felt, was tightly drawn, that his cheekbones protruded unnaturally, that the muscles that allowed for normal human expressions were in spasm, locked together by life's hand-outs. He thought he would never laugh again; that some *laugh manager* who doled out the stuff like medicine was doled out on a once-only prescription and now the medicine was all gone. It was like someone had taken away his ability to enjoy married life, raise children, indeed, enjoy life itself, like a man is struck in a hit-and-run and is left paralysed by the accident. He can no longer walk or run as he once did. The tragedy that took away his pleasure, his humour, his smile, took away his family, his happiness, his reason for living, in one devious, vindictive act.

How he hated that cruel ocean for mismanaging his happiness.

Instantly, he felt guilty for being so selfish. Elizabeth and Stephie would *never, never* laugh again! Anger surged into his chest and throat. That the ocean, the familiar waters that filled the bay in view of his home, would repay his sweet wife for her loyalty by rewarding her with such contempt! How could the very entity that Elizabeth loved—the sea, the waves, the boats that she let sail on her liquid energy, the multitudinous creatures that she sustained—how could the sea be so malicious?

Didn't the sea *know* that Elizabeth loved her many moods and marvel at her wonders? Did the sea *not know* Elizabeth was in awe of the setting sun on her waters, spreading its orange hues across its placid ebb tide? Did the sea not know that Elizabeth *appreciated* the cooperation between the sea and the sun to give pleasure to people; how her waters reflected the blues, reds, greens, and greys—the continuum of the beautiful variety of colours—of the sky throughout the year?

His mother watched his face tighten in contorted anger, his eyes narrowing in hidden disapproval, his lips taut over teeth ground together, vexed. She could not tell what he was thinking, but she knew it wasn't good. Not wanting to provoke a reason for his portrayal of anger she let it slide, wishing he'd allow his emotions to calm. Instead, Rosa aimed a forced smile at her son and let the moment find its own answer.

Would Elizabeth have blamed the sea for taking her daughter alive and disgorging the once happy toddler onto a heartless and cold beach dead? Ben agonised. Or would she have blamed the wind? After all, the *wind* stirs up the waters; the storm creates monster waves that capsize boats and sink ships; the rip wrenches inexperienced swimmers out to sea.

No! Elizabeth would not have made such accusation against the sea nor the wind nor anything else!

'This is all in *your* head,' Ben heard his thoughts echoing down a narrow tunnel of reality. He found himself at the end of the tunnel, forced to recognise his reasoning was faulty, despite the infringement on his view of justice, distorted or not. Elizabeth's fairness helped him to reach the right conclusion. He closed his eyes and wished she were beside him now, carrying Stephie on her hip, as she usually did when they welcomed him home from work each afternoon. Savouring the image for as long as possible, he covered his eyes with his hands to block out all knowledge of light from entering and so spoiling the vivid pictures of the two people he loved most.

It was too painful to keep watching, imagining. He became conscious of his mother across the table, a few feet away from his face, and wondered did she know his thoughts. Drawn to her eyes, he mapped her face, examining her features. There were features of Stephie around his mother's cheeks; her nose, too, was a reminder of Stephie's.

'Mum, have the police come up with anything else?'

Rosa was temporarily stunned by the sudden change in his demeanour. It took her a few seconds to adapt to the unexpected switch of emotions that reflected pain on his pitiable face, to a serious, matter-of-fact question on police investigations. All the information she passed on to him over the last few months clearly had little impact on him. Nothing, she concluded with a mother's understanding, could get past his broken heart. *Now* he seemed focused. Minutes, no seconds, earlier he was silently agonising over his loss. She stammered at first, to regain her composure, and then considered the question.

'Well...no. Nothing...nothing more than what Inspector Plinter said. Remember I told you, Ben. They...the police...called off any further investigation. Lost at sea...was their verdict. They said someone would come and talk to you...but it was too much for you at the time. The Inspector said he'd write. Have you checked your mail, Ben? I put the last lot on the sideboard...with the other letters.'

Ben glanced towards the living room through the glass panels. That he wasn't eager to get up was obvious, so she offered to get the mail for him; half way to the closed doors she turned to acknowledge his 'thanks, Mum'. She picked up a stack of unopened letters and several wrapped copies of *Reader's Digest* and one on bridges and roads. A letter slipped from the bundle and slid down between the timber top and the wall. Rosa stooped to retrieve it from the floor but she couldn't see it. She got down on her knees and saw two envelopes resting on the skirting board. Stretching in, she salvaged the letters from anonymity and placed the wad of mail in front of Ben.

He showed no interest in the envelopes that looked like bills and shoved them to one side as he fingered through them. Casually, he asked what she was doing on her knees in front of the sideboard. Rosa pointed to the delinquent letters, saying she retrieved them from the floor. The magazines he ignored and piled them in a neat stack on top of the demands for payment. He held a brown envelope, embossed with the police insignia, for an extended few seconds, then put it with the others. Elizabeth's name appeared on the next letter. He bit his lip to ward off any further flow and affectionately rubbed his forefinger across her name in the envelope's window, then passed it quickly to his mother.

'You open this one, Mum. Tell me what it says.'

Rosa searched for something in her handbag. She found a nail file and began to read. 'It's from a book club. Doubleday. They regret that the book Elizabeth ordered is unavailable at present…'

'What book?' he asked with heightened interest. Rosa scanned the page.

'*Oceans of the World*,' she shot out without thinking, and as if to punish her tongue for an inexcusable offence, she immediately grabbed her mouth and pressed hard against her lips. Ben leapt up. Once again, his hatred for the sea welled up in his chest. Rosa was taken aback. She stood up slowly. His face filled with rage and then the rage subsided, one part of his personality yielding to another.

'Elizabeth loved the ocean, Mum. I've been blaming the sea for taking her and Stephie. The *sea*! How stupid can a man get? She loved the sea; she loved nature, animals, the mountains, the natural surroundings. She has books galore on everything that hints of people and places, the earth's ecosystems… everything!'

Rosa leant forward to hold him. He fell into her arms and wept on her shoulder. Gently rocking him as though a little boy who had a cherished toy crushed, she attempting to help him overcome his loss. How she wished that's all it was; a toy, something that could be repaired or replaced. But who was able to replace Elizabeth and Stephie? Rosa discarded the thought quickly before she was of use to anyone, before she ended up a blubbering mess in her son's arms. It was *he* who needed the specialised attention now. Hers would come later.

But where could she start? After all, the police came up with nothing solid. Elizabeth's movements on that fatal day were explored ardently; everyone who had come in contact with her and Stephie came forward, from the time they left the house until little Stephie's body washed up on the beach. Some had brief conversations with Elizabeth. Others had marginal contact: a 'good morning' or a wave from across the street as the young mother pushed the stroller towards the town centre. Nobody, however, offered tangible clues for what really happened; and yet, someone out there knew and had not come forward.

And how? How did they end up in the water? Did Stephie fall in, somehow, and did Elizabeth jump off the wharf to save her child? Did she let the stroller go for just a second and turn to see it roll over the edge? Didn't anyone see *that* happen? Besides, even if it did happen that way, Rosa queried, as she did hundreds of times during the past several months, how did Stephie—she wept along with her son as she thought of her beautiful granddaughter's lifeless body on the sand—how did Stephie get two hundred metres from the marina?

And what happened to the stroller? It wasn't sunk at the quayside; divers found a supermarket trolley and other bits and pieces, but no stroller. Rosa stopped herself thinking on what *wasn't* discovered, what answers remained *hidden*. While the *unknown* disturbed her, it did her no good to re-examine questions the police had already investigated and had come up with nothing conclusive. The last person who *thought* she saw Elizabeth and Stephie—it could have been another mother and child—was Mrs Freda Oughter.

Freda had a reputation for knowing *everything* and *everybody*; the elderly lady believed the person she saw pushing the pram along the promenade *was* Elizabeth. When asked to positively answer, she couldn't say with complete certainty. Twenty metres or so turned out to be nearly forty metres when angles and locations were established. Anyway, it was a *fleeting* glimpse the old lady had, and had she not been startled by what she described as the noise of a car backfiring, she wouldn't have looked behind her to see the mother and child in the distance.

Freda complained she might have gotten everything wrong, being distraught by the news of the tragedy later and imagining there was a connection between the drowning and the sighting she had of the young mother and child near the bus-stop. Rosa had a vivid picture of Inspector Plinter offering to clean Freda's glasses for her. The old lady declined the offer. He did, however, draw out of her the last time she had an eye test. Apparently, she wore the same glasses for the last fifteen years!

What made things even harder was the rainstorm that followed. Before Mrs Oughter had reached home the rain drenched her and the tote bag she carried bread and milk in, and a packet of gingernut biscuits. Elizabeth and Stephie were very likely caught in the downpour, it was surmised. Possibly, Plinter had said, Elizabeth had lost her grip on the pram and it was swept by the strong wind, careered into the promenade railings, and tossed the child out and into the water. It was only guesswork, Plinter reminded her, but a plausible outcome in view of the available evidence. Rosa recalled telling Ben what the police had said, but she was convinced his grief blocked any or all reasoning or comprehension.

Ben drew away from his mother and thanked her for coming. Rosa took a seat again and he did likewise; he toyed with the two envelopes as though undecided what to do with them. He put one on the pile; the other was addressed with scrawled handwriting. On the reverse side, the letter B was written in equally untidy script.

'It's from…I'm not sure, probably Billy. It looks like his scribble. Yeah, must be.'

Rosa nodded, acknowledging it as the one hidden behind the cupboard. 'Billy wanted to see you, Ben, he asked me over and over. Then he stopped asking.' She thought before saying anything further, in case it made Ben feel bad about isolating himself. Ben vaguely recalled the door being hammered, the bell ringing, piercing his eardrums, Billy's worried, high-pitched voice pleading with Ben to open up, and he, wishing the caller, albeit his friend, *would simply go away*. He had a vague recollection of something his mother told him about Billy wanting to see him but couldn't recall what it was exactly. Something about his mother dancing in the rain and when Billy had taken care of her, he'd be over to see him.

At what point he disconnected the doorbell he couldn't remember, but its silence reminded him he didn't want interfering busybodies telling him how to deal with or how to overcome his pain. Taking the phone off the hook was the only way to stop them creeping into his domain, to extinguish their invasive voices blaring at him down thin wires, pounding his ears with offers to help, to console, to pity. What he wanted was *not* pity, *not* soothing words of consolation, *not* hope, *not* deliverance from mental trauma or heartache that time allegedly would take care of. No! None of these things! What he wanted was his wife and child back home, close to him, to hold and hug and kiss.

Two

'Will you read it for me, Mum?'

Even as he asked, his mind went back to the first time he met Billy. They shared a common denominator in their teens, which drew them together, slowly at first, but merging into a solid friendship. The death of his father one warm sunny day was Ben's loss; the departure of his father from home one rainy night was Billy's. Theirs was a long friendship borne of tragic backgrounds. Each lost their father in different ways at an early age.

Hey, you! Send the ball back, can't you?

The soccer ball, worn and discoloured from being kicked about on the hard tarmac of the school playground, came to a stop between Ben's feet. He looked up at the group of boys, most with shirts hanging out and all waving their fists and shouting names at him. In a daze now, having been in his unhappy world on the hard steel bench for most of the lunch-break, he left the sadness his dead father brought him behind and shook his head to revisit the present. Why are they calling me names? What have I done? I'm not even *playing* with them. He sat up from his slumped posture on the seat, confused, and asked, 'What?'

'The ball, stupid! The ball at your feet!' One of the boys roared; they mob-chided him some more. Ben looked down at the leather football and stared at it. A tall boy ran over and nearly tripped over his shoelaces, which made him even angrier. He berated the seated boy with a stinging tongue.

'Are you blind or what? And deaf as well! What is your problem?'

Ben made as if to stand up and explain but he couldn't stand up nor explain. The taller boy didn't wait for a reply to his rhetoric and bent down to pick up the ball. Ben automatically tapped the ball with his toe, unaware of the other's plan.

He kicked the boy's hand, forcing an expletive yell from him. Billy Turner pushed Ben, who thumped hard against the back of the steel bench, but he didn't flinch. Billy repeated his question, this time demanding an explanation.

'What is your *problem*, shorty?'

Ben stared up at him defiantly at first, then bit his lip and said: 'My Dad died.'

Billy looked sternly at him, then dropped his eyes. He faced the motley group of aspiring Beckhams and Ronaldos and after throwing the ball towards them, threatened: 'I'll be there in a minute. And don't forget, we're winning 4-3.' He sat down and eyed Ben for a few seconds before speaking, with an attempt at empathy. 'You must be *him*…the one the others were talking about. A car crash, wasn't it? Sorry about that.'

Billy said he found it hard to talk about *his* problem. It embarrassed him that others would whisper about him and avoid him if they knew. 'I don't tell everyone but my…my…my dad left home.'

Ben nodded sympathetically and asked, 'When?'

'Six months and two weeks…no, nearly three weeks now. My Mother drove him out, I think. They—she used to fight with him a lot, yeah, she gave him curry. Always picking on him, saying he was with other women and stuff. But I know that wasn't true; I was with him at times he was supposed to be with someone else. Then she started to accuse him of taking her son away from her—that's me. In the end, my dad couldn't take it. I hated him for leaving but that's mainly because he left me behind, with her! He's moved up to Scotland. I don't see him anymore. How about you? Sorry…I mean, how do you manage without your dad?'

'Not very well, sometimes. My Mum's great, though—I don't mean yours isn't—'

'Hey, don't worry about it. She isn't! I think she's got worse since Dad left. Talks to herself and that. And badmouths my dad all the time…never gives up. I wish I were older; I'd go up to Glasgow, maybe, or just find a place in London to stay. I have an aunt; she's not a real aunt. I think she's my Mum's cousin or something…in Manchester; she might take me in for a while. On second thoughts, forget that! She's as bad as my mother! That's what my dad told me, anyway. Runs in the family. I hear the guy is in jail?'

'*Pardon?*'

'The kid who…you know? The kid that knocked your dad over…that one.'

'Oh! Yeah…I…try not to…think of him…but he comes into my mind all the time. My Mum says I shouldn't…but he killed my dad.'

'What's your name? I'm William Turner. Billy for short. I'm fifteen. I'm behind in school. They kept me back to repeat a year. I'd rather be working on engines and stuff. My dad…we used to work on his boat but since he left, I fiddle with any old thing that's broken. I fixed our washing machine while my mother was out doing the shopping one day. She nearly took my head off, said I'd get electrocuted or something. She called the repairman but he said it was working fine and charged her for the service call. Mother could have saved that money if she believed me or even switched the thing on to see for herself, but no, she didn't even say thanks to me! After the man went, she said he was making eyes at her and said that all men were fools. She said I wasn't though. Said I was different—'

'Hello! Earth to Billy! You sure do say a lot. I'm Benjamin Tavistock. Everybody calls me Ben. Except my mother. She shouts 'Benjamin!' when I annoy her.' He attempted to mimic her voice but it was a woeful rendition. Billy kept going.

'Who's your favourite teacher? I don't have one. Well, not exactly true…I like the science teacher, Mr Blackton. He has a small boat. We talk about fixing things. Yeah, I like him a lot. He gives me the time of day, not like Waterson! He tries to bamboozle everyone with fractions and decimals and pi R squared, whatever that means—don't tell me *you* like him—oh, I suppose he's alright. I'd imagine he needs *some* fans to keep his head swelled up. Go on, then, you're not going to tell me he's your favourite, are you?'

'As a matter of fact—'

'How old are you, Benjamin? I've seen you in my science class. Have you got Blackton, too? I think he's the best. Don't you think he's a brilliant teacher?'

'Which question shall I answer first, Billy Turner?'

'You choose. It doesn't matter to me one way or the other. One thing for sure. Neither of us has a dad anymore, so we might as well be friends. What do you say?'

Rosa sighed within. She felt somewhat embarrassed being asked to read her son's mail. Firstly, because of an innate respect for privacy, and secondly because she had a fair idea what Billy had written. Billy *finally* responded to her suggestion to write, Rosa reflected, since he had no other way of contacting his friend, apart from breaking down Ben's front door. What should he say in the letter, he had asked her? She told him to simply say he'd be there for Ben. 'Remind Ben you were friends from your early teens and that *had* to be worth something; Remind him of your fishing weekends together and coming home with everything else but fish!'

As Rosa slit open the envelope, she recalled helping Billy put a few thoughts together, expecting words from Billy along these lines. Now, she felt, was a good time for Ben to hear these things, for it seemed her son was, at last, beginning to open up his heart to another persuasion: that there *was* life after personal loss, even after painful, catastrophic heartache.

The letter began by expressing his sorrow for the man, any man that loses such a treasure. That a man should lose a beautiful woman and the prospects for adorable children of his own was a tragedy no man deserved. Rosa scanned the printed page without relating its contents. It was not the words she read that started to bother her, as much as the intensity of the sentences, the deliberateness of the language he used. To Rosa, it seemed that it was almost poetic in its structure, the like of which a man would speak to his lover.

Rosa held her breath and her thoughts back as she turned over the page. She gave Ben a quick glance in order to ascertain his attention, to check whether he was curious or not by her delay in reading the letter out loud. He appeared apathetic, with only a surface interest in Billy's letter. She skipped to the last few sentences and decided that Ben was not ready for what Billy had written. She was aware her hesitancy was about to be questioned, as shown by Ben's raised eyebrows so she quickly made light of the contents and paraphrased Billy's flowery poetry, reinventing the sentiments to suit the occasion.

'Oh, you know Billy's way of saying how sorry he is for your loss, Ben. He would very much wish you would see him, if only for a few minutes. Do you think you are a little nearer to that? Might I tell him you will?'

Rosa felt the need to divert Ben's attention from the letter so she could read it privately, either to clarify her fears or squash them. She hoped her face hadn't betrayed any guilt and hoped he wouldn't ask for the letter. He answered with indifference.

'Probably, Mum. Just give me a few more days to think about it.' Rosa pointed to the bundle of letters and asked him did he need to pay some of the utilities. She said she noticed REMINDER in big red print on a few of the envelopes. He gave a procrastinating 'thanks' to the offer and fidgeted before his memory went into action to fetch his chequebook. Rosa was glad the diversion worked; the letter from Billy had begun to distress her. She slipped it into her bag as he turned towards the bureau, and covered it with her scarf.

This behaviour, she told herself, was not a true reflection of her personality; withholding information with stealth and creating diversions to detract and trick her son was not at all like her. Perhaps what Billy had written was harmless anyway. 'Maybe,' Rosa queried her reasons for being suspicious, 'maybe I'm being foolish. After all, I don't really know Billy's style, his persona, that well! It's probably normal to Ben, he knows him better than anyone.'

With that, she realised she didn't know Billy all that well, despite the long friendship he and Ben had together. She knew that Billy was more the mechanic than the academic, more of a doer than a writer. Yes, she does remember Ben telling her his pal was slow in some areas but brilliant in others.

Ben got the chequebook ready while Rosa read out the amounts due to BT, the electric company and Sky Digital. Rosa suggested he replace the phone on the hook and switch on his mobile, to which he responded positively at first, but then said 'maybe tomorrow, I'm not ready for much, Mum. Just be patient with me. I know I have a long way to go…if I can just get these…awful thoughts…from my mind—' Rosa stopped short of snapping at him, angered by what he might mean. She concealed her distress that his abysmal thoughts might mean another awful reality. As delicately as her emotions let her, she probed him.

'What do you mean, son? What awful thoughts? You mean about Elizabeth and Stephie? Are you reliving…are you imagining their plight in the water, son? Is that what you mean?'

Ben was hesitant to answer what felt like a barrage of missiles lobbed to flush out the enemy; the effect his mother's questions, however caring and innocent they were, struck him with interrogative intent. His lips quivered at having to explain his innermost horrors to another person, albeit his own mother, whom he loved dearly. His reticence lingered, partly hampered by embarrassment and shame but mostly by the shocking truth that he had gone appallingly near the perimeter of self-destruction. *Something he knew Elizabeth would never have condoned.* Her love for life, her desire to remain as active as she possibly could, was paramount, especially during her illness, and more especially to be there for her husband and her daughter.

'I...in one of my dark moods...I thought of ending it all. You must understand, Mum, I couldn't bear it...I couldn't! I still can't...it's so hard...my chest is tight... aches all the time...no let-up...ripping my heart...like it's going through...a shredding machine.' Rosa leant forward to comfort him but he avoided her hand. 'I'm trying to spill my guts here, Mum. Just let me be, can't you? It's hard enough admitting this, just let it come out!' He paused to stabilise his emotions and continued, commanding her attention but allowing his mother her dignity; she, in turn, respecting his.

'I was hooked up to the Internet one night. It was late, very late. I hadn't been sleeping much. I was very low, mentally and emotionally exhausted...physically drained. There was this group... a suicide pact was agreed upon...six of us. It was euphoric, Mum. Absolutely. It's difficult to explain the power I felt...a feeling so overwhelming, so irresistible that I...somehow all my grief, my aching heart...it disappeared.

'This...exhilaration...spread throughout the group. We all experienced it, slowly at first, and then it was...it was there. We all shared it. For the first time since...the accident...I was focused, I was clear in my thinking. Nothing would stop this... enterprise...this vision of serenity...' Ben paused to answer the concern on his mother's lips.

'Ben, *tell* me I needn't worry about you?'

'A date was set and a meeting place picked. The mode of death was unanimously selected—'

'Ben!'

'Mum! The meeting place was London. The weapon selected was cyanide. The date was...two days ago...'

'Two days ago? You mean—'

'Yes, Mum, I got scared and backed out. I came to my senses. Elizabeth wouldn't want it that way. I was in the deepest pit. I'm not out of it yet. I recognise the power of deep depression...the grip it can hold you in is... frightening.'

'I'm *so* glad for you, Ben.'

Rosa put a hankie to her cheeks. It drew a warm response from Ben; he gathered his mother in his arms and told her how sorry he was for the anguish he caused her.

'See Dr Ames, Ben, and get back on the tablets he prescribed. Seeing you cope is my greatest wish for you. All the pain I felt for your grief, and my anxiety will go away, once I know you are making headway.'

Rosa made an excuse to visit the bathroom. 'I'd better clean up my face before I let the neighbours see me.' The letter from Billy was far too tempting to be left unexamined until she returned home. Secure behind the bathroom door she sat on the edge of the bath and opened the letter. Now, she would read it slowly, deliberately. To try to gain a clearer picture, a fuller meaning of the writer's mindset, she read several lines repeatedly.

By the time she had finished the four-page wordy letter, she was convinced it was written to a *woman.* She flipped the envelope over and squinted to make out the date on the postmark; December 10, two weeks after the tragedy. The *timing* did not coincide with the suggestion she gave Billy to write to Ben. Straining her memory, she reckoned it was well over a month after the tragedy when she had encouraged Billy to write Ben.

Her face was pale when she checked the mirror; the tension was showing. She managed to cover her cheeks with powder, freshen her lipstick. At fifty-eight she looked well, inheriting her lovely skin from her mother. In the hallway, she met Ben with a bright and cheery smile; albeit put on for the purpose of disguising her true feelings, her anguish about the contents of the letter from Billy. Whatever joy she got from Ben's new and near-determined approach was partly nullified by the latest development.

'You should see to that broken window in the bathroom. The draught in there cuts like ice! It must be three months since the break-in.'

Rosa left with a promise that Ben would get the glass people in, that he'd open the windows and let some fresh air permeate the house. She said it was refuse collection today; she'd put the dustbin out, and she promised to come back later with bags for the vacuum cleaner and spruce up the house. And maybe, he would come and have dinner with her? She'd get his favourite; pork chops soaked in plum sauce. At the door, she remembered Elizabeth's mother called again for any news of Ben.

'Lucy Ackridge called. She asks for you. She hopes she can—I know it's awfully hard for you, Ben—she'd love to talk to you about…she needs to talk about her last… well, the last things you and Elizabeth…planned together. Lucy needs closure, too, Ben. I'm sorry! That didn't come out the way I meant it to.

You understand what I mean, don't you? Lucy was very close to her daughter. Please think about it, Ben. Goodbye, love.'

When his mother left, he went to the mantelpiece where his favourite photo of Elizabeth stood. The clock next to it read ten forty-two. Touching her smiling lips he gave out a mournful groan, spilling a little more angst from his heart. He imagined Elizabeth's soothing voice telling him he was making the right decision, that he would always have their sweet memories as he moved on in his life. His eyes switched to the family snap of the three of them, new-born Stephie in his arms, Elizabeth leaning on his shoulder.

He would always treasure the times spent with them, the two years when he and Elizabeth were husband and wife, the pregnancy that seemed to last forever, and finally, the two happy years they enjoyed as a family. Ben clutched the photo frame and felt his chest heave uncontrollably. Taking on Lucy Ackridge's pain, or anyone else's pain, was not an option. Other people's heartaches were not able to enter into his sentiments because there were no empty spaces left. His personal grief used up all the crevices where pain lurked. He wept profusely onto the hearth and when his tears subsided, he sucked in a confident breath.

Having confessed his self-deceptive error in thinking suicide was the only way to cure his grief relieved him of an enormous burden. It was as though he underwent a major operation to remove a blockage from his lungs; the culprit obstruction was eliminated and now he could breathe again. Now he had another chance at life, and although he still hurt from the surgery, recovery was in sight. Like a patient convalesces on the hospital bed and reaches to feel the raised scar tissue on his torso; nevertheless, it was only a matter of time before he would walk out on his own. For now, he had no more tears to spill. That's what he would try to convince himself to believe.

How he would handle not having Elizabeth and Stephie was another matter, but deal with it, he must! If he was to survive! He heard it said that in time the pain eases, the memory fades and new relationships are formed. 'What utter rubbish!' Ben spoke aloud, arguing against such a heartless proposal, finding his nemesis in the mirror. 'How could I *ever* forget Elizabeth and Stephie?'

'You won't forget the good things you did together, the memory of your pumping heart when you first met Elizabeth, the awesome pleasure in seeing Stephie come into the world! No, those things you won't forget. You'll always cherish them but the pain of losing them ought not to be endless, now ought it?

Ben stared at his reflection and kept his disagreement alive. He started to build up an intense dislike for the image that strove to twist things, to confuse his thinking and disfigure his loyalty to his dead wife and daughter.

'The pain may subside but it will never die completely,' he said sharply, directing his words straight into his own eyes, accusing the other of gross contempt. 'If I don't feel anything, if I don't hurt, it would be tantamount to forgetting them! Can't you see that?'

'Don't put pain and memory in the same basket, Ben. How fair would it be for you to suffer continually the pain of losing the people you love, in interminable anguish until you grow too numb or old to feel? How fair is that, Ben? That every time you think of the ones you loved, pain echoes into your heart's chambers! It would be like losing an arm and then having to undergo the awful throbbing pain, like some cruel surgical aftermath. How fair would that be? Give yourself a chance to separate your feelings. You will come through, trust me.

He dropped his eyes in submission, grateful for the advice but hanging on to his deep-seated view that he should feel *some* pain. 'I've heard of a man who lost his leg in a car accident and complained of pain where his knee used to be. See! That's proof!'

'Yes! That is 'phantom pain', but is not real pain where nerves are pinched or bones are crushed. The memory of the pain is recalled in the brain and feels real. It won't kill a person, however. It'll just make fascinating dialogue.

'You expect me to forget them? You want me to let their memories fade? Like the snow disappears in front of the sun, or the red rose that loses his scent and drops off the bush to become part of the soil, gone forever? Do you really expect me to let Elizabeth fade into oblivion, and little Stephie, too? Is that what you want?' He glared at his image in the mirror, demanding an apology for accusing him of disloyalty to his wife, desertion of his daughter.

'I'm not your enemy, Ben! We are in this together. No one is asking us to forget those we have loved. Of course, there'll be memories, happy ones, ones that will bring a smile to our lips, or make us cry sometimes. There'll be flashes of sadness, too, but not an overwhelming, crushing sorrow that devastates us, as if the pain had never eased! Warrior Pain doesn't have the authority to take out its sword whenever it wants to! That kind of pain is not normal because it is self-inflicted. No one should be exposed to that agony because they have the misfortune of losing someone to death, as though they were being punished for

not taking care of their family because they didn't give twenty-four seven attention to the ones they loved! Now, isn't that the case with you? Elizabeth didn't think that way. She wouldn't want you to think that way, either. Isn't that the truth?

Ben fought hard to demonstrate that *his* side of the mirror portrayed the real Ben, the one whose thinking wasn't altogether misdirected, that he still had a good argument for his feelings. Yet he couldn't repudiate the power of reasoning from his twin in the glass, especially when he brought Elizabeth into the fray. He tried one last-ditch effort to defend his fears.

'I could never love anyone but Elizabeth, so how could I possibly enter into a *new* relationship? How could I form a relationship with *another woman*, have children with *another woman*, bring *her* into the home that Elizabeth and I shared together? It's too hard to think about it! Will you not even concede that?'

'Of course, it's unthinkable! But are you expected to live like that indefinitely? No one wants you to rush out and marry. It's not like saying 'I do' to another woman would end your grief. That won't happen. Your natural grief has to find a resting place. Only then can you move on. You need time to heal from your pain; everyone does, whether it's physical or emotional. We all need time, Ben, time to fit back into as normal a routine as we can manage. Don't remain isolated; that's a real downer. Take advantage of family and friends to lean on until you are stronger…

Ben stared at his own image to allow his analytical tête-à-tête settle. He could not deny his own intelligence; that it made sense to come to terms with the solid advice his mother gave, similar to what the doctor recommended, that the woman counsellor from the police department offered him, that the man in the mirror presented to him. The inner need for personal pity from others was denied him by his continued remoteness, he now recognised, which left room only for self-pity.

Consequently, depression overtook him and armed him with a weapon to self-destruct. He thought, even whispered, how grateful he was for not yielding to his negative feelings, grateful that his mother kept coming to him, and despite getting no answer from the doorbell, from his phone or from the rapping on his window, she kept up her vigil for her son's sake. Having felt her concern, it replaced some of the sting in his heart. Instinctively, he went to the phone to tell her how much he appreciated her persistence, how much he loved her. He had to be content with his desire to tell her because the phone rang on and on, unheard, unanswered.

He decided to call Elizabeth's mother. Lucy was overcome on hearing his voice. Her tears hijacked the first few minutes. Her time, she emphasised, her every spare minute was pretty much taken up with caring for her husband, Gordon, who suffered a stroke several months before the tragic events. Lucy bemoaned the fact that his progress was minimal, if one could call it progress. She complained it was hard for her to cope with the succession of distressing occurrences in her life. First Jordan dying so young, then Gordon's stroke and now this—this awful thing with Elizabeth and Stephie!

Ben found himself trying to comfort her, saying that Gordon wouldn't die on her and lots of people recover from strokes. Whether it helped or not—the conversation taxed Ben's emotional reservoir. They talked for ten minutes, Ben purposefully selecting happier moments, special moments with Elizabeth and Stephie. Here he was advising his mother-in-law to be strong when *he* was the one needing reinforcement. Gradually, the verbal tonic seemed to work on both of them. Lucy felt somewhat better at the end of the call and Ben's desire to find answers about *that day* climbed to a higher level.

Going from room to room he presented a heightened zeal and opened every window to allow fresh air in. Heavy clouds outside didn't dampen his new eagerness, nor did the pouring rain diminish his passion for answers. The cold air from a winter that fought to cling to its power filled the house, rushing down corridors and across walls and over carpets, exiling the stale air that had built up in musty rooms. Ben felt the breeze sweep through his body and all its chambers; he had awakened from the dark mood that kept him oppressed with grief, with depression, despair, and misery.

The worst, and longest, winter he ever experienced, he hoped, was almost over. The other winter, the one outside, was fighting hard to stay but knew it had to give way to the spring.

Three

With re-invented vigour, Ben threw on a raincoat and attacked the plywood he nailed over the broken window in the bathroom months earlier, removing it with more gusto than he secured it. On the phone to the glass company, he considered, for the first time, the oddity of the burglary. Nothing of value was taken, none of Elizabeth's jewellery, no electrical goods or other items thieves take for resale. His mobile phone was where he left it the day he went to the doctor, a visit he remembers, to please his mother, for he had no heart for his own welfare. That was the day he found the bathroom window smashed.

Ben struggled to recall the following day two policemen came, again by his mother's request, to check the house for clues the intruder may have left. He remembers walking torpidly through each room with the two men and his mother in tow, trying to care whether things were missing or not. It was easier to say nothing was missing than to try to get his head around the questions. *Didn't they know the important people in his life were missing: his lovely wife and his adorable child?* What else mattered, he remembered thinking; he didn't voice his angst on that occasion.

Why break into a house if not to steal? He argued, pulling the last nail out. *There were some nice things to take, too. Antique furniture inherited from grandmother, jewellery, an expensive DVD, the plasma TV, all good stuff. Why? Why leave the valuable things?*

'Yes sir, we'll be out soon. Our repairman is working in your area,' the woman from the *All Hours Glass Company* replied. He responded with a curt 'thank you'. What took up more space in his head was a decision to relive his tour of the house for things missing, this time with a fresh, no, a fresher mind, and a new pair of eyes. Starting in the bedroom, he was instantly appalled at the condition he found it in and quickly took the blame for his neglect, without scolding himself. He would leave all that behind and try to undo his negativity with constructive changes.

The sheets he literally hauled off the bed and threw them into the laundry basket. Next, he did the carpet a favour by gathering up a pile of dirty shirts and underwear, whiffy socks, and slippers that had gone way beyond their use-by date. In a short time, the basket was filled and placed outside the door. His mother would be surprised by the start he made to clean up the mess. Secretly, he knew Elizabeth would have been proud of him.

Animated by the exercise, a little glimmer of hope surged through his chest, and swelled into an optimism that now, *today,* might be the beginning of tidying up his emotions, too.

Maybe the burglar was scared off by…a noise, maybe a neighbour's dog? That would explain why nothing was missing.

Ben double-checked Elizabeth's dressing table as though for the first time. Her mobile phone gathered dust; Ben hadn't touched it in months. He remembered the detective asking him questions he barely heard or was interested in, even if he did hear. At the time, and vaguely, he recalled the Detective asking to see Elizabeth's phone; something about calls made or received; might throw light onto possibilities of foul play. The phone turned up nothing unusual, his mother said later.

Again, another memory of the policeman mumbling something or other; his mother interpreted the question about jewellery and money. Even now he wasn't sure what answers he furnished. If his mother hadn't been there, he was sure he would have been unable to think straight, let alone give rational replies. Now, he had to pretend he was the policeman asking the questions. Now that he was thinking a bit clearer.

So, Mr Tavistock? I know you've a lot on your mind, what with your bereavement and that. Take your time and look around. Do you notice anything missing, anything out of place?

He concentrated on her things spread neatly in front of the mirror. His eyes went from her favourite colour in among a colonnade of lipsticks to several shades of mascara in an opened make-up case. He touched the little bottles of nail polish and quickly pulled his fingers away. Elizabeth probably used that red on Stephie's tiny toes. Instantly their faces appeared in his head, clear and fresh and alive. He shook his head, trying extra hard to keep their images from his mind, but he couldn't, so he worked around them.

Must work through the grief, he whispered, forcing his thoughts back to Inspector Plinter's question.

Anything missing? Anything out of place?

The words rang in his head like he was too close to a dinner gong. His whole being responded with flagrant disapproval to intrusive, heartless probing that echoed down spiralling chambers to his middle ear. He wanted to scream at the policeman that, *Of course, there was something missing, of course, things were out of place! My wife and child are gone! My life is disordered! Does that answer your routine enquiry, Mr Insensitive Inspector Plinter?*

He put his hands to his ears.

How long will this anger swell my intestines?

Permitting reason to discipline his thinking, he reclaimed control. Plinter was imagined, nothing more. The question was a normal one; a job had to be done; the questions have to be asked. Ask the question, Ben. Take over the investigation. Seek the truth.

You do want to know what happened, don't you? You want to know, are the rumours true or not? Was Elizabeth so distraught with her illness that she ended her life and took Stephie with her? The room began to turn in slow circles. He fought hard to regain composure, at least a measure of it. As a climber clings to a vertical cliff face, gripping the wall for dear life, fighting a strong wind, an icy wind that would scrape him from his perch and plunge him downwards, so he hung on to his sanity. He had to maintain clarity of reason. What the papers intimated could not be true. Elizabeth loved life! She adored Stephie! The media thrives on gossip, anything to sell their product. Everybody knew that! So, too, was this fabrication part of the media hype. No one who knew her would believe such blatant lies!

The bed came to his rescue, to sit and collect his thoughts. The room stopped spinning. Plinter's question returned. It seemed less harsh this time, more bearable. He engaged with the dressing table again. The image in the mirror appeared surprisingly calm. He was grateful for the little chat he had earlier. It convinced him he hadn't succumbed to total despair, that he still had his sanity, despite his anger-lined sorrow.

Leaning over, he pulled open and closed the drawers one by one, skimming over the contents inside. Elizabeth's chair, covered with a soft floral fabric, was pushed into the gap where her knees would normally be when at the table. Pulling out the chair as Elizabeth often did (he thought he could feel the spot warm where she held the back of the chair), he sat in front of the mirror, running his eyes over the items, concentrating, trying to remember. He flipped open her jewellery box and ran his fingers over the various rings and necklaces.

Which one, do you think, Ben, the gold chain or this one? The sweet echo of her voice rose and fell in his ears. And he would reply, 'the silver one suits your eyes'.

Smell this perfume…now this! Which do you prefer? And he would usually say, *White Diamonds* smell gorgeous, mainly because it was her favourite, and besides, when she sprayed two different scents on her wrist, it always confused his sense of smell.

That was it!

He made a thorough search of the drawers again and confirmed his doubts. Something *was* missing! *Her new bottle of White Diamonds!*

Maybe it's in the en suite? He rushed in and surveyed every corner, every shelf. No bottle. Then where? He darted downstairs to the bathroom off the hallway. Nothing. The draught from the broken window cut across his face and made him shiver. Decidedly, it was time to shut all the windows; they were opened long enough to clear the air and send the mercury hurtling to match the temperature on the outside.

So, really, what's the problem with the missing bottle? She must have had it in *her handbag* when she left for the shops *that* day. What an obvious solution! Nothing mysterious at all!'

With each room he searched, he did so with the mindset that he wished he *could* report a valuable item stolen. At least the police could trace the item through a pawnbroker or however they tracked down stolen property. But no, everything was in order. Not even the diamond engagement ring was touched, and really, the only expensive piece he could afford to buy her. Elizabeth had complained the ring was a bit loose, that it slid along her finger and she'd be angry with herself were she to lose it.

Ben was to take it to the place he bought it to have it resized but forgot. It was still in her jewellery box; he saw it for himself. Oddly, the eternity ring he bought her was also loose but not enough to worry about, he remembered her saying. The day they exchanged eternity rings with each other leapt into his mind. It was an echo of their vows to love and to cherish, in front of the jeweller's assistant.

The chill in the house prompted him to flick the switch for the heating and having done that, he changed into fresh clothes. The rain had stopped when he opened the door to a sharp knock-knock from the man to replace the windowpane. Ben offered the tradesman, who introduced himself as Trevor, a warm drink. Apart from his mother, Trevor was the first real human he had seen in months. He eyed the tradesman awkwardly, suspiciously.

The man was a rough-looking character, older than Ben by ten years, with potholes in his face and looked at his customers through big black eyes. He had the habit of staring when he interacted with people, a practice that was not client-friendly. Trevor tried to remember that but he wasn't always conscious of his deficiency but he made up for it by the softness of his speech, and besides, he wore a nice uniform, green, like rich grass. Trevor declined the offer of tea, saying he was behind schedule and had tea and cucumber sandwiches at the previous job. Ben was amused by the man's answer; he could have simply said no thanks.

Ben was sure Trevor would have said yes had Elizabeth offered him tea and scones. In a very short time, the list of Trevor's peculiarities grew. It was more than he wanted to know about the tradesman slash stranger. The glazier made the usual chat. The weather. Local news. How did it happen? Meaning the glass. Ben said it was a foiled burglary. Trevor said Ben was lucky and proceeded to relate a burglary where the owner was not so lucky but then got lucky. Later the police caught the culprit, a known thief, when they found his wallet. Somehow, he dropped it; landed under the wardrobe. An honest housekeeper accidentally fished it out when vacuuming the bedroom, thus ending the burglar's two-year adventure in acquiring other people's property.

Ben had the crazy notion of checking under his cupboards. He dismissed the knee-jerk idea because *nothing* was missing since the would-be burglar apparently hadn't entered the house! Ben acknowledged it was a good story the glass man related. Trevor showed Ben the frosted glass and said he didn't have the same pattern as the broken pane and would it be alright. Ben said fine.

Heavy clouds darkened the room even further as Trevor completed the job; he swept up the debris he made and reminded Ben slivers of glass turn up long after the breakage, due to their size and being hard to see. 'Get your Missus to run the vacuum over it a few times. If your kids run around barefoot like my boy does, then there's sure to be big tears on little faces.' Ben writhed in a moment of mental anguish when he imagined little Stephie howling with a fragment of blood-stained frosted window pane protruding from her tiny foot. To save himself unasked-for trauma, he quickly thanked Trevor for his input. The repairman left with his cheque.

At first, he thought the man's comment was insensitive; he mentally berated the repairman for assuming there were *children* in the house. Had he not heard of his loss? Does he not read the papers or listen to the news? Do his friends not communicate with him, swap tragic tales with him? Or is his only interest in life, *glass*? And giving advice to concerned parents about *glass* particles ripping open toddler's feet and toes, as he went from job to job? Was that *his* job satisfaction?

Would Mr Tactless Repairman change his tune on child suffering if he knew Stephie was forced to swallow the salted tide until her lungs were saturated with the bitter and angry, surging, foaming, merciless waters of our local bay? Waters that one day were calm and inviting, surf that let the people who lived near her fringes, and strangers from far away, enjoy her liquid massage, and the next day raid the shores of normal, happy families and plunder their children, never to return them!

What would you think of that, Mr Glass Man!

In the dining room, he sifted through the mail once again and returned them to the neat pile. Four cheques in one day! The electric bill, the telephone, the TV, and finally the payment for the broken glass, all handled with the stroke of a pen. That had to be a record for him. Elizabeth usually took care of the bills. She was so efficient! His mind raced to her lovely profile as he pictured her adding figures and double-checking the accounts. He put his hand to his mouth to try to stop his chest from emptying a heaving sob into his throat, but he was unable to and let it happen.

He was glad his mother urged him on; he was happy she took care of the mail and other domestic chores, but now he felt he could venture outdoors to post the letters. The letter from the Police Department demanded his attention! Perhaps this was the follow-up letter his mother meant. It had Inspector Plinter's name at the top.

Dear Mr Tavistock,

I wish I were speaking to you face to face. I tried several times at your home before resorting to writing. I doubt if I could sympathise with you enough for the loss of Elizabeth, your dear wife and of your little daughter, Stephie, whether by the spoken word or through a letter such as this one. I understand why you couldn't answer the door or speak to me. I suspect your mother conveyed some of the information relating to our investigation of your family's tragic circumstances. The enquiry is finished from the point of view that we invited the public to come forward with any information that might help us to piece together the events of that day, November 26th, 2015, along with other inquiries by a team of detectives and constables. There was no evidence of foul play. Duty is laid upon us to inform you of the coroner's report.

The Coroner was left with only one option, i.e., to conclude with a verdict of death by drowning, therefore, death by misadventure, in Stephie's case. For Elizabeth, the coroner reached a verdict of 'missing, likely drowned at sea'. It is believed that Stephie got into difficulty, perhaps fell into the water, Elizabeth went to her aid, and died in her attempt. The other possibility is that Elizabeth had a blackout, and being near the water, fell in. These are offered as reasonable but speculative approaches to the accident in view of the lack of solid evidence, no eyewitnesses having come forward, if indeed there were any.

I cannot express my commiseration in terms that will bring you relief. Please, however, visit my office with questions that trouble you, or with any further information you may have. While the case has been suspended it is by no means closed. Should you wish to go over the case as we handled it, or to have a chat, I'd be glad to do that as a public service.

Once again, my deepest sympathies go to you and your mother in your time of grief.

CA Plinter, Chief Inspector

Ben had been neither emotionally or mentally well enough to keep up with the investigation. He sought solace with his own company, cutting himself off from the community. His only contact was his mother, who wasn't always welcome but who gave him snippets of information. Anything that included him to think deeply on matters he couldn't deal with. Snippets were all he allowed his mother to tell him and if she hadn't come at all, he felt in his direst moments, it wouldn't have mattered one iota.

Now, he realised, she was his lifesaver; a treasure he didn't appreciate during his darker hours. In a turnabout that even surprised him, the decision to take up Plinter's offer to go over the details of the accident looked more conceivable than earlier. And if he could manage it, he would follow Elizabeth's and Stephie's footsteps on that fatal morning.

It would take a certain kind of strength to do that but he believed he owed it to the two people in his life that meant so much to him. Being out of circulation at a time when he should have been more involved, he let self-pity overtake his grief, became unbalanced with his feelings. It was incumbent upon him to make up for lost time.

Four

Inspector Plinter was somewhat surprised to hear Benjamin Tavistock's voice on the end of the phone, but as usual, he took every development in his stride. The last he heard from Rosa, and that recently, was that her son was deeply depressed and had become a virtual recluse. Coping during the past few months had been hard, she had told the Inspector; Ben's depression had worsened and she felt useless as a mother to persuade her son that he should open up and talk. Plinter expressed his experience with persons plagued with depression, one who is so filled with remorse to the point of taking responsibility for the tragedy, one whose thinking becomes a burden to themselves and those close to them.

'You know, Rosa, sometimes I wonder why I do this job…police work, I mean. There's nothing glamorous about crime and criminals. We see the full gamut of people who find their names and activities on our paperwork: the hardened criminal, the ordinary person, young people, pensioners; people from all walks of life who either break the law or are victims of lawbreakers. Car accidents, boat accidents; lonely old people found dead in their flats, the TV still on, pouring the evening news into ears that have stopped listening days previously; domestic arguments and fights leading to injury, to wife beating, to child abuse.

'The list is endless and every day police officers face a multitude of scenarios that, over time, can harden them, harden their senses, and even numb their feelings. Some see the writing on the wall and get out before it happens to them; others stick it out, like me—and don't ask me why!—I suppose it becomes a *job* after a while…'

'You don't sound like a man without feelings, Corish. And believe me, I for one, am grateful for what the police do for the community. I can't imagine—well, actually I *can* imagine—what life would be like without law enforcement and the brave people who are in the front line of attack against crime. It would be anarchic, I'm sure of it.'

'It all gets down to people, doesn't it?' Plinter responded. 'People just don't seem to get on anymore and anyone who argues with that only has to spend a day in court, be it civil hearings or High Court litigation. People just can't agree! People just don't work hard to get on with others. To me, that's the biggest crime, not punishable by law, of course, but it would eliminate all sorts of problems were there greater cooperation. Don't you think, Rosa?'

'Yes, definitely! Much of it has to do with how well we teach our children. Teaching them right values when they are young, that's where it starts. When they are *young*. There are so many pressures put upon young people these days from outside forces. What with the attitude to drugs and sex, and the violence on TV that is portrayed comically in cartoon form or outright brutal murders in crime dramas. I really believe seeing violence portrayed so openly, so often and…what I mean to say, it…desensitises people, people of all ages.

'Young people—and old—are bombarded with these things on a daily basis, it's no wonder the crime rate is climbing. We both know that decency and respect for others must be started early in life if the desired results are to be seen in later life. Children need the right guidance; they need to have respect for themselves and for others. Parents have the hard task of teaching their kids good values. It means the parents, firstly, practice those values; otherwise, well, it sort of defeats the purpose, doesn't it?'

Corish Plinter had had numerous discussions with Rosa Tavistock from day one of the tragedy, and over the period of their acquaintance he came to admire her. He saw her as strong-minded but gentle; readied to support her son in a time of need; not bossy or belligerent in manner; and not demanding justice nor blaming anyone for the tragedy. Angered by it, yes, but contained.

Being the steadied intermediary between the police and her distraught son, Rosa used her influence to get information from Ben about Elizabeth, what plans she had for *that* day, whom she would see, what shops her daughter-in-law visited; all things helpful to construct a map of the missing woman's activity on that day. The detective found it easy to get to know Rosa because she didn't hide her persona, nor hold back from cooperating as best she could, in view of her own grief. If the Inspector were asked to summarise Rosa Tavistock in a few words, he'd have to say she was 'steady as a rock'. He liked that about her. Very much so.

'Ah! Mr Tavistock, Sir! Glad to hear from you. I hope you are feeling… a little better?'

'Yes, thank you, Inspector. I have to admit, though, I've had worse days. I received your letter and, eh, I want to thank you for all the good work your department did. The reason for my calling you is to take you up on your offer to answer a few of my questions. There are a couple of things that, eh, I suppose you could say…a few things that *trouble* me. It's probably nothing at all but I'm sure you can clear it up for me.'

'Certainly! I'll do what I can to help. I'm free for the rest of the day. Tomorrow I'm off to Spain for a well-earned vacation. Would you like to come in, say, well, shortly, if you are able to, and we'll…chat?'

'Ok, I'll come in directly. Let's say, 15 minutes?'

'Fine. Just ask for me at the desk. I'll let the Desk Sergeant know you are on your way. Eh, as a matter of interest, what is it that bothers you? I can give it some thought while I'm waiting for you.'

'As I said, it may be nothing, but here goes. When I went along with my mother to formally identify…my daughter's body'—Plinter waited patiently during the pause that followed. He could only imagine the torment behind Ben's faltering speech—'I…noticed some scratches on her body…a row of scratches on her right side. I…had a flash, a recall I suppose, of the thin lines of dried blood. Probably happened when her body washed across the pebbles or rough sand, yes, that was likely the reason.'

'Ok, I'll check on the autopsy report. Was there something else?'

'Yes. You might also check what it says about the dark area on her underarm and around her shoulder. My mother thought it might have been bruised from falling, or perhaps when Elizabeth tried to grab her from the water. At the time, I was unable to function normally. Today…I had this flash of memory. It suddenly struck me as odd, I don't know why, it just did. I was in shock for weeks after the tragedy, and…as you know…I was in a…a bad way for months.'

'They weren't *normal* circumstances, Mr Tavistock. You had a lot on your plate. I will look over those points you raise, OK? See you shortly, then.'

Ben grabbed the car keys from the hook on the Welsh Oak hallstand and pulled the door behind him. A strange awareness consumed him. He hadn't left the house by the front door in months; the need to readjust his thinking to the scene that met him besieged his mind. Even the air seemed different. To all appearances, nothing had *changed*. The houses on the street below his were the same colour as before, the same shapes. Nothing new or different about them.

Over the horizon of the rooftops, a line of toy cars moved in slow motion in the distance, along the road in front of the promenade and came to a stop at the traffic lights. Ant-size people waited at the bus stop to take them into town and disappeared inside the toy red bus that held up a line of vehicles. Elizabeth and he used to sit at the bay window and take turns with the binoculars and 'spy' on the little people walking their tiny dogs.

They played a silly game they called 'find it' and claimed it as their own invention. Each would pick out a setting below and give a clue, sometimes several, and the other had the task of locating the scene. Three minutes was the agreed allowance and they timed each other meticulously, to the last grain of sand in the egg-timer. And if either went overtime, then they had that much less time for the next scene. They joked about marketing the 'game', but reckoned it would be impossible to patent it. Their hillside position, two hundred and fifty feet above the ocean, gave them the vantage point to have hours of fun with other peoples' lives, where they were going and where they had been.

A large lump grew in Ben's throat as he robotically went in and out of reminiscent mode. Elizabeth is gone! He couldn't believe she was *gone*. She would never look through the binoculars again and laugh aloud in her unique, infectious way. Water surged into his eyes; he struggled to hold back his tears. Then he realised what the strange awareness was that overtook him. *He was on display*. Outside in the open, where he could be seen, where his vulnerability was on public view, suddenly he felt threatened.

For months, the inside of the house was his haven of private pain, his shelter from would-be comforters who knew nothing of the hurt of having one's family wrenched away, torn away without warning and having to endure the painful grip death has on one's every fibre. Losing Elizabeth and Stephie was far worse than losing his father.

The debate he had in the mirror returned. 'You are allowed to cry,' the man in the mirror the reminded him. 'The flowing tears take away a little more grief. Little by little, not in one swift retreating wave. Much like the tide goes out. *It is all right to cry.* But not be consistently overwhelmed with sadness to the point of destroying quality of life, of being denied life's pleasures, both for you and those nearest you.'

With renewed determination to keep his thinking forward-moving, he swept his wet cheeks with the back of his hand and stepped into the cool, damp air. The rain had all but stopped. It wasn't until he reached the Rover he realised the car hadn't been driven for months; the battery would be flat. He got in and tried the ignition switch. The engine growled once and died. *Ring Billy* was his first thought; he'll come with jumper leads and have it sorted in no time. Billy is always prepared for that sort of thing.

Ben recalled the times when they worked on his boat in the garage (Billy loved his boat. He said he inherited it from his dad but later he said his dad just left it behind when he went to Scotland). Billy said he found a lot of comfort working on his father's 'mini cruiser', as he nicknamed it. Oddly, Ben recalled Billy saying he felt closer to his father when he was in the garage, working on one thing or another. Unable to relate to that line of reasoning, Ben didn't ask why Billy felt like that, because *he* didn't have a special place where he missed his dad; there were many good memories, though.

Anyway, Billy was quite the handyman when it came to engine repairs. He'd be sure to get the car going. And besides he wanted to talk to his friend. A few things needed explanation, particularly his isolation. For now, the car was the main priority. He rang Plinter and told him about the failed car battery. Plinter offered to come and pick him up. Ben declined.

The policeman said, 'Come in when you can, then. I'll be here.' Next, he phoned Billy's house. His mother answered and said he was out somewhere. She didn't know where but he might have left home for good.

'He's always going out, that man! Never here when I want him! We'd all be better off if he stayed away!' Her voice was sharp and full of condemnation for her son but Ben knew the reason why. He was surprised she answered the phone in the first place. Billy said she had become fearful of picking up the phone in case it was her husband and she'd have to tell him to stay away from her, that she didn't deserve what he had done to her, leaving her to fend for herself, and she with a young child to bring up on her own.

'Should he come back, and I don't think he will, I'll tell him you called. Who are you? Who are you really?' she finished sharply.

'It's Ben, Mrs Turner. Ben Tavistock.'

'That name is not familiar to me. Does Billy know you?'

'Yes, we've been friends a long time. Since school.'

'School! You must be very old. William finished school over forty years ago! Or maybe it was longer… I can't remember now…'

There was a long pause. Ben respectfully waited. Mrs Turner was getting her son and her husband confused again, he privately sympathised. He recalled Billy jokingly referring to her as Sal Zheimers but Ben detected a barb on the end of his friend's tongue. Billy used to get cranky with her *disease*, believing she knew *exactly* what was what. The memory thing and the wanderings, he felt, was her way of getting his attention.

At other times, she lived up to the medical name experts gave her illness, a condition that placed her miles from home seeking directions from strangers but often taken as crazy, or a homeless woman, and ignored accordingly. Occasionally, someone who knew her would call the police, who would invariably take her home. More often than not, it was up to Billy to play hide and seek with her, frustrating the patience out of him. Other times he was convinced her forgetfulness was purposefully designed to upset him. Oftentimes she demanded her medication minutes after he had given it to her; other times she accused him of lying to her, saying he was *holding back* the tablets from her.

She seemed to have a fetish for the rain. Whenever it rained, she'd wander. Billy got so used to that feature of her quirky nature that he took an avid interest in the weather report and when showers were forecast, he'd keep her in sight, or, strategically, he'd lock her in her room for the duration. That was in earlier years when her actions embarrassed him, when he walked the streets trying to find her and having to call the police to help locate her. Now he stopped caring about the antics she got up to.

On the day Elizabeth and Stephie died, Billy returned from an errand in town and found her at the bottom of the garden—he told Rosa, who related it to Ben—dancing in circles around the rosebush in the downpour. It was later that day when Billy rushed over to see Ben, to commiserate with his friend over his awful loss. Ben was beside himself, emotionally unable to hear any apology or sympathy from anyone. When Billy left without seeing Ben, Rosa tried to explain why Billy wasn't over sooner; he had to tend to his mother: she was frolicking in the rain again.

'*I know!*' Mrs Turner blurted. 'That name, Tavistock! There was a young woman…wait a minute, will you? I have difficulty remembering. Elizabeth! That's it… I think. Elizabeth Tavistock! A good-looking child. She was here, you know.'

Ben wanted to correct her memory but felt he'd be banging his head against a concrete wall. He wanted to tell her that his true love and his darling child were no longer alive but the words died in his throat before the thought was complete. A surge of grief thumped his chest but he fought his way through the ordeal like a phobic stands up against his worst fears, meeting them head on.

'I saw her in the garden. I asked her to dance with me, but Billy said she was sick and wasn't able to dance. He always tries to spoil my fun. Jealousy! That's what it was; jealousy, unadulterated jealousy. He wanted her for himself! And she supposed to be married! A man should give a woman a ring, that's what I think…'

Ben reeled at the woman's injection of lies. He wished he could scream at her vulgar insensitivity and chastise her for having a disease that caused her to disregard human feelings. Her version of reality distorted by senescent dementia, however, didn't abate.

'She didn't look at all well, either. Serves her right for choosing to dance with him and not me!'

Ben fought hard to guard his ears against Mrs Turner's perverse words, but he couldn't. Instead, he forgave her mental absence and tried to explain his loss to her. 'I know you have a tendency to forget things, but my wife Elizabeth passed away…some months ago—'

'Don't fool yourself, mister! She left *you* just like William left *me*! We are better off without them.' The old woman broke into a melody of her own making, raising and lowering her voice in tuneless discord. Ben knew he had lost contact with her. Next thing, he took a sharp smack in his ear and yanked the phone from his head. *Must have dropped the phone*, he thought; *must have struck the table?*

Then he heard Billy's harsh tone ring out, snapping at his mother, telling her *not* to answer the phone. 'I've told you repeatedly, mother! Don't pick up the phone! If I'm not here to answer it, then leave it alone! Who is it, anyway? Some salesman trying to sell us something, as usual, I suppose.' He tempered his tone somewhat.

His mother said, 'It's *that* woman's husband. All men are fools!'

'Who?'

'Elizabeth's husband… calls himself Ben something or other.' She started to sing again; her demented sopranino squeal drifting into the bowels of the house.

Billy almost yelled into the phone. 'Is that *you*, Ben?'

'Yes, it is. Your mother is…she's a bit off today. I'm sorry.'

'Listen! It's great to hear from you. I thought we'd lost you—go away, Mother! Sorry Ben, she's back, trying to get the phone from me—' Ben heard what sounded like rubber soles screech across the floor, followed by the sharp crack of glass crashing on ceramic tiles. He figured they had to be in the hallway where the second phone was kept and the beautiful crystal vase Mrs Turner inherited must now be a thousand jagged slivers.

The woman screamed out: '…and…his mother…take…'—the phone thumped against something hard—'care of…face needs make-up…her hair…' Mrs Turner gasped, for more air to spit out her venom.

Ben worried for Billy and imagined that he was fighting to keep her calm but was doing it tough. *It's time I hung up*, he thought. The scuffle quietened to stifled whispers. Meredith Turner cried out again.

'Her hair needs a comb—' Her words became muffled as though a hand was placed across her mouth but she managed to stutter again, 'and her wrists… bleeding… …hates life!' Ben heard the sound of a door slamming; he wasn't sure if the next sound he heard was a key clicking a lock shut. Meredith's subdued screams no doubt came from behind the locked door, he reasoned. Must be a nightmare for poor old Billy!

The urge to put the phone down and let the family deal with their personal affairs without him eavesdropping was his next thought. Even though he knew Billy well and his mother to a lesser extent, he felt that every family should have their privacy; he accepted their right to that. Billy came back. 'Listen, Ben. Can I call you later? I need to take care of Mother.'

'Why, of course, Billy! I understand. My car battery is flat and I thought—'

'—and you need a kick-start! I'll be over soon…soon as I get Mother sorted.'

'I can call a mechanic, Billy…'

'…wouldn't hear of it, Ben! I want…to see you...I need to. It's been…so… long! It must be awful for you…not having…Stephie around, I mean. I'm sorry, you don't need reminders…I'm sorry. Look, I'll see you later and if you want to…to… talk, then we'll talk. If you don't, then that's OK too.'

―⁓⁓⁓―

Forty-five minutes later, Billy knocked on Ben's door. There was a brief moment when the two men stood awkwardly on either side of the threshold. The extended gap since they saw each other felt like a lifetime to Billy, but a blur to Ben. Although eye contact was in milli-seconds, Billy made snatching glances at Ben's face, unable to fix him with a solid stare. Ben stuck his hand out. Billy hesitated by first rubbing his palm along his trouser leg. He quickly stuttered it was dirty from handling the spare battery.

Ben pulled him inside and put his arm around Billy for a hug. The reaction was negative, Ben thought, but he quickly confined it to his own lack of response towards Billy during his dark winter months. Billy may have felt hurt that his long-time friend had avoided him and hadn't shown trust in him. Either way, Ben thought it better to express regret for his depressed state. Billy told him not to be daft, saying no one could blame him for reacting that way to his loss.

'Losing a child as beautiful as Stephie would make any parent depressed, Ben. Everyone…with any sort of feelings would understand your…despair and… sadness. You've no need to apologise, Ben. Not one bit!'

'Thank you, Billy. I need to phone my mother. Pop into the kitchen and fill the kettle. We'll have a cuppa.'

When Ben returned, having failed again to contact his mother, Billy said he'd much rather get the car going; he had a few things to attend to at home. Ben gathered up the letters spread out on the table to make space and put them beside the telephone in the hall.

They got on with the job at hand. Billy said they needed to get the two vehicles nose to nose so they pushed the Rover out and swung it onto the lawn in order to connect the jumper leads. Billy's mechanical mind automatically worked out the procedure. It was this approach with everything he did. When it came to fixing things, he was a natural whizz.

Ben had once told him he had an amazing brain when it came to engines, vacuum cleaners, radios, anything of a mechanical nature, and often praised him for his ability. When he repaired Rosa's washing machine, Ben said, 'You seem to know what's wrong just by the sound it makes!' Billy simply said all he did was to replace a faulty part, nothing spectacular about that.

Expecting that the battery was already dead, Billy put a voltmeter across the terminals as a matter of course and promptly decided to fit the spare one he brought. The engine roared first time; Billy grinned and Ben left for his appointment with CA Plinter. He thought for a moment on Billy's mood. It felt odd at first; he was usually talkative, often hard to shut him up. Restrained, even reserved, accurately described his manner, Ben concluded. He mentioned Stephie but not a word about Elizabeth. 'Maybe Billy thinks I feel a greater loss for Stephie than I do for Elizabeth?' He pulled up at a set of traffic lights at five minutes to one.

Maybe he avoided Elizabeth's name because he thinks I cried more for her than for Stephie?

Ben gave himself a dilemma he virtually brought on himself, *whatever* he imagined was on Billy's mind. *Did* he love one more than the other? Could he separate his feelings for them into two parts, two halves? Did he not love them the same amount? Equally? Did he love them in different ways? Someone beeped their horn behind him. He glanced in the rear-view mirror at the framed scowling face of *Impatience* deified. The green light glared at him, prompting him to force the gear stick into drive. At the next left, he swung hard and brought the vehicle to a stop in a parking space, forcing the handbrake back, not conscious of the clicking sound it made.

Realising he hadn't left the blackness that descended upon him in his self-exile from society, distress returned with a vengeance. There was no comfort from a steering wheel that soaked his sobbing cries and offered no solace to his heaving chest that was ready to burst his heart wide open. He heard a knocking sound and tried to locate it. The man in uniform was speaking but no sound came from his lips; his fingers waved in a circular motion while he knocked on the glass. Ben was reminded of the charades Elizabeth and he played when friends came for dinner.

What was this policeman trying to tell him? The clues the man in uniform gave were hard to understand. Elizabeth would have got them right away. She was very good at charades. She used to show Stephie how to play, pretending to be a tiger, an elephant, or a bird. Stephie learned well. She was quick to get the answers. Ben felt his face and looked at his wet hands. Tears were never part of the charade game! Elizabeth never played games to make him cry. Then it twigged; the man outside wanted him to wind down his window. He touched the electric button.

'Are you alright, Sir? You looked distressed. Can I help you?' Ben took out a handkerchief and mopped his face.

'Yes, I'm fine now.'

'You are in a designated parking space. Police cars only. Please move on, sir.'

Ben looked out and saw the sign for the police station on the ornate sandstone building. He was where he set out to be but now he didn't want to be there. How could he face Plinter in this state? He managed to tell the policeman he had an appointment with Inspector Plinter. The young copper said to pull into the gate on the left. 'You can park inside the compound, sir.'

The engine fell silent; he wiped his face again. The handkerchief was soaked. Stephie's cream dress was dripping wet, too. Her blonde hair was discoloured by the sea water and matted with sand. Whoever pulled her from the surf had the kindness to wipe sand and weed off her face, and pull her dress down to cover her body. Ben's thoughts transferred images of her into his mind and showed her little white, lifeless face aimed towards the sinking sun.

For all the world, she could have been asleep; her tiny features looked so peaceful. Missing was the gentle rise and fall of her stomach; the occasional twitch of a curled finger; the slight movement of her mouth; the blue eyes behind closed eyelids that could no longer see and sparkle. How could he go in to meet with Plinter feeling like this? Going home seemed to be the best thing to do. His house was, paradoxically, the safest place for him because it was a haven from his 'nightmare' stress, yet the worst place for him because it was where he experienced his darkest hours. He reached for the key but stopped to see Plinter waving to him from the window, beckoning him to come in. The decision had been made for him.

'Got your car going, I see, Mr Tavistock?'

Plinter didn't wait for an answer. Instead, he pointed to a chair. 'Have a seat, sir.' Someone knocked and muttered something Ben couldn't understand nor wanted to. Plinter said he wouldn't be interrupted.

The grey-haired near-retiree with fashionable glasses said, 'right, Guv'nor' and made no noise shutting the door. Plinter lifted a file from a tray. 'This is the autopsy report on your little one, Stephie.' Ben tried to stand up. The edge of the table came to his support. He wobbled a little and pulled himself erect, then promptly buckled at the knees and collapsed in a heap on the floor.

―⋙⋘―

'I called your mother, Mr Tavistock, but there was no answer. I'll try again in a few minutes. Are you feeling any better?' Ben nodded. The light-headedness from earlier persisted. The autopsy report flashed into his mind. He groaned. He couldn't remember giving Plinter his mother's number. Plinter waved the police doctor to one side and said he would make sure the patient got home safely. The medic nodded and left quietly and obediently.

The Inspector encouraged Ben to sit up on the couch, placing a cuppa near his elbow. Ben sipped on the hot liquid and asked, 'What happened?' And then he remembered the report on his child's death; *it* had triggered the blackout. He told himself he wasn't ready for such things. And where was his mother? She was always available to help out. And what did *that* woman mean when she said his mother's hair was messy, and what did she mean about her 'bleeding wrists'?

And, could she have *really* seen Elizabeth in the rain, or did she simply have a flashback to the wedding and saw Billy dance with Elizabeth, and got thoroughly mixed up? Did she see Elizabeth *that day* and no one believed her, no one even asked her? Is it because she is not considered compos mentis? That her state of mind would make her an unreliable witness even if she were near the 'accident scene'? Too many questions. Too many *difficult* questions.

Ben's head spun. He took the blame for the latest scenario. He *should have* hung up when Meredith Turner answered the phone. No one should have to listen to such drivel, especially from a person who had a history of 'crazy'. Hadn't Billy told him enough stories about her moods and idiosyncrasies over the years to fill a book? Hadn't he seen first-hand her eccentricities, that strange way she had of peering at him when he visited Billy's house?

'Are you feeling better now, sir?' Plinter asked again, not having received a positive reply the first time. The man's tone, Ben heard, was a fatherly one, like his own father's soft tone, but the voice was different. He looked up at the policeman and saw the concern in his eyes that matched his tone.

Maybe I should put these questions to Plinter, Ben reasoned. *Let him sort them out. That's his domain, his expertise! No doubt he would approach the matter professionally, unemotionally. Not like me, a disorganised mess, an emotional watering can.* He let the thought slide.

'I think so. Yes, the tea is helping.' The phone rang. Plinter answered with curt replies. He stiffened and glanced at Ben, who continued to struggle with the idea of telling Plinter about Meredith Turner's behaviour.

'Is that right, now? Did she leave her name? Where did she find it? Ok! Get the plod who spoke with her to my office and the recovered items.' He turned to Ben and said, 'we might have found something belonging to your wife, Mr Tavistock! He opened a file and speed-read the pages. 'Ah, here it is, Mr Tavistock—'

Ben snapped at him and said, 'You can call me *Ben*, for goodness sakes, don't be so officious, Inspector!'

Plinter nodded to his request and carried on. 'This, Ben, is the list of items you gave us, that is, your mother gave us, from your memory of what Elizabeth and Stephie wore that day. Now, you said, among other items, Elizabeth had a ring, an eternity ring on her right hand. Rosa…your mother that is…said she heard Elizabeth complain it was too loose sometimes but she wouldn't remove it because it meant so much to her and you.'

Ben nodded. He unconsciously rubbed the ring Elizabeth gave him. Plinter went on. 'Someone found the ring less than an hour ago. Sergeant Brighton made the connection. She's good like that.' Ben straightened upright, spilling the tea.

'Elizabeth's ring? How can that be? How do you know for certain it was hers?' He stood up, demanding an explanation. Plinter read from the file. 'The inscription on the inside reads; *My Treasure, My Love. Ben.*'

Ben tapped his forehead. 'How? Where?' He stammered several times, trying to get the sentence out. 'Where was…it…it…found? In the water? How? I don't understand!'

'No, it wasn't like that—'

'You're not saying someone found Elizabeth's body…after *all* this time?

'No, Ben. That's not what happened. Please relax and let me explain.' The policeman touched his shoulder and gently encouraged the distraught man into the chair.

'From the little I know—that was the phone call I had just now—a woman was walking her dog, the dog knocked over a garbage bin and a nappy, still inside the panties, fell out. The curious animal sniffed the bundle and picked it up. The ring fell out of the nappy. The woman stopped PC Denham and handed it to her as a lost item. That, basically, was the eh… message. We'll have more details when we talk to the woman again. They are on their way here, as we speak.'

Ben covered and uncovered his face several times, finally drawing his hands down his cheeks and stopping his fingers on his chin. He eyed the cup at his elbow and put it to his mouth robot-like, and sipped. 'The tea is cold' he said unconsciously and placed it back on the saucer. The tinkle echoed in his head. Plinter asked him did he want a refill. Ben said no. A tap-tap-tap struck the door. PC Denham walked in and introduced Mrs Angela Perkes and pet, Tipsy, and gave a brief summary of the fortuitous find.

Plinter shook the short woman's hand and eyed the brindled terrier-cross suspiciously, and wondered how the small creature had the power to upend a garbage bin. After declining the offer of tea and digestive biscuits, Mrs Perkes was installed in a seat. She tied the lead to the chair, saying Tipsy had been naughty lately. 'It's not his nature to pull the lead from my hand like that and go…well, sniffing!'

She went on to give the history behind the dog's name. Out of a respect for the aging widow but more out of a desire to get information, Plinter listened to the tale. The little fellow, it appears, walked around *most delicately* on tip-toes, thus earning the name Tipsy.

Ben hadn't been introduced; he felt invisible, but it suited him that way. All he wanted from the woman were answers. The squat woman, he thought, gave truth to the expression that dog owners begin to look like their dogs at some stage. She had a hat on that mimicked the dog's ears and her eyes squinted as if peering through folds of hair. She made furtive glances at Ben as though she considered him a junior detective or some such, who needed the experience, and wasn't allowed to ask questions just yet.

'Mrs Perkes, we thank you for coming in, we appreciate the cooperation the public renders. Can you tell us how you came to find the piece of jewellery?' Ben half expected him to either start or finish with the phrase 'in your own words'. *Whose* words would he expect her to use! Why do policemen and barristers *say* that? He meandered for a moment and returned to the woman's story.

'It's very simple really. I was taking Tipsy for his daily—he needs the exercise, you know. Well, when we came to the old Thornley house he became a little….agitated, jumping at the fence, that sort of excitement, you understand. I thought it was a bird or maybe a mouse that brought the hunter out in him'—

she rubbed his head and shook hers as a team. Ben had the theory confirmed instantly; they *did* look alike!

'What happened then, Marm?'

'There was this small hole in the fence. It was too much for Tipsy to resist. He squeezed through it...well, I had to let go of the lead, otherwise, he'd have pulled me with him into the garden. He's so strong—aren't you, you great hunter, you! Any road, I could see through a crack in the fence and there he was attacking the plastic lid on the rubbish bin. He had it off very smartly and this...this child's...white nappy thing fell out. Then, to my horror, Tipsy picked it up, jumped through the hole, and laid it at my feet. I would NEVER train a dog to do that! NEVER! I don't know where he learned such a disgusting habit!'

Ben waited for the dog to copy his owner's antics, but he didn't. He did, however, mimic misery enough for both of them.

'And that's when you found the ring?'

'Well, yes! It must have been wrapped up in the... nappy.'

Ben silently told the old woman to be very careful when she referred to the nappy that had once belonged to Stephie. He could feel a seething anger climb steadily up his chest coupled with a horrible sense of loss and grief. He cautioned himself to be calm; he *would* trace Elizabeth's footsteps from the time she left the house with Stephie, right up until the 'incident'. That was his determined mission; for Elizabeth and Stephie's sakes.

Plinter quizzed PC Denham. 'You checked out the garbage bin. What about the rest of the garbage? I assume it spilled onto the footpath too?' She remained at attention behind Mrs Perkes, as she answered her boss. 'No, Guv. There was nothing on the concrete and nothing else in the bin. The address is 26 Ridge Terrace; it runs off King Street further down. It's near the corner. I was patrolling with PC Jones when Mrs Perkes approached me. I had Mrs Perkes show me exactly where she found it.'

'I also checked the hole where the dog ...Tipsy, that is, got through. The narrow wooden fence panels could be pushed aside with no difficulty at all. Most of the nails that fastened the panels were rusted. The footpath referred to is the path leading to the house, not the public footpath outside the property. The gate was locked; in fact, it's been vacant for years, apparently.' The other woman nodded in agreement and verified the age of the Thornley house and the number of years it was unoccupied.

'That house has been vacant for three and a half years. I've been walking Tipsy that same route for that long…he's nearly four now. We started when he was a pup. Before Tipsy, I had faithful Hamper.' Ben's first thought was, 'Plinter, don't let her explain that dog's name, too! Find out who owns the house and the garbage bin, for goodness' sakes.' The investigator must have read his thoughts and quickly moved on.

'Mrs Perkes, you've been very helpful and, indeed, very honest. We need more with your…eh…cooperative spirit…in the community.' He addressed the policewoman. 'Check with the Council and see who owns the house.' Mrs Perkes intervened. 'I can tell you *that*. Ever since old Edna Thornley passed away her two sons have been fighting over the house. James wanted to sell it; Sydney wanted to keep it for investment. Neither of them needs the money, so it's a case of stubbornness. They've always disagreed with each other.'

'Well, thank you for that and….'—he helped her from the chair. She untied her pet; they toddled through the doorway— '…and may we call on you again Madam, should we need to clarify some statements?' She said yes into the air and gave Ben a salutatory glance, and was gone.

Ben's mind was littered with questions. PC Denham produced a plastic bag she had been holding and a smaller one containing the ring. Her boss asked her what state the nappy was in when found. She said it was dry and unsullied, both it and the child's panties. Plinter told her to give the items to the Duty Officer for testing. He intimated to Ben that the possibility of finding DNA at this point was slim.

Ben was more interested in the ring he gave to Elizabeth. Plinter handed him the sealed bag and asked him to identify the ring. Ben rolled the petite golden circle in his fingers until the inscription was the right way up. He read the love message and then repeated it aloud for Plinter's benefit. *My Treasure, My Love. Ben.* PC Denham screwed her face up in sympathy and closed the door behind her.

'How! How did my wife's ring end up in a garbage bin, Inspector? How? And why would a DNA test be necessary? Elizabeth's ring wrapped up in Stephie's nappy! Who else *could* the nappy belong to? This development raises huge questions, man. Tell me I'm not wrong!'

'It does, indeed, Ben. It does indeed. It changes the whole perspective of the case. I don't wish to alarm you but it has the scent of foul play.' Ben got to his feet as if to challenge the policeman's allegation. He ran his hands through his mop of black hair and moaned his horror. 'And I thought I might be starting to come to terms with the whole accident. What? What really happened to them?'

He fell back onto the couch asking no one and everyone and breathed out a mix of frustration and anger. He jumped to his feet again and demanded that the Inspector and he do a full and detailed retrace of Elizabeth's movements, from the moment she left the house to the water's edge, where Stephie was found. Plinter told him to hold his horses; the police would handle things. Ben didn't like the response Plinter gave. He decided from that moment he would do his own research. He plied Plinter with more questions. 'Show me the paperwork on what they wore. I don't remember all the details; you said I gave a description to my mother.'

Plinter flicked through the file and handed a single sheet of paper to Ben. In seconds he slapped the A4 with the back of his hand and said accusingly, 'My…my child had a nappy on when she left. Why was the missing nappy not queried?' The moustachioed detective ran his eye over the coroner's report.

'Says here the child's underwear most likely came loose in the water; possibly pulled off by her mother while trying to save the child. The coroner admits it was speculation, though.'

'Was it not reasonable to expect the tide would bring it ashore? I mean, you would have had the beach watched in case…Elizabeth…'

'Yes, of course. Police divers and the Coast Guard were on hand for days after the accident. Nothing else showed up except the usual debris…bits of wood, plastic items, that type of thing.'

'Not even a baby blanket, sir? You'd expect an item like that would float to the surface and end on the sand, wouldn't you? Surely you found it strange at the time, sir, that not only did Elizabeth not wash up, but also the stroller didn't, the nappy didn't and neither did my baby's little pillow or blanket turn up! Surely you were asking yourself some serious questions months ago! Is that not a reasonable assumption, Sir?'

'I can understand how you feel—'

'You *cannot*, sir, you most certainly cannot!'

'Be assured we did all we could under the circumstances. Remember the investigations came to a halt; the case has been kept open, however. It is exactly public input like what occurred today that gives us what we need to continue. And continue we will!'

Ben was fired up. He outspokenly emphasised his ambition to find the truth and didn't wait for Plinter to chastise his zeal. 'And what about the row of scratches on her left thigh or the dark bruises under her arms? What did the coroner say to that?' Plinter turned to the appropriate page and passed the file to the irate but revitalised man. Ben finished reading the theorised explanation and said, '*This had to raise questions, Detective*! Surely?'

'What do you mean?'

'The coroner says, and I quote, *Mrs Tavistock likely grabbed the child under the arms to raise Stephie from the surf, thus the reason for the bruising. The child must have got away from her and she made another attempt to get hold of her and frantically did so but the child was the wrong way up at this point. The marks are very likely the result of the mother's fingernails digging into the skin in a desperate attempt to draw her up. The skin was torn with the fingernails of the right hand from the upper part of the left thigh and down towards the knee, to a length of one hundred and four millimetres. The right-hand side of the child's dress had several tears in it, consistent with being punctured with sharp nails, likely from the same source; those of Mrs Tavistock.*' Ben found Plinter's eyes and stared straight at him. 'End of quote,' he finished succinctly.

'Just how *thorough* was your investigation, Mr Plinter? Did it never strike you that someone tried to snatch Stephie from her mother? One pair of hands placed under her arms and Elizabeth feverishly trying to grasp her child…by whatever means she could? I ask *you*, I ask the *Police Force*, just how *thorough* was your investigation?'

'In hindsight, I have to admit you have a point—'

Ben didn't wait for him to finish. He strode towards the door and glared back at Plinter and declared, 'I'll find the truth myself.'

Plinter hardened his tone and spoke directly to Ben's back, 'This information throws new light on the subject. If a case of foul play can be established, it means we now may be looking for a motive. There will be questions that will need answers. You may be able to help us in our inquiries. We hope you will continue to make yourself available, Sir.'

Ben turned abruptly and laughed at the insinuation. 'You are *seriously* demented, you are! You'd think for one moment I would bother to be here in the first place—you are one sick person, do you know that? The mere idea that you now have me as a suspect in the death of *my own family*—and don't bother telling me you are just doing your job! You've let all this time go by, months wasted, when you should have been doing your *job*, sir!'

Five

Rosa Tavistock grew hoarse from shouting. Her throat felt like she had sandpaper where her larynx used to be. Every time she breathed in or expelled, the harsh, grating sensation scraped inside her neck. She lost track of the time. It felt late. There was light coming through the narrow window, she remembered, when she was shoved into the foul-smelling room and tied to the hard chair. It was bright outside then.

Hunger gnawed at her stomach lining but what she wanted most was a soothing drink for her throat. Someone came in earlier and shouted at her to stop screaming and squawking, that no one could hear her shouts anyway, that she should save her voice. Rosa couldn't tell whether or not the person was a man or a woman. At some point during her imprisonment, she thought she heard the sounds of a woman crying.

The ropes had made her wrists bleed; partly from the tension applied, but chiefly from the violent effort she made trying to undo the bonds. It seemed that several hours had passed since she struggled with the ropes; the blood had dried and seeped into the jute cords, but the odour, that earthy odour, remained in her nostrils. There was another smell, a strong one; one she couldn't put a name to, but nevertheless oppressively present and unpleasant. It hung in the air; like a gassy smell, or was it petrol, or weed killer? A smell of rotten fish now? Or was it a mixture of several odours?

Whatever it was, there was no good complaining about it, the ropes were the real problem. Getting free and searching for a way out was the thing to do. She let out an audible groan, appealing for someone, anyone, to come to her aid, and for the thousandth time since she began shouting for help, she heard the dull echo of hopelessness bounce off several walls. A new struggle took over from the one with the ropes; the battle to remember who she was. The mental effort to think, to comprehend the situation, to concentrate, was too difficult. Much easier to try to sit still, and wait…and maybe sleep. Her head hurt…

The throbbing in her temple had stopped. Had she slept? She must have dozed, at least. She remembered the hard thump to the back of her head, getting awfully dizzy and nearly blacking out, but she was working hard to recall why. Why would someone hit her? Why was she here in this place, this room that felt more like a cave? Black, pitch black, and cold. And damp. Her hair irritated her eyes and it felt dirty, tangled and wet; blood must have flowed when she was struck. The blow came from behind but there was another face in front of her, threatening her. 'It was a man's face. It was getting clearer...' Yes, they were arguing. 'About what though?' she asked herself aloud.

The fog was clearing. She focused hard in the blackness but the face was elusive. The man's voice had a familiar ring to it but it was vague. The mist was lifting now, her thoughts clearer now. It was Ben's voice! She almost yelled her son's name and remembered she had a son who was in deep trouble but she couldn't say what the trouble was. 'Keep thinking, keep focusing,' she urged her captive mind to come forward and sort out her dilemma.

Ben's image came back; she tried to fit it on the faceless man who threatened her but the voice she heard was not Ben's. Ben's voice was softer. And yet, she recalled anger in his tone, lots of anger, and harsh words, raised against society. And weeping. Why? Why was Ben angry? Was it with me? Did I let him down in some way? Why was he crying? Did I upset him? Why didn't Elizabeth do something for him? My God! Elizabeth is dead! And Stephie too! That's why he's upset and angry. His family is gone! They drowned in that cruel bay!

Rosa tried to sit up; her muscles wouldn't cooperate. How long had she been in this position, slumped forward with her chin leaning on her chest? Slowly she eased her stiff neck and aching head into an upright posture, to manage the pain as best she could. Her long silver-black hair irritated her nose and mouth: she made an automatic attempt to flick her hair from her face. The rope cut deeper into her bloodied wrists; her neck hurt even more.

'If I just sit quietly and let the moment pass, perhaps my thoughts will unravel,' she whispered, to urge the real Rosa Tavistock to take command of the situation and not an impostor.

The smell! Ether! *That's* it! He put the cloth to my mouth. I struggled and kicked. Yes, that's when I felt the peal of metal against my head. I must have fallen, for I remember being dragged and tied. Then he...Billy! It was Billy! I felt the pleasant smell of ether in my nostrils. That must have been how it happened. Meredith! *She* was the one who struck me! Ben doesn't know where I am…'

Ben needed to talk with his mother. Why wasn't she *answering* the phone? The waitress brought him tea and scones which he devoured quickly and ordered another helping. Ben tried his mother's mobile again. Maybe she has switched it off for some reason he couldn't fathom; it had to be a good one for she *always* had her mobile switched on. He left a message with BT to pass on when she came back on air. It was important that she knew about the ring and the nappy; he also wanted to tell her what a jackass the whole policing system was, or that Plinter was.

On the way home, he made a detour and rapped loudly on his mother's door. Getting no reply he peered through the windows at the side and back, making a racket on the glass. At least she wasn't lying on the floor unconscious. That much was a relief, although he couldn't see *upstairs.* The emergency key she left with him years ago was hanging on a hook on his hallstand; he promised himself to include it on his key ring with the car keys.

Reasoning, or rather hoping, she was likely at his house, he recalled her promise to return and help him clean up. Her phone was either damaged or lost, he concluded, and she'd be waiting for him when he got home. That had to be it! He rang his home phone. No answer. He drove fast. Swinging into Vista Hill Drive, Ben saw a grey car parked outside his gate. It wasn't his mother's Volvo. As he pulled into his drive, two men got out and approached him, one in a suit, one in uniform. They identified themselves with names that meant nothing to him, except they were from King Street Police-station. The Policeman in the suit requested that Ben accompany him to the station. Ben mumbled that Plinter hadn't let the grass grow under his feet; the men ignored that remark.

'What for?' he demanded from the fatter of the two, knowing the answer but resisting strongly.

'Inspector Plinter wants to ask you a few questions, sir. Routine stuff, you understand.'

'No, I don't understand! I was in his office barely half an hour ago. Why didn't he ask me so-called 'routine questions' *then*?'

'I don't know sir, I'm following orders.'

'Am I under arrest?'

'Not that I'm aware of, sir. Do you have reason to think you are?' Ben held his tongue in check for a moment then let loose. 'I suppose you learned that remark from detective school. Have you any more smart-alecky clichés you'd like to get off your chest. Then again, you probably can't remember the *other* one!'

The officers exchanged glances, stepped away and began muttering to each other. The plainclothesman put a phone to his ear, said a few words into it, and then listened for a longer period. He came back to Ben and said his boss would like to see him in his office around nine in the morning, and would that be suitable to him. Ben scowled and left the men gaping at his back. A final search up and down the street for his mother's car was met with further disappointment. Except for a few cars parked here and there, there was no approaching traffic. At four-thirty-five, and not a word from his mother, he felt more than a little agitated. She was always around of late, even when he didn't want her to be.

The house was chilly, prompting him to light the fire. Armed with a brass container he went to the wood shed to fill it. Every evening during the winter, and often into the early spring, he lit a fire. The thought of not having Elizabeth with him anymore plunged into his psyche. Grief saturated his vital organs like a tap fully opened. He quickly turned it off before it flooded his insides with negativity and self-pity again. Tonight, and even if it takes all night, he had plans to draw up and complete a sketch of the route Elizabeth took.

Tomorrow, he would walk that route and retrace her footsteps. He had traversed her journey many times in his head during his dark and angry hours alone, negotiating her every step from the door of the house to her last known port of call, the doctor's waiting room on King Street. He needed his mother to confirm the route the police had built. Plinter showed Rosa the likely route Elizabeth followed, all known data considered. There was, the man explained to Rosa, and she repeated it to Ben, the possibility that Elizabeth did something differently than planned or met someone not on her list. His mother did pass on the information but, he conceded, his deep sorrow didn't allow him to be responsive.

Now, he was in a better frame of mind, more focused on his new agenda and fired up, ready to start his own investigation. He would start, maybe not first thing tomorrow, but certainly after he satisfied Plinter of his utter disgust at the policeman's insinuation. He also had a score to settle with Copeland Publishers. They would *retract* their lies about Elizabeth's sickness and her state of mind. Some upstart busybody, some gossip-spreading reporter would wish he had chosen a different career!

First, however, he would trace the owners of 26 Ridge Terrace; there was no time like the present.

'Good afternoon, Madam. Would you connect me to Jim Hartnett, please?'

'Please hold, sir. May I ask who is calling?'

'Tell him it's Ben.'

'Thank you. I'll get him for you.'

'Hello, Ben!'

'Hello, Jim.'

'How *are* you? So sorry about your loss. We missed your face in Town Planning. I saw you at the funeral. I thought it better not burden you with my commiserations. You really looked…'

'Thank you, Jim. I need a favour.'

'Anything I can do for you, just ask.'

'Give me the names and addresses of the owners of 26 Ridge Terrace. I believe it's owned by two brothers. Thornley I think. The house is vacant and I'm interested in the property.'

Jim from Planning was not a man for protocol. 'Bear with me, Ben. I have to go to another computer. Just a mo.' He came back and said, 'Got a pen handy?' Ben scratched the names of James and Sydny Thornley and their respective addresses on a notepad and said thanks to the sixty-something Jim and hung up. He was tempted to drive the fifteen miles to Stauntonbury, the village where disagreeable Sydny lived and then onto Cayfield, another twenty miles north to see his equally argumentative brother, James.

But, no, his mother's absence delivered anxiety. He would talk to her *first* and make sure she was OK. On the other hand, were she in trouble of any sort, she would get to a phone-box. 'Why didn't she?' he worried, and reasoned that Stauntonbury was less than twenty minutes away.

Half way there he filled his tank and sped on to his first interview. He might even get there in front of Plinter, he thought, enthused by the hunt for answers. A ripple of nervous excitement zigzagged down his spine; he was a Private Investigator now. He suddenly realised he couldn't give his name to Thornley; an alias was required. This heightened his nervousness and it also struck him that the man might recognise him from a newspaper clipping. The press had run a story on the tragedy; they even brought their nosey cameras into the cemetery.

A wave of distress rolled up from his deepest parts and moved relentlessly up to his chest, heading for his throat. He wanted to, needed to, open his neck and let the flood of pain pour out in savage groans of anger at having to bear the same sorrow over and over again. He gripped the steering wheel and slammed the brakes on without thinking, without looking. The car came to a screeching halt on the narrow road. A vehicle overtook the Rover, the driver blasting his raucous horn and waving a clenched fist out the window.

Ben was oblivious to the threats. His knuckles turned white from the grip he had on the wheel, his mind fighting the onslaught of the images of little Stephie being lowered into the ground. His mind was losing the battle to calm his system. In a short time, he was plunged back to the funeral parlour where a misled vicar attempted to persuade his audience that humans can recover from the passing of a beloved child.

He felt his mother clasp his hand as he staggered as though drunk from the black limousine to the edge of the 'hole' that would imprison his daughter forever. Watchful eyes tracked his wooden movements towards the neatly dug trench. Twice he felt his heart would burst and twice strong hands helped him off his knees. Someone brought a chair. He didn't see anyone to thank for it.

Diminished concentration caused him to relax his hold on the steering wheel. His mind took him back to the graveyard; slumped in a seat metres from the grave, the only one sitting. His mother massaged his shoulders from behind, willing herself to be brave for her son's sake. Ben felt her hands and fingers caress his neck and tried to reciprocate support but couldn't. Her hands quivered in her task and he felt her anguish; he couldn't help her and that made him feel useless, powerless. The small lacquered box with ornate silver handles came between him and the burial pit. He thought he heard someone say 'one final goodbye, Ben?'

He wanted to stand up and thrash the person who made the offer but he was physically unable. If his voice hadn't been strangled by the ache in his heart, an ache that made his larynx spasm, he would have shouted 'No! What do you think I am? A monster? I will *never* say goodbye to my baby. You want that I should say goodbye to Elizabeth, too, do you? You heartless, merciless, callous, cold-blooded fiend!'

He wished he'd had the strength to push the man away and have no part with Stephie.

A car roared by, jolting him into the present. Ben followed the vehicle until it disappeared around a corner. He had a vague recollection he asked his mother that evening who was that fiendish man at the graveside. He thought at the time she was reluctant to say who it was. He didn't register the answer she gave until today. Until now. It was his friend, Billy Turner.

And here he was, in his car, disconsolate, on his way to meet a stranger who may or may not have met Elizabeth and Stephie. How could he carry on with his foolish enterprise, attempting to do the work of a professional investigator! Ben summed up his qualifications in an honest appraisal of his ability to produce results. Lacking greatly in emotional stability, continuously distraught mentally by his loss, and the consequential physical strain on his body and well-being gave him no right to solve the mystery surrounding the tragic end of his two loves.

Thinking about where his mother might be and anticipating her disapproval for his rash actions, he decided to turn around and go home. There was nowhere to turn around; road too winding, too dangerous. He looked up and down the narrow and twisting road for somewhere to reverse his car but found none; he drove on to find a suitable place to turn. A gated entrance loomed up on his left. He slowed down and threw the car into reverse. The sign on the gate said *Twin Pines*, the address that he had on his notepad. It was Sydny Thornley's house! In an instant, he changed his mind again. This was too much a coincidence to ignore. He hoped the man wasn't as disagreeable as Mrs Perkes suggested.

'The bottom line is, Mr Davis, the house is still lying idle. My brother stubbornly refused to see things my way and get tenants in. The time isn't right to sell. It's that simple.'

'It's been vacant for how long? Three years?'

'More or less. I put tenants in for a few months and James put it on the market. The tenants left, disgruntled by the bad manners James showed and I wouldn't agree to sell it for the greatly undervalued offer. And so it lies, vacant. I'm sorry you made the journey for nothing; the house is not for sale.'

Ben was not good at this. He racked his brain to work out how he should proceed without giving the game away. The garbage bin sprung into his mind. The proverbial straw loomed in his mind; he reached for it and stuttered to bring up a question about the rubbish bin.

'I…eh…had a look at the house earlier today in fact, and I noticed the rubbish bin in the garden. A small dog knocked it over…and eh, I…a nappy fell out…I thought the Council truck forgot to pick it up?

'They don't collect garbage unless it's on the footpath. The last time it was emptied was three months ago. I know, because I cleaned up the garden last and I cancelled the collection. It was empty. Is there something specific you are getting at here, Mr Davis? Why all the interest in rubbish collection?'

Ben was stymied for an answer; he didn't prepare himself well enough. Plinter and his trained boys wouldn't get into this predicament; that was a given. They didn't have to pretend who they were; they were the real McCoy, with powers to ask questions. Now, the man in front of him was demanding an answer. One thing was certain, however, Ben believed, Plinter's boys hadn't been to see Mr Thornley yet. *He* may have reached Thornley first but he wasn't getting anywhere.

Take a chance, Ben. Ask the question. Put the man on the spot. If he knows anything his face might show guilt.

'Can I be perfectly honest with you, Mr Thornley? The truth is…I believe a woman was at your house. She had a child with her, a young child. A girl—'

'—and you want to know, Mr Davis *alias whatever*, did she apply for a room to rent or the house to rent. Is that it? Why didn't you say you were a private eye?'

'Did she?'

'No! The house has been idle for *years*. *Nobody* has applied for tenancy. End of story. Maybe your friend with the child put the nappy in the garbage bin, and *her* little dog knocked it over! Have you thought of that? *Good day* to you, Sir!

On his return trip, Ben pondered that question. If Stephie had soiled her nappy, would Elizabeth have changed it for a fresh one in the street, in a public place? Possibly. If the situation were dire, perhaps. But to discard the nappy in a garbage bin *behind a fence, on someone's private property?* No way! Not Elizabeth! She would had to have seen that the bin was there and the only way that was possible was to know there was a rubbish bin in the garden, which meant she had to look over the fence. The gate was locked, besides. He couldn't see her pulling palings off and climbing through the gap…just to discard a dirty nappy. Besides, there were counsel bins dotted around the town.

Anyway, Elizabeth had bags especially for the purpose of containing the old nappy and its contents. Elizabeth would have carried the dirty nappy in the plastic bag and put it her own garbage bin. Wait a minute. The nappy was inside Stephie's *panties*. Elizabeth wouldn't *throw* them away, not unless they were damaged badly. That was something else! Where was the bag she kept the nappies and baby wipes and cream in? Did it fill up and sink? Would it have floated? If so, why was *it* not washed ashore?

Ben felt his reasoning was correct but it was circular. The argument still got back to whether Elizabeth would discard the nappy in the first place. And he kept coming up with the same answer. No! He *knew* Elizabeth wouldn't do that.

And the ring? Mrs Perkes said the ring definitely fell out of the bundle her dog brought to her. Why would Elizabeth put the ring she loved in the nappy and then place it in a stranger's bin? Why would she want to get rid of it? There's no logic in that.

Another dark thought entered the arena.

Was there any truth to the rumour she was so sick that she contemplated suicide? No, not my Elizabeth! Yes, she *was* ill. The discomfort she had in her stomach was attributed to the uterus not returning to its original position after Stephie was born. It was a 'muscular thing', Elizabeth explained to him, 'it should sort itself out'. Then there was the constant tiredness and the aches and pains all over. Still Elizabeth's nature was such that she didn't complain. In all her sickness, her motherly character always displayed itself; Stephie was never neglected.

Ben remembers the many nights she was deprived of sleep because Stephie needed attention and she didn't want to wake him because he had work to go to. Or she'd blame her sleepless nights on the 'stomach thing', saying it will get better soon. There were the lovely meals she cooked for him but picked at her own food. 'Go to the doctor, darling', he urged her on several occasions. And she did. Each time she went she came back with: 'it's just a bug' or 'Doctor thinks I might have that Chronic Fatigue thing', or something similar.

Was he so busy at work designing buildings and roads that his sweet wife's health was slowly deteriorating before his eyes and he didn't see it? Was he so blind not to see her weight loss, see her buy new clothes because the ones she had no longer fit? Why didn't he take more interest when her rings easily slipped off her fingers? How could he have missed all of those symptoms? What planet was he on? Why didn't she tell him something was wrong? No! It was *his* place to find out; *his* role to make sure his wife was getting the right treatment!

Ben condemned his negligence. He wished his mother was available. Elizabeth may have confided in her. The family doctor came to his mind. One person who should throw light on Elizabeth's health was Dr Ames; he was one of the last people to see her.

'Surely if Elizabeth had a major medical problem, he would be obliged to tell me now.'

Ben determined the person he would definitely call on tomorrow was Dr Jeremy Ames.

The light had begun to fade and still, he hadn't heard from his mother. Anxiety climbed another rung up his worry ladder. Relegating some of his concern to his mother visiting Carla in London, he reasoned that's where she must be. She had spoken to him about the visit earlier that morning and yet… she promised to return to help him clean up his house. That didn't sound right either. Unsure of her real intentions he called his Aunt Carla. The number rang and rang. Not home. He'd ring again. Ring until she answered.

Driving through a set of traffic lights he saw the two overweight policemen from earlier. He guessed they were heading for Stauntonbury. The dustbin entered his thoughts again. He decided to take a detour past the abandoned house and see first-hand the 'mystery' bin for himself; if nothing else, it would put him in a space that, perhaps, Elizabeth and Stephie once occupied.

The fence was about five feet high. Able to see past the few scraggly and neglected trees planted behind the fence, which did nothing to obstruct his vision, he could see comfortably into the garden. And there it stood; the short, round, lonely witness to curious activity, the lowly black plastic refuse container that may or may not be the guardian of criminal goings-on. It struck him as odd that it was still there. *Why* was it still there? He guessed it must at least be considered as *evidence*. Why hadn't Plinter commandeered it for testing? Maybe the wind and rain had done enough to erase any tell-tale fingerprints, if there were any at all; who knows? At any rate, the bin was no longer upturned as Mrs Perkes had described. *Somebody* must have reinstated the lid.

Hunger pangs made their presence keen on Ben's belly. He could rustle up a tin of beans to satisfy the hunger. Or, he remembered, the remains of the soup his mother gave him. Home was a good place to be, he thought. The fire he started ninety minutes ago would need stoking or relighting and he could sit and enjoy the flames and plan his agenda for tomorrow. In this familiar, natural setting, Ben allowed himself the luxury of recalling him and Elizabeth curled up on the couch late at night, having put Stephie to bed, and soaking in the heat from the burning logs, while they talked of future plans. Forcibly breaking into his reverie he tried to remember what his mirror-image said about the pain of memories and the joy of memories.

He wept a little; he smiled a little.

Where was his mother?

He needed to know.

He would ring his aunt again.

Aunt Carla was overjoyed at the sound of her nephew's voice. After standard family chit-chat, Ben asked was his mother in London and received the reply he wasn't looking for. He played down the fact his mother was due to visit him by saying she probably got delayed at her pottery lessons. Carla signed off saying she'd love to see him and when can he come to London. Ben said soon and his dead father's sister told him how bad Uncle Stan's health was. There was, he thought, a whimper of despair; he found it hard to offer sympathy.

For now, he kept all the pity he could muster up for himself. At least Carla still had her husband with her; she could look after him, comfort him and be there for him when his hope waned. *He* could not give any help to Elizabeth or Stephie. *None at all.* His last few words to his aunt included a visit 'when he could', and yes, he was coping as best he could without 'Liz'. Carla was the only one who called her by that name despite repeated efforts to convert her.

The revitalised embers grew into a blazing fire. Ben sipped on the hot soup and silently thanked his mother for being there for him, in more ways than one. The heat from the fire and the warm soup in his belly made him drowsy, and when the tiredness brought on by the day's anxieties joined in, sleep overtook him. And with sleep came unsolicited dreams.

He and Plinter were together. After they left the house, they waved to Mrs Crampton from across the road. It was nine-thirty and as usual, she was in the garden tending her roses. She cultivated a magnificent display of deep reds and bright yellows, mingled with pinks of various shades, and whites dotted here and there. The garden was alive with colour and equally pleasurable to the senses were the perfumes that filled the air. Elizabeth generally stopped for a chat with her and usually came away with a few cuttings and how-to tips for her own garden.

Ben and Plinter leaned casually over the fence engaging the elderly lady in the usual greetings of the day. Her mood, Ben noticed, did not reflect the happy colours of, or the perfumed aroma from, her floral estate. An obvious sadness hung from her eyes and mouth. She spoke a few words of regret for 'a beautiful mother and an adorable child'. Plinter asked her about Elizabeth's demeanour.

'Was there anything different about her that day?'

'No, she was her charming, usual self. She would have sat down with me for a cuppa but she hadn't the time that morning. She did say, however, perhaps later in the afternoon. I told her I looked forward to her company.'

Ben considered himself part of the team and felt the urgency to establish his role by asking: 'Was that the last time you saw her?'

'No, Benjamin. I glimpsed her briefly when I went to the nursery for a few things. My secateurs needed replacing; the spring mechanism fell apart. The blades were losing their cutting edge anyway, so I bought myself a new one.'

'So where did you actually sight her, Mrs Crampton?'

'The nursery, as you know, is on the corner of Green and King Streets. I did my business and saw her on the pedestrian crossing on King Street. Elizabeth was pushing the pram and heading to town. I think she said the post office was on her list of things to do.'

Plinter took over and scribbled something in a notebook. 'And what time was that, do you remember?'

'About eleven o'clock, Inspector.'

Subconscious meanderings took another direction and Ben was splashing in a turbulent tide hysterically searching through misted vision. His eyes were at water level frantically scanning the surface for a face, a lock of hair, a tiny raised hand. Every muscle in his body warred against the swelling waves, just to keep afloat. His nose kept filling with liquid. He thought he saw a small head bob through the heavy rain on a frothed wave. For the briefest of moments, the petite but terrified face of Stephie stared back at him. The words 'help me Daddy' were framed on her lips but salty water blocked any speech. Ben struck out for the little tot…

Plinter pulled him from the water and led him to meet Jan Avery, an acquaintance from school. Ben dripped water; the water sloshed in his shoes, he wanted to stop to empty them and go back for Stephie, but Plinter insisted since Ben asked for this case, he must soldier on.

Jan Avery was crying when she came to the door. Plinter invited he and Ben in for a quick chat; she didn't object or couldn't. It didn't matter because Ben was assigned to make a pot of tea while Plinter began his inquiries. From the kitchen he heard the woman sobbing over Elizabeth and Stephie, she wishing she had talked a little longer with Elizabeth or had decided to go with her to the shops or the post office; then this awful thing would not have happened.

Ben opened several cupboards to find cups and saucers but gave up and opted to wash the dishes lying in hot sudsy water in the sink. He shouted out to Jan did she have any biscuits. Plinter translated her tears into 'No, but I'll go to the mall and get some!' Ben said it didn't matter and it instantly struck him that he saw no sign of Elizabeth in the stormy sea. And worse still, it distressed him that he didn't look for her. Did he treat Elizabeth's ordeal as though it didn't matter, like not having biscuits to offer to guests? Why didn't he scream out her name? Why? Did he think that because he didn't see her, he believed she wasn't in the water? Was she still on the promenade clinging onto the railings, saving her own life and not trying to save Stephie's? He blamed Plinter for interfering in his search. He left the kettle boiling in Jan Avery's kitchen and dashed back to the wharf and plunged into the bay again.

The water was calm.

Calm like a glass pond.

Hundreds of people had lined up along the promenade railings laughing at the fully-clothed madman's antics, as if they paid their money and were being entertained, as at a circus; and he was the clown bobbing gently on still waters. Leaning over the rails, the sounds of ridiculers reverberated across the water. The acoustics were perfect; he heard every mannerism, every accent, every chiding remark.

'Did you find what you were looking for, Mate?'

'What a novel way to go fishing!'

'You forgot your snorkel!'

Mrs Crampton yelled in applause with a yellow rose between her teeth. Jan Avery laughed out loud with a wet handkerchief hanging on a hook from her cheek. Rosa Tavistock hauled him from the ocean and said 'Inspector Plinter needs you to help in his inquiries'. She pointed him towards the shopping mall where the policeman introduced him to Rick Saunders, the chemist. The man spoke as if Ben wasn't present.

'Yes. They came in about ten o'clock. Elizabeth is…was, a very personable woman. I know her husband by sight, but Elizabeth and little Stephie… were regulars. Most of our staff knows them. We were all shocked when we heard the news.'

'Did you fill out a prescription for her?'

'Yes.'

'What was it?'

The chemist eyed Plinter and then Ben suspiciously. Plinter told Ben to buy a tube of toothpaste for him. He went off obediently and tried to shake the water from his shoes. Taking his place in the pay queue he could hear the salesgirl explaining and demonstrating the merits of an earthy aromatic perfume. Ben could feel the spray on his wrist; Elizabeth asking him to choose which one he liked better. He swooned.

The sea felt cold.

The waves rose high.

It was dark.

Ben's clothes were heavily laden with water, like a lead suit pulling him down; he had to tread water with all his strength to keep afloat. There were boats everywhere, big and small, liners cruising, yachts sailing and canoes paddled by two-man crews. A captain dressed in full regalia with a megaphone hiding a sea-hardened face called out to survivors in the water. Ben's first instinct was to call back. He started to raise his hand and yell 'over here' when he realised they were using Elizabeth's name, then Stephie's.

'They are searching for my family!' Ben spat more water from his throat.

'Mrs Tavistock! Can you hear us? Please make a sound. Call out if you can.'

Great searchlights poured a beam of light onto the water and picked out quaint reflections on the surface.

'Stephie Tavistock! Please cry out! We are here to save you. You and your mother!'

There were no answers, no cries. The beam of light was extinguished and a great sound cancelled all other sounds; the engines in the bowels of the ship roared into life. The vessel turned in a giant circle and glided into the darkness. The captain appeared at the stern in full regalia, his peaked cap reflected the light from a lonely bulb above his head. He dropped the megaphone to his side and touched his hat with a fair-well salute. Ben gasped at the face of Billy Turner staring into the water. Ben was sure Billy caught his eye, but he made a gesture of no importance. A mocking grin took hold of one side of his mouth, aimed at the woman on his right. It was his crazy mother, Meredith. She was singing one of her tunes and begun to dance in the spray from the sea.

Elizabeth pulled him from the tide and left him lying on the sand, next to Stephie. His mouth was pressed into the sand, he immediately withdrew his head. There was a nappy lying next to the child; a shiny circle of gold fell out and glinted in the light from the esplanade. Mrs Perkes and her yappy little dog breezed by, rapidly shaking her fist at the exhausted Ben. 'You don't need that Plinter fellow! You should find out the truth on your own, for Elizabeth's sake! What are you waiting for?'

The mug slipped from Ben's hand and jolted him into consciousness; then into an upright position on the edge of the couch. The fire was blazing; his mouth was dry and salty. The sensation of grains of sand on his tongue and crunching between his teeth made him want to spit out the imaginary grit. Beads of water did a downward ballet on his forehead; sweat rolled down his arm to collect under his wrist watch, the watch that Elizabeth bought him. He had to clear his eyes before reading eight-thirty-five. In the kitchen he rinsed with several mouthfuls of clean, fresh water before the last of the salty sand was eliminated.

There were so many puzzles competing in his head he felt it would explode. So many unanswered questions, so many doubts. Staying alert was his main target; to stop allowing the grief to overtake what common sense he had left. He fancied the notion of working along with Plinter to solve the riddle and bring matters to a close, and then maybe he could move on. Plinter put the kibosh on their partnership by virtually accusing him of harming his family! Well, Plinter can work without *my* services, Ben's ego stormed.

He didn't believe his dreams had a deep or mysterious meaning, but rather his thoughts to resolve the ambiguity of what occurred on that fatal day were clarified and his dreams only emphasised what his subconscious state indicated. Besides his own feelings on the matter, he *knew* that's what Elizabeth would want him to do; find the truth! The inclusion of the nappy and the ring that his dreams conjured up supported his own notion that the two items found together must be a key factor in solving the mystery.

Maybe he could get Billy to help him. He discarded that idea as soon as he thought of it. Billy seemed nervous today, not his normal self, if it could be said that Billy was ever normal. It was the quirkiness of the man that he liked. From their first encounter as boys in a schoolyard right up until he and Elizabeth were married, he and Ben enjoyed the oddest friendship, sometimes hot, sometimes cold, and rarely in between, but never vindictive. Since then Billy showed a certain amount of reserve, the in-between status, and that for the past four years.

Rosa explained, as did Elizabeth, Ben recalled early in his marriage, that once a man gets married, other relationships generally go on the wane, often taking second billing. At least until the newly-weds settle into their relationship. Had Billy also married, then perhaps the couples may have become close friends. As it turned out he and Billy saw less of each other, for obvious reasons.

Ben yawned and checked his watch again. Not even nine o'clock and he felt so tired! The few hours he slept on the couch clearly did nothing to energise his body or his mind. The activity, both physically and mentally, were probably more than he needed for his first day back into life. He resigned himself to a night's sleep and while he prepared for bed he pondered on the next day and what it might bring.

Then he remembered more of his dream.

The picture of Billy and his mother standing high above him while he languished in the water flashed into his head. The images were distinct. The faces were... gloating, he thought. Was that really the case? Is that how Billy really felt about him when Elizabeth and Stephie died? Or was it just about Elizabeth? *Was* he gloating? Was he glad that she was gone? Is that why he didn't mention saying goodbye to *Elizabeth* at Stephie's funeral? More feelings and memories bombarded Ben's tired mind; it rejuvenated his thought processes into action.

The cutting remark Billy made about Elizabeth six months into their marriage returned to wound him once more. The memory was so vivid, it resounded in his ears.

We've reached a crossroads in our friendship, Ben. Your wife has come between us.

The comment still stung. Instead of being happy for him and Elizabeth, Billy as good as said she was an *intruder*, someone with no right to be there! There were other incidents, too, Ben panicked as he recollected the one visit that resolutely put Elizabeth off going to Meredith Turner's house. Ben fought to piece together the events of that evening. They had been seeing each other for six months.

It was at Meredith's invitation to come for tea; she *wanted* to meet the love of Ben's life. Before they went in Ben reminded Elizabeth of Meredith's idiosyncrasies, her wayward mind and even gave details of the poor woman's recent 'journeys', and the subsequent 'searches' Billy made to find her. When she wandered physically or mentally, he explained, it was all a result of her illness; Alzheimer's disease is what the doctor called it.

In the course of the evening and the natural law that women have to talk about the man in their lives, Elizabeth and Meredith became detached from the men shortly after they had eaten desert. When they returned from Meredith's bedroom it was Elizabeth's white face that primarily worried Ben; the other thing was the look of contentment on Meredith's. Elizabeth made the pretext that satisfied everyone; she felt quite ill and needed to go home and lie down. Meredith made a sarcastic comment that it wasn't her cooking that made her guest ill. Both Ben and Billy were unaffected by the remark and automatically put it down to the older woman's unpredictable temperament. On the way home, Elizabeth explained to Ben that the woman was right about the food; it was *very tasty*. It was rather the way she cooked her words; they were hard to digest.

'She was cruel, Ben! The woman said hateful things against you. She implied very subtly that I was marrying the wrong man! Can you believe that?'

'I tried to warn you about her, Elizabeth. She's a weird one, is Meredith! I think she's harmless, though.'

'Benjamin, don't be fooled! Despite what you say and know about her, she sounded very lucid to me. She was articulate and calculating. I'd prefer to have as little as possible to do with her! I know Billy is your friend but his mother is toxic! Please don't ask me to make this a regular thing…I'd have to say no.'

'I'd never ask that of you, you *know* that. I'm incredibly surprised she could have this effect on you, that's all.'

'Do you imagine it's my fault, Ben? Do you think I'm making this up and painting the woman blacker than she is? What *possible reason* would I have?'

'No, darling. It's not *anything* like that! We don't have to go if you don't want to.'

'Thank you, Ben. I really feel that strongly about it. What will you tell Billy?'

'I'll tell him how *I* feel about his mother's treatment of you, that it's unacceptable, that he should talk with her. Billy will understand.'

'I hope so, Ben. I don't want to be the reason for breaking your long friendship with Billy. I think he has a lot on his plate. He might be married, were his circumstances different.'

'Yes, maybe so? By the way, who did Meredith suggest would make you a better husband?'

'She said Billy would.'

It was nine-forty when Ben pulled the duvet over his tired body. The pillow engaged his head that throbbed with questions and his brain that pulsed with potential answers. Billy's stinging remark made over four years ago and other 'innocent' barbs since then dominated his thoughts. He worked hard to oust his friend from his mind, not wanting to think badly of him and yet, finding a series of isolated incidents to criticise his behaviour, even outrightly condemn his manners.

Elizabeth's face was the last image he wanted on his mind before he slept. He summoned up the happier times, the memories without the pain, and closed his eyes. She was as beautiful as ever. Standing on the veranda in the summer sun she looked stunning. It was the year she gave birth to Stephie; her body was in full bloom and with two months to go she was the image of motherhood. A light breeze blew her sandy hair across her clean skin and with one sweeping motion she waved the tresses to one side, revealing once again her sparkling blue eyes and infectious smile.

Elizabeth had the most outstandingly easy birth, Ben recalled in vivid pictures. Underwater in the spa-bath and surrounded by her family she groaned and grunted her way to the spectacular arrival of Stephie Jordan Tavistock, named after Ben's grandmother, Stephanie, and Elizabeth's deceased twin, Jordan. Ben held her hand throughout the whole ordeal, having had all the blood squeezed from his fingers by Elizabeth's strong grip. To Elizabeth the experience was exquisite; to Ben it was painful. And he sweated a lot. Afterwards, in a quiet moment together, he recalled how her ecstasy oozed when telling him she'd have all his babies. Despite the pangs of childbirth and the exhaustion afterwards, she thanked Ben for loving her.

Ben nestled into the latex bed and thought back to their early courtship. It was easy to remember but it hurt to hold onto the images. The *real* person was the one he wanted to hold in his arms again, even for a moment, and not her image. But the memories would have to do. Elizabeth never knew her sister, the new-born Jordan dying in her mother's arms in the hospital at twelve weeks. Jordan's heart complications barely allowed her to live three months; she didn't have the strength to fight and on a spring day in April she closed her dark blue eyes.

Stephie had dark blue eyes.

Ben wept into his pillow.

And as determined as he was to keep his tears in check, he realised more and more that some decisions were not his to make.

He had no more dreams that night.

Six

The floor was cold against her face. And hard.

Rosa felt a strong sense of bewilderment in the dark room. The dull throbbing ache in her shoulder only added to the confusion that ruled her thoughts. When she tried to move her head the ache in her left shoulder took second place to the sharp pain in her cheekbone. It made her whimper, which further moved her head, which in turn, scraped her face on the rough concrete. She moaned again. The side of her face felt sticky and a whiff of blood leaped into her nostrils as she drew in a new lungful of the room's rancid air.

Now she figured out what happened. A rope was tied to one wrist, brought under the seat of the chair and tied to the other wrist. Her ankles were secured, one to each of the front legs, and a third band strapped around her chest and under her arms forced her against the back of the chair. The idea was to knock the chair over and cause it to break up. Her plan to get free didn't work. The wooden chair was stronger than she thought and the steady rocking motion she moved her rigid body didn't break the chair as she'd wished.

When she finally toppled it, she remembered falling in slow motion as her body, firmly anchored to the seat, tilted at a weird angle. Her only defence against crashing to the floor and striking her head against the unforgiving stone was to close her eyes and wait.

How long she lay unconscious in this awkward position was hard to work out; all sense of time eluded her. Hours, she guessed, maybe three or four hours since she struggled with Billy and his mother. Maybe longer. She called out with what little power she had. No more than a weak plea for help escaped her lips. After a few attempts she gave up and resigned herself to her captive state; and her captor's good pleasure. In time, Rosa thought, Billy would give her a little food or maybe a glass of water. In despair, she wept for the awful mess she was in, trying hard not to think that Billy was altogether mad, that this whole scenario was a hoax of some kind. Reality, however, convinced her it was not a hoax, not of any kind.

Whatever Billy's problem was, it was not a recent one. It might easily have stemmed from the family background. Meredith was never an easy woman to get on with. Not that she had much to do with Meredith, but general rumour and Ben's own experience with the Turner family didn't paint a pleasant picture. Her husband, William, left, she understood, because Meredith was jealous to the point of paranoia; it was rumoured William never did have a chance. Maybe Billy has inherited bad genes from his mother.

'Could that be the reason for the madness that ensued after I knocked on Billy's door? Rosa queried the dirt-ridden floor inches from her mouth. 'He's gone over the edge. But what would move him to hurt his best friend's mother?'

The memory of the encounter flowed back to Rosa. After she left Ben, she contemplated how she would approach Billy, because surely, she reasoned, Billy's letter was more than the average sentiment to a bereaved friend. It was not to a friend at all! It was to a lover; the sentiments spelled out in romantic terms the writer's deepest feelings. *Therefore, it wasn't meant for Ben.*

Oddly, while the envelope had Ben's address on it, the letter itself didn't begin with a 'Dear Ben'. She recalled that some of the expressions were in a mixture of prose and poetry, and very well written in words that expressed profound feelings for a love that wasn't to be. *Who* wrote it wasn't a riddle; William (Bill) Turner was typed in neat script at the bottom. Who was the letter intended for? And how did it end up in Ben's letterbox? Ah yes, *it was addressed* to Ben, even though he was not the intended recipient. Was there a mix-up? Did Billy have a girlfriend nobody knew about, a girl who clearly didn't respond to his advances?

Rosa couldn't quiz her weary mind any further. She needed water. Even more than that, she wanted out of this prison; she needed to know her son was safe from the Turners. The door opened behind her; she wished she could turn and see a friendly face, a familiar face, someone to help her.

Meredith Turner stood over her.

Rosa swivelled her eyes up to see the woman's scornful glare staring down at her, shaking her head mockingly. It wasn't the human face she wished to see.

'You pathetic heap of pretence, you! Don't look so la-di-dah now, do you? You excuse for grandeur, you!'

Rosa forced her throat to speak. 'Meredith, what are you doing? You *know* me. You know *Ben.*'

Of course I *know* you. *And* that selfish brat of yours, who parades his sweet wife around like a prized possession! And his purpose?'—she let loose an ear-piercing scream—'to humiliate my boy Billy! That's what I know, only too well.' She deepened her voice like a man's, ending with a quiver in her throat. From under a wide-brimmed hat that came from a distant past Rosa picked out the white features of madness, the light from the opened door showing the wrinkles through the powder lavishly applied, but carelessly.

Framed in a white mask of powdered dust, two dark orbs aimed their hateful gaze at her. Rosa felt totally powerless and absorbed the smell of death near her, around her, ready to ensnare her. She closed her eyes to block the evil that was above her, the badness clothed in a long and badly fitted dress that draped on the floor.

Meredith spoke sternly again, 'Open your eyes when I talk to you, d'you hear me!' Rosa obeyed and tried to focus on the figure that began to roll the long creamy-yellow gloves down her skeletal-thin arms. The woman softened her tone, much like the soothing words of the villainess in a fairy tale.

'That's better, now. What are you doing on the floor? Not trying to escape, are you?' She started to dance on septuagenarian legs that resembled broom handles, making little circles with petite steps, then went into song, singing shrill notes of the alleged Banshee, her mouse-squeak voice rising and falling, devoid of harmony.

'If you were standing, we could dance together, Mrs Tavistock. I wanted to dance with Elizabeth but Billy wouldn't let me. He's the spoilsport, that one!' She stopped twirling and offered to help Rosa to her feet. Rosa didn't know how to answer. The woman could hardly lift her own feet off the ground. Before Rosa could say 'get Billy to help me', Meredith had bent over her, grabbed the chair with both hands, pulled hard, and hauled it upright. Rosa marvelled at her strength.

A thought came into her mind, straight from Ben and Elizabeth's wedding; it was of Meredith dancing, hardly off the floor, changing partners frequently. If she wanted to dance with Elizabeth, why would *Billy* stop her? Indeed, why would *anyone* stop the old woman? It was a happy time, a celebration, and yet… Elizabeth did appear somewhat relieved when Ben got between them and waltzed his bride into the kitchen.

'He did that before, you know?'

'Did what, Meredith?' Rosa muttered the question along the sandpaper channel that was her throat. Giving full attention to the woman's face was hard work. Although a thousand times more comfortable back on the chair, her entire body ached; Rosa was certain her shoulder was badly bruised and the side of her face throbbed with the pain of a broken cheekbone. She couldn't remember slamming onto the concrete but she figured it must have knocked her unconscious. The pain verified that.

'Stopped me dancing with Elizabeth! Aren't you listening to me?' Her voice climbed higher.

'I'm sorry, Meredith, but I don't feel well. Can't you see I'm hurt? I need medical attention. Will you help me?'

Meredith placed her bony hand under Rosa's chin and raised her head. It hurt and brought a groan. She studied Rosa's features, especially the bloodied cheek, then she slowly wiped away some of the dust from her lips and chin. She looked quite intelligent at that moment, Rosa was convinced, like a medic examines for injuries.

'I once trained to be a nurse, Mrs Tavistock. Did you know that?' Rosa made some attempt to move her head.

'You have lovely skin, Mrs Tavistock. I had beautiful skin, too, when I was young. Mr Turner told me so, but he didn't *appreciate* my beauty or my talents, not then and certainly not now. However, back to your plea for my help! I *will* help you if—if you get Elizabeth to dance with me.' Rosa saw the intelligent eyes change shape; the shape of insanity.

'Meredith, that's not possible. Don't you remember the accident?' Rosa pleaded for an intellectual response. Meredith stamped her foot and demanded an answer.

'You sound just like Billy! None of you want me to have fun! *Will you or will you not ask her?*'

'I can't! Elizabeth is gone! Don't you understand that?' Rosa closed her eyes and lowered her head in despair.

'Gone? No! She can't be!' Meredith's incredulity forced her towards the exit. Rosa perceived that the meagre light in the room became sparser. She opened her eyes and spun her head as far as she could.

Billy's bulky figure darkened the doorway.

'Billy! She says Elizabeth is gone! Where did she go? How could you—she moaned a sorrowful moan—'how could you let this happen to me. You planned it! I know you did! *Anything—anything* to hurt me!' She screamed at her son and shouted abhorrently. Billy took her by the thin arm and quietly said to her: 'Mother, go and get Rosa some food and bring a glass and a jug of water, please. You may get your wish to dance with her yet.' Rosa felt invisible. Mother and son carried on an obscure dialogue as if she weren't there. She interpreted Billy's response as humouring the old woman. And who wouldn't, to keep her calm?

Billy took in the situation with a brief study of Rosa's face. He went outside and returned with a sponge in a bowl of warm water in one hand and a small white box marked *First Aid* in the other. He said nothing to his friend's mother while he daubed the broken, bruised skin on her cheek. She winced several times and waited for him to talk his way out of the position he had put her in. Gently, he moved the matted hair from her eyes and mouth, cleaned her face of dried blood and grime and applied a band-aid to the cut. Rosa felt no better for the treatment but the new situation honed her tongue.

'Why, Billy, why?' I don't understand any of this—I don't know what to think!' His mother returned with the requested food items and spat in Rosa's face, calling her a vicious liar. Rosa grimaced. Stunned by the foul woman's action, she stiffened before she made the automatic move to wipe the spittle off her cheek but hurt her wrists, the rope searing her skin.

Billy stepped in once again and bodily lifted his mother; the tray carrying the sandwich and water crashed to the floor. He carried her from the room and closed the door. A touch of the switch on the wall and a twenty-five-watt globe issued a dull but ample beam of light across their faces. Rosa waited for his reply. The words came slowly, almost shamefully, but he kept contact with her eyes.

'Rosa, it went all wrong. It wasn't meant to be like this. No one should have been hurt, not Stephie, and certainly not Elizabeth. You *must* understand this! Do you think you can? Do you think Ben will understand?'

Rosa shook her head, weeping and unable to cover her face. 'Take these ropes off me, will you? You have me tied like a dangerous convict!'

A woman's scream, long and anguished, sent a shiver up Rosa's spine. The scream echoed into the dank basement; she thought it came from upstairs. She looked to Billy for an explanation. Instead, he breathed a deep groan and hurriedly untied her wrists. Rosa guessed the old hag was giving vent to her anger, having being dismissed expeditiously by her son. Clearly, his behaviour infuriated the wrinkled woman.

With the door locked behind him, Billy left Rosa free to massage her wrists but her feet and chest remained tied. Attempting to undo the cords she found she had neither the strength nor the dexterity to get her fingernails into the tight knots. She gazed around her prison cell in the new but dim light, squinting into the darker corners where an assortment of tins and boxes made unruly columns on the floor. Large silver cans dotted with rust spots marked WEEDKILLER and FERTILISER, with labels peeling off, stood on a crooked shelf three feet off the ground; a rusting jerry can with the word DIESEL scrawled in big letters with black paint leaned against the wall.

Rosa guessed the wet spot beneath it was a direct leak from the can; one of the fumes that burnt her nostrils and the back of her throat. On a table that used to be a butcher's block, a long knife lay at one end. The rotten taste of old fish climbed into her nasal passages; she reckoned Billy scaled his catch of fish in this room before storage in the ice box.

Individually, the odours were nauseating but the combination of petrol fumes and fetid fish remains, toxic weed killer and the dank and mustiness made her gag. Not once did she hear neither Billy nor Meredith complain about the rancid, sickening stench. She figured they were used to it, which was sickening even to think about the possibility, or else both of them suffered a serious olfactory disorder.

To her left a gap in the wall that would easily accommodate double doors opened into a larger space. The light just about picked up the grey aluminium surfaces of a boat trailer. Behind it, Rosa saw the outline of Billy's Mazda 4x4, its chrome aerial reflecting the sparse light. A broken propeller lay by the wall opposite her; half a dozen tyres were heaped on top of each other in an awkward tower; thick ropes hung from large hooks embedded in the brick. Rosa ran her eyes around the walls and the floor area and took in the general mishmash of household debris strewn carelessly about; broken chairs intertwined, piled up like spaghetti; newspapers three feet high and yellowed on their edges.

Her overwhelming thought was; *how could anybody be so unhygienic*?

The rough concrete beneath her feet had several wall-to-wall cracks; she guessing the work was done by a DIY-er who had way too much alcohol in his veins. The floor hadn't been swept for eons; the dirt and dust and grease filled the gaping cracks. How she wanted out of this hole! She felt something creeping down her face and quickly wiped Meredith's spit before it reached her lips; with the other sleeve she dried her eyes. And thought of Ben.

Seven

Ben woke up.

In the distance, he heard the clock in the Town Hall tower give out the faintest of chimes and complete its cycle. He checked his digital watch; it showed the numbers 10:01. Incredibly, he slept for only a few minutes; it felt like hours, even days. Unusually refreshed, and uncomfortable by it, he missed doing something he should not have missed at all; he actually went to bed without knowing where his mother was!

Dressing quickly, he grabbed the spare key from the hallstand and drove to his mother's house. There was no logic to her leaving, he decided. Having not seen her all day, and especially when she promised to return and help him spring clean, he could reach only one conclusion: *she had to be at home.* When he came into range the security light lit up the garden and gave a new perspective to the shrubs and flowerbeds.

It seemed like years since he'd been to his mother's house. Nothing had changed except the spring had brought new life to the cherry blossom tree and the rose bush began to bud. The lawn was neat and the brick path showed little signs of wear since Rosa had it done five years ago. It was a weird feeling of déjà vu and yet there was no reason for it. He grew up in this house! Knew it back to front!

Why won't the key fit the lock? He fumbled with his left hand and rapped on the panel with his right. 'Mum hasn't changed the locks, has she?' he whispered to the door panel. Concentrating harder he saw his error. The key was the wrong way up. Expecting his mother to be in bed and disturbed by the knocking, he stepped back onto the brick path and waited for a light to come on in her bedroom. The house stayed dark. Going inside, he tapped the light switch and called out to his mother in his best least anxious voice. By now he was racing up the stairs, thinking he might have to wake her up to be convinced she was all right.

The bed was empty. The room was cold; no heating had been turned on today, which meant she was out all day. Where is she? Ben became agitated by her absence. Where can she be? If she joined a club of some sort and the meeting ran late—yes! That would explain it, he thought. Maybe she mentioned it but I wasn't taking much in. Dot Layton! She'd know. They're friends, they do things together. He checked out every room in the house before he rang Dot.

'I was just heading off to bed, Ben—oh, I'm *so, so* glad you are up and about. It's just *wonder*ful. But no, Rosa and I do the pottery classes but not today. Anyway, they finish by four o'clock. We play bridge now and then but never *this* late. Are you sure she hasn't gone to see your Aunt Carla? She said she would.'

Ben hung up and thought about ringing Plinter but changed his mind. The police do nothing about missing people until they are truly "missing". For now, he could only hope she's not lying ill somewhere, in an alley, or collapsed in her car and slumped on the wheel on a lonely road or in a ditch where people drive by minding their own business, either because they fear involvement or they don't care at all.

A new thought came to him. She's had a car accident; she's in the hospital and can't remember a thing. That's it! He rang the local hospital and waited and waited for the night nurse to check. She came back with a negative response, which was disappointing in one way but at least his mother wasn't in a sick bed. He tried two more private hospitals and received the same answers. Questions continued to pummel his brain for answers.

'Where, then?' he anguished. 'Since the hospital hadn't checked her in with a traffic injury, then it seemed unlikely the police would know anything. What other reason would she have to be away from home at this hour, and why, why didn't she ring me?' He decided that it wouldn't hurt to call the police. The policewoman who sounded like a young person listened for a minute and said it was too early to qualify as a missing person.

'Well, will you take the details at least? Someone on the beat may see or hear something—I don't know!'

'Ok, Sir. Give me your mother's name and address.' Ben did so.

'Mrs Rosa Tavi—is that Tavistock, sir?' Ben said yes.

Another voice, a man's, interrupted. The young woman must have only part-covered the mouthpiece while she spoke to the other because Ben picked up their muffled sounds. The next voice he heard was Plinter's.

'Ben! Is that you? What's this about your mother?' Ben imagined the inspector's voice softened but he went on to relate his concerns about her, saying he hadn't seen her since nine-forty and they had a prior arrangement to meet in the afternoon.

'Hold on, Ben, I'll have the call transferred to my office.'

The woman said, 'Right sir!'

'I was just clearing up a few things before leaving and heard PC Brimley mention your mother's name. Listen, where are you now?'

'I'm at my mother's house—'

'—I'll be there in ten minutes.'

Plinter arrived in twelve minutes and seemed different somehow, more relaxed, as though they were old friends. He began to look around the roomy foyer, apparently for clues, and said, 'the kitchen', then promptly assumed where it was and headed for it. Ben raised his voice and got the policeman's attention. 'And a very good night to you, too, Inspector!' Plinter checked his pace and turned to face Ben, who had his hands apart, showing his palms. 'I'm sorry. I'm probably overreacting.'

Ben eyed him squarely and said, 'You seem to know your way around. Have you been here before?'

'Yes. I had reason to call on your mother.'

'In connection with …the accident?'

'You could say that, Ben.'

'What was wrong with the police station?'

'The truth is, Ben, I am quite fond of Rosa…your mother.' Plinter shifted his feet.

'And how does *my mother* feel about you?'

'I don't rightly know. I sort of hope she likes me. Don't put me on the spot. Ben. My interest in her is genuine. I'm not to trying to sneak behind anyone's back, including you.' Ben scoffed at him. 'So let me see if I've got this right, Inspector. Tonight you'd woo my mother and tomorrow at nine a.m. you'll interrogate me as a suspect in the strange case of Elizabeth and Stephie Tavistock! A conflict of interest, methinks, Inspector Plinter?'

'I'm here as a friend, Ben, an admirer of your mother. I can offer my services. Consider me a friend with a history of police experience. You choose whether I stay or leave.'

Ben grew angry instantly. 'Let me tell you my deep feelings on the matter. Are you prepared to listen?' Plinter nodded. Ben poured out his disgust on past injustices. 'I rang the police station to report my mother was missing, yeah? I was told she wasn't gone long enough to get your flatfoot underlings off their rear ends. YOU come along and I get IMMEDIATE attention! But wait! There's more. Almost twenty years ago my father was mowed down on a pedestrian crossing by a drunken teenager. The lout did six months of an eighteen-month sentence in a correctional institution after which he got straight back into a car. I received no special treatment back then and I don't expect it from you now!'

'Ben, I've been in the business of crime and criminals for nearly forty years. I've seen things that would curl your hair; I've seen people get off who were guilty as hell. I've seen poor innocent folk end up as victims. And I've been *powerless* to do anything. I *also* have a deep sense of fair play and justice and more than once I felt like packing the whole thing in, and getting a job in a factory sweeping floors…with no responsibilities! I'm not much different to you in that respect; I also hate that those with limited resources have less opportunity in court than rich people. Of course I do! I hate that even more than I hate to see the criminal get away.'

'Excuse me if I sound cynical, Plinter, but why didn't you leave the force since you hated it that much?'

'Don't get me wrong, Ben. The police force is not the problem! The law is in place to protect the innocent, to punish the thief or the murderer, or the drunk driver who maims and kills. Rules and regulations are vital for a smooth-running society. We need them. The law is a reminder to everyone to be decent members of the community.

'Without law and law enforcement there would be anarchy, every man a law unto himself. So I decided to stick with it because while the guilty may get away sometimes, eventually they will have to answer for their crime. It will come back on them. By staying with the force I help put the bad guys away, some, at least, which translates into helping the rest of the community.'

Ben was impressed with the policeman's reaction. Behind the dark suit and the stern exterior, he seemed to have a heart for what he did best. Perhaps he didn't treat it as a job that put food on the table and a few quid away for retirement. Ben concluded, for the moment anyway, that the man was sincere, that his career had become a vocation and not just a job.

'I thank you for your straightforwardness. Whatever you think of me, I appreciate your assistance to locate my mother. What can you do here?'

Plinter relaxed. He was on the verge of offering the young man his hand, as a token of acceptance, as an introduction into the family. Instead, he went into investigator mode. 'Let's look for tell-tale signs, anything to suggest her itinerary for today. You said she left your house around nine-forty. Did she say where she was going…shops, hair salon, things like that?'

Ben thought for a second. 'Yes, uh, she took the model number of our—my… vacuum cleaner, so she would go to Berkley's to pick up dust bags. There was something else. Oh yes, she invited me to dinner so I guess the butcher was on her list. She often goes to Mac's Meats in Grand Street Mall.'

Plinter acknowledged it was a start but checking it out would have wait until the morning. He suggested she probably made a list of things to do. 'Where does Rosa… your mother… keep a notepad, appointment diary? Near the phone?'

Ben got a little excited by the basic method of finding information; instantly he found the man intrusive. Still, in his mind he pictured the end result: his mother appearing out of nowhere and asking what the fuss was all about.

Plinter moved to the telephone table and gestured to Ben. 'May I?' Ben said go ahead; Plinter read through the appointments. There were several entries; a trip on the Moonlight Cruiser with CP on the 18th, a surprise visitor to the pottery club on the 20th and *Carla* (underlined)—*tentative date 23rd*.

'Who is Carla? Her sister?' Plinter asked.

'No, she's my aunt, my dad's sister. She lives in London. Mum said she would visit her soon. My uncle is sick. It's a dead-end anyway, I rang Carla earlier.'

'There's nothing for today, Ben. She must have planned a day at home. What about other activities? I know she does volunteer work with some old folks in the area. Was this on her regular agenda, not something she'd necessarily have to be reminded to do?'

The reply came, she spent time with him in the morning; her only plans, as far as Ben understood, was to come back and help him clean up the house. 'There was no mention of other things she had to do. I think she would have told me.'

'Was she upset in any way? Did she have something on her mind, did you notice if she was… distressed in any way?'

Ben guffawed in his face. 'Come on, man! *She* lost Elizabeth and Stephie as well. Or hadn't that crossed your mind? And then there was *me*! *Of course* she had worries on her mind! Now her son was deep in the pits of depression for months on end, and you ask was she upset!'

'Forgive me if I sound insensitive, Ben, but if there's no logical reason why she hasn't kept her appointment with you, and the hospitals haven't admitted her, then *something* must have occurred to change her mind. And since she hasn't told *you* why she's late then it's likely because she's unable to do so. Does that sound a reasonable explanation to you?'

The younger man stared at the floor searching for another conclusion. 'I suppose what you say is true. I can't reach her by phone. My earlier fear had her in a ditch unconscious after an accident—'

'We can't rule that out... but let's not speculate. How's her health been? She's an active lady, by all accounts, isn't she? Does volunteer work and plays bowls too, I believe?'

Ben watched Plinter rub his neat moustache, a routine the man had when asking questions. He wondered whether or not it was an unconscious mannerism that came along with the job of interrogation, or was it body language? Ben continued his secret thoughts. *Perhaps it's a nervous habit, his way of saying that he's been courting my mother and he's worried about my approval. After all, he seems to know a fair bit about her. Has he been getting to know her these past months while I was out of the picture, isolated from reality?*

Ben's thoughts went black again. *The awful feeling of utter loss and hopelessness took up residence in his chest cavity. Images of Elizabeth and Stephie flashed on and off like a neon light on a tall building, images of his darling loves struggling in unrelenting, merciless waves. Plinter saw him sway. Ben didn't feel the policeman ease him into a chair; rather, he kept reeling in his anguish, his head spinning, his stomach heaving.*

In his ears, his brain replayed Elizabeth's desperate cries for her child. Her voice was so clear. Over and over he heard her apologising to him for not being able to find their infant in the chaotic tide, for not being able to see her, for not being able to save their little baby. Vivid pictures of her forlorn face appeared above the waterline, her head turning hysterically to locate Stephie. Her eyes, once blue and sparkling, now miserable and sad, sank below the surface and reappeared as she fought to keep afloat.

Ben's disordered, tangled thoughts showed him her eyes, her mournful eyes, searching his face for forgiveness for being careless as a mother. He tried to grab hold of her white hand with red paint on her fingernails, to pull her from *the cruel sea, but her ring came off in his hand. He wanted to tell her there was nothing to forgive; he wished he could reach down to her lips and kiss away the awful, ceaseless pain that distorted her lovely mouth and carved her beautiful smile into a perverse mosaic of remorse.*

From somewhere—he couldn't discern the direction—he thought he heard the whimper of a child across the churning waves. Someone shone a strong light on the foam and he caught a glimpse of Stephie's blonde hair with her blue ribbon neatly tied to it. Then she was gone. Another tormented scream came from Elizabeth's heart and faded.

Ben's mental video pictures showed him the wispy carpet her sandy hair left on the surface. Then she was gone. He plunged into the water, calling out their names each time he resurfaced for air. In the watery conflict where salty waves sting eyes and fill nasal passages, he heard a male voice calling his name.

'Ben! Ben.' *Plinter pulled him out of the water.* Ben shot upright. The big hand on his shoulder gently shook him.

'Are you all right, Ben? You look pale.'

'I'm…fine now. I was a bit dizzy… a headache.' That was his way of saying to the policeman 'you'd never understand should I explain the torment I have dealing with losing my family'. He wasn't prepared to try to explain the entrenched ache that regularly and systematically wrenched his heart in two. How could a hardened flatfoot of forty years' experience who deals only with facts and motives, crimes and punishments, really comprehend his personal loss?

'Can I make you a cup of tea?' Ben smirked inwardly at the man's offer. *Yeah, why not? You know where the kitchen is and I'm sure you can source the cups from the right cupboard, too. Need I tell you that the teabags are in the green tin next to the Nescafé jar, or do you know that too!* He found Plinter staring at him; it was as if the man was reading his thoughts. No one is that good, Ben thought, not even the best body linguist at the top of his game.

'A cup of tea would be… nice, thanks.'

At the kitchen table, Plinter suggested a pill to help ease his headache and asked where Rosa kept them. Ben held back his jagged tongue from insulting the man out loud. He wanted to tell him to leave his mother alone, that she was all he had left after the ocean killed his family and he wasn't about to surrender her to the clutches of a stranger! He stared at the figure across the oval table and saw no malice in the man's eyes. In fact, they were soft, they were sympathetic; they were a bit like his father's eyes.

Ben hadn't thought about his father in months. Not that he chose not to, no, but rather he and his mother spoke less and less about him as the years went by. Occasionally they would dig out the photos and reminisce, but all too often emotions got in the way; the excursions through the photo albums became rarer. It was hard work for Ben to recall his face sometimes but he did remember his eyes. Panic struck him. Would he forget what *Elizabeth* looked like, what *Stephie* looked like? He vowed a secret vow that he would not forget!

Plinter began to look around again. Ben knew the man was thinking *clues,* anything to suggest where his mother might be. Then he stopped and aimed his next words directly into Ben's eyes.

'Can we check her room?'

'You mean her bedroom?'

'Yes.'

'I'm not sure she'd like you to do that.'

'If it bothers you, we can do it together.'

'If it bothers my mother, it bothers me.'

'She'd understand if she knew we were trying to help her.'

'What do you hope to find there?'

'Don't know until I look around.'

'Let's just say the idea bothers me, Inspector.'

'Call me Corish. Remember, I'm here as a friend…with experience.'

'Corish?'

'Yeah, blame my mother for the name, but hey, I'm used to it by now.'

'Do you have a middle name?'

'You don't need to know.'

'You are not ashamed of your *given* names, are you?'

Plinter smiled at this. 'No, of course not.'

'Then why don't you tell me what it is?'

'Are you serious about locating your mother, Ben?'

'Are you the CP in my mother's diary?'

'Yes, I am. Does that bother you, too?'

'What really bothers me is that you feel the need to check out or… double check *my* whereabouts the day Elizabeth and Stephie drowned. Something you didn't think of doing until the ring was found half a mile from the Marina!'

'Ben, if you really want to talk about this now, so be it! We can leave your mother wherever she might be and discuss exactly where you were that day between the hours of twelve and two. Let's not wait for tomorrow. Shall we begin?'

'Is solving the case more important to you than finding my mother, Mr Corish Plinter?'

'No, it's not, but seeing as you prefer not to accept my help, then why not use the time eliminating *you* as the chief suspect: your words, not mine!'

'What do you mean, *eliminate* me?'

'Ben, I don't believe you had anything whatever to do with the incident.'

'You don't?'

'Listen to me for a minute. I've been dealing with the criminal element for many years, do you understand? You get to *know* people; a kind of mixture of gut feeling, intuition and an ability to see through the lies they tell or the body language they give off…indiscretions that eventually convicts them. I can't see *you*… hiding away for months from friends and work colleagues, barely letting your mother in to see you, behaving and looking like a hermit, not taking care of yourself, and virtually starving yourself to show others you are grieving! I saw you, what, twice, in the days after the accident.

'You were not *acting,* Ben! Besides, I had constant feedback from Rosa; let's face it, she was the link between you and the police investigators; it was she who conveyed the torment you were suffering. I saw that in Rosa's—your mother's eyes. I believed her. She described your anguish, your pain. I understand pain of that sort. I had a daughter once. I know! Drug overdose, that sort of thing.'

'I'm sorry for your trouble, your daughter, that is. I had no idea. But…why did you as good as accuse me—'

'—I didn't *accuse* you. I simply asked you to be available for questions in the event that it was more than an unfortunate accident. If I sounded brusque it was because I didn't want you storming out of my office on a mission of truth! Firstly, I don't think you are emotionally equipped to do it, and secondly, you might do more damage by talking to people. You might scare *someone* off. *If someone had hurt*…Elizabeth and Stephie!

'That's it. Maybe *now* we can reconstruct their steps, this time from a different angle. With this new information…we can use a wider lens, a zoom lens, so to speak, and focus more on the *individuals* Elizabeth spoke to or had contact with and not just the superficial information they gave us when interviewed.'

Ben slowly nodded his head while he kept his eyes fixed on the Inspector. The man had a bit more to him, he thought, now that they had talked together and feelings were spread and explored. But he only lost a daughter. Does he really know what it's like to lose a devoted wife and an adorable little girl…in one day? He tried to feel for the man, really feel for him but he could only feel his own pain. And now his mother! My own mother in some sort of danger! What an awful thought!

'Inspector, do you think my mother's disappearance is connected with Elizabeth and Stephie's accident?' Ben didn't try to disguise his agitation.

'Ben, don't rush into conjecture. You'll give yourself undue worry! At this point, there's no relationship between the two incidents. You need to get a grip. Let's first of all talk about your whereabouts that day.'

'Ok, Inspector. What do you want to know? I'll try to… recall. I said goodbye as usual but I left a little earlier that day. It was a little ritual we had before work. We kissed and hugged, and waved before I drove off. I'd lower the window as I turned into the street and blow a final kiss. Little Stephie would… wave to me…in her comical way.

'My day began at half past eight but I had an important appointment on that day…Thursday. The extra time allowed to me to go over my presentation and make any minor changes. A meeting with the Town Clerk and the owner of a shopping mall for final approval on a four-story car park was scheduled for ten o'clock. That took just under an hour, I think. I drove back to the office; Diana, she manages the office, brought me a snack from the deli. Tom Marnier and I…he's my boss…we discussed some details about the house we designed for my next appointment, Aubrey Tanzin, the banker.

'After that, I got the blueprints ready and went to meet Tanzin. Let me see now, oh yes! Diana rang me on the way and said the client had been involved in a squabble with a Ford at the traffic lights and both cars needed to be towed away, but Mr Tanzin would keep his appointment, but an hour later. I walked around the park to kill some time. I thought about meeting up with Elizabeth and Stephie but then the storm hit.

'People dashed for cover. Within minutes the place was empty; wait a sec…the blind man! There was an old man with his guide dog. We were near the bandstand so I helped him to the shelter. The rain was so heavy it was impossible to drive so we sat together during the downpour for twenty minutes or so. I offered him a lift but he said he'd be fine. I remember he rubbed the Labrador and said 'we didn't get very wet'.

'After that I went to the bank and used their facilities to clean up and dry my pants and jacket and then I met the client in his office at one pm; Tanzin manages the show. When I returned to the office at three o'clock…it was then I heard the news.'

Ben took a breath and sat back into the armchair. Gripping the armrests tightly, in an effort to ease the tension revisiting that awful day brought him, only worsened his stress. Making a conscious attempt to relax, he began tapping the armrest instead. That didn't help either. He stopped tapping and waited nervously for Plinter to question him. He couldn't think of any reason to be fearful; he knew he was nowhere near his family on that day. The last time he saw them was ten minutes to eight when he left for the office. Recalling the events of *that day* that made him anxious.

Why the policeman wasn't taking notes caused him to wonder. Maybe he paid some memory expert to teach him the tricks of the trade. And now he has perfect recall and doesn't need written reminders. Forty years of interviewing, interrogating, and probing punters must also help, or maybe he has all the answers and the questions are superfluous! Is *anyone* that good?

Plinter pulled out a small, cheap notepad. A pencil appeared between his fingers like a magician pulls something out of a hat. He licked the graphite and swung the pencil into the readied position, hovering over the paper. Ben divorced all his opinions about the man's memory. Maybe it was only old plods near to retirement that licked the lead tip; putting it down on paper seemed to make what they heard official, more authentic. Or maybe they *just had to* write it down, otherwise they'd forget it. They probably needed a memory course!

'Now, let's talk about the schedules you had with your clients, and particularly the second one. You left your office when?'

'That appointment was for twelve; the bank was minutes from the office so quarter to twelve sounds right.'

'Before you reached the bank you had a call from your office. How long was that after you left?'

'A few minutes, no more.'

'So let's say it was close to ten minutes to twelve, OK? How long were you in the park before the rain started?'

'About twenty minutes. I checked my watch a number of times before…before the rain started.'

'Did you get the man's name?'

'I told you! Aubrey Tanzin.'

'No, I mean the blind man.'

'Oh, him…no, I didn't.'

'Think about this, Ben. It could prove to be very important.' Ben thought about it.

'No, I barely talked to him. He just stared straight ahead and talked to his dog more than me.'

'Did he mention the *dog's* name? Think, man!'

Ben thought hard. 'I don't remember him addressing the dog by name. Occasionally, he took a biscuit from a paper bag in his pocket and fed the dog.'

'What did he look like?'

Ben gave him a queer look. 'Well, he was big and black, and he wagged his tail a lot! How does one describe a guide dog, Inspector?'

'I didn't mean *the dog*, Tavistock! The man! The blind man, how would you describe *him*?'

'Oh, sorry, I misunderstood. Eh…he was…short, old and grey…I don't follow you, Inspector. What has this to do with anything?'

'He can verify that you spent time with him during the storm, that's what! The next person you had contact with was Tanzin at one o'clock. The point I'm trying to establish, Ben, is that you may need an alibi, from the time the storm started until you met with your client, the banker.'

'Plinter…pardon me…Corish, may I ask a stupid question?'

Plinter nodded, a little frustration crept in beside his patience. 'Please do!'

'Is the cart not before the horse here? I mean…you *want* me to have an alibi! What for? Unless you know something I don't—wait a minute. Where is this leading to? What *did* happen to my family, Inspector? Did someone hurt them? Tell me! When you said *foul play,* you really meant that, didn't you? What do you *know*, man!' Ben leaned forward, his manner demanding.

Plinter spoke slowly, softly, 'At the time, it *was* suspicious. Finding the ring and the nappy together caused alarms bells to go off. Whoever put the nappy in the dustbin didn't know the ring was inside it; that's the theory for the present. If it was Elizabeth who did it… well, that's another story. I can't think of any reason why a loving mother would do such a thing, can you? I know this is all delicate stuff with you, Ben, but you understand there are all sorts of questions raised when we start looking into the tragedy that no longer reads 'accident'.

Ben sat back again, his thoughts changing from demanding answers to yielding to questions. Questions he knew were aimed directly at him, like arrows fired from a bow, questions that hurt, questions about Elizabeth's mental health, questions he would have to face from rumours the media spread to sell newspapers; lies and innuendo that sold printed gossip to mindless readers who had nothing better to do than read and pass on the woes of others!

And why! Why did he have to answer twisted, provocative and offensive queries about his dead wife and child? No! He didn't have to nor would he entertain the masses who bought the paper for the headlines that tantalised their sordid curiosity, which excited their brief but grimy interest, until the next edition. Was Plinter the law enforcer any different? He looked at the man twirling his self-styled upper-lip fuzz and wanted to ask him just where his police work crossed over the borders into curiosity fantasy-land. But he kept his thoughts inside.

Ben anticipated Plinter's first question and immediately went into reverie. There was nothing wrong with Elizabeth's mind! Nothing weird about the love she had for the beautiful child she cared for and for a certainty, there was nothing dishonest with the deep feelings she had for him!

'Ben, as hard as it is for you to think about it… Did Elizabeth show any sign of depression before the terrible mishap?'

'Do you mean did she shows signs of pre-suicidal behaviour, isn't that the real question, sir? Let me set the record straight! Elizabeth did not drown herself and take Stephie with her! Are you a madman or what, to ask such a thing as that? Ask anyone who knew her! She loved *life*, she loved *Stephie* and she loved *me*! *She would not have taken her own life.*'

'These things have to be explored, Ben. Once we eliminate them, then we move on. I had a word with her doctor, Jeremy Ames, one of the last people who spoke to her. He prescribed antidepressants for her. You *knew* that, of course?' Ben was disappointed that the policeman would be so insensitive by asking him; and now, shocked by this new information.

'I wasn't aware of that. She would have told me. I've never seen her take anything like that. No, I don't believe it!'

'Maybe she didn't *want* you to know, not wanting to trouble you or give you cause for alarm. Withholding information from a spouse could also be seen as a sign of love and concern; perhaps she didn't want to worry you. Perhaps she felt the feeling would pass; oftentimes people with depression are the last to accept it.'

'Read my lips, Plinter. Elizabeth did not suffer from depression, no matter what the doctor said or prescribed. She did not, I repeat, DID NOT, swallow those tablets. I will talk to Ames myself! Tomorrow!'

'I think you *should* talk to him, Ben! He has things he wants to discuss with you but he put off talking to you because you were…grieving; the opportunity for him to do so was not…convenient, let's say.'

'What things, Plinter? Tell me what you know or so help me!'

'Has not your mother spoken to you yet?'

'My mother? What does my *mother* know? She *wouldn't* withhold things from me. Not about Elizabeth!'

'Ben! She wanted to tell you. But she told me you weren't ready for it, the timing would have to be right.'

'Do *you* know? Are you telling me *you* know something about my wife, something my mother told *you* and not *me?*' Plinter stood up and paced the floor, caressed his thin moustache and stopped with his back to Ben. He turned abruptly and said he regretted that Rosa wasn't present.

'Ben, Elizabeth was pregnant. Your mother—'

The enormity of the statement forced Ben out of the chair. He rushed at Plinter, grabbed him by the collar and shook him back and forward. No words left his quivering lips, but he continued to shake the taller man. His face was fixed with a contorted, twisted expression that translated into speechless but angered disbelief. Corish Plinter took Ben's wrists in his big hands and steadily eased them from his jacket. He held on to them for a minute, trying in some way to give the younger man a sense of stability, an attempt to inject strength into him to help him cope with the sudden burst of data on his brain.

But no, he unwittingly infused Ben with a weakness that reached his leg muscles and made him wobble. Plinter steered him towards the chair then let him go. He couldn't tell what thoughts went buzzing around Ben's head, what synapses were bridged to deliver more and more grief to his already blistered heart. Ben stared into emptiness in front of him. Wasn't it enough that the cruel ocean took Elizabeth and Stephie? Why an unborn child should also suffer, should be barred from seeing the outside world, should be deprived of joining its sister in growing up together in a happy family structure?

In a heartless eruption of three words, *Elizabeth was pregnant*, Ben's family was increased instantaneously by one. And now, in his mind, the tragedy multiplied and the loss amplified a thousand times. There was a flagrant newness to his pain, a ruthless inventiveness that hurled him back into the throes of heartache that infested his being months earlier. It left him cold and numb, and angry. Angry, yet again. He started to shiver as his head reran images of Elizabeth struggling to save Stephie, all the time holding her stomach to protect the new life in her womb.

What an awful decision she faced! To save the infant sinking in waves of fury or the infant floating in calm embryonic fluid? The picture of Stephie appeared on the shore once again, only, this time, he saw the lifeless embryo lying beside her, nestled into her body. It was as though he had been shown a photograph of Stephie and he missed seeing her sister the first time round. Now it was so obvious.

He looked up at Plinter without taking in his presence, silently questioning the man's temerity to heap more pain on him. He thought of his mother with annoyance and wondered why she hadn't the courage to tell him about Elizabeth's pregnancy; why she let Plinter, her new boyfriend, do her dirty work. What would Dad have thought about this betrayal? He checked his attitude towards his mother then forgave her as quickly as he condemned her.

'She must have had a good reason for not telling me,' he promptly concluded. 'She also loved Elizabeth and Stephie…and…' A name for the unborn baby didn't readily come to mind. Plinter interrupted his gloom.

'Ben, your mother doesn't know about the pregnancy.'

Eight

Rosa's body leapt into consciousness, awakened by the wailing coming from the bowels of the house. Somewhere—she couldn't pinpoint where—but it sounded like the old woman crying in an empty room. The echoes resounded like a wind howling along bare corridors, bouncing from one hard surface to another. Rosa thought her sense of hearing heightened; the screams reached her ears in a crescendo and then faded to an eerie silence. A cold breeze iced its way across her neck and shoulders.

Straining, she swivelled her head towards the door. It was wide open. There was no sign of Billy or his mother. The light had been turned out. One of them must have been in the room while she slept. The tray was still on the floor from the last visit; the sandwich compressed into the cracks in the concrete. She couldn't avoid thinking it was deliberately trodden on. The spilled water left its stain.

The pain in her cheek had subsided to a dull ache; she massaged it with sore fingers. The blood on her wrists had congealed and crusted on the wounds; she touched them tentatively. The wounds were sensitive. The chair was hard against her back and the pangs of hunger and thirst continued to grip her insides. Billy had been gone for quite a while, as far as she could tell, it was hours. If she could reach the crust of bread that survived the fall, then gladly she would have devoured it. Her mouth was desert-dry and her lips craved for moisture; she mustered up a frothy saliva to moisten them.

Rosa began to dwell on the madness that breathed in this large Georgian house; she sobbed in between her thoughts. The stories Ben told her over the years, some of which she felt were far-fetched and sometimes outrageously untrue, were now taking on a new shape. She recalled the times, and it was often, when Billy came home with Ben after school. They would get lost in the garden shed tinkering with an old lawnmower, or broken radios and clocks Billy brought along.

Occasionally, she heard Ben explaining, or trying to explain to Billy a few tips on fractions and decimals, but rarely had success with him. Normal things, healthy things, she thought, that boys engage in when building and reinforcing a camaraderie. What did disturb her were the tales Ben used to tell her about Billy's home life. It reached the point where she told him not to repeat any more boys' tales; she wasn't interested in gossip about Mrs Turner! But memories of the tales of the woman's so-called antics were etched on her brain. She could hear eighteen-year-old Ben's version of what happened when he went to pick up Billy for the end of term dance…

…Billy had finished dressing and needed a final hand with his bow tie. Mrs Turner intervened when I offered to help him. She gave me the foulest look, a real look of jealousy, Mum. It was such a contrast to the way she treated me earlier. In the kitchen, she was flirting with me! Billy's mother is fifty-six! It wasn't just the fact that she admired me in a suit but it was the way she touched my collar…my arms.

She actually pressed her fingers into my biceps… and squeezed. There was a glint in her eye. I was starting to shake inside. It was scary. When she sorted Billy's neckwear, she took his fingers in hers and turned him in a circle. She was showing him off, comparing him to me as if there was a competition, a rivalry between us! Billy was so embarrassed. Then Mr Turner knocked on the door!

Her husband came back after four years. Meredith ushered him into the sitting room; we heard her arguing at first. He could hardly get a word in. then she began screaming. Billy couldn't believe his father was back. He hadn't seen him for ages. His first impulse was to go in there and defend his father against his mother's vitriol but he looked at me and said 'she'll never change'. We could hear Mr Turner's raised voice arguing he only wanted to see his son. Billy took me into his games room and shut the door. He asked me to wait with him until the row was over. We heard some noises, more shouting and then doors slamming.

A few minutes later, Mrs Turner called out for Billy, saying he'd be late for the dance if he didn't hurry. Billy asked her where his father was. She replied he had left and, as if addressing a large visible audience, she continued, 'good riddance to him; he'll never be the man Billy had become'. She kissed his cheek and winked at me and then we left for the school dance...

Rosa pondered; the account Ben related to her years ago now had substance. There *was* something odd about the woman, something seriously wrong with her and not just the state of her mental health; something more than senile dementia inflicted by Alzheimer's disease. The woman had a quirky, calculating, menacing dimension to her persona. Rosa had seen it for herself. What reached her ears as a giggle caused Rosa to look behind again but no one was there. The giggle turned into a laugh. It came from the shadow in the corner of the room. Meredith stepped into the sparse light. Rosa visibly jumped with fright. The chair moved several inches. Meredith shuffled in front of her and spoke.

'I was *watching* you, Mrs Tavistock. You looked so *worried,* like a little child who has lost a precious possession. I saw your every expression. What were you thinking? Nothing unpleasant, I hope?'

'Meredith, please tell me what I've done to deserve this?'

'You *interfered.* That's what you did. You stuck your nose in where it was not invited.'

'I was—where is Billy? I need to talk with him. Please get him for me.'

'Look who's giving the orders now! And you all tied up! Where did you ever get such confidence, Rosa? Billy is not in charge here, anyway. *I am!* So let's get our priorities right, Rosa, shall we? *I* tell Billy what to do. I have *always* controlled my son. It is better for him that way. It protects him.'

'Protects him? From what, Meredith, from what?'

'From his father's influence, and ultimately from himself! From himself! Do you hear? Boys need to be sheltered from wayward fathers. Are you blind as well as stupid? I shielded him from his father. His father was a womaniser and Billy was not going to follow in his footsteps. I would make sure of that. He would not be happy until the right girl came along; I would screen his girlfriends and decide if she was the right one for him! That is how a real mother protects her son. Protection of the highest order, Rosa Tavistock, but you wouldn't understand that, now would you? You didn't save *your* son, did you?'

'What do you mean, Meredith? My son is not in danger, is he?'

'Will you listen to yourself, Rosa? You didn't save your son from *that woman*, did you? You didn't vet her properly. She got past you and ruined his life. *You* ruined *his* life by being irresponsible. You should have seen through her! We mothers must stick together and protect our sons. For you, dearie, it is too late!'

'What are you saying? You can't possibly mean Elizabeth!'

'Can't possibly mean Elizabeth, can't I? You make her sound like a goddess, that butter wouldn't melt in her mouth! She is the most unfaithful creature that ever walked!'

'Unfaithful? Not to Ben she wasn't. Never!'

'I'm not talking about Ben, you dimwit!'

'Then who, Meredith? Who?'

The older woman guffawed into Rosa's face, shaking her head with contempt, belittling Rosa for her ignorance.

'Billy! Who else? She was unfaithful to *Billy*, my *son* Billy!' She ended in a shrill crescendo, leaving Rosa as puzzled as ever, and very vulnerable. The thought that the old woman in her present rage might strike out at her face raced through her mind. The ropes that bound her to the chair emphasised her helplessness. Her hands, although free, had no wish to defend herself either, for she was frail from lack of food, and she had seen the strength the older woman displayed earlier.

'She was married to Ben, not Billy, Meredith. What—'

Rosa's puzzled face provoked more anger from Meredith's malicious lips.

'What nothing! Billy saw her *first*! Can't you see that now, surely you *must*, after all the damage that has been done.' Rosa remained wide-eyed, her face still begging for an answer that made sense. Meredith supplied an answer that made sense to *her* and to no one else.

'Billy fell in love with Elizabeth. He told me about her over and over. I told him: 'bring the girl home to me and I will run my eye over her for you'. He complained he hadn't formally met her; he hadn't even talked to her but rather saw her in the bank one day and *knew* she was the one. And just as he got up the courage to introduce himself to her, in struts his *so-called friend* and steals his girl from him. Yes, *your son* stole Billy's girl! Isn't that the truth, Mrs Tavistock?'

A rush of thoughts came to Rosa; some clearly, others hazily. The one clear thing that struck her was the noticeable change in Billy's attitude towards Ben.

She recalled mentioning it to Ben but he discarded any hint of jealousy on Billy's part as ridiculous. He knew their relationship ran hot and cold, but Billy was never vindictive. Sometimes Ben wouldn't see Billy for weeks on end. Rosa didn't see it as Ben explained it at the time, and now, after hearing the poison from Meredith's tongue, she realised that Ben had gotten it wrong. It was the ongoing *irritation* in Billy's demeanour she saw when Ben and Elizabeth were together, not that the two men's relationship had switched to the temporary "off" position.

She remembered putting Ben's theory to the test on one occasion, to see if Billy was happy for Ben and Elizabeth. Billy and his mother were invited to a meal at her house. Shortly after the food was served, Ben announced his engagement to Elizabeth. There was a moment of stunned silence quickly followed by a subdued applause, followed by animated congratulations by Meredith. Billy hardly joined in at all.

Rosa distinctly remembered the look Meredith gave Elizabeth, almost hateful in its nature but she smartly recovered with a fond smile. Rosa now understood that it was a disguise to hide her contempt. She hadn't seen the obvious jealousy back then but now, five years later, the link was made; *Meredith really did believe that Ben stole Billy's girl!*

It was later in the evening she got the opportunity to ask Billy what he thought of the engaged couple. The answer he gave didn't match up with his reaction when Ben made the announcement initially.

I think it's wonderful for them. He's a lucky man to find a girl like Elizabeth.

It was the lack of eye contact with her that caused her to doubt him. She put it down to the man's shyness and then quickly erased it from her mind. That was *then. Now* gave a different picture. Rosa's mental register had Meredith off planet earth and heading for the lunar globe; maybe she arrived there twenty years ago? All the signs were in place. She had a vicious streak for such a wizened woman; life hadn't taught her any lessons in kindness, in human decency, and if the dementia she supposedly suffered brought her sympathy, then her calculative, manipulative and maniacal mindset earned her none.

Rosa concluded Meredith Turner was psychotic, and probably psychopathic. What things she knew and read on the subjects convinced her that the old woman's behaviour matched the description. She wasn't in the habit of judging or condemning anyone; still, Billy's mother's actions warranted reproach. What she was doing was unconscionable. Rosa was sure Corish would agree with her.

And Billy? Rosa was worried about Billy. He drugged her then tied her up and for what? A letter? A love letter from him? And to whom? *That* was a mystery. But why the anger? Why did Billy get so physical? He must have something to hide. No one behaves that way over a love letter. No one does. Unless…unless it's a forbidden love…or a suitor who didn't get the desired response.

The more Rosa thought about the sentiments the letter produced the more she believed the writer was making a plea for the woman's hand, and although he felt unworthy of her and didn't fancy his chances a whole lot, the words were sincere; the request was a plaintive one. Who was this woman, this creature of unsurpassed beauty that had the man's destiny on her tongue? Just one word, one nod of her lovely head, one smile of approval from her delicate lips was all he wanted, was all he needed, was all he lived for.

Rosa looked up at the woman staring down at her. Staring, and waiting for an answer.

'Can't bear to admit it, can you, Dearie? Your son robbed my boy of the happiness he deserves, isn't that so?'

Rosa was tired of the woman's rhetoric. She couldn't answer *yes* because she didn't believe it and she feared answering *no* because the woman might attack her as she had done earlier in the day. The dried blood that matted her hair was proof of that. Diplomacy was the half-way house she dared enter. Rosa closed her eyes to conjure up a tactful response. Billy's voice came to save her. She opened her eyes.

'Mother! I told you to give our guest some water. Go, do it now!' Meredith glared at him, her face stiffened and for a frozen moment, *she* was the painting of the matriarchal head hung above the fireplace. The eyes narrowed and the wrinkled mouth slowly cracked and became a smile, not a real smile but one that said 'my time will come, just wait and see'.

She left the room and immediately Billy began opening Rosa's cords. He took a penknife from his pocket and sliced through the tough knots then helped her to her feet. He muttered something about circulation and began to move her around. Rosa complained she was stiff and her body ached, gesturing to the chair indicating her preference to sit. The smell in the room reached her nostrils once again; nausea tried to overtake her abdomen and spill its juices into her throat. She held her neck and swallowed.

'Billy, how could you allow this to happen? You lock me in a filthy, dirty, foul-smelling place—an animal wouldn't live here—and why? We are supposed to be friends—why? Why are you and your mother so much against Ben and me? He'll be worried about me, Billy, you *know* that. Ben will be out looking for me as we speak. Just call him and let him know where I am. He'll come and pick me up. Please?'

Billy turned his back on her; she watched the man's shoulders heave; she heard his breath whistling in and out and quicken. Rosa heard him sobbing. He rubbed his sleeve across his face and said, 'Rosa, come with me. You are right. This place stinks.'

In the kitchen, he pulled a chair out from the table. 'You need food.' He poured a glass of water shakily from a beaker and passed it to her. Exhausted, Rosa took in slow sips at first then gulped the remainder greedily, then waved the glass at him for more. He filled the glass a second time and began carving thick slices from a leg of cooked ham, placing the plate before Rosa. 'Can I make you a sandwich, Rosa?'

She said no, could she wash her hands first. Pulling her body from the seat, she waited for his permission. Billy was quick to apologise for not offering her the bathroom facility. Meredith entered the kitchen with a tray, an empty glass on top. 'You're not *feeding* her, are you? She deserves nothing for raising a lying thieving rat for a son!'

Billy answered sharply then softened his tone. 'Go to your room now, mother. It's twelve thirty. It's time to sleep. I'll look after everything.' Meredith fairly threw the tray and tumbler into the sink; glass splintered in all directions. Billy didn't move a millimetre; Rosa jumped back a pace. Meredith deliberately brushed past the nervous Rosa, nearly causing her to topple. She grabbed the back of the chair for support and steadied herself.

Meredith's parting shot was a firm reminder to Billy 'not to let that two-faced lying, thieving shrew out of your sight. She'll be out the door and telling all her friends false stories. Be careful, Billy! Be *very* careful!' Then she was gone. Her footfall on the oaken stairs faded, to be replaced by the sharp thump of a door slamming. It resounded into Rosa's ears; she secretly wished that was the last sound the old woman made.

The mental leg-room the bathroom offered, gave Rosa the chance to try and collect her thoughts and come up with the worst-case scenario for her plight. There were too many blank spots to fill in between the time she knocked on the Turner's front door, and wakening up in the malodorous room that smelled like an abattoir, tied and tired, beaten and aching. Her head spun searching for possible reasons for Billy's uncharacteristic manner. The question *why* circled her mind without finding a landing strip. Only Billy could provide the answer, if he wanted to. So far, nothing that made sense materialised. She would implore him to explain.

His mother clearly had a strong influence in what went down, Rosa concluded, and it struck her for the first time that evening as to which of them had the remote control. Billy *seemed* to be in charge, judging by his impatience with his mother and the way he ordered her about. Rosa allowed her intuition to kick in; she was sure, however, that Billy was not the prime mover. Whatever questions remained, one thing was certain; the malicious language Meredith aimed at Ben for 'stealing' Elizabeth from Billy was the key factor in this whole charade. The old woman kept bringing up her *perceived* view of events, which could be put down to confusion that dementia brings, or the woman has this *crazy* all on her own.

'What did she mean, Billy?'

'What do you mean?'

'Your mother, Billy. What did she mean when she said you need to be careful of me, that I might tell stories? You must tell me what this is all about!'

'It's too hard to explain, Rosa…too complicated. I can't let you go just yet…can't decide what to do either. It's…far too complicated.'

'She talked as if you and Elizabeth were an item that should have led to marriage. Where did that come from?' Billy straightened up and snapped back.

'That part is true! I did fall in love with her. From the time I saw her I was…I was smitten. I could not believe it when Ben introduced me to her…I was mortified at first, then ashamed for being jealous of Ben. Then I felt embarrassed by the situation…then humiliated, *even betrayed by both of them*. You have…no…idea, Rosa. None. I tried to be happy for them, truly, you must believe that, Rosa'—he nearly reached for her hand to urge her to feel sympathy for him—'you really should try to understand how I felt.' He ended with a look of despair, a soulful plea for recognition that he was entitled to feel dejected, to be miserable.

Rosa shook her head rapidly, her natural motherly role taking over.

'I had no idea you were in that awful position. And you kept it to yourself all this time?'

'What else could I do? It was a hopeless situation.'

'Elizabeth rejected your…I mean…did she discourage your interest?'

'I hadn't spoken to her until Ben…I only *saw her*. That was enough for me. Didn't I tell you that already?'

'So she never *really rejected* you; she never really *knew* you, Billy, *to* reject you. Isn't that right?' Billy didn't respond to the insinuation.

'I have a room ready for you, Rosa. It will be…comfortable…at least. I am sorry for the way you were treated. Mother…it was her idea. I panicked…yes… I panicked. It should not have happened that way.'

'The letter, Billy, tell me about the letter. Why did you send it? To Ben? Why to Ben?'

'I didn't send the letter. Elizabeth did.'

'Elizabeth?'

'Yes. Elizabeth.'

'What are you saying, Billy? That it was an old letter? That she sent it to Ben before she died?'

'No, I'm not saying that at all! Besides, it was not written by Elizabeth. You read the letter. It was written by a man to a woman. Surely that was obvious, Rosa.'

'Yes. I see that. I'm confused, Billy. Your name was at the bottom. Help me understand. Why was it addressed to Ben?'

'I told you. Elizabeth sent it. Besides, it was not meant for Ben's eyes, not ever.'

'Billy, please! You're not making any sense. You say Elizabeth sent it but didn't write it. It had Ben's name on the envelope but it wasn't meant for him. It had your signature on the bottom…and you didn't send it?'

'It did *not* have a signature, Rosa. It was typewritten. The whole letter—all four pages—were typed. Have you not figured it out yet, woman? '

'No! I can't! I must be delusional from lack of food, lack of sleep. I can't think straight. Just tell me, Billy. Tell me!'

'Eat the ham, Rosa. Then get some sleep. I have a nice bed ready for you. You might work it out in the morning.'

'I *can't* work it out! *Billy, just tell me, please?*'

'I won't get any sleep tonight unless you know the truth, Rosa, isn't that right? Eat the ham *first*, you need it; then I'll show you the truth!' In exasperated submission, he hammered his fist on the table.

Rosa gazed at the pink meat, dazed. Nourishing food lost its appeal. Hunger and thirst were the least important items in the present order of things; only a simple answer to a simple question was all she required. And here, she complained, this man with a mouth full of riddles dangled truth before her to tantalise her curiosity even further. She caught his eye and followed his nod towards the plate; he was determined she should eat first.

Her stomach heaved again; the sight of the pink pig meat with its thick layer of white greasy fat hanging loosely, the two slices alongside that looked like two fleshy tongues intertwined, only worsened matters. She put her hands to her head and pressed hard against her temples to ease the new pain. Her knees wobbled. She made a grab for the chair and, with a weak exhalation of air, called out Ben's name and fell to the floor.

Nine

'Why didn't Elizabeth tell me she was pregnant? That…that would be the most natural thing for her to do…to tell *me*! We had no…*reason*…to hide things from each other. We loved each other, Plinter. We were partners.' He paused to collect his thoughts. 'Tell me, did my mother tell you Elizabeth was…?'

'No. I told *her*. I spoke with Dr Ames recently, part of the investigation, you understand?' Ben stared into emptiness.

'You had no idea she was pregnant, no discussion, no hint, no signs… anything?' Ben left his reveries.

'We didn't plan…that is, we planned to have another child, but not just yet. Elizabeth didn't enjoy the best of health, so we thought it better to wait…a few years anyway…give Stephie time to be more independent. Elizabeth would find it easier that way.'

'Yes, I understand, but did you notice any change in her…routine, her…well, you know how women get when they are expecting. Morning sickness, stuff like that?'

'Inspector, I had no idea she was pregnant. And no, I didn't see any…signs as you put it. Elizabeth didn't…some women don't have all the traumas of early pregnancy. With Stephie, she hardly put weight on, her…morning sickness was minimal. She had the best nine months of her life! The baby was born at home; it was perfect. Possibly…no probably, I didn't detect it. But I *can't* understand why she didn't confide in me. That's the hard part.' Plinter prepared Ben for the next question. It wasn't an easy one to ask but as a policeman for decades it was routine. He half apologised to soften the blow.

'Ben, don't go off the deep end on me but I need to ask you a…a sensitive question—'

'Do you think I don't know what it is? Do you imagine I don't know where you are going with this? The answer is NO! The child was mine. There was no other man in her life! End of story.'

'It had to be asked, Ben; it needed to be established. I know it's hard for you. But we have only your word on the matter.'

'Let me get this straight, Plinter. You were *hoping* I would confess that Elizabeth was unfaithful to me. That she had someone on the side, that I'd be jealous and do her in! And my little girl, too! That this would give you and your staff a new line of attack on a crime, a murder? You madman, Plinter! You are one piece of work! And you have not even established that a crime was committed. You have a ring, found in a rubbish container by a yappy little dog and now you think you have a motive?'

'No, Ben. That's not my way. Like I told you before, I'm trying to *eliminate* you from a crime that may or may not be. I'm not trying to pin anything on you. Will you work along with me on this? Just answer calmly.'

'You, Sir, are making some appalling allegations against me! How do you *expect* me to react?'

'We are in a peculiar liaison, Ben. I'm acting towards you as a friend of your mother, but I'm also a policeman with investigative fire in my veins. If your family *was* victimised then there is a criminal out there, and questions like the ones I'm putting to you will be put by the Police. I will excuse myself from the investigation, of course, *should there be one*. I'm preparing you now, Ben, because *you are the chief suspect.* Crime stats show that people are usually killed by someone they know. It's a fact of life, Ben.'

'Thanks, Plinter, that makes me feel a lot better. But what you haven't told me, and what I sense is—you *really think* there was a criminal act. Am I right, sir?'

'Yes, I do. I sent a forensic team out to the Thornley house. We tested for fingerprints on the dustbin. They matched with the prints on the teacup you drank from in my office this afternoon.'

Ben stared long and hard at Plinter, piercing deep into the policeman's eyes, demanding a logical doctrine from the man, and getting a blank, stone-faced response from him. He laughed loudly, nervously. Plinter kept a poker face while Ben laughed in it; then watched the younger man's demeanour change shape into utter incredulity. Ben raised his hands and curled them into fists.

'*My* fingerprints? Tell me you are winding me up. Why are you doing this, Plinter? What is your purpose in life anyway? To shock? To get a reaction from me? You are not seeking a promotion, are you? Just how low can you go?

'I'm just stating the facts, Ben. The evidence is real. Some would say it puts you at the Thornley house. In the garden, to be exact.'

'I…was…at the house today, it's true. I did not, however, enter the garden!'

'You were seen by a neighbour who thought you looked suspicious. The woman saw a car outside and took note of the number plate. It was your car, Ben. We got a phone call from her husband shortly after six. He saw a fire in the Thornley garden as he pulled into his driveway and quickly doused it. The dustbin was set alight by someone and all that's left is a small heap of melted plastic and a black circle of burnt grass. The man said he smelled petrol. Our boys confirmed it. Did you set the dustbin on fire to get rid of your fingerprints?'

Ben tried to equate the ruthless questioning with the so-called friendly approach Plinter said he was operating under; he remembered what Plinter *said* but he found it hard to believe the man. It was almost like the old fox was cajoling him into a confession, under the pretence of amity, and subtly, deviously, bringing damning evidence to bear against him where there was no evidence at all. He decided to play Plinter's game.

'I agree, Inspector. My fingerprints were on the *cup*. The Thornley dustbin is foreign to me; I did not touch it,' he ended sarcastically.

'How do suppose they got there?'

'I have no idea.'

The two stared at each other; neither man flinched. Plinter continued, 'Did you cause the death of Elizabeth and Stephie Tavistock? Be careful how you answer. It may be used against you.'

The question hit Ben like he'd been electrocuted and hurled into the air only to crash against a wall. His mind reeled at the suggestion, yet this grey-haired senior detective peered over the rim of his glasses coolly waiting for a *yes* answer. Ben's whole chest fibrillated from the pounding of his heart. His breathing shortened into rapid panting. He had insight into the kind of panic the asthmatic person has and wished someone would give him a ventilator for relief. *Slow down*, he heard an inner warning whisper to him. *It's not real,* the voice continued, *Plinter is really a friend, he's only preparing you for the worst-case scenario.*

'No! I did not! I'd rather have my hands severed than use them to hurt my family.' Plinter paced the floor while he thought up his next line of amiable slash fierce attack.

'Your secretary, Miss Diana…Silvester—we talked to her today—she said your boss wanted you to return to the office. He had blueprints he wanted to discuss with you seeing you had an hour or so before the next appointment. You chose not to return. Why not?' Ben stuttered, a little confused by the statement.

'I…I can't think why, I can't remember…that. I was passing by the park and thought it would be nice to enjoy the moment. There was a tree there planted by a dignitary some years ago, a Eucalypt. Elizabeth loved the aroma from it …and…I thought of her. That's all. Nothing covert about it. I must say, Inspector, you have been getting around, haven't you. No doubt you talked to Tanzin the banker, and his Missus. All you need now is to locate the blind man to confirm my whereabouts, or have his guide dog visit your office for tea and doggie biscuits!'

'My office will be vacant for the next three weeks, Ben. I have a well-earned holiday waiting for me. So, no chasing old blind men or guide dogs for me. That is, in a purely professional manner. There is a whole team of men and women quite capable of that. In my absence, and without my help, they will, I'm sure, follow through on that line of investigation. In the meantime, I would like to offer my services to help you and your mother.'

'My mother! D'you mean help to find her?'

'That is important, of course, but there is something else.'

'Which is?'

'Ben, there were *two* sets of fingerprints on the dustbin lid. The other set belongs, I believe, to your mother. It's not official yet, I haven't spoken to my colleagues either, but I do have a gut feeling on this one.'

'You are beginning to intrigue me, Mr Plinter. Why on earth would my mother's fingerprints be on a *stranger's* bin?'

'Well, follow my way of thinking for a moment—'

'—don't tell me the police imagine that my mother and I…hurt Elizabeth and Stephie, including the baby—'

'Don't be foolish, young man. Rosa—your mother—would not hurt a fly! Just listen until I'm finished. Ok! Would I be right in saying you also have a black plastic ten-gallon dustbin?'

'As a matter of fact, I do. Doesn't everyone?'

'And your mother has been assisting you with household chores during the past few months? Yes? Including putting the rubbish out at the appropriate time?'

'Yes...she has been a rock... always there for me.'

'Ah! Therein lays the solution! Someone stole the lid of your dustbin. I *guarantee* you will not find Thornley's lid in your yard. I believe the lid was taken, not swapped.' Ben was flabbergasted by Plinter's turnaround. In one broad calculated deduction, he became the protagonist instead of the avenging angel from King Street Police Station. He had to know how the man arrived at Sherlock Holmes' school for detectives.

'It's a bizarre notion, but I'm eager to hear your line of reasoning, Inspector.'

'Well, there are two things. One, your fingerprints were preserved from the weather to some extent, because they were *under* the moulded handle. Four fingers gripped the handle; the thumb presses down on the top to complete the grip, much like a man would pick up a briefcase. The thumbprint was smudged and unrecognisable.

'Second, the smaller prints were *fresh* and obviously were not found on the handle because they would have obliterated your prints. Rather, when the whole lid was dusted, a set of prints on each side of the lid were evident, and inches apart the same set of prints were repeated. It was as if the lid was removed using both hands, put down on the ground and the rubbish placed in. Picking the lid up again put another set of prints on it, again, inches apart. Why—I believe it was Rosa—chose to do it that way, well, only she knows? There were no other prints; the garbage man wore gloves?

'Which leads me to conclude the lid was stolen before the collection. There was a print on one of the two side handles on the bin itself, enough to match it with the prints on the lid, forcing me to conclude Rosa...your eh, mother...dragged the bin rather than lifting it. I imagine the reason for that was the weight of it. A few inquiries told me the Council picked up your garbage around twelve.'

Ben nodded and said that his mother would have put it out for the collection truck before she left his house this morning, that he had no interest in it or anything else for that matter.

'You would *not* have seen it when you returned home today, Ben.'

'Why not? Not that I actually thought about it to look for it, but why not?'

'I had my men take it into 'custody', so to speak. For testing, you know?'

'And was the lid missing, as you suggest?'

'I'm *sure* it was, Ben. The boys will let me know tomorrow. Officially I'm on leave but I'll be keen to hear the results.'

'So, let me get this straight. IF the lid is *missing* it won't be because some school kids decided to have fun with it, like kicking it all the way down the hill, but rather because someone took it to fit it on top of Sydny Thornley's dustbin. Which means, I suppose, old Sydny has two lids instead of the usual one. Lucky him! *And*, may I finish…IF the lids have been *swapped,* we would expect to find, not mine or my mother's fingerprints there at all, but perhaps good old Sydny's, providing usable fingerprints, or some other form of DNA can be found on it to show it once belonged to the man OR, wait a minute! All the above may be guesswork, another of your hunches…unless the lid survived the arson attack in the Thornley garden today! Really, Inspector!'

'Sarcasm, in this instance, Ben, belittles you. Remember, we lifted your fingerprints off the lid found in Thornley's garden, and the other prints on the side of the lid, as I described. *That much is certain.* Someone removed your dustbin lid and yes, it *was* destroyed in the fire. *That is also a certainty.* My men were thorough, Ben.

'When you stop treating this case as a joke, you'll see that someone deliberately took your lid to incriminate you. It's that serious! I'm here to help you, and your mother. Otherwise, I'm off to Spain for three weeks and you'll be left to prove your innocence to others. I might add, it does not look good for you, in view of the present findings. My colleagues won't be as lenient as I. Say *yes* to my offer and we'll get serious about it.'

'Are you doing this for my mother, Plinter, particularly for my mother?'

'Yes. Particularly. I like her more than I like you. Maybe I'll change my opinion of you in time. Maybe you'll change your opinion of me.'

'In that case, I admire you for your candour, however blunt. At least it's honest. I respect you for that. I'm not a matchmaker for my mother's happiness; she deserves to be happy, but I am naturally protective of her, and suspicious besides. So, I do accept your offer to help us and I will make myself ready. Where shall we start?'

Plinter sported a triumphant grin and like an eager, impatient schoolboy about to dissect a frog in the science room, said, 'Now! Let's search for clues.' Ben led him to his mother's bedroom and, like a hawk the policeman's eyes were focused. Ben queried what he was looking for. The senior sleuth surprised him by saying he didn't know. 'Not sure…yet. Anything at all, anything to indicate whether she came back here after she left you, something that might tell us where she went from here, if she did return home. You say she may have gone to the butchers.'

Ben said yes, or to Berkley's to buy new vacuum bags.

'We'll have to wait until tomorrow to talk to them, but in the meantime, we can check the fridge for fresh meat. What time did she leave your house?' Ben answered, before ten. Plinter hardly stopped. 'Do you remember her shoes? What shoes did she have on?' Ben didn't know for sure. He thought they might be black, with a low heel. Plinter went into the en suite. Ben followed. Plinter picked up a pair of black shoes. 'These them?' Ben said yes, he thought so. Plinter said, 'They are wet' and passed them to Ben for inspection. Next Plinter opened a tall cane laundry basket and pulled out a cream skirt, then a lilac blouse and a cream jacket to match. 'She wore these to your house today?'

Ben replied, 'Yes, they are the clothes she wore.'

'She was caught in the rain, came home and changed. Let's check the fridge.' He left Ben standing; the younger man had only begun to descend the stairs when he heard Plinter give a victory shout from the kitchen. 'She got the meat! The label has today's date on it. Mac's Meats. Look around for the vacuum bags, Ben. Where would she keep them?'

'They were for my machine, so I suppose she'd have them with her when she left here. She would have, I'm sure, come straight to me and got into the cleaning.'

'Ok, let's make a few assumptions; something we shouldn't do but for the present let's forget the rules. She left your house, went shopping, and was caught in the rain. She came home; she was soaked to the skin, judging by the wet clothing and shoes. The time could have been anywhere from shortly after ten until the rain eased up fifteen minutes later. Getting home and out of those wet clothes being the first priority. So what would you do, Ben?'

'I'd...have a shower. Put some warm, fresh clothes on and...well, I'd light a fire. I love a roaring fire. Elizabeth and I would listen to *Turandot* in front of a scorching fire.' He stopped talking and bit his lip; he remained silent.

Plinter touched his shoulder and shook him gently. 'And what if you had to go out, Ben? Like your mother had to. Remember she was coming back to your house with the vacuum bags. What time would she have arrived, do you think?' Ben looked at Plinter beseechingly before he took the hint to get back on track. He needed a cue to work out a possible time schedule. 'Let's say she arrived home wet around ten-thirty' Plinter tapped his watch face.

Ben agreed, then added, 'A change of clothing, freshen up, maybe a quick cuppa…I'd have to allow an hour, give or take. That would make it about eleven-thirty.'

The tall policeman said that sounded reasonable and went on. 'But she didn't arrive, and your friend Billy came, got your car going. He left.'

'Yes. Then I went to meet you at the Station…that was about twelve-fifteen. We had our little differences and I left. So where was my mother all this time? It's not like her. She keeps in touch with me!'

'She hasn't a key to let herself in?'

'Yes, she does. But I…when I got back home there was no evidence the house had been cleaned, except for the little I did earlier. When I couldn't contact her by phone—and I tried numerous times texting—I came by her house but didn't have the spare key on me. Anyway, she was not home; her car was not there either. I was anxious about her and came back a few hours ago to check the house thoroughly.

'That's when I rang the Station. I thought she might have fallen over or she had an accident, I don't know…it was a worry, and I continue to be afraid for her. She's not like this, never! She would let me know if there was a problem. The total lack of communication with her is really what bothers me. It's been well over twelve hours since she left my house; it's too long, much too long.'

Plinter picked up the kettle and filled it from the tap. 'Let's have a cup of tea, shall we. Nothing like a cuppa to get the grey cells into top gear, I always find.' Ben didn't object and pulled a chair away from the table. A white piece of paper under the table caught his eye. He read the words on the torn envelope:

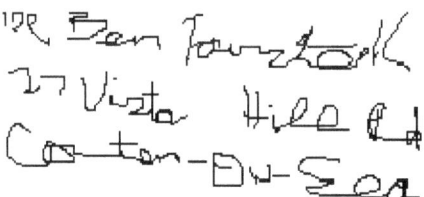

The writing was untidy, scrawled as if in a hurry. Some of the strokes looked familiar. He showed his find to Plinter, who snatched it from his fingers and MRI'ed the envelope, back and front. 'Do you recognise the writing?'

'No…it's got touches of Elizabeth's hand but it's too…too sloppy for that…and yet, she makes her *aitches* just like that'—he pointed to the *aitch* in

Hill—and the *Ess* in Corten-on-Sea—'but that can't be! Look at the postmark!' Plinter squinted and read, Dec 10, 2015.

'That proves it!' Ben exclaimed. 'That was two weeks after the…accident. Couldn't be Elizabeth's writing! The writing is…it's just a coincidence.' Plinter flicked the envelope over a few times.

'There's no sender's address, just the letter B and, yes, your name and address appears to be carelessly written, and as you say, perhaps hastily. I'll hold on to this, Ben. It may be a coincidence but it won't do any harm to have an expert look at it. Can you, if it's not too painful, that is, can you give me something with Elizabeth's handwriting, a postcard, a letter, anything at all.'

'I'll find something tomorrow for you, but it'll be a waste of time. How could it be…Elizabeth's?'

'The postmark doesn't prove it's not hers, Ben. All it shows is that the Royal Mail stamped it. Until we have the actual correspondence we can't tell much. My question is: what's it doing in your mother's home?'

It suddenly dawned on Ben where he had seen the envelope before. 'I must be losing it, Inspector! My mum found it under the old Queen Anne cabinet in my living room. It slipped between the wall and the sideboard and lodged there. It must have been there for the whole winter. The B is for Billy…Billy Turner. He's a long-time pal of mine. That's it! I asked Mum to read it for me, yes, now I remember. She said Billy sends his best wishes. Billy has the sloppiest handwriting *ever*. Well, that's solved that problem.'

Plinter kept up the argument. 'The question still remains, Ben. What's this— he waved the envelope in front of him like he deliberated between war and truce—doing here? In your mother's house? The natural thing to do was to *leave it with you*, not take it with her, don't you think?'

'My mother…simply… must have forgotten, and slipped it into her bag by mistake. Easily done, Plinter.'

The detective got cross. 'Try calling me Corish. You'll find with a bit of practice it'll roll off your tongue. Either that or stick with Inspector, alright?'

Ben offered a smirky smile and said, 'Ok, Corish, I'll try.'

The tall policeman carried on. 'I don't buy that. I don't think Rosa would absentmindedly pocket your private mail. *Is* she absentminded?'

'No.'

'I thought so. Which leads to the obvious question; where is the letter? Why is it not in the envelope? You know what I think?'

'No, but I have an inkling you are about to tell me.'

'I think she took it out to read again.'

'Is that another hunch?'

'No, it's not a hunch, it's intuition…instinct, if you prefer.'

'So it is a hunch, Corish.'

'Ok, then, it is a hunch.'

'Now that we're on the same page, why do you imagine she read the letter again?'

'Because she wasn't happy the first time around. If it were simply a greeting from your friend, then why would she be that interested in it? To take it away with her, bring it home and go through the contents a second time seems rather strange to me. What could possibly move her to do that?'

'You're the detective, detective. I'm just your humble pupil. For what it's worth, I think she's a caring mother; she probably was looking for some points of encouragement to pass on to me the next time she came by. I had very little heart for listening, talking, or reading for that matter. I hadn't opened my mail for months, until Mum coaxed me. *You* know how hard it was to see me, let alone talk to me. The letter will turn up and Mum will tell you exactly what I have told you; she just cares a lot.'

The bulldog wouldn't let go. 'How many pages, Ben? Was it a single page, two pages? How many?'

'I don't rightly know, now that you ask me. I think…I think there was more than one. I wasn't following too closely, but she did appear to be lost in thought, I seem to remember.'

'Tell me again, Ben, what did she say Billy said?'

'Corish, my man, you certainly don't give up easily! I think she said something to the effect that…let me think now…that he had a roundabout way of saying he'd like to see me, if only for a few moments. Something like that.'

'Do you see my point, then, Ben? What's hard to remember so simple a message that you'd have to re-read it? To me, the answer is plain. There was more to the letter than she told you. She wasn't happy with what she read and didn't want to upset you. I believe she went to see your friend Billy Turner.' Plinter sat back and folded his arms.

'You got all that information from one piece of white paper, an envelope with my name scribbled on it? Excuse my scepticism, Corish, but I think it's way past your bedtime. Lack of sleep is affecting your brain cells. You are now insinuating that Billy has what? Ulterior motives? Some secret agenda, a coded message that sends my mother off running to him for explanations? Get real, Corish. Seriously?'

'You admit you didn't read the letter, Ben, isn't that so?'

'That's correct.'

'So how can know there was nothing untoward in it?'

'My mother *told* me what was in it.'

'Well, prove me wrong, then. Go pay your friend a visit tomorrow and ask him about the letter. Then watch his reaction.'

'And what will you do? Tag along for company?'

'No, better you go alone. It must be kept as normal as possible. Thank him for the letter…that you just found it. Say your mother read it and told you the gist of it. You should be able to tell if he wrote the letter. Play with him until you come away with a positive answer; a *yes* or a *no*.'

'You *really* believe he didn't write it, Corish!'

'I believe the first thing you said is closer to the truth.'

'Go on. Who *really* wrote it?' Ben's face showed amusement but his heart was anxious.

'Your wife did.'

Plinter handed him the envelope. Ben read the address over and over and studied the handwriting carefully. Finally, guardedly, he looked at Plinter and said in a worried tone, 'I'll talk to him tomorrow.'

'Good. There's no need to tell him I'm helping you. There are a few items I need you to get for me. First, your mother's hairdryer; I noticed it on the dressing table and plugged in. There will be, all things being equal, fresh fingerprints on it. We can compare Rosa's prints with those on the dustbin lid. Also, we'll go past your house and collect Elizabeth's hairbrush and, as we discussed earlier, a sample of Elizabeth's handwriting.'

Ben was tired, almost too tired to query the inspector's rationale. Still, the hair brush bothered him. 'What do you need the hairbrush for?'

Plinter carried out his usual routine with his moustache and pondered his own reason for a few moments. How much does the young man need to know? He thought, and quickly discarded all arguments. 'Ben, if Elizabeth did write the address on the envelope, then it's reasonable to conclude she licked the stamp too. That means DNA. Is she a stamp licker, or does she brush it on a wet sponge?'

Ben queried the man's sanity for a second time since they met. 'Do you actually believe what your reasoning suggests? Are you trying to torture me, Inspector?'

'Ben, I'm a copper. I think this way, not to upset you or put doubts in your head. So far, it's a theory. From everything I know about this case, and hear me out! I am not convinced your wife is dead. She's not *able* to contact you.'

'You *are* here to torment me! The coroner—'

'—the coroner gave his expert opinion! Coroners have been wrong before, Ben, and they'll make wrong conclusions again. They're human, just like you and me.'

'I don't—I can't believe you, Plinter! You're making this up. You are trying to lay a trap for me, confuse me. You think I killed her, don't you?'

'I don't think she's dead, Ben.'

This protracted scenario was a whole new ball game for Ben.

This guesswork-policeman dressed up as a friend enters my domain and tells me blatant lies! To confuse me! To give me false hope! Next, he'll be telling me it wasn't Stephie they buried! When will the man control his ego and stop this charade? Always guessing at outcomes. Damn his hunches, his fabricated clues! Why wasn't he a farmer? Farmers don't hurt people with false statements and innuendo. They provide milk and eggs and beef, foods that build muscles and breed stamina and good health. Or why didn't he opt to be a bricklayer? Bricklayers build strong houses which give protection from the elements, which provide a haven for little families. But not our Inspector Corish Plinter. Not he!

But what if he's right?

What if his instinct is not just guesswork? What if the information he has does point to something sinister, someone sinister, someone who set out to hurt Elizabeth, and Stephie got in the way? Where could she be? Plinter said she would call me if she was able. Is she some dark stranger's prisoner? Is Plinter right after all? Or is he a policeman gone mad, like in the movies? Is he really on leave, or has he been fired from his post for a reason he has not revealed...?

'You are mad, Plinter! If Elizabeth were alive, she *would* contact me.'

'Nobody killed her, Ben. I think she's still alive and wants to contact you but can't.'

'Where is she, then? Where, Plinter? Tell me if you can?'

'If I knew that we'd be there already. You know that. Let me first prove my theory. I have a friend who will fast-track the DNA test—'

'—a friend? You mean a forensic man with the police?'

'No, a friend in the private sector; a research scientist. I can have the results in a matter of hours. Quicker than our boys.'

'You are an odd fellow, Corish. I'm not sure I want to know too much more about you. You have weird ideas and you change your appearance like a chameleon. I don't know if you are here to help me or arrest me. I wish my mother was here, she'd know what to do.'

'I wish she was here, too, Ben. But she's not! She could be in danger and that's why we have to act, and quickly!

'You *do* think my mother's disappearance has something to do with the accident, don't you?'

'I believe it has something to do with the *letter* your mother read. She said she gave you the gist of the letter. You said she *turned* a page; it had to be, at least, two pages. There could have been more than two; that's conjectural, however. For my money, that's more than enough just to say "hello, I hope you feel better and I look forward to seeing you". There was more, Ben, in that letter. I stick by that.'

'Not another hunch, Corish? You're prone to that of late.'

'I'm a copper, Ben. I have a nose for this work, backed up by many years of hard grind, and I get a bad smell from this case.

Ten

Rosa awoke and threw her eyes wide open. She was in a dark place. What were the sounds, she queried, no, the *voices* she heard? Raised voices from…there they were again…from her right…and…they seemed as though they sounds were floating. The softness beneath her surprised her; it was warm and comfortable. She was in a bed, a big bed. The pillow under her head was remarkably soft, like her head rested on a cloud. The wonderful sensation that she was restored to her own bed was a fleeting one. *This* bed was different; the onset of a sinking feeling in her stomach matched her worst thoughts.

Her body felt tight, encumbered. Then she realised she was fully clothed. The foul smells of the pseudo storeroom no longer assaulted her senses, but hung in the air nonetheless. The stink must have clung to her clothes. She felt dirtied and had the strong urge to change out of her jeans and tracksuit top. Her first thought to sit up was rejected by her aching body. The events of the previous night filled her mind. She put her feet on the floor; she had one shoe on. Odd, she thought, and then remembered feeling dizzy. Billy must have carried her onto the bed.

Slowly, her eyes managed the blackness; ghostly outlines of furniture began to make their appearance as a full moon gradually emerged from behind a mass of thick clouds, extending its rays through the opened curtain and revealing the antique treasures on the walls, the golden edges of picture frames. Scanning the floor she saw the missing jogger lying on its side under the legs of an old chair with worn old-world fabric on its seat and back.

The last thing she remembered was talking to Billy. Yes! His statements were contradictory; the frustration in trying to make sense of them angered her. Now her head spun and nausea joined in. The voices seemed louder now. They were difficult to decipher; the wall between was clearly the major deterrent to sound waves.

The fluorescent moon lured her to the new light coming in the window. She slipped on the delinquent jogger and tried to raise the sash window. It refused to budge. She couldn't decide if she lacked the strength or the window had a lock on it. Nor had she thought why she went to the window in the first place. Was it a subconscious lunge for escape? She quickly discarded the notion; two storeys up made that decision for her. The portrait painted in the window framed the slender shape of a tall decorative pine tree and behind, the silhouetted hills in the background. Fields stretched into the distance; some large, some small, bordered by dark hedges and stone walls.

Rosa knew the Turner property was a large farm at one time but had begun to be neglected once Meredith's grandfather passed on. Her father died in a tractor accident, leaving no sons to carry on. Meredith quit her nursing career to care for her ailing mother, who died slowly and painfully before succumbing to a premature grave. Rosa remembered Ben telling her. Billy told Ben. Meredith told Billy. Now it was she and Billy living in a big house on the edge of town, on a large acreage that drew the attention of several land developers. Ben came home one day telling Rosa he'd upset Billy. He jokingly said if his mother sold the land, she'd be worth millions. Billy said she'd never do that; she'd never give up her property.

Rosa left her thoughts dangling in the past.

'Even if I did scream for help, no one would hear my cries out here,' she conceded. The voices continued as if they were a long way in the distance, thin and fading. The moon and its halo disappeared behind the clouds, its powerful beam slowly succumbing to the building up of thick cumulonimbus masses that swept by. The thought of escape returned. Rosa squinted in the blackness, searching the wall for the door. Maybe it wasn't locked, and maybe she could slip down the stairs and onto the road and hail a passing car.

The idea excited her. She moved around the room in the near dark, groping at the furniture. The light from the moon made its presence shine briefly upon the door. Rosa started for it and gripped the handle; it was locked. The voices crept into the room again. Her eyes followed the sounds to a vent above the moulded picture rail and close to the ceiling. A chair next to the dressing table, she decided, would make a suitable ladder to climb and get her ears near the vent.

The effort to get her aching body onto the chair and haul herself up into an upright position was barely within her strength. Pressing her ear as closely as she could, she listened intently. Meredith was speaking but the words were indistinct.

There was another voice. It was soft and weak; and pleading. Rosa strained to hear more. The words were broken; she had to get nearer. She looked for something to stand on to reach higher. Against the opposite wall stood an ornate bookcase filled with old books. She clambered down and made a platform of several large and thick volumes then reclaimed her position by the vent.

The old woman's voice was clearer but the words were distorted; the sentences were broken, senseless. Her voice rose and fell as though she was reasoning to herself in a mirror, half talking, half in song and not paying attention to the other person. Was she talking to herself? Well, that was possible, knowing the nature of the woman, and yet…the other voice was different, weaker, and barely audible.

Meredith's squeaky voice fluctuated. "…see…dear…bet ….baby… belong here…no Billy…you…get used… night…" Then a pause, a long one. Rosa pressed even harder against the grill. Quiet pervaded. She heard a door click. Then sobbing, very faint, but very definitely a child sobbing, followed by a louder wailing, and then silence. Rosa was thoroughly convinced there were two people next door. She heard a second clicking sound, a louder click. She pressed her ear even closer to the vent.

'What are you doing up there!'

Meredith's shrieks came from the opened door. Rosa's body jolted with the sudden, unexpected entry of the old woman. The book-platform twisted under her feet. She grabbed at the picture rail and missed, and then made a frantic attempt to grasp the picture of a vase with yellow roses. Tumbling backwards, still holding the frame, she fell through space in slow motion. Somewhere in her descent, she heard her own voice begging for an easy landing.

The thump her body made on the floorboards echoed through the house. Her head bounced on the edge of the mattress and catapulted her head and shoulders forward and then back again, like a rubber band. Her finished posture left her sitting on the floor with her head against the mattress. Dazed and disoriented, she tried to focus on the wrinkled face above her. The scowl on the old woman's face told Rosa she was in for another venomous mouthful. The door sprang wider and Billy jumped into the room.

'What have you done to her, Mother? Move away!' He pushed her to one side and examined Rosa.

With an uncharacteristic fear in her eyes, Meredith backed towards the doorway. 'She was up there with her ear to the vent, sticking her nose in again.

She fell over. I didn't touch her! She deserves what she got! All busybodies deserve what they get!' The old woman clung to the moulded architrave on each side of the threshold, insolent in her stance, defiant in her view of accounts. Billy told her to be quiet. She took hold of the door handle. 'This is *my* house. I'll do as I please!' She screamed out the last few words. 'Ask her what she heard. Ask *her*, Billy. Go on!'

He said quietly, 'Shut the door, mother.' The door slammed and shook the picture frames on the wall; the crystals on the small chandelier above the bed tinkled together as if applauding a demented cause.

'Are you alright, Rosa? *Did* you fall?' She managed a slight nod.

'Can you move? Can you get up?' She shook her head slowly. Billy glanced at the books on the floor, then at the vent. He was averse to making eye contact with her. Instead, he surveyed her face with a quick scan, concentrating on her mouth, from where her next answer would come; he didn't like the questions her eyes asked.

'What were you *doing*? Were you *listening*?' She touched her neck and groaned.

'I heard voices, Billy. A girl I think—she was crying. I was…concerned. Who is she, Billy? There are so many questions…and you haven't been honest with me. Why is that? What's going on? What's *really* going on?'

He stared at her for a full minute, not moving, just thinking. Then, as though someone threw a switch in his brain, he said, 'Try to get up, Rosa. You need to get up now. There is something you must know…something you should see.' He helped her to her feet and sat her on the bed. The ache from her previous fall in the basement-cum-storeroom and the current pain in her head and neck went into remission. A stronger, ominous character jumped onto the stage in this awful drama, a feeling of impending gloom took over when personal pain was relegated to understudy.

Rosa limped into the dark corridor, holding onto Billy's arm. She thought how this man, who is now so gentle, could do what he did to her. Drugged her, tied her up and left her in foul conditions, let her be abused by his mother or at least didn't or couldn't control her, a woman who is plainly unstable—and yet he keeps his best friend's mother prisoner!

Billy opened the door into the adjoining room, pointed to the bed and led her to it. He pulled a chair closer and said, with a mixture of sorrow and torment tearing at his throat: 'I'll leave you now.'

Rosa gazed at the ruffled duvet on the bed for a moment, not knowing what to do, what to expect. She swivelled her eyes around the room, into the corners the light missed. A tall lamp with a heavy shade on it radiated the only light available. There was a form under the duvet that took up the shape of a thin figure. A child, no more than the space a child would occupy, Rosa guessed. A lock of hair lay across the girl's cheek, whose face was towards the wall. Her breathing was shallow with long gaps between breaths.

Rosa swung her head towards the door, prompted by the snap of the lock, and then back to the bed. She sat down and panicked at what she might find under the bedclothes. Is this the mystery, the truth Billy spoke of? Whose child is this? Billy's? Where is the mother? Why isn't she here? And who is the other voice she heard talking to Meredith through the vent? Was *that* voice the mother of this child? 'And why would Billy want me to meet this young person?' she argued with her thoughts. 'What had this to do with the letter sent to Ben?'

The petite figure stirred and murmured a string of unintelligible, frenzied sounds, and as a result of the product of disquieted dreams, the duvet was thrown forward. A girl's arm swung into open view. Rosa's maternal instinct moved her to restore it to the heat but the sight of the child's skin startled her somewhat. Her hand was not the hand of a child at all. Unless…the person was ill? The hand was…older looking, the skin was sallow. She touched the hand lightly.

Immediately, the delicate fingers wrapped around hers and held on. Rosa leaned forward to get closer. Still holding the small hand, she brushed the hair from the child's face. The child turned her head in response to the touch and opened her eyes. Rosa gasped and drew back, pulling her hand from the child's hand, gripping her throat with her other hand. The girl let out a feeble cry of subdued delight then used Rosa's name.

A stifled scream came from Rosa's diaphragm. '*Elizabeth!*' Instantly, she hugged the thin body of her 'dead' daughter-in-law. Rosa cried heartrending tears. 'My *dear, dear* Elizabeth! What have they *done* to you?' Elizabeth spoke with all the excitement she could muster. Her lean, gaunt face etched with the strokes of a death-brush, managed a narrow smile. Cheekbones that were once covered with healthy, pink flesh now protruded behind skin stretched taut across her face; her eyes sunken into deep sad sockets rimmed with black circles.

Rosa stared closely at her, studying the features carefully, as though she couldn't believe the sight before her. If it wasn't for the blue eyes and the familiar but diminished sparkle, she would not have recognised Elizabeth at all. She raised her up and gathered her into her arms, as a loving mother cherishes her sick child. Restraining her mouth from blurting out how thin she was, how light her body felt, how sick she looked, so as not to discourage the girl any further, Rosa wept and let her tears express her emotions. She held onto the featherweight girl who was as a daughter to her and heard Elizabeth's weak but tender words of gratitude pour into her ears.

'Rosa, I am so glad you came to save me. Where is Ben? Is he here? He must hate me for what happened.'

'My darling Elizabeth, Ben could *never* hate *you*! He's not here yet but I'm sure he'll be here soon.' Rosa, the mother, continued to rock her back and forth, saying, like a lullaby, 'Ben will be here soon, very soon, and get us both out of here.'

Elizabeth tried to pull away from Rosa but was not able to. Rosa sensed the intelligent gaze in her eyes, laced with a question. 'What do you mean, Rosa? Can't we leave now?'

The distressed look on Rosa's face told Elizabeth her captivity had not ended. She hauled a sob of utter regret from her stomach to her throat. The new anxiety caused her to breathe rapidly, panting for air. Rosa took hold of her again and whispered soothing words, to no avail. She fell limp in her arms; Rosa laid her head on the pillow. The two women sobbed together, neither getting any comfort from the other, nor any hope from the dismal situation they were in. When emotions calmed, Elizabeth whispered, 'Ben doesn't know we are here, Rosa, does he?' Rosa shook her head helplessly; her hand to her mouth, her teeth biting into her fingertips.

'Did…Stephie…did she drown, Rosa…did she?' Rosa nodded, her eyes filled up. Wild with anger she rushed to the door and pounded the panels with her fists. 'Billy! Billy Turner! Where are you, you monster! Get a doctor here NOW!'

Billy sat on the floor next to the door, his back tight against the wall, a sentinel who let no one in and no one out. His eyes were wide and stared into nothingness in the darkness, as in a trance, where nothing entered his mind and nothing escaped. He had committed an unforgivable crime against the very person he claimed to love, and now there was no flight from his guilt. At one level, he had owned up to it by allowing Rosa to see her, but he knew there were greater consequences to face. Not the least was the wrath of his own flesh and blood, his mother.

'Billy!' Rosa sobbed, clinging to the door. 'Please…get help for Elizabeth…please?' She slid to the carpet, imploring him to get a doctor, and wept bitterly for Elizabeth. The cries from behind the door no longer had meaning for the beaten man. How many years had he heard the tears, the snivelling complaints about his father, the accusations escorted by weeping, weeping to reinforce how badly *she* was treated? How often *she* moaned about having to quit her nursing career to look after her sick mother.

He was glad he wasn't alive to hear her then and not thankful at all for having being born. But heard it he did! All his growing up years when his father was at home, and all the years since. How she has not changed one iota with the passing of time. And how could she? How she never did learn to live and love graciously, to treat people with dignity and to be loved for it in return. And how could she? He wondered if he ever did love her as a boy should love his mother. He *knew* she didn't love him.

If manipulation, followed by shielded threats, was a sign of affection, then Billy supposed she called *that* love! He thought of the fifteen years of life he had with her and his dad and how bad those years were. But nothing compared to the onslaught that came after his dad moved out. Or more correctly, after his dad was *forced* out. Billy's anger was still raw, after finding that bundle of letters addressed to him. Recalling his confrontation with her, he could hear the argument she presented to convince him she was only trying to *protect* him from his father's wayward influence. How he hated her for that!

From his eighteenth birthday, when he found the letters hidden under a loose floorboard in the attic, until now, a man of thirty-four, his loathing for what she concealed from him hadn't abated. The night he returned from the school dance, when he was nineteen, added a new dimension to his revulsion of her. He could never forgive her from that night on…and yet he felt trapped.

Rosa raised her chin with renewed determination. She looked around for something suitable to smash the door. In the shadowed corner a long brass lamp-stand with a heavy, round base, caught her eye. Ripping the wire from the power socket, she took aim, with the base of the stand readied to strike. The splintering timber crashed into Billy's private, ugly memoirs. Frightened by the raucous intrusion into his thoughts, he jumped to his feet to see the metal fixture poking through the door panel.

Rosa tried to pull it back for a second strike but she couldn't pull the thing back; the base was stuck. Billy unlocked the door; Rosa stood back, quivering. Elizabeth kept murmuring, 'What is happening?' Billy gazed at the scene and swiftly went into the corridor again and ripped the lamp-stand from the door. He was angry and it showed. His anger was not directed at Elizabeth or Rosa; it was his mother he resented. If not for her, none of this would have happened. And yet, he allowed it to happen.

He could have nipped this whole affair in the bud months ago; brought Elizabeth home and taken his medicine for his crime. He looked long and hard at Elizabeth, whose life was drifting out of her like the ebb tide fades into the vast waters of the sea.

He knew she was dying.

He knew he would have to stand up to his mother. And if not him, then *someone* would have to restrain her.

She was the problem in his life, all his life.

Deep down, he knew that.

He sat in the chair, let his head drop forward, and wept. Elizabeth turned away from him and thought about Stephie and the infant inside her. She asked Rosa to take Billy out of the room; she couldn't bear to listen to his weeping.

Rosa was in a quandary. For the first time since she was incarcerated, she now had choices. Would she, could she, slip out into the darkness and get help? At four in the morning, who would be out at this hour? What about the old woman? Where was she? Is she such a heavy sleeper that the disturbance didn't rouse her? What if she *had* to confront her? Could she fight off the wiry Meredith? And, more importantly, could she leave Elizabeth in the clutches of these people, they knowing she who escaped into the night would return with the police?

The stage was set for escape. Rosa persuaded her mind to act, one way or the other. Billy was virtually incapacitated with a grief she didn't understand. Meredith was probably asleep. The door was wide open. The stairs were only metres away. Her heartbeat accelerated. She reviewed the risk over and over; indecision returned. She looked at the treasure in the sick bed once again. Her mind was firmly set now.

She couldn't possibly leave Elizabeth.

As soon as she decided to stay, her pulse rate slowed, her breathing became manageable. She sat on the edge of the bed near Elizabeth. Maybe there was another way, she wondered. My mobile phone! Where is it now? 'If only I could get to it', she whispered audibly. Billy sat shaking his head; he didn't hear Rosa ask for the phone. She shook his shoulder. His head moved up and sideways, like a mime artist. His eyes were red; his face was plagued with guilt, his reason for living misplaced, his mind stuck in a lift that neither went up nor down. Rosa shook him again. 'Billy! My phone! Where is it? I must ring an ambulance for Elizabeth!' He continued in his dazed, trapped condition, searching Rosa's face for clues, for explanations.

'*Please*, Billy,' she roared in his face, 'the phone!'

He dropped his head into an apathetic wilt and uttered the reply Rosa waited for. 'It's in my room'—he pointed a lethargic finger to the door opposite—'in the drawer by the bed.' A fresh supply of adrenaline urged her aching limbs into Billy's bedroom. She attacked the drawer and grabbed the phone, switched it on and waited for the network to kick in.

'Not much battery left,' she moaned and tapped in triple 9.

The clear and business-like voice at the other end said 'Emergency, which service do you require?'

'Ambulance, please! Quickly!'

'Can you repeat that, please? You are breaking up.'

'I want the Ambulance!' Rosa shouted louder.

'I'm sorry. I can't hear you. If you are on a mobile, you may need to change your location or find a landline. Are you there?'

The phone let out a series of beeps. 'Wait! Please, you must hear me. You must!' The phone went dead. Rosa never swore. She swore now.

'The house phone! That's what the lady said.' Spinning around, she stared into the grisly, grey eyes of Meredith Turner. Stunned by the old woman's appearance, as if from nowhere, Rosa was slow to react to the solid thump to her arm. She saw the rifle in Meredith's hands but did not comprehend its significance. Then came the pain; the resultant scream came from the blow to her elbow that sent a stinging sensation up to her shoulder and down to her fingertips.

'Who gave YOU permission to use the phone, Miss la-di-dah Tavistock?' The old woman's squawk rose to a crescendo. 'Get back into your room! I don't know what that boy is thinking of. Move it, NOW!' She poked the barrel into

Rosa's ribs. Rosa yelped again and hobbled out. Meredith's voice behind her sounded like chalk across a blackboard. 'I should have known you'd get up to your tricks, little Miss Grandiose! First, you listen into private conversations and nearly kill yourself into the bargain, and NOW! You make sneaky phone messages. To your friends no doubt. Or… perhaps the police! When will you learn, Mrs T for treacherous, that some things don't concern you? Now move! Move into the other room and keep your tongue still!' She screamed and poked Rosa again.

Billy suddenly came to life on seeing the two women. 'Mother, what are you doing? How did you get the gun?'

She pooh-poohed him with a scathing flash of her tongue. 'You think you can take what's mine and hide it from me? This is my grandfather's rifle. Then my father's. Then mine! They used to shoot foxes, didn't they, little thieves who ate the chickens, that's what! I have a few foxes of my own to deal with, don't I, Rosa?' She strung the syllables out and pointed the three-o-three at her chest.

Rosa whimpered. Billy went to stand up but he was met with a threat via his mother's glare. From her bed, Elizabeth said with surprising awareness: 'You are aiming the gun at the wrong person, Meredith.'

'What! What is that you said! You! The one who started all of this!'

'You should shoot me, if that's what will please you. I'm near to dying anyway. Then you can let Rosa go and that'll be the end of it. Don't you agree?' Meredith was momentarily stymied for an answer.

'And pray tell me, Elizabeth dear, why would I want to hurt you when we all know that you belong to Billy. It's Billy's happiness I want. Do you think I have no *feelings*?'

'If I belong to Billy, Meredith, whose baby is it?'

Rosa was agitated by this line of reasoning and said, 'This is ridiculous, Elizabeth. Where are you going with this?'

Elizabeth ignored her mother-in-law and continued, 'Whose baby, Meredith?'

'You know whose child it is, you vixen! You were unfaithful to my son, that's what!'

'So! You see now. You should shoot me for being unfaithful. Yes?'

Rosa moved forward. Billy stopped her; his body language begged her to stay put. He whispered, 'She's mad, Rosa. She *is* mad!'

Meredith screamed at her son. 'Billy! Tell her to stop saying these things. She wants me to shoot her. Tell her!'

Billy said alright, he'd talk to her. 'But I need privacy, mother, a man and a woman need privacy, don't you think?'

Meredith eyed her son cautiously and then relented. 'Ok, but she leaves too.' Rosa's stomach heaved at the thought of being *near* the woman. She offered to be locked in her room again, using tiredness as a pretext.

'What a good idea! I don't trust people who eavesdrop and sneak around. And YOU especially! You didn't protect your son! Mothers ought to protect their own flesh!'

Morning light began to make slicing gaps in the darkness. Elizabeth sensed the new day dawning and asked Billy to open the curtains. She wished with all her heart she could stand on the hill above her house just before the sun came up. Ben and she did that many times, although getting Ben out of bed that early was no easy task. Recalling his antics to hold onto the blankets made her smile. Despite her debilitating illness, her smile remained contagious.

Other things too came to mind. Like sitting with Ben at the bay window overlooking the sea in summer playing the "find it" game. A boat was selected by either one and the other had to identify the size, the type, the name, the colours on the sails, and how many were on board. Binoculars scanned the waves while the other followed with the telescope. Sometimes, the game ended when the yacht wasn't spotted at all. And how she would laugh when he became irritable because he couldn't find it. When Stephie was born, they didn't play so often. They had a new game to play: mummies and daddies.

Elizabeth tried to sit up but she lacked energy. The view, she thought, must be approaching the glorious stage, when the sun juggled its innovative rays to dance on the edge of gliding clouds, to filter in among the trees and chase the darkness away. She wished Ben were here to lift her into position in front of the window. He knew how much she loved the sunrise.

For a strange moment the idea of Billy, the only available person, lifting her onto the soft armchair was acceptable. But only for a manic moment. Her thoughts switched to waking up in Billy's house. She staggered, with his help, out of the Mazda and into the rain, past the dancing matriarch and into the door at the rear of the house. Meredith said something cruel to Billy—it was in her voice—something about 'having Elizabeth all to himself'. Climbing the stairs was a vague memory but she must have climbed up somehow. The next thing she felt was being laid on a bed. She relived waking up in the dark hours screaming Stephie's name, and everything became clear in one blinding flash of mnemonic renaissance.

It began to rain, lightly at first, when she left the shopping mall. It wasn't much, she thought, just a shower. The weathermen don't always get it right.

(Be over shortly. Stephie is wrapped up in her little blanket and the hood is waterproof. A walk on the esplanade will give me a chance to digest Dr Ames' concerns. Ben will be surprised! A new baby in the summer. I know he'll be over the moon. But can I tell him about the danger? I don't know if I can, and yet he has to be told. Sooner or later. What's that? Sounded like gunfire. A car, probably. Oh, there's Mrs Oughter. She's waving. Always with that black bag, that environmentally friendly bag from Tesco's. I hope Ben…I know he won't mind, he loves children and we did say we'd have more. I need to keep things together. The 'weight' thing worries me, my desire for food, I know, is not normal. I just don't feel like eating. Doctor Ames said I should be eating more, not less, seeing as I'm pregnant.)

It's alright, Stephie darling, it's only rain.

(The wind is getting up and those clouds look heavy. I wonder if I should go back. No, the bus shelter is near.)

We'll wait here and watch the rain for a while, Stephie. Rain is exciting to watch. Oh no, there's Billy! Stephie, see! That's him. Across the street. Don't look, Stephie. Don't look!

(Mustn't let Stephie see my annoyance. I wonder what he wants. He's waving and coming over. I hope he's not going to bother me again.)

'Hello, Billy.'

'Hello, Elizabeth. How are you? Hi, Stephie!'

(He's staring at me. What does he want? If he wasn't Ben's pal, I'd tell him to go hike.)

'I'm fine, Billy. And you?'

'I'm fine, too. Listen, I eh, saw you just now and I thought of a brilliant surprise for Ben.'

'Oh, and what's that?'

'I thought we could jump in the boat and take a spin across the bay and surprise him for lunch. He'd really like that.'

(Would I, Billy. Would I? That's the question. Oh, why did he have to be Ben's friend? It makes it so hard to avoid this man.)

'Oh, I don't think so, Billy. I think he has appointments out of town today.'

(Take that forlorn look off your face. Ben and I are happily married. Don't you get that?)

'Did he tell you that? He may be in his office. Let's take a chance. He'll be surprised. Come on, Elizabeth, let's go. Grab the stroller.'

'It's pouring the heavens down, Billy! No one goes out in this weather.'

(Take your hands off Stephie!)

'Come on, Elizabeth. Ben said you love the ocean. Don't let a little rain stop you. I'll take Stephie.'

'Billy! Put her down! You'll upset her. See, she's starting to cry.'

(Oh, God, he's walking away with her.)

'Come on, Elizabeth, the boat's not far.'

'She's getting soaked, Billy. Give her to me!'

(Somebody stop him, he's heading for the marina. Why has everybody disappeared? The stroller! I'll ask him to put her back in the stroller.)

'Nearly there, Stephie. Have you out of this weather in a jiffy.'

'I'll carry my daughter, Billy Turner. She wants her stroller. She's safer with me.'

(Why did I say that? He'll take offence now, I'm sure of it. I can't keep up with him.)

'Watch your step, now. Hold onto the rail. Here, pass me the stroller.'

'Billy, wait! I can't…keep up…with you. Don't cry, Stephie. Mummy's here.'

(Can't breathe…wind…rain…too heavy. He's… taking Stephie…down below. I'll grab my phone from the stroller. Where is it? Must have left it at home.)

'How good is this, my little princess? Out of the rain and soon we'll have you warm as toast. And don't worry; your little stroller is on board too. A bit wet, yes, but nothing a towel won't take care of. And here's your beautiful mother coming down the steps.'

'Billy, I need… to go home and…get Stephie into fresh clothes.'

(I need to be calm. Ben should know what's happening. Billy has a mobile.)

'No, no, we'll be having lunch with Ben soon. Stephie is not too wet. There's a towel in that box, Elizabeth.'

'I want to use your phone, Billy. I need to ring Ben.'

(I don't want your towel. I want my baby. You are holding me against my will.)

'You are NOT listening to me, Elizabeth! We'll be seeing Ben very soon. Don't keep mentioning his name, do you understand? Let's have a nice time together, like a little family on an outing. OK?'

'What is it you want from me? I'm married to Ben. Doesn't that mean anything to you?'

(Must stay in control. Billy is delusional. Can't reason with him. This is the worst he's been. Can't upset him. No one to help me.)

'What do I WANT from you? You have the gall to ask me that! You know what I want! WE were supposed to be together. You and me. Ben was not part of the deal. This baby should be ours. I was cheated out of a family, that's what!'

'Billy, please let me hold my baby. Please?'

(I must keep it together. I have to. For Stephie's sake, she's scared in his arms.)

'OUR baby, Elizabeth!'

'Yes, Billy. I understand. Our baby.'

(Say nothing to anger him. Just coax him to hand her back to me.)

'As long as we feel the same about each other, then that's all that matters, isn't that right, Elizabeth?'

'Yes Billy, that's right. I would like to pacify Stephie. I know you love her and you'd never harm her in any way. Now she needs a hug from her mother. Let her come to me.'

(The steps are steep, the hatch is wide open, but I must take a chance and run.)

'Ok, take her while I close the hatch. The rainstorm is not letting up; we don't want to get swamped, do we?'

'No.'

(What now? He's blocking my only escape. Get behind the steps and push him off before he closes it.)

Whaaaa!

(Quickly. Up the steps. Hold on tightly, Stephie. Nearly there. Shut the hatch. Run, Elizabeth, run!)

'Elizabeth!'

(God help me. He's upon me. Run!)

'You lied to me, Elizabeth. Trust is so important in a relationship. And now, look what you've done?'

'I'm sorry, Billy, you are… hurting… my neck! You CAN'T have my child! That's final! We have no relationship. We never had one and we never will. So, back off!'

(Stay firm. Confront him with the truth. Fight as though your life depended on it.)

'My mother was right about you, after all. I didn't believe her when she said you were unfaithful. You've shown your true colours, Elizabeth. Give me the baby!'

'Nooo!'

(Scream, Elizabeth, scream your lungs out! Hold onto Stephie. Oh, no, he's too strong for me.)

'Let her go! You're hurting her!'

(Keep a tight hold, Elizabeth. Hold her legs! Oh, I'm losing her, she's slipping.)

'Don't keep fighting me, Elizabeth. We're too close to the side…the deck is treacherous…I'm slipping…'

'I want my BA…BEE! You are mad like your mother! Give her to me!'

(He's falling backwards. I can't hold on to you, Stephie. Oh no! Stepheeee!)

'She's in the water, Billy! Get up! I can't see her. I'm going in!'

'It's too dangerous! I can't let you! You are all I have, Elizabeth.'

'Let me go! You're mad, mad…you're mad…'

Elizabeth emerged from her nightmare, too exhausted to cry. The last thing she remembered was the surging waters crashing against the boat; the ceaseless rain lashing into her face, unable to keep her eyes open. Thunder clapped in her ears; lightning lit up the pelting rain for an instant at a time. She had a vague recollection of clinging to Stephie's nappy. The lethargy that now inhabited every muscle, every bone, every fibre in her body had crept gradually into her being.

Every thought and craving had been overtaken, robbing her senses of the normal desire to feel. Slowly, day by day, from the first day Billy locked her in this room, until today, her natural cravings had deteriorated into apathy and finally, into numbness. Thinking about Stephie didn't help. Neither did thinking of Ben. It was less painful to push what happened into hidden recesses and reserve whatever mental energy she possessed to think of a way out from Meredith's grasp.

Decidedly, *the old woman* was the vicious streak in her son's persona, and while she couldn't forgive Billy for what he did, she could sympathise with him. He was weak. He was made weak by years of manipulation by his psychopathic mother, who trained him from an early age to think and act just like she did. How he ever made friends with another human Elizabeth couldn't figure out. What drew him to Ben? What drew Ben to him?

Pushing the physical pain into the background was much harder, even impossible. Keeping her illness from Ben, she admitted, was the hardest thing she ever did. Since they shared everything, withholding her medical condition from him was tantamount to disloyalty, she thought. And then finding she was pregnant, and the danger her illness could mean to the baby, well, it was that much more difficult to tell him. Better wait for the specialist's opinion.

When all the variables were calculated, when the all the symptoms were diagnosed, *then* she would tell him. She wished to heaven she hadn't detoured along the esplanade *that day,* the day she would explain her weight loss to him, her limited energy, and her fears for the new baby.

In hindsight, had she decided to go straight home when the rain started—that's the trouble with hindsight, she yielded—you have to make the mistake to benefit from it. Even so, it would have meant *no* Billy. *No* boat. *No* struggling to fight for Stephie in a rainstorm. *No* Meredith. And maybe treatment for the diseased ovaries…

She watched Billy slumped in the chair, asleep. Asleep, like a relative sits near the sick bed of a loved spouse, or child, hoping the fever will break. *But he was no relative.* People who care do not behave like him. Elizabeth silently condemned both the man and his mother.

Billy didn't speak a word to her after Meredith marched Rosa out; he had nothing worthwhile to say to her or do for her. Even if his ruse to get his mother out of the room worked, it was mainly due to the divisive tactics Elizabeth used. At least for the time being, Meredith's threat to hurt Rosa was diverted. And yet there were no guarantees the matriarch wouldn't. Elizabeth turned her eyes toward the morning light filtering through the mesh curtains, her ears to the music the birds sing, to bring in the new day.

Eleven

Ben woke to the annoying bell of the alarm clock and struck it hard with his fist. He didn't object to being woken at seven; that time was pre-ordered, but he must buy his mother a new *clock,* one with a musical alarm, soft music to *ease* one back to a conscious state, not one to start a revolution! However raucous the alarm sounded, it made little difference to the snoring policeman downstairs.

Ben dressed quickly and set about using the time profitably. This was a day when every minute would be accounted for, a fresh start to find his mother, a fresh start to find out what actually happened to Elizabeth and Stephie, a fresh start with an unlikely partner; a detective on holiday who also had 'feelings' for his mother.

He approached the rumbling policeman, who sounded like a portable generator with no muffler, with every intention of waking him. He hit the RADIO button and tuned to the local pop station, then hit the volume. Plinter jumped several inches on the settee and sat up straight, ready for his attacker. Ben turned the radio off and said, 'how does scrambled egg for breakfast grab you, Corish?' Plinter said something unpleasant under his breath. He threw the blanket aside and made a series of sweeps with his fingers to restore the creases in his pants.

'Did you sleep well?' Ben chided. 'You could have used the guest room, you know.'

Plinter grunted, 'I'll freshen up first. Coffee and toast will be fine, thank you, and, I *hate* burnt toast.'

Having eaten, Plinter reminded Ben they'd make a detour to his house to pick up a hairbrush and a sample of Elizabeth's writing. Ben placed a *can't-miss-it* note on his car, which he left in his mother's driveway and then phoned his mother's mobile. It rang in the drawer of Billy's bedside locker. A voice said the phone was either out of range or it was switched off. Ben left a text message.

When Plinter touched the brakes of his Jaguar at Ben's house, Ben's first port-o-call was to check Plinter's theory on the missing lid. While Ben busied himself with that, the policeman rang ahead to Sue Brighton; there were errands she could expedite better than anyone he knew, and keep quiet about, too. More than once he persuaded her not to retire; managing his role would have been near impossible without her. Thankfully, for him, she was still there.

Recently, however, she told him he should think of her replacement. The south of France was her retirement plan. It took a certain class of woman to deal with all the goings-on in the Station; being a Tarter to the crusty cops and a mother-figure to the rookies were just some of her talents, a balancing act that was second nature to her. Few could successfully step into the shoes of Susan Amelia Brighton.

Plinter paced up and down, as those using mobiles habitually do. Ben waved him into the house while he looked for the items the inspector requested. In the hallway, he acceded to the man's judgement. 'There's no sign of a lid, as you suspected, Corish. In fact, there's no dustbin! But then again, your men may have both the lid *and* the dustbin *in custody*, as you put it. Top marks for your…instinct!' He opened his mouth to speak further but hesitated.

Plinter prompted him, 'Did you think of something, Ben?'

'No…I…eh…I was actually thinking of what…you said…last night. I hope your instinct is right, Corish. That…Elizabeth is alive.'

While Ben saw to the items for DNA testing, Plinter used the ground floor bathroom. And while others took a walk to begin their day, the inspector started his by brushing his moustache and removing wayward hairs. He carried a small bag for this purpose, and like the saying goes about the famous credit card, or more accurately the debit card, Plinter never left home without it. The ritual took less than two minutes to complete. When Ben passed by the bathroom door it was wide open. Plinter sat on the toilet seat in the pensive position, except he massaged one end of his moustache instead of copying the statue of the man with his hand on his chin. In his free hand, he seemed to be contemplating his handkerchief. Ben jolted the policeman from his thoughts, but not disturbing them.

'Inspector Plinter! What on earth are you doing?'

'Ben, this window pane is new, yes?'

'Yes! The man came yesterday.'

'The same window you reported broken some months ago?'

'The same.'

'Did the repairman cut his hand?'

'No! Why do you ask?'

'How do know he didn't?'

'Because, Inspector, he gave me a friendly warning about stray glass and little children's toes, that's how. He didn't show me a bloodied finger either.' Plinter went on, with more determination.

'When you discovered the breakage, did you get cut, perhaps by a sliver of glass?'

'No! As usual, Corish, you are in enigma mode. Get to the point, will you?'

'I found this—he showed Ben a tiny dark-red object—under the vanity unit.' He held it out on a white handkerchief. Ben declared: 'A piece of dirt, Corish. I see a piece of dirt! Please explain, and for mercy sakes, don't offer me another *hunch*.'

'Don't belittle the mind of a criminal investigator, Ben. In our business, sometimes insignificant things are really major clues. If the blood on this sliver is not yours, then it could be the burglar's.'

'It could also be my mother's! She swept up the broken glass the next day, after the two plods left. You remember, don't you? Nothing was taken. The burglar must have been interrupted. That was the logical conclusion.' Plinter was quick to respond. 'The logical conclusion *now is*: the blood on this sliver of glass belongs to the *burglar!* After we see the doctor, I want you to come with me to the Marina.

In King Street Police Station, Plinter said 'good morning' to the regulars; someone asked what he was doing back. Someone, with more gall than the others, murmured to a colleague, 'Spain wouldn't let him pass their borders.' Whether he heard it or not, the Inspector waved at a senior policewoman who followed him into his office.

'Sue, any results come back from the dustbin yet?—oh! This is Mr Tavistock; he's helping with our inquiries.' She gave Ben a perceptive nod. She knew his history.

'The Keystone Cops—I mean Sims and Baines—haven't reported in yet. The garbage bin is probably still in the car boot. I'll revive them when they get in, Guv'nor.'

At that moment, Baines walked into the general office with a bulky black plastic bag. Brighton turned to sort him out. Ben heard the plainclothesman argue he got held up with a call to apprehend two teenagers shoplifting at the supermarket, and that he had left his Spiderman uniform at home.

'Don't try to be smart, Baines, it might give some people the impression you are! The Guv'nor wants you to get *that* to the lab ASAP. That means *yesterday*! And leave shoplifting to the plods on the beat. You and Sims are *supposed to be* investigating serious crimes!'

Baines knew better than to argue with the mentally robust and resolute queen of King Street Cop Shop. Instead, he muttered something under his breath and headed for his vehicle. Plinter came forward with Rosa's hairdryer in a plastic bag and stopped Baines at the exit. 'Baines, wait up! Give this to Arty at Forensic. Tell him I suspect a match with the prints on the dustbin. Get him to ring me with the results.' Plinter asked and Baines replied no, there was no lid.

Behind the Venetian blinds in the Inspector's smart office, Ben switched his gaze from the various characters who paraded through the Station to a picture of a smiling woman gazing into the angelic face of a small child, a tender moment, he guessed. It occupied the central position on the large polished desk. 'Must be his wife,' pondered Ben. And the child? His daughter, probably.

A wave of sadness swept over him. He remembered that particular occasion, when he attempted to change Stephie's nappy. Squealing with glee, she tossed and kicked her chubby legs. Ben was convinced her frolics were all part of a master plan to make life tough for him. Maybe by then she'd had enough nappy changes to know her father was putting the thing on back-to-front and in the only way she could she was letting him know!

It was hard for him to put a seventeen-year-old face on the child in the photo; Plinter's adorable and only child who overdosed and didn't survive the onslaught to her brain. What kind of torture did Plinter go through? Ben mused sadly. Was he over it? Can a man *ever* get over the loss of a child? An only child? And whatever became of his wife? Where is she now? Just left him, like Billy's dad left? Did they divorce? Maybe she's remarried and has a new family? And Plinter? Was he too filled with anguish to start a new relationship?

'Until he met my mother!' Ben brooded, and was instantly angry at the man who had lost so much. He didn't hear Plinter re-enter his office.

'In case you're asking, it's my wife and daughter. The only photo I kept…'

'I…I was curious, yes. You and I…we both lost children. We understand.'

'And you also wonder about Karyn, my wife?'

'Only if you want to—'

'Helicopter crashed. She and a friend took a tourist ride, part of a weekend package to Snowden. No survivors. She was forty. Cindy just turned sixteen.'

'I'm sorry—'

'That was thirteen years ago. Cindy went out of control. She worshipped her mother….couldn't handle the loss. Before she was halfway through her seventeenth birthday, I pulled the plug from the machine.'

'I…I can't imagine having the guts to do that. I…I could have done with your input, your understanding…your sympathy when I…needed it.'

'I know. I was knocking on your door, Ben, but you weren't answering. I suppose we have to *want* it at the time. I know *I* didn't. Nothing gave me comfort when Karyn died and nothing gave me comfort when Cindy died. I just had to go back to work.'

'I hear what you are saying, but I'm not ready to go back to work. I want to find the truth. I want to locate my mother, and if you're reasoning is correct, I need to find my wife!'

'Let's make a start then; we have an appointment with a butcher! Let's go!'

Off-Duty Inquiries

The head butcher at Mac's Meats personally served Rosa.

'Yes, I *do* remember Mrs Tavistock. She said she was 'aving a special guest for dinner and she wanted the best lamb chops in the shop. I asked 'er was she cooking for the boyfriend—I take a bit of cheek wiv me old customers—and she looked at me in a funny sort of way and said, "As a matter of fact, you're not far out." A lovely woman, absolutely lovely. And I mean that in a *good* way, Inspector.'

'And what time did she leave, Mac?'

'Aw, I'm not Mac. Mac's Meats is a franchise name, a business name, pulled out of an 'at, I believe.'

Ben interrupted the man, sternly. 'We are not here for a history of the meat trade, Sir. Just tell us the time, as accurately as you can, when my…em…Mrs Tavistock left your premises.'

'About ten o'clock, Guv'nor. 'Ere, what's up wiv Mrs T? Don't tell me she's got food poisonin'? We are very strict 'ow we 'andle our meat. We 'ave a reputation to fink abouh!'

'Are you sure about the time?'

'Of course! Didn't it rain cats and dogs five minutes later?'

Plinter took over. 'We're sure you have the finest meats, Mr Mac. Thank you and good day.' Outside Ben apologised. Plinter said, 'That's ok; just let *me* do the talking. Now for Rosa's other errand, the vacuum bags. Next stop: Berkley's.'

'*Why* are we revisiting the shops Rosa—my mother—went to? We…you, that is, you already established she was drenched by the rain, went home, changed and went out again! You've worked out, more or less, the *time* factor!' Plinter twirled his moustache before speaking.

'She may have said something to indicate to these people her mood, or where she went from here. And…well, to be honest with you, Ben, I wanted to meet the people Rosa spoke to, you know, to interact with them first.'

'Would I be impertinent to ask WHY?'

'It might help locate her, I just explained that.'

'No, man! Why did you want to *interact* with these people?'

'Don't think me absurd, will you, Ben, but it's important for me to know how people view your mother.'

'You are *rating* her? By butchers and bakers and candlestick makers?'

'I *knew* you wouldn't understand. And it's not a rating at all! It's simply a…I just want to see how she is perceived. Mr Mac certainly thinks highly of her, and, I'm pleased with that report. Can we change the subject?'

'Wait 'til I tell her she's under investigation by the Chief Inspector of King Street cop shop.'

'You, Sir, will do no such thing! And that's a warning, my boy.'

'We'll see! Shall we *interact* with Mr Vacuum-Bag man?' Plinter kept quiet for a few minutes while they walked to Berkley's. He had decided on a different approach this time. He would let Ben do *all* the talking; he would listen.

'My mother came in here, I think, to buy some bags for my machine. I was passing by and thought I'd make sure. Otherwise, I'll get them now.' After establishing the make and model and a brief description of the 'mother' in question, the owner said; 'Ah! Mrs Tavistock! Yes, she came in shortly before the rain came. I was surprised she didn't wait for it to stop or at least ease off. Did *it* come down! I shouted after her did she have an umbrella, but she didn't hear me. She just raced out.'

'Ok. Did you actually sell her the bags, sir?'

'Oh yes! But not at first.'

'No?'

'No. When she gave me the Hoover model number, I was sure we had none in stock. She looked disappointed, so I told her to take a seat while I double-checked. I found a box of them behind some other supplies. I told her so and passed the bags to her but… she seemed to be miles away. I asked was everything OK. She said yes quickly and took a twenty-pound note from her handbag and that's when she dropped what she had been reading. Then she ran straight into the rain. It had just started. *Would* that be your mother, Sir? She went without taking her change from the twenty.'

Ben wanted to assure the man that his mother was not like that, but he said yes anyway and thanked the man. On the way out, Mr Berkley said, 'Goodbye for now, Inspector. Be sure to come again.'

Plinter turned to the shop owner and offered an offhand reply. It seemed people had no problem recognising him. But not a word of the Tavistock tragedy. It was clear Berkley knew Rosa, as did the butcher, and yet not a word of condolence from either of them. People are strange creatures, he thought to himself. He quickly jumped to the riddle of the letter.

'There's that letter again, Ben. Now, do you see! She's worried so much about the content of that letter she just has to read it again and again. It's almost like she has to convince herself there's something amiss but she's not sure how to handle it.'

'Why? Why didn't she speak to *me*, tell me what *troubled* her? I *can't* understand it.'

'Nor can I? Only the writer of the letter can help us there—wait here!' Plinter went back into the shop and came out minutes later.

'What was that all about? Do you need vacuum bags as well?'

'No! I don't. I have a cleaning lady for that. What—'

'Don't tell me it's *another* hunch!'

'What I *now* know is…your mother is really concerned with that letter! What *I* call good police investigative work, *you* may call a hunch. I asked Berkley about the letter, and did he see it. He said he got a good look at it when he leant over the counter and offered to help but she'd gathered them up in a flash. I asked him how many pages were there. He said he saw three, then changed his mind to four. It was too far away to read anything, he said, but it was printed material. Think about it, Ben! *Four pages* of typed material to say a simple greeting! No, Ben! I say again, no!'

Twelve

Rosa was wakened by Meredith after what seemed a short while. She complained to the old woman that she was kept up most of the previous night and she needed more sleep. What she really wanted was for that woman to leave. Meredith replied coldly she had enough rest, that she didn't trust her even while she slept.

'The gun is not necessary, Meredith. You don't have to worry about me. I have no intentions of leaving. I had a chance earlier and stayed for Elizabeth's sake,' Rosa finished.

'Oh you did now, did you? How thoughtful of you!' Again, Meredith Turner unleashed her caustic tongue. 'Do you imagine I've been neglecting the girl? *No one* gives her better treatment than I do! Every day she gets her pills. Like clockwork! I was a trained nurse, you know!'

'I'm sure you are a wonderful nurse. What…pills do you give her?'

'Why, the ones Billy got for her. What else?'

'Where did he get them, I mean, were they for Elizabeth?'

'Of course they were for her! They were in Billy's Mazda.'

'The pills were in his vehicle? Why?'

'Because the silly girl left them there. *Some* things are obvious, woman!'

'Forgive me for being so slow, Meredith. Why was Elizabeth in Billy's car?'

'Because she was soaked to the skin. Billy was showing her kindness; he's that sort of person, you know. Not like some of the men I've known. Cruel men! Perverted men! Call themselves fathers and husbands, men you'd expect to love their children and wives! Not so, Mrs Tavistock, not so. That's why *we* have to keep them in check, isn't that so?'

As she vented her spleen on men—likely her own father, her own husband, Rosa concluded—Rosa studied the old woman's features; the twisted mouth, the insane delight in her grey eyes, the scorn that oozed off a pink-white tongue, and for a moment Rosa imagined the long, thin, forked tongue of a viper. Something in this woman's past, Rosa thought, must be the reason she is so filled with hatred. Something distasteful occurred, or maybe she was crazy from the beginning, all on her own. Diplomacy, then, was the safest course to take when walking near the volcanic edge of Meredith Turner.

'Yes, Meredith, I think you have summed up very nicely what men are like. I suppose that's why we need to mollycoddle them. So…you were explaining about the pills and Billy taking care of Elizabeth—was she caught in the rain? Is that it? Billy gave her a lift?'

'Yes, he gave her a lift! Wasn't the woman fighting him, arguing with him, and not cooperating! Billy tried to save the child, but that wretched, ungrateful vixen threw the baby into the water, just to spite my son. If *she* couldn't have the child, then *no one* would! That was her evil side coming out, the part of her that showed up her true colours. She does not deserve to have children! That shrew! And to think that my son had thoughts on marrying her! What a fatal mistake that would have been. A real tragedy!' Her voice reached a high note and trailed into a guttural depth.

Rosa knew she'd have to listen to more of the same to find out what medication the old woman was giving Elizabeth. It grated her senses to listen to the vulgarity seeping from between the woman's yellowed teeth, but she'd persevere.

'Meredith, as a nurse…what do you suppose is wrong with her? She looks pretty sick, to me that is, but I'd respect your opinion.'

'You see! That's how clever she is. Don't you see that? There's *nothing* wrong with her at all. Nothing more than stomach cramps. Or period pains.'

'She says she's dying, Meredith. Why do you think she says that?'

'Be…cau…au…se! She wants to go home! Are you dumb or what? She thought I'd fall for that ruse. She is trying to get out of her commitment to Billy. *That's* why she feigns illness! No faithfulness anymore! Is it too much to ask for a little loyalty these days?'

'Yes, I know what you mean. There are so many people getting divorced and playing the field and…well, you know what I mean, Meredith. Tell me, what medication have you got her on? For her…cramps… and things?'

The old woman wasn't ready for that. She dropped her eyes then glanced away and shot back with an accusative scowl. 'That's privileged information between me and the patient. Why do YOU want to know?' She scowled, rearranging the deep wrinkles around her mouth and eyes. Rosa urged herself to tread softly.

'Oh, no, I wouldn't try to interfere. It's just that the girl might need a new prescription. Tablets have a tendency of running out and, you know, she'll need some more, I suppose. But I'm sure you have that all under control, Meredith.' Rosa managed to make a forced laugh sound real and waited for the other's tongue to cut her down.

Instead, the woman stared at Rosa as though she was making a decision at an audition to recruit a medical partner; she made several attempts to remove something from her deep-brown nightgown, a plain knotted cord tied up her narrow midriff. An abbess with a weapon, Rosa mused. Meredith produced a small printed form and passed it to Rosa for inspection.

'I give her these.'

Rosa examined the prescription. Elizabeth's name and address were evident, as was the doctor's. A scrawl that imitated *AR Ames* unjustifiably spread the short signature across the page. The dosage was clearly stated.

'How often would she take the pills, Meredith?'

'Whenever she complains,' she answered professionally and placed the gun on the bed. Rosa didn't agree or disagree with the deluded woman. Nor did she mention the pills were anti-depressants. Tactfully, Rosa asked her was there a good supply left. Meredith made a cautious glance at the rifle and went to another pocket and fished out a plastic container. She rattled it and said, as if conferring with her partner, 'I think we'll be OK for a few more days. It depends on how much she bellyaches.'

Rosa nodded, maintaining a casual composure. She guessed Elizabeth must have swallowed most of the supply. Inwardly, she reeled at the thought of poor Elizabeth under the auspices of this depraved, self–appointed Matron. Her poise was difficult to hold onto, her self-control fought to break loose and swap for a rampant attack on the old hag. The gun was in reach. Only two feet away. She was younger than Meredith. Maybe stronger. Maybe quicker. Maybe not stronger. Maybe not quicker. She had never handled a weapon before. She doubted she could pull a trigger on another human, even if she reached the gun first. Can't take the chance. It would ruin everything. Better to keep up the pretence and cajole the woman into some sense of trust. Yes! The only *practical* course left open. The *only* course. For Elizabeth's sake.

Rosa coughed to clear the anger in her throat and make way for a new line of discreet attack. She passed the prescription back to Meredith and asked her what else she did for the *patient.* 'I see by the date the prescription is several months old. We'll need the pharmacist to issue a fresh batch. Will you get in touch with the doctor? Or will you simply ring him, Meredith? I do that sometimes. It saves waiting in his surgery.'

The woman got to her feet, grabbing the rifle as she stood up. Like a switch was thrown, Meredith Turner resumed her former belligerent persona. 'You are crazy, Tavistock! She's dead! Don't you read the newspapers? You want me to waltz into Ames' office and ask for a repeat prescription for a *dead person*! Anyone who did that would be certified! Like a loony! What are you trying to prove here? You dimwit! I *know* what you are up to. Trying to catch me out, aren't you? Get up! On your feet, Mrs T for Tricky Tavistock!'

Rosa jumped to her feet and stood erect; not out of strict obedience but rather due to a surge of adrenaline. For the first time since her imprisonment, fearlessness joined the blood rushing through her veins. Suddenly, the gun lost its power to terrorise her. The weapon that kept her in fear was not the enemy. *It was the woman herself.* The feral tongue she possessed, along with her cruel disposition, is what herded her victims into a corner, like a trapped and defenceless animal. It's no wonder Billy lived a life of trembling under her control, Rosa assured her new confidence.

'You don't frighten me anymore, old woman. All you've got is malice and spite, a jagged tongue to threaten, a cruel heart to manipulate and a damaged, vindictive mind to plot your evil schemes. An old and decrepit specimen of a human being is what you are; you'll end up wasted, with no one to care for you or about you! Some nurse in a mental home will have the task of feeding you tablets that suppress your poisonous tongue and malicious mind.

'You'll be pushed around in a wheelchair from the dining hall to a boxy room by a person you don't know and, quite frankly, who doesn't want to know you. And why? Because your reputation will precede you. Decent people will shun you, even in your old age, even in your deformed physical and mental state. Someone will spoon-feed you and afterwards clean up the drool that runs down your chin, and yes, they will perform the task out of duty, not out of pity, and certainly not out of kindness.'

Rosa threw her head and shoulders back to reach her full height of five feet five as she finished her speech, and looked down upon the petite, thin, bony figure of her nemesis. An unpractised twinkle involuntarily appeared in Meredith's grey eyes and grew until the sensation of amusement filtered into all her facial creases. She cackled a guffaw into Rosa's face and stood back a pace.

Rosa was still trying to figure out the quirky Mrs Turner when she felt the sting of the rifle butt on her kneecap. Her body folded like cardboard. As she tried to stop herself falling and grasp the injured leg simultaneously, she toppled towards the old woman. The seventy-year-old deftly stepped to one side and watched Rosa strike the floor; using her hands to break the fall helped, but not much. The pain in her knee kicked in; Rosa screamed.

Elizabeth heard her mother-in-law cry out. She moaned within herself and closed her eyes. Pain was something she learned to submit to; pain of body brought on by disease, pain of heart brought on by the loss of Stephie, of missing Ben, and the depressing pain to her mind brought on by the decision to die rather than abort her baby. The excruciating cry she heard from Rosa's lips was easy to bear. Nothing else could compare to her own pain. She succumbed to sleep and hoped that tomorrow would take longer to arrive. Much longer. Or not arrive at all.

The sting to Rosa's knee didn't abate. The old woman stood grinning above her, revelling in her control. The rifle she placed against the wall; she was relishing the exhibition of Rosa's body writhing on the carpet.

'You like being near the floor, don't you, Lady Tavistock? Haven't been our guest very long and... I believe you've hugged the floor at least...three, no, four times is it? That has to be a record. I'll call in the man from the Guinness Book, what do you say? Even if you haven't set a new record, you've given me a good laugh. So it *was* worth it, don't you think! YOU are the one needing help now, aren't you, my dearie? Maybe *you'll* be shoved around in a chair and someone will clean up *your* excrement! And don't accuse me of having an audacious tongue, you foghorn, you handle yourself pretty well when it comes to expletives.'

Rosa groaned and held her leg, endeavouring to rub healing into it. Nevertheless, she plunged into another attack. 'Those pills you gave Elizabeth did nothing to help her! What else did you force down her neck?'

'Force! You say *force*? How *little* you know. That selfish girl doesn't want help! You heard her ask me to shoot her, didn't you? Living for her meant that she'd have to stay with Billy. She would have none of that! Too *good* for my son! If that's her attitude then she deserves *no one*. No one! Do you hear me?'

'She is sick, Meredith. You're a nurse; you can see that, surely?'

'Not sick! Stubborn! That's what!'

'Help me up, Meredith. You are taking me to see her. Let *her* tell us how she feels.'

'You stay where you are! In my house, you obey *my* rules, and that's the final word on the subject. That's the way it has been and that's the way it will stay.'

'What about Billy? Does he obey all your rules? He challenged your will today and there wasn't much you could do about it.'

'Billy is putty in my hands, Mrs Tavistock. I say and he does. That's the only way things work around here. He has always obeyed me. He knows it's for his own good, otherwise…'

'Don't stop now, Mrs Turner. Otherwise what?'

'Never you mind! You busybody gossiper! That's *our* little secret.'

Rosa glanced at the door. 'Why not tell Billy to his face! He's right behind you.'

With uneasy fear in her eyes, Meredith looked behind into an empty space. Rosa grabbed her ankle, digging her nails into layers of old skin, and squeezing the skeletal bone with what strength she mustered, she pulled hard. Meredith fought to keep her balance, teetered on one foot and fell backwards, striking her head on the skirting board. She tried to scramble to her feet but Rosa held on. The pain in her knee dulled while she dug her fingers deeper into the old woman's flesh.

Like an eel, the old woman wriggled until Rosa's arm was at full stretch. The gun was within inches of Meredith's grasp. Kicking and screaming, she managed to inflict several blows on Rosa's hand and forearm with her free foot; each movement brought her closer to the weapon. The butt was in her hand. She swung the three-o-three blindly, in a vicious arc, over and over, catching Rosa on the shoulder, freeing herself from Rosa's grip in the process. Meredith was quick to get into the sitting position, yelling and shouting abuse. Her finger massaged the trigger.

Rosa rolled her body at Meredith, crushing the other's feet and bony knees then steamrolling onto her stomach. Meredith squeezed the trigger. The momentum of Rosa's full-framed ten stone on Meredith's midriff sent the old woman's arms flailing; a bullet whizzed over Rosa's ear. Rosa continued to roll; she came to an abrupt stop on Meredith's chest. The rifle struck the wall, bounced and landed on Rosa's back. She slid off the old woman; deep down she hoped she hadn't hurt her; the thin figure didn't move.

Using the door handle to bear her weight, Rosa made an attempt to stand up. The throbbing pain returned. Through her jeans, she rubbed the sore area and came away with sticky, gooey fingers. The blood left a large wet patch as a reminder the skin was also broken. The effort to stand was excruciating; she moaned to ease the pain and didn't hear the old woman behind her. She turned to see the barrel aimed at her; the owner had an evil smirk on her face. Rosa instinctively moved through the doorway for cover but she couldn't support her weight and slumped to the floor.

Billy appeared in the doorway; he took the bullet instead, full in the shoulder. It sent him staggering across the corridor. The wall stopped him going further. He fell against it and slid down slowly, jerkily, attempting to grip his shoulder. His eyes rolled like a boxer hit on the head too many times. Meredith yelled, 'Billy!' She let go of the gun and crawled to her son, crying and muttering, 'I'm so sorry Billy, I'm so sorry, Billy. My son! My baby! My boy!'

Rosa heaved her body past the wailing hag and back into the bedroom. Partly afraid the weapon might go off and mostly afraid the old woman would attack her again, she cautiously pushed the rifle under the bed as far as she could.

Thirteen

On the way to Dr Ames' surgery, Ben quizzed the policeman, 'Tell me, Corish, I'm curious about that piece of glass. How did you manage to find it? It seems an extraordinary piece of good luck.' Plinter eyed him sideways as he swung the car round a left-hand bend.

'The soap fell and it slid under the vanity unit. When I retrieved it, bits of dirt and glass stuck to it, including our friend in the plastic bag here.' He tapped his jacket at the chest.

Ben smirked in disbelief. 'I mean, you crawling on all fours, soiling your pinstripe pants, chasing a slippery bar of soap! If nothing else, it says a lot for your dedication.'

'Don't mock, Ben, it does not become you. As an architect, I'm sure you get your hands dirty from time to time.' Ben smiled. The law enforcer was getting more human by the hour, Ben mused. He began to think of the *policeman* side to Plinter's persona. And about all his hunches. The dustbin lid and his mother's fingerprints. The saliva under the stamp. The letter with its scribbled address. Elizabeth's ring and Stephie's nappy turning up in the same place half a mile from the water's edge. And now, the bloodstained sliver of glass.

Were they simply gut feelings the man had, was he groping in the dark? Was he too long in the force, worn out? Had he chased clues all his life and this was the sum total of his career? Was he smitten with infatuation so late in life that it blocked out intelligent reasoning? Was he secretly carrying on a private war to find some justice in the death of his own wife and child? Was he taking on Elizabeth's and Stephie's tragedy as though it was his own? Why didn't he go to Spain as he planned? Does my mother mean *that* much to him? Why couldn't he enjoy his holiday and come back to pursue his love interests?

Ben's mind got tired. What good is a folder full of questions, he thought. Each question only raised another one. Besides, it was all conjecture; his head spun with other people's questions. Not much made sense to him. He wondered what the doctor would say. Maybe he could shed some light on Elizabeth's mood the day she…? The only thing…the only thing that didn't make sense was the dustbin lid! And, the ring in the dustbin. That, too! There had to be a logical explanation for *his* lid being in the *Thornley* garden! Had to be! Had to be a reason why Elizabeth's ring, and Stephie's nappy, was in the Thornley dustbin. Just had to be! If Elizabeth didn't put it there, then someone else did! If so, then who? And why?

Ben peered at his tall partner with another head full of questions. Plinter looked at him expectantly. The doctor's office loomed in front of them. Plinter had the door open for him. Ben shook his head and said 'not now, Corish. Later.'

The hundred-year-old building they entered was a splendid one. Leased by a large practice of medicos, it housed a variety of specialists in the medical profession. On a shiny brass plate, polished daily, the name Jeremy Roland Ames M.D. invited the public to knock on his door for advice and cures. Before he knocked Plinter said 'promise me you'll keep a cool head on your shoulders?' Ben nodded he would try. He didn't know how he'd react; he hadn't planned to be angry.

'Thank you for fitting us into your busy schedule, Doctor—'

'Please! Call me Jeremy, Inspector, we're all professional men. Ah! Ben! So glad to see you again! Come, now, take a seat and we'll start. I'll get Jayne to make some tea.' He spoke into a box and turned back to the men.

Plinter said, 'Not for me, Jeremy. Ben has some private things he needs to know, so I'll wait outside. I'm his chauffeur for today.' Plinter gave him an energetic smile. The doctor assumed the policeman's presence meant whatever he discussed with Ben included an interest by the constabulary while at the same time submitting to privacy.

'What do you want to know, Ben? I'll tell you all I can about Elizabeth, her condition, her state of mind.'

'Start with her pregnancy. I found out from Mr Plinter. Apparently my mother didn't know.'

'Ok. First of all, you knew she wasn't well?'

'Yes, she said it was something to do with her womb. Slow to return to its normal position, she said.'

'That was part of the problem but there was more. I sent her to a specialist, a very thorough man. He performed a biopsy. I gave her the results of his findings the day…the day she drowned. Everybody…and I mean every member of this practice…was devastated by the tragedy.'

'Go on, doc, what was wrong with her?'

'Ovarian carcinoma. The advice, the only viable advice, was to perform an oophorectomy. In her case, it meant also the removal of…well, a hysterectomy, to be exact. Elizabeth left my office that day with a heavy heart. She said she didn't know how she would tell you. I urged her to tell you.'

'But she was carrying a baby, doc. She would not have killed her baby! Tell me, doc, why did you not inform me after the accident? *Who* decided not to tell *me*?'

'I did try to contact you, Ben, but I was not able to. I spoke to your mother—'

'My mother knew about the cancer! You are not serious, are you?'

'No! Only Elizabeth knew, Ben, unless she told others. I would not inform your mother ahead of you. I hoped your mother could get you to come in—'

'So! How did Plinter know? *He* told me!'

'The police…Inspector Plinter…I told him. Yesterday…we spoke. It was part of his investigation. I felt obliged—'

'So *why* didn't you tell me? Why? You could have written or something! Suddenly you've become very unpopular, Dr Ames.'

'It was a very delicate situation, Ben. You were depressed, isolated. From my perspective, you didn't need to know. I felt it would have been inappropriate, unkind. Elizabeth had died; your little child had died, you didn't need the bad news then. Not…not that you…ever need bad news. Sorry, I didn't mean it to sound insensitive. The point is, I'm glad you came to speak with me. One is never ready for news of this sort…but now is a good time, I hope, Ben?'

'Why the hell didn't you ring me at the time? My wife must have been beside herself with anxiety! She must have been depressed, deeply depressed! And you let her go? You are in a *care* profession; you showed little care *that* day. I hope this comes back to haunt you. I hope, at least, you learn a strong lesson from this!'

Ames took the rebuke on the chin. 'In hindsight, you are right, no doubt. There was, however, doctor/patient privilege; I felt bound by that. *And*, I had every belief she was on her way to tell you; she *said* she would have to tell you. Perhaps a little walk along the promenade, to gather her thoughts, was her way of preparing herself to talk with you. That is only my view, Ben…I'm…sorry for your troubles.'

'The press came out with the story she took her own life. How do you suppose they came up with that? *Somebody* must have hinted she was depressed.'

'Ben, I must stress that it didn't come from my office. In fact, the media did not speak to me at all.'

'What about your staff, your secretary, the receptionist? Perhaps one of them let it slip?'

'No. Not possible. Elizabeth's file has been locked in this drawer. I maintained the privacy between us. Apart from the gynaecologist who saw her, no one else knew. Dr Sandlier respects privacy, too. We are professional men', he defended.

Ben sucked in air. His temperament soothed somewhat. The good doctor made a plausible defence. Ben offered a solution. 'The media thrive on stories, I suppose. The more emotion they can squeeze out of it, the more papers they sell.' Ames nodded in agreement.

'One more thing, doc. *If* Elizabeth were alive now, at what stage would her…cancer be?'

'According to the report from Sandy, eh Dr Sandlier'—he sifted through the file to quote the specialist, to give extra authority to his answer—'*without surgery, he gave her three to six months.*'

Ben flinched. He asked again, 'If Elizabeth were alive…what would be the state of her health?'

'Ok. She'd likely be very weak…eh…very thin…her weight loss, dramatic.'

'And the pain, doctor, what about the pain?'

'With proper treatment, the pain would certainly be lessened, but she didn't experience the end stages, Ben. It's not much consolation, I know. Had she opted to have the operation, it would have saved her life…but…there was the child to consider. An awful decision to be faced with…a frightful dilemma.'

Ben did his best to let the doctor's version sink in. Accepting it was another matter. However professional the medic made it sound, Ben found fault with it.

'You made the wrong decision, doc. You should have told me!'

'I'm sorry, Ben. I gave Elizabeth the status on her health. I pointed out to her the options. I did my job towards my patient. I stand by that. I am really, really sorry for your loss.'

'Are you? What medication did you prescribe for her?'

'Elizabeth first complained of deep stomach pains for several weeks; after more thorough examinations and tests, I grew suspicious. I decided the problem was serious enough to warrant a specialist so I sent her to James Sandlier. It was clear she was depressed and I prescribed accordingly.'

'So, she was taking anti-depressant pills?'

'Yes.'

'Why couldn't you have *said* that? I'm *so angry* with you. If you thought she was that depressed, why did you just let her go off on her own? If I'd been in your place, doctor, I would have at least called a relative or put her in a taxi. She walked out of your surgery and into her death! A paradox, don't you think?'

Ben got up and left the interview. On seeing him emerge, Plinter x-rayed his face and saw one angry young man on the verge of detonation. He reached out his hand to provide some kind of comfort; Ben pushed his hand away. Plinter surrendered to Ben's angst, suspecting that all did not go well with the doctor, that there were unresolved issues.

They sat on a bench for five minutes, neither saying a word. Plinter rightly held his tongue while the cooling down period took its natural course. After a while, Ben said, 'I was very hard on the man. But he was so self-righteous! Had all the answers…took none of the blame.'

'What did you find out, Ben? Was there no good news?' The policeman probed carefully, to explore the young man's delicate, raw regions.

'Cancer. Elizabeth had cancer.' He wept openly, unable to stop the flow. Several passers-by gaped in natural curiosity. A woman kept on walking and looking back. One old man and his dog stopped for a good long, hard look. He knew the policeman; probably thought Plinter had given the unfortunate man some very bad news, but he didn't wait to hear Ben next words.

'She…had to decide…between…having her insides removed, effectively killing the baby…and saving herself. Elizabeth, *I know*, would hang on until our baby was born. I *know* that's what she would have done.'

The Inspector told Ben he applauded that brave decision but to get the full benefit they had to find her alive before any further complications set in.

'Come, Ben! We have more people to talk to.'

Ben felt Plinter take his arm and steer him to the car. He tried to find a word that described the policeman. *Madman, raving lunatic,* came to mind. Not dogged. Not strong-minded. Not gritty. Not without clues. Not without knowledge. The passenger seat cushioned his body when he slumped into the chair. Plinter helped him with his seat belt and urged him to keep his courage alive.

'We are heading for the Marina. We'll talk to every boat owner who rents a space on the dock, Ben. Someone must have seen something, or heard something. I'm sure all they need is for us to jog their memory!'

Ben wanted to tell him he was mad for thinking Elizabeth was alive. He wanted to shout at him the reasons given did not convince him of any such thing. Not even a glimmer of hope. Even the doctor gave him no hope, so how could Plinter? Ben knew he was more distraught than confused. He knew that. Deep down he wanted to know about the garbage lid and the ring. The two things that puzzled him. Really puzzled him. Someone set out to implicate him! That was it! And his mother got in the firing line! So Plinter thinks.

Plinter parked and got out. Ben made no attempt at moving so he opened the door for him and urged him to be strong. Ben wanted to say what's the use? It's a wild goose-chase, Corish, and we both know it! He could read Plinter's firm but persuasive answer and imagined what he might say. *One of us thinks it's a useless cause, Ben. I don't! But, for the moment, let's assume your wife is dead. We still have to find your mother, isn't that true? So get up and starting walking! When we find her, she'll have you to thank, too!*

As the two men walked along the row of boats, Plinter asked Ben what he was thinking before he entered the doctor's office. 'You were about to say something to me. I could see it in your eyes. What was it? What worried you? Was it apprehension at meeting Ames?'

'Yes, I was a bit shaky going in…but…you are…I think you are right about foul play. Someone removed the ring and nappy and placed them in the garbage bin. I also think that they were meant to be found. The police would add two and two together and come up with my name. I see that now.' He sighed deeply as though he'd been carrying a great weight and let it fall off his shoulders.

'And your mother?'

'I'm not sure why she's missing…you might be right about the letter, too…I don't know. I can't believe…no…*if* the letter came from Billy…no, I can't imagine him hurting…I can't!'

'Listen to me, Ben. Go and see him like we said. Do that, now! I'll continue with this line of investigation. I'll take you back to your mother's house. Get your car and go see him. Just behave normally. Play it cool and relaxed, as if nothing happened. Suggest your mother has probably gone to see your aunt, something like that. See what you discern. And make the visit brief, casual. Only stay as long as he allows.'

'You really are a suspicious character, Corish. Is everybody a suspect?'

'In the realms of crime, young man, everyone is, and no one is. However… we can only follow what clues we have. Now, let's go!'

'Pick him up! Take him under the armpits, Tavistock!'

Rosa struggled to lift her own weight off the floor. The pain in her knee throbbed throughout her whole body. Unable to stand, and fearful of displeasing the woman, she lamented that her kneecap may be smashed. Meredith told her how useless she was and that her refusal to help Billy was her way of taking revenge on Billy for tying her up in the cellar. Blood oozed from his shoulder; he lay limp against the wall and groaned. His face was white, his eyes rolled and he was near to passing out.

'Call an ambulance, Meredith, for goodness sakes! He needs expert help!'

In a nasty, angry attack, the woman responded by spitting at her. 'That's what I think of your suggestion. I'm a nurse! A trained nurse! I don't need anyone's help. Billy is in safe hands with me. Now move your useless body out of my way!'

Rosa moved as close to the wall as she could, sliding her injured leg behind. Meredith forced her legs between Billy's back and the wall and slowly twisted his torso until her hands fit under his armpits. Despite his groans and pleas to stop, she dragged him through the doorway and stopped only when she had reached the bed. Rosa wondered where the woman got her strength; she could only come up with one answer. It was a mixture of relentless and turbulent anger, and malevolence in its vilest form. Billy's groans came to a sudden halt; Rosa guessed he passed out. She listened for a while to the grunting sounds from Meredith's coarse tongue, swearing at the dead-weight body of her son. 'Wake up, Billy! I need you to help me get you on the bed. I have to stop the bleeding. Get up, will you!'

Rosa pulled herself into Elizabeth's room, keeping a watch on the old woman as she tried to lift Billy onto the bed. Meredith gave up and let him fall in a heap on the carpet. Then she screamed abuse into the air. Catching sight of Rosa crawling into the bedroom, she darted in a mad frenzy and pulled the door shut, locked it and screamed that Rosa would not leave that room again! Rosa let out a thankful sigh of relief, albeit a temporary respite from the demented woman. Through the hole in the splintered door, she watched the old woman straighten Billy's body on the carpet.

'That bullet has to come out, son.'

Meredith left the room; Rosa gaped through the hole in the door. She heard the footfall down the stairs, and secretly hoped the hag was not able to climb back up! Minutes later, she returned. Rosa peeked again and saw Meredith stand over her son. She had a bottle in one hand and a knife in the other.

'Guess what Nurse Crazy is about to do,' Rosa whispered derisively, 'with a sharp knife and a bottle of Johnny Walker; what a surgeon worth his salt would give for those instruments.' She turned away in disgust and crawled over to the bed. With much effort, she climbed into the chair and sat back, exhausted. Needing to talk to someone but not wanting to disturb Elizabeth, who was more like her own child, Rosa tried a whisper. If there was no reply from Elizabeth then she would leave it, and sleep instead, while the butchery in the 'theatre' across the hallway got under way. Elizabeth lay still.

'Elizabeth!' Rosa touched her shoulder gently. Elizabeth moved a little and responded further to Rosa's hand. She opened her dark-ringed eyes and stared.

'Rosa, I thought you were…I heard the gun go off…I'm glad…you are…ok,' she panted, drawing in short breaths.

Rosa rubbed her cheek affectionately. Again, Rosa recoiled at the touch of her gaunt face and tried not to show her distress. It was hard not to. The thin, emaciated features had replaced those of the woman, who, only a few short months ago, radiated warmth and beauty. They stared caringly before Elizabeth said with clarity: '*Rosa, you know I'm dying, don't you?*'

Rosa objected passionately, 'No, Elizabeth! Don't talk that way. Ben will come and get us. Please don't say that, now that we've found you.'

'*Listen to me…have you…does Ben know I am pregnant?*'

Rosa apologised, 'Pregnant! No, I had no idea. Ben never mentioned—'

It's alright, Rosa. Dr Ames…he mustn't have told Ben. Tell Ben I would never harm our child. Be sure to tell him for me, won't you, Rosa?

'My dear Elizabeth! I know you'd *never* hurt Stephie. Ben *knows* you loved Stephie. Where…where did this come from, my darling?'

I'm not talking about Stephie, Rosa. Billy wouldn't…give her back to me. I…I tried to…I tried to get her from him…but she…fell. The water…Billy stopped me from jumping after her…

Rosa was not able to contain her emotions. The tears swept over the banks and flooded her face and onto the bedclothes. She had an overwhelming desire to hold Elizabeth in her arms and wipe the pain from the child's heart but she was the one needing the calming embrace. In a reversal of roles, Elizabeth reached up to Rosa's neck and drew her anguished friend to her bosom. Rosa tried to talk; Elizabeth told her to cry instead. Rosa obeyed.

I've cried all my tears, Rosa. I have none left for myself. I've cried myself dry for Stephie. What tears I have left are tears are for Ben and this little life nestling inside me. I'm sorry I can't give birth to my little baby…I don't think there'll be enough time.

Rosa lifted her head, sobbing in between words. 'Please…please, Elizabeth, don't talk like this. It's…not going to happen. Help *will* come. I can't let you say you'll die!' Her emotions switched to anger. 'Did that vile woman do something to you? What medication did she make you swallow?'

It has nothing…nothing to do with her, Rosa.

'What then, what did you mean when you said you'd never harm Stephie? You weren't so depressed…that you'd take your own…? Elizabeth, please tell me…please?'

No, no, Rosa. She took her mother-in-law's hand and placed it on her swollen stomach. *I mean this little baby. It is nearly six months, Rosa. Only six months…so tiny…only half made. This is the baby I'm talking about.*

'Oh! I understand now, darling, but you'd never deliberately harm your baby! You'd never hurt your child! You are just not like that, Elizabeth.'

Elizabeth focused on Rosa's eyes. When she had her full attention, she said, *Don't misunderstand me but…I was given the choice, Rosa. The doctor…he gave me a choice. But I would never choose to kill our baby.*

'Now you are confusing me, Elizabeth.'

Rosa, I really am dying. I have cancer. A hysterectomy meant our child's death. I chose to not to kill our baby. The decision was easy, Rosa.

Her mother-in-law threw her hands to her face and suppressed a desolate cry. It came out as a guttural squeal. She stared at Elizabeth and with a new look in her eyes she tenderly kissed her cheek. Resolutely, she told her that her worst fears would not happen, her baby would be born and this awful cancer would go away. What she didn't tell Elizabeth was *how* Meredith Turner would be stopped. She, Rosa Tavistock, would find a way to contact the outside world. The police, Corish, Ben! One or all of them! Somehow, *somehow,* she would find a way out of this nightmare.

Even if it meant sacrificing her own body.

Among her determined thoughts came the loudest, the most agonising scream she ever encountered. Billy shrieked the pain of his mother's knife into every corner of the house. Rosa covered her ears because she *knew* what Meredith was attempting. The man's cries continued as Rosa grabbed the lampstand, as she did before, and pounded the door panels with maniacal fury. With the kind of strength that anger musters, Rosa forgot the aches in all the parts of her beleaguered body and stretched her arm through the splintered door to reach the key.

Billy's door was closed. Meredith hadn't heard the pounding nor the door open; Rosa guessed the old woman was preoccupied with her 'surgical' skills to hear anything, or Billy's screams blocked out the pounding on the door. That didn't matter now; Rosa had other plans. Sucking in a deep breath, she limped along the corridor to retrieve the gun from under the bed. Her heart somersaulted when it wasn't there.

'*She* must have found it!'

The doorbell rang. The jangle echoed up the stairs. Billy's door flew open. Meredith stood in the doorway. She waved the weapon at Rosa's chest. Rosa froze in the kneeling position. The pain in her knee returned. The bell rang again. Meredith told her to get up. Rosa was slow to move. Too slow for Meredith's liking. She aimed the gun. Rosa moved faster. Billy called out in pain. Rosa thought he heard him say the bleeding wouldn't stop.

His mother pushed the gun into her ribs and prodded her back to Elizabeth's bed and shoved her into the chair, and told her if she moved, she'd regret it. Meredith left the room and returned with a rope and sticky tape. The caller seemed impatient. The bell rang a third time and for much longer. Tied and gagged, Rosa could only offer Elizabeth a disappointed, forlorn gaze. Elizabeth managed a thin, forgiving smile. The doorbell rang continuously, annoyingly. Meredith left the gun behind the front door and opened it a smidgen.

'What do you want? Oh, it's YOU! What do you *want* I said?'

Ben squinted through the narrow gap. 'Hello, Mrs Turner. I was hoping to see Billy. May I?'

She said, 'No, you may not. He's sick.'

Ben asked, 'What's the matter with him? He was OK yesterday…when he fixed my car. Remember?'

'He fell and hurt his shoulder. He's resting. Not able to see anyone. Go away, now!' Rosa heard the voices. She rocked the chair back and forward. Well-practiced at rocking chairs, she, however, had a poor success rate at falling safely.

'Is there anything I can do for him?' Ben continued.

'No! He'll be fine. Now go! I have a house to run.'

Billy yelled out 'help'. His mother glanced behind her, up the stairs, and looked back at Ben.

'Was that Billy, Mrs Turner? Sounds like he's in real pain. How did he fall?'

'He tripped on the carpet. Now go!'

'Ok. Will you ask him to ring me? I'd like to see him, to thank him.'

'No! The phone's dead. He tripped and fell…on the phone…the wire. Can't ring you. Can't ring out.'

Rosa's chair crashed to the floor. Her head struck the carpet, creating a muffled thump on the carpeted floorboards. Ben put his hand on the door. 'Mrs Turner, what was that noise?' He exerted a little more pressure.

'That was nothing…we…we have a new cat. Now will you please go! I have Billy to tend to.' She pushed on the door.

Ben relented. 'I'll…call again…' His voice faded as she shoved against the door and secured the latch. Ben's insides were shaking. At one point he wanted to storm the house, throw the woman to one side and confront Billy, and scream into his face, *Where is my mother? She came here! What have you done with her?* He opted out on that move; better to stay cool, like Plinter said. How could this wizened old hag have so much control, he questioned. What lies she told to keep him from seeing Billy. First his accident then the phone then the cat. He reminded himself what Plinter had warned: *keep calm, act normally, don't overstay your visit.*

Ben decided to leave. Knowing she'd be watching, he sauntered to his car as casually as he could, fit his seatbelt and drove down the long driveway before swinging the vehicle towards town. When he'd driven for a few hundred metres he pulled over and parked under an elm tree and tapped a few numbers into his phone. A sweet voice from the telephone exchange sang 'how may I help you'. Ben explained he was having trouble reaching a number and could she check it for him. The contralto came back within seconds and replied, 'The number is ringing, sir.'

'Could the phone be damaged and still ring?'

'Yes, it will ring at the exchange. Hold on. I'll check for any complaints on that number. Please hold.' Ben listened to his breath disappear down the line while he waited.

'There have been no complaints with that line, sir. Please try the number again.' He took the advice from the young woman and waited. It was ringing. As soon as he heard *her* say hello, he would hang up and go back for the big confrontation. He had to make sure she was lying to him. Still ringing. Ten, fifteen, twenty times. 'Either the phone is really damaged,' he thought aloud, 'or she won't pick up because she has to carry out the lie. She's cunning enough to believe I'd be the caller.'

A four-wheel drive shot by. It took Ben several seconds to identify Billy's vehicle. 'What the heck! She said he was sick.' Ben turned the key and took off after the Mazda. Two cars separated his Rover from Billy's vehicle. One, then the other made left and right turns. So as not be seen, he indicated left and slowed down to let a car pass him, then re-joined the queue. Three or four minutes later, the Mazda pulled up at the lights on King Street, the right blinker flashing. It shot forward and swung hard in front of oncoming traffic. Several horns blasted warnings, followed by the sound of tyres squealing.

The Mazda got away with it. Just. As the vehicle turned the corner, the shape of Meredith Turner behind the wheel shocked Ben. Firstly, he expected to see Billy and, more importantly, Meredith no longer qualified as a driver, for medical reasons. *And* forbidden by Billy to boot! No wonder the driving was erratic!

Ben waited his turn to follow her, anxiously thinking he might lose sight of her; but she pulled into a parking bay. With a raised, arrogant hand—he watched her bring traffic to a halt to cross the road. She disappeared inside the pharmacy. A parking spot became available. Ben was quick to secure it and waited until she toddled out. A brown paper carry bag with *Rick Saunders, The People's Pharmacy* sprawled on it hung on her skinny arm. She drove away as recklessly as she parked. Ben got out. He wanted to know what she was up to, what she bought, what she needed in such a hurry.

Rick the chemist welcomed him with well-practiced courtesy. 'I'm supposed to meet my mother here…a small thin lady…black dress…Did you serve her?'

'Not me personally but I did see her—hey, Jarma, you took care of that little old lady, didn't you?'

The assistant approached with a genuine smile. 'Yes, she left a minute ago. You've just missed her, sir.'

'Um…she's a little absentminded…Did she buy some…eh…skin cream, I have a rash on my…my leg. Did she?'

'No, no cream. I'll get it for you. What size tube?'

'Em…I gave her a list…what exactly did she get?'

'Ok, there was a large roll of bandages…antiseptic solution, and…yes, painkillers, Paracetamol. That's it, sir. I'll show you our range of creams?'

Ben left the shop with the distinct opinion that something *did* happen to Billy, *and* a tube of vitamin E cream for a rash he didn't have. He thought it best to report to Plinter with the latest from the Turner house. When he finally caught up to him Plinter was talking with a young man who owned a speedboat. Ben stood off nearby to attract the policeman's attention. Plinter casually waved him over and explained to him, with sympathy, the young man's boat was seriously damaged by the storm and the insurance company was not coming to the party. The young man said he was at work at the time; he couldn't offer any assistance ID-ing the 'woman with the little girl'.

'That's another one we can scratch off the list, Ben. So far, of those I spoke to, none of them were on the wharf when the storm hit, which is understandable—look! There's an old man tying up his cabin cruiser. Let's talk to him.' Ben wanted to get back to the Turner house immediately. With the top-notch policeman to support him, Old Mother Turner couldn't palm him off so easily. Plinter insisted on interviewing the last man on the Marina before he listened to Ben's episode with Old Lady Dementia.

'Ah, good day to you, sir! Pleasant jaunt on the waves?' The old man didn't seem to hear but he knew he was being addressed. He put his hand up like a traffic controller does and touched his ear and rotated a tiny dial on his hearing-aid. 'That's better. Now, what did you say?'

'I say, it's a nice day for a jaunt on the water. Were you out fishing this fine morning?' The old man turned and lifted a plastic bucket from the side and proudly raised a large fish. Plinter remarked on the size of the John Dory and said how lovely it would be, seasoned and wrapped in foil and in *his* oven! The old man laughed and said he could have the bones after he'd finished with it.

Plinter didn't have to make introductions. 'So, how I can be of assistance, Inspector?' He glanced at Ben and nodded. Plinter began quizzing the man in his casual manner.

'We are continuing with our on-going investigation of the tragedy on the day of the great storm, Thursday, November 26th.'

The man aimed his bushy eyebrows at Ben and said, 'I'm sorry, son…sorry for your loss', and switched his gaze back to the Inspector's question.

'I know it's been a little while now, but were you on the dock that day, before midday?'

At seventy-six, Martin Greenwell was unable to stand to his younger height of five-eleven. He leaned forward and tried to straighten his curved backbone. His legs were unconsciously separated wider than normal to give him an easier-to-handle centre of gravity.

'I paid special attention to the weather forecast the night before. Next morning, early, I came here to secure my boat with a few extra lines. Fortunately for me, I suffered very little damage, not like some of the other boat owners.' He pointed to one in particular. 'That one there, yeah, the blue and white one, the man who owns that one still hasn't got it repaired. Think he ran out of money.'

'So, you left before the storm hit.'

'Wouldn't you?' he replied, with a grumpy grin. 'I was at home, finished my breakfast and the cryptic puzzle by half-past nine.'

'Right, eh, sir. Did you notice anything, anything out of order… anything unusual?'

The old man shook his head and scratched behind his ear. He rubbed his white-grey stubble, took another look at Ben and addressed him as if to reemphasise his commiserations and give the young man *some* hope of finding out what caused the death of his family. 'No, but you might want to see Tommy Blake.'

'And who is he? Ben asked. The old man got a little excited when Ben spoke, sort of glad the bereaved man didn't *sound* as depressed as he looked.

'Oh, Tommy ties up three down from me. He's a bit older than me. We share a few pints together now and then in *Jemser Finnegan's,* the Irish pub near the roundabout. He slept in his boat the day of the storm. I think…I got the impression he heard a commotion coming from the boat next to his, but he wasn't sure. He can't always be trusted, though. He's fond of the Guinness.'

'Do you remember any of what he said, Martin?'

'Well, at first he thought he heard a baby crying, then he changed his mind and decided it was a dog howling. Then he was convinced it was the wind. He told me he lifted the hatch and had a peek out but the rain was pelting down and the wind blew the hatch shut. Slept like a log for the afternoon, he said, and between you and me, anyone who drinks like a fish can outlast *any* storm.' Plinter asked Martin for Tommy's address; a pen and a notebook was at the ready.

Back in the car, Plinter listened carefully to Ben's account of what happened, from the time Meredith answered the doorbell to Ben's exiting the pharmacy. Plinter conceded that apart from the woman being a mental hit-and-run case he found nothing unusual about buying medical supplies.

'And the noises I heard from upstairs? It was Billy's voice, and then a thump on the floor like he fell out of the bed! Surely, that's suspicious?'

'Actually, Ben, it appears to me that he hurt himself, perhaps a nasty cut, his mother went out for a proper bandage and some painkiller, like any good mother would do—and the noise on the floor could very possibly be…a frisky cat knocking a piece of furniture over. All very normal things.'

'Whose side are you on anyway, Corish? You strongly recommend I see Billy and suss him out, and then you totally disregard everything I saw and heard.'

'No, no, no Ben. It's not like that at all. Try not to read something into a set of circumstances that is, in itself, perfectly normal. The things that grab my attention are the *odd* things, the little things that *seem* innocent, but really are powerful clues. For instance, Ben, could *you* tell the difference between a baby's cry, a dog howling and a gale force ten wind?'

Ben was perplexed by the question. To think that someone had heard Stephie crying and did nothing about it appalled him. To have heard her cry out for help and say it was a *dog* made him livid. Already he hated the Guinness-soaked boat owner from Ireland.

'What are you thinking, Ben? Remember, we know there was a baby in the vicinity of the marina, the man-made reference to hearing a baby cry. A coincidence? I think not!'

'I'm thinking that you are full of…full of…hunches, Inspector, and not much sensitivity. It doesn't bother you that the baby in question was mine, does it? You should know how I feel. You had a daughter, once.'

Plinter apologised profusely for his candour. 'I take your point, Ben. It was rather callous of me. I need to know when to take off the policeman's uniform and show a little tact. Forgive me, sir.'

Ben shrugged and said that life is not all about clues. Plinter acquiesced. Ben suggested they go immediately to visit Tommy Blake before he died, or absorbed an unhealthy amount of the creamy black stuff into his bloodstream.

Fourteen

Meredith Turner barged into Elizabeth's room. She took a step back at the sight of the thin, delicate figure of Elizabeth kneeling next to the fallen chair. Attempting to undo the knots on Rosa's wrists, and having no success, she turned to face Meredith with a whispered plea to let her mother-in-law go. The old woman scolded her for being out of bed. She lifted the fragile Elizabeth off the floor easily and placed her on the bed.

'Must keep you fit and well, child. For Billy's sake…for his sake.' She bent down and undid the knots. 'Get up, Mrs Tavistock! You are going to help me with Billy's wound. Up! Now! I'll show you what to do, you just follow orders. You're in my theatre now; you might even learn something, girlie.'

Billy lay still. The carpet was wet under his shoulder. Rosa grimaced at the dark stain. A strong smell of alcohol stung her nostrils. His shirt was torn to expose the right side of his upper body. A white pillowcase was made into a pad and shoved into the wound. It was saturated in dark-red ooze. The old woman removed the pad and threw the red cloth against the wall. It part-covered the small missile that tore through the deltoid muscle and lodged in the joint where the humerus meets the scapula. The blood-stained cloth landed near the knife used in the operation. The blood had congealed on its long, sharp serrated edge. Meredith checked the area and decided the bleeding had all but stopped.

'Here, take this—she passed the rolled-up bandage to Rosa, told her to get busy unwrapping—we haven't got all day,' she scowled and saturated a cloth with the antiseptic solution. She ordered Rosa to hurry up with the bandage and slapped the cloth on Billy's wound. He made some movement in his unconscious state. Rosa unrolled a metre of the four-inch-wide bandage; Meredith snipped it with scissors and told her to 'keep going, we need enough for a sling.' Getting behind her son, she raised him to the sitting position then began to wind the bandage.

In minutes, the bullet wound was neatly bound, his arm slung in a vee. Together, they struggled to haul Billy's fifteen stone dead-weight onto the bed. He made no audible complaints. Meredith went to the bathroom and came out with a basin of warm water. She thrust a clean hand towel into Rosa's hand and ordered, 'Clean up the blood and don't get the bandages wet! And don't get any smart ideas about leaving this room.' She closed the door. Rosa heard her trundle down the stairs.

With one hand pressed to her mouth, she began to dab Billy's exposed skin with the towel, whimpering in between rinses. Billy opened his eyes, slowly at first, blinked and stared at her. A look of wonder filled his eyes as he ran his gaze around the room, and realising where he was and who it was standing above him, he muttered, 'Did you do this?'

Rosa thought he meant the injury. She answered firmly, 'No, your mother did.'

He repeated, 'I mean the dressing.'

She said, 'Oh that. No, your mother did. I helped…a little.'

'My mother shot me, Rosa. My own mother!'

'Don't take it too hard. She meant to shoot *me*; you got caught in the cross-hairs. And now, even if you had the guts to stop her and let us go, you're in no condition to do that now. What did you *do*, Billy? *What have you done*?' Billy turned his head towards the window.

'It all went crazy. All I wanted was to get away from *her*…have a life of my own…a family of my own, where everything was fine, everyone was happy. When I saw Elizabeth at the bank, I believed she was the answer. She was *so* different to my mother, the very opposite. Caring eyes, warm smile… she looked happy. I watched her day after day. I found reasons to go the bank and when I ran out of reasons I'd go anyway. I'd pretend to fill in withdrawal forms. I'd even join a queue and leave before my turn. I'd—'

'Explain the letter to me, Billy. The letter! Isn't this what it's all about? Why did you send that letter?'

'I already told you. I did not send that letter. Elizabeth did! I could not put words together like those. That was poetry, Rosa, *poetry*. I did poorly at school in English and maths. I was good with mechanical things, motors, taking things apart, fitting them back together. When it came to…reading and writing…well, they were…a different matter. I was…I am dyslexic.'

Rosa remembered Ben saying something to that effect years ago. She had paid more attention to his talents with machinery than to his poor writing skills. It didn't seem to matter since his natural ability would always guarantee him work. Now she believed him. *He* was not the one who penned the four sheets of romantic prose.

'Ok,' she said patiently, 'explain to me how it reached Ben's mailbox?'

Billy collected his thoughts and carried on, 'This is what happened. We had the usual bills that had to be paid. My mother had the habit of fixing stamps to a pile of envelopes—don't ask me why, it was just one of her quirks—she'd have up to twenty envelopes with stamps at one time. She kept them in the bureau downstairs. So when it came to sending off mail, bills or whatever, she'd methodically write the addresses on each envelope and slot in the cheque that went with it. They were left on the kitchen table for me to post.

'I posted the letter that was addressed to Ben. I had no idea it was there. It was later my mother asked did I post them. I said *yes*. She said, "All three of them?" I said there were four. My mother went berserk. "I only wrote three!" she screamed at me and accused me of lying.

'I told her again there were *four* on the kitchen table. Well, she went to her drawer and swung around wildly. "Who took my letter? It was on the table. I bet it was that vixen!" She rushed upstairs. I just wanted to leave the house at that moment; the woman made me want to…I needed to get away from her, for her sake…I couldn't trust what I might do.

'I heard the commotion from upstairs, and then Elizabeth crying. I got up there as fast as I could and pulled my mother off her. "What are you doing, mother?" I remember yelling at her. There was fear in my mother's eyes, like a vicious, wild animal ready to pounce. She pointed at Elizabeth and screamed: "Sheee…took my letter and sent it to her lover!"'

Billy took a breath to get the image of his mother from his brain but he couldn't. In her mind, Rosa tried to fill in the missing pieces.

'Billy, are you saying Elizabeth sent the letter?'

'Yes. My mother forced the truth from her. That's what all the screaming was about that day. I remember. Later Elizabeth told me she undid the straps on her wrist—she'd been working all night on the knots, stretching them until there were loose enough to finally slip her hands out—she crept downstairs, saw what my mother was doing, and waited for an opportunity to get to the door. My mother answered the phone—a telemarketer wanted to sell her something, and you know how they can talk.

'When my mother's back was turned, Elizabeth tried the door but it wouldn't budge. My mother had secured every door and window. Elizabeth had to think quickly. Then she saw a way. If Ben received the oddest, weirdest message in the post from me, his friend, then surely he'd come running to my house? That's how Elizabeth figured it. It was a desperate move, she told me. There was barely enough time to scribble the address and seal the envelope and hide from my mother.'

Rosa asked him when it was sent.

'Middle of December. Tenth, to be exact. I know because my mother wanted me to get the letter before Ben did. She was crazy. She suggested I wait and ambush the postman. I told her she was foolish. Then she suggested I wait by Ben's gate and pretend to be him; the postman, she said, would place the letter directly into my hand. She got excited by that idea of hers.

'I told her the postman *knows* Ben and that it was a stupid idea. She didn't like being told that. I said we'll have to wait a day or so to see the reaction. If Ben did come around, we'd have to come up with an excuse of some sort. Wires got crossed, or something. Nothing happened for a few days, so I thought the letter may have gotten lost in the post. That's what happens to lots of mail, so I was prepared to let it go at that. *But not my mother.* She made me break into Ben's house and look for the letter.'

'It was YOU! You came in through the bathroom window?'

'Yeah, but I didn't find the letter. I looked through a pile of unopened mail and felt sure that it was not delivered at all! Until you turned up at our door. Where was it?'

Rosa kept shaking her head at the man. She wanted to berate him for disloyalty to her son, his friend, but the break-in was nothing compared to what he had allowed in this house. He said his mother *made him do it*. She tried to imagine what kind of hold Meredith had on him, that a shrivelled, wrinkled old hag like her could exert so much power over another human. Then it began to dawn on her. The truth was slowly emerging.

Meredith Turner had controlled Billy from his birth onwards. She was the inveterate manipulator. No wonder her husband left. No wonder her own son couldn't stand her. Rosa stared at the man in the bed. No wonder this man, this full-grown person was in agony; he never really was allowed to grow up to be a man.

'It fell behind the sideboard. It stayed there for months. I found it quite by accident. The writer…the writer was…your father, William, wasn't it, Billy?'

'Yes.'

'But he left years ago. Why did your mother keep it? She wasn't…or maybe she was? Does she… still have feelings for him?'

'Feelings? You've got be joking! She has feelings only for herself! She…she drove my father out'—Billy twisted his body, his face contorted with anger—'she…she wouldn't let me see him. He came home especially to see *me*, not her. She said my father was a bad influence on me and I'd be better off had I never known him. My mother was…is sick! She's never been anything but… sick, crazy—'

Rosa said he should slow down and take control. The dressing showed a spot of red; it quickly grew into the size of a large coin. 'You need to lie still.' She pressed a cloth to his shoulder. He gave out a short groan. It wasn't the pain of his wound; it was the hurt he had inside, the things *she* made him do. Things he did for *her*. He wished he had died when he was young.

'The truth is, Rosa, my mother hated my father. I think she hated all men. She told me, more than once, how she hated her own father. Sometimes…sometimes…I think she hates *me*. I could see it in her eyes. She just didn't say it. The letter…*that* letter. How often I wanted to burn it, destroy it out of my life. When I was young, after my father left, she'd sit me down and read it out loud. Over and over, day in, day out. I got so annoyed with her I told she'd better stop or I would rip it into a million pieces. She stopped after that, but she continued to read in her room or I'd find her in the kitchen and catch her trying to hide it behind her back.

'Yes, my father wrote it to her. He told me that he fell in love with her but she showed no interest in him. It was a sort of a…a farewell letter, a do-or-die plea for her hand. The letter seemed to change everything. Suddenly she was all over him. He thought it was the real McCoy and when she said yes to marriage, well, even now, I can remember the joy on his face when he related it to me. After I was born, he said, things went downhill, and fast.'

Billy paused. Rosa felt there was so much pain in recounting the ordeal that he had to stop and regroup. She asked why his mother kept the letter all these years.

'I believe my mother truly hates men, but I also think she loved the idea that one day a real man would come and rescue her from…I don't know…from the person she was. You know, make her into a loving, warm and happy person. She said to me one day, and she never said it again, that she was *so* unhappy. The letter, the words, the way it was expressed, yes, I think she was in love with the idea of being *in love*, being looked after by, I suppose… her version of what a man should be. In reality, she could never be fulfilled. Her *personality* would always get in the way. That's the best way I can explain it, Rosa.'

Rosa was somewhat taken aback by Billy. There was an inconsistency in the man. She had to ask him.

'Billy, can I ask you about your dyslexia?'

'What's there to know, I just am.'

'Who told you had a problem that way?'

'Mr Waterson, my math teacher…he told my mother. She told me.'

'Was anything done to help you?'

'She said I got it from my father…there was no cure for it. I just had to live with it…like she had to live with the problems her father gave her.'

'Billy, you didn't get it from your father. You got it from *her*, your mother.'

'I…I don't follow you, Rosa. What are you saying to me?'

'Billy, Billy, can't you see what's been happening? For the last five minutes, your speech has been fine. You explained *very well* the dilemma behind the love letter. I think…yes, I think you have offloaded a big burden. You told another person how you really feel about your mother. Can't you see she's held you in fear for most of your life, blaming your father for everything that went wrong? She manipulated your thinking from an early age and compounded it when your father left…or was driven out, as you put it.

'You have an intelligent mind, a very clever mind. But…you are thirty-four years old and you…*you need to break free from her*, Billy…you need to confront her. It's not her size that scares you, is it? She's half your size and probably half your weight, but that's not the problem, is it? No! It's her tongue! It's what she *says* to keep you scared. She is the ultimate bully. She got you young and she got you frightened. She got you believing you needed her, and it worked. Now is the time to confront her, Billy. Now!'

Billy rolled his head to the side, escaping Rosa's eyes. 'You don't understand. It's easy for you…to talk…and tell me what I should do. You don't know what…what… happened. No one does. No…one…'

Rosa spoke softly to him. 'Isn't it time someone does, besides you and your mother?'

The door flew open. Meredith stood wielding the gun, her eyes aimed at Billy, the weapon at Rosa. Rosa searched Billy's face. She knew by his demeanour that he would obey his mother above all else. She had lost her plea to provoke Billy into defending his life from Meredith, thus losing the chance to get Elizabeth proper medical attention.

'What's she been filling your head with, son? You and me must stick *together*, d'you hear me, son. Together. *No one* can hurt us if we stick together. Tell me you agree with me, go on? Tell me, son.'

Billy raised his head and found her eyes briefly. He said 'yes, mother' and lay back again, and closed his eyes in a vain attempt to block out her presence. The last words he heard before she closed the door were from his mother's mouth saying that Rosa's brat came knocking on her door but he was sent packing.

'Poor Ben,' Rosa heard him whisper, 'all the trouble I've caused him.'

Fifteen

Tommy Blake shuffled his short, round body to answer the doorbell. Without saying a word he expressed jolly surprise at the callers. His cheerful face said it all.

'Now, what can I do you gentlemen for?'

Plinter raised a curious eyebrow at the little Irishman and his agreeable approach. *Darby O'Gill and the Little People* quickly came to mind; the send-up on leprechauns he saw at the cinema in his younger days.

Ben recalled the two weeks he spent in County Clare with Elizabeth, setting up a project, so he was familiar with the hospitable heritage the Irish shared. The client took Elizabeth and him on an outing to visit the *Cliffs of Moher* on the rugged Atlantic coast. The joy Elizabeth had that day flooded back to him. In his head, he saw in her face the picture of absolute awe. They walked up the hill, past the old stone tower and gazed across at the ominous yet breath-taking, craggy perpendicular cliffs. A young tourist couple dared to walk on the narrow grass verge on the cliff side of the safety fence. A keen photographer, aka a hyperactive, frenzied hobbyist, lay on his stomach on a rock platform, his head and shoulders hung out over the vertical rock face that went down 30-40 metres.

With his camera aimed at the activity below, he snapped pictures to make *National Geographic* drool with envy. For the man, the risk was clearly worth the end results, but for Ben, the exercise was sheer madness! In the far distance, tiny dots of white representing kittiwakes seemed to hang in mid-air, an exhibition of aerial acrobatics for the ancient rocks to witness. Speckled wings of parent birds flew effortlessly, in apparent slow motion, back and forward to nests that housed their young on shale and flagstone.

Through hi-tech binoculars, Elizabeth picked out the white bellies of the penguin-like guillemots that stood in line as though in a queue for handouts. Their bearded and bespectacled client-host, Seamus, pointed to the choughs and passed the glasses to Elizabeth once again. She marvelled at the black bird with bright red beak and matching legs. Divers zipped into the water at high speed, emerging with tasty bites for their young. Ben recalled they forgot the camera that day but he clearly remembers Elizabeth saying she would *never* forget the pictures in her memory banks. All she had to do was close her eyes, and press the *play* button.

An instant scene of the foaming surf far below filed his head. The surf crashing against the rocks was, from his perspective, distant, surreally gentle, hushed, but reality had other claims; the turbulent tide was angrily pounding against prehistoric legs that supported precipitous cliffs. He knew the power of the sea. He knew what the sea had done to his beloved wife and his child. The memory was no longer pleasant. The songlike accent of Tommy Blake brought him back to the present.

'Sure, will you gentlemen not come in and join me for a little drop. I hope you haven't come to take away me boat lishenshe. Sure I'd absholutely fall apart at the sheams if ya did daht.'

They followed the retired sailor into a large space, which used to be the living room, but now a veritable museum of marine artefacts. An old but beautifully polished brass bell hung from the ceiling; a plaited cord dangled temptingly for the curious to ring eight bells; a ship's wheel pivoted onto the wall at waist height, offering the adventurous landlubber instant sea legs. Exotic shells from far-flung beaches and remnants of fishermen's nets decorated an entire wall, the whole collection enclosed in a glass case to deter experimental fingers.

Above their heads and looking a threat was the bust of a white pointer, displaying most of his teeth. Tommy waved at pictures of famous disaster ships hung at scattered levels on another wall, with a brief history printed below each photograph. He explained he let the public see his collection on the last Saturday of each month; the entrance fee was their solemn promise to come back and polish the big brass bell once a year. The bell always gleamed, he chuckled through old and thin lips. All the while his tongue rolled around inside his mouth as if searching for a safe haven in a storm.

He took them along the hallway that was littered with marine memorabilia and into a small room at the back of the house where the sun shone through the glass. There was a two-seater cane chair against the wall facing the window and a single wooden one opposite with barely enough space to sit if one kept one's legs in. A double bar heater gave out the extra heat the old man needed.

'Sho' he said with a markedly inebriated lisp; a twinkle filled his eyes, 'whatshall dhish about? Shnot every day I have the pleasure of poleesh company.'

Ben wasn't sure they should talk to a man sipping stout in the early afternoon, and how long before that did the man start also crossed his mind. He began anyway. 'Mr Blake—' Tommy got up abruptly and excused himself.

'Don't go 'way. I'll be back in a flash.' True to his word he returned with a jar; performing a jig in a cleansing solution were his teeth. One dip and he fished them out, shook them vigorously onto the polished floorboards and manoeuvred them into position. 'That's much better,' he said in the clearest of English with an Irish lilt. Plinter and Ben almost burst out laughing. Tommy joined in and said he had his first drink of the day after lunch and would they care to have a pint. Still smiling they declined and restarted the interview in earnest.

'You were saying, young man…?' Tommy prompted Ben to continue.

'Yes, I…we spoke to a friend of yours, Martin Greenwell. He said you stayed on your boat the day of the big storm in November'—Tommy nodded he did—'do you recall that day…is it fairly clear in your mind?'

'Indeed it is, my good man. As clear as I can make it, at my age, it was a Thursday.'

'He said you told him you heard noises outside. Is that right?'

'Well, it was very stormy. The wind was howling and boats were getting a bit of a bashing…and the rain lashed down like nobody's business! Yes, it was a boisterous night.'

Plinter adjusted the question. 'Did you hear a baby cry, Mr Blake?'

Tommy was quick to reply. 'I'm not sure what I heard, gentlemen. I did try to have a look, but…it was too hard to see anything. Visibility was practically nil.'

Ben thought the old man who loved the sea was a little uncomfortable on land. His twinkle disappeared momentarily then returned at half-mast. Ben thought Plinter brought in the *baby's cry* too soon; he spoke to relax the situation.

'I *will* have that pint, Mr Blake; I do feel a little thirsty.' Plinter's eyes widened; he almost said 'we're on duty, Tavistock', but checked his thoughts. Ben said his colleague will have a pint as well. Plinter's eyes widened further. The little man from Waterford got his sparkle back and impishly looked from one to the other. 'Well, that'll be a first. Anyway, I always hated that part in the film when the cop says "no thanks, I'm on duty". It's such a crock! When all the time the man would *love* a drop.'

For a rare few moments, Tommy Blake became a barman. 'What'll it be, gentlemen? I have bottles of stout or cans of Heineken.'

In between emptying a few glasses of Guinness and several cans of ale, the two investigators learned that Tommy had been to sixty-two countries and never married, that he joined the Navy when he was under age and that he was lucky to survive the bombing of his ship in '44. Without indicating he was changing lanes, Ben switched the conversation, bringing Tommy back to the storm and the accident. Tommy seemed to persist with his Navy days, the 'old days'.

'It was such a tragedy,' he lamented between sips.

Ben asked, 'Did you lose some mates in the bombing?'

'I'm not talking…I mean the baby…on the beach. I saw the crowd standing around on the sand, then the police came…I didn't know what the matter was until I got closer.'

Ben leaned forward. 'Mr Blake…Tommy, I'm the baby's father. Can you help me?' The old man nearly let his glass slip, a near tragedy seeing that it was more than half full. He stared sympathetically at the young man then reached for his shoulder to offer condolence.

'I'm *really* sorry for you, son. Really, really I am.' He paused for a moment; his mind seemed to be working overtime. 'I…I…did hear something that morning. There was a commotion. It sounded like a man and a woman arguing, but you must remember the rain was pelting down and the wind was howling a gale force.'

'That's alright, Tommy. You can understand that I want closure on the whole affair. If I know *how* it happened, or *why*, well, *anything you remember might help.* Could you…make out any words in the argument?'

'I thought I heard a child crying…then a…then a scream…like a Banshee! It was all in quick succession. I checked to see if I'd left me radio on, but no, I didn't. Then I had to find me glasses. I lifted the hatch—I could barely keep it open a few inches, the rain was so fierce! The wind made the rain go every which way but, I think…I'm not absolutely certain…but I think I saw a couple of shapes on the boat next to mine. It was only a fleeting glimpse, you know. It could've been the lightning, do you think, throwing shadows.'

'Did you have much to drink that morning?' Plinter put in.

What a stupid question, Ben thought. He wanted to ask Plinter did he have *any* brains this morning. Tommy replied as he did earlier. 'I don't have my first drink 'til *after* lunch. Weren't you listening to me at all?' Plinter said he needed to ask. Tommy gave his attention to Ben. 'Is there something else you want to ask me, son?'

The policeman shuffled his body. Tommy sent him a message to button it; it was Ben Tommy was addressing. Still, Ben struggled to come up with another question. 'No, Tommy, you've been very helpful…I can't think of anything else. Thank you.'

'There is *one* more question, isn't there?' the old man asked, warily.

'I can't think…'

'You want to know why I didn't come forward with this information the next day, don't you?' Clearly, the old man wanted to get a load off.

'Ok. Why…why didn't you?'

'Truth is, son, I felt bad about it. I only made the connection when I saw the little tot on the sand. And…and I thought…well, I couldn't *identify* anyone…I didn't *see* anyone, so what use would I be? I wasn't even sure where the sounds came from. Still, I know now I should've said something.'

Ben thanked him again, and saddened, got up to leave. Plinter wasn't quite finished with the old salt.

'Mr Blake! What were you doing on your boat that day?'

'To tell you the truth, I was out fishing from early morning. I got the storm warning on me radio and I headed back to the Bay. I tied her down and went for a snooze.'

'Did you talk to anyone?'

'Ah, yes. As a matter of fact, I had a few words to Martin. He came down to check his moorings. I helped him with a few ropes and then he left. The wind was getting up by then, so I climbed into me bunk for a nap.'

'Did you see anyone else?'

'There was a man with his dog…yes, that was after Martin came…and later on a couple of women. Could have been mother and daughter, those two. The younger woman was pushing a little pram…about eleven o'clock, I think.'

'Did you see the child? Could it have been the baby on the beach?'

'Ah, no! It was a baby boy.'

'How do you know…it was a *boy*?'

'Sure the little fella wore blue, officer. *Blue* it was.'

'Why didn't you go home? You *knew* the storm was coming.'

'Ah sure storms don't bother me. I lived through worse ones than that, I'll have you know. A lot worse. So there!' The little man stamped his foot to hammer home his defiance. The cheeky little leprechaun, Ben thought, and came to Plinter's rescue.

'Just one more thing, Tommy. The boat you thought the commotion came from, which one was it?'

'It was *The Fish Tale*...yes, that's the one. Right next to mine.'

'Are you sure about this? Could it have been another boat?'

'Well, to be perfectly honest with you...I can't state categorically that it was, but I think so. It's normally tied up right next to mine and the sounds came from that direction. That's the best I can offer to you, son.'

Climbing into the Jaguar, Plinter said he'd get Sue check out the boat's owner. Ben told him not to bother. 'It belongs to my friend, Billy Turner.' Plinter saw the implication and gave Ben a worried stare. Ben sat quietly, thinking. Plinter's phone rang. It was his colleague in forensics.

'Corish, I have the results from the handwriting samples; they *do* match. The scribble on the envelope matches the postcard; the B on the back was also written by the same person. It has the start of an upward stroke, suggesting there was more to come...like the start of the sender's details. The saliva under the stamp...did *not* match the DNA from the hair sample—'

'What! That surprises me, Tim. I had hoped—'

'Let me finish, Corish! The saliva used to *seal* the envelope *did*, however! I'll get back to you on the piece of glass. Cheerio for now.'

'I knew it!' Plinter triumphed. Excited by the relevance of the test, he filled Ben in on the scientist's findings. Ben was agog at the new twist in the tragedy. Half stunned, he asked Plinter what it meant.

'Well, number one, it *does* mean the envelope with your name and address on it was written by your wife. The handwriting and the DNA sample prove that. Number two, it was written on or before the Tenth of December. The postal date confirms that. How long she wrote it before that date, however, we don't know. If she had perished in the storm, then she wrote it before the accident. Was it written before the accident and then posted in December by someone unknown? Why? It does *not* make sense, Ben.

'Another thing; why would your wife send you a letter when she could talk to you? An anniversary card or some other family event around that time'—Ben shook his head—'I can understand, but an address in scribbled text? No, that does not gel with my reasoning. *This was written hastily because time was short.* The letter B on the back is unfinished, which also strongly points to insufficient time to complete the sender's name. And why would Elizabeth *type* four pages of information and then *scribble* the address? Do you know what I think, Ben?'

'Yes, I think I do.'

Plinter prompted an answer.

'I think Elizabeth was trying to get a message to me.' He spoke like a robot, disbelieving his own words, words that virtually said *Elizabeth is alive!* Plinter punched the air in agreement. 'Yes! Exactly!' he shouted. 'And your mother was caught in the middle. She sensed something was wrong, didn't want to upset you and naturally went straight to where she thought the letter came from. The *Turner household!*'

Ben remained stunned by the inferences, not wanting to believe but unable to refute them. There were too many questions unanswered. About Billy: his peculiar attitude toward Elizabeth over the past few years, in fact, since he and Elizabeth were married. About his mother: she was an odd person who said the oddest things. Like wanting to dance with Elizabeth. The phone conversation he had with her yesterday was very strange, he realised. What was that reference she made about a ring?

'A man should give a woman a ring', that was it… that's what she said, but…what did she mean? *She said she wanted to dance with Elizabeth but Billy said she was too sick to dance.* What on earth was that about?' Ben moaned within, perplexed by the old woman's innuendo.

'And what did Billy tell my mother the day of the accident, when Billy tried to see me, to offer his condolences, he said something about Meredith dancing in the rain. Yes, he would have come sooner had he not had to take care of his mother. *She was dancing in the rain*! *On the day of the storm? Was THAT the day she saw Elizabeth, in her garden? Did Billy bring Elizabeth back to his house after…after Stephie…no*! *This can't be*!'

Plinter saw Ben was highly agitated. 'What is it, Ben? You look troubled.'

'I want…I need to go home…need to think…work things out. Where's my car? I have to go.'

'Slow down, Ben! Talk to me! Do you remember something?'

'Yes…you are the detective…you think clues, don't you? That's all you do. You are good at that.' He stopped short and then calmly said, 'Corish, we need to compare notes. I'll get my car. You follow me to my place…yes, *we have to compare notes.*

Sixteen

Meredith Turner tightened the knots. 'This is the only thing you understand, Mrs Tavistock, isn't it? Whenever you are free to move about, you are at your most dangerous. You either snoop around or make for the telephone. I wonder what Billy told you, Mrs T? Something juicy about me, perhaps? The trouble with Billy is, of course, he's not sure of his own mind. He *needs* me to guide him. Wouldn't you agree with that, Rosie dear?'

'You know how I feel about you, Meredith. I haven't changed my mind, either. I still believe you are a vile person. You have shown yourself to be malicious, vindictive, scheming. The last person Billy needs is YOU. One day he *will* stand up to you, mark my words. Deep down he knows what you are. Whatever it is you hold over him, be assured that one day, and I hope it's soon—one day, he will break out of the prison you put him in. And then… watch out!'

'Let *me* worry about my Billy. You should worry about *your* little horror! He thought he could wheedle his way into my house today. Poor boy doesn't have a clue what's happening here, does he now? Serves him right for taking what didn't belong to him! It's all come back on him now, hasn't it, girlie? Lost his little child, lost his little wife and by the looks of her he'll probably lose what she's carrying. All because he stole what didn't belong to him. Your boy! Yes, *your* brat caused all this damage.'

Elizabeth kept her eyes closed throughout the old woman's foul speech. The one thing she clung to was the part where the hag mentioned Ben being at the door today. *Tomorrow* he would be in this house, in this very room, lifting her up and taking her away from the madness that permeated these walls. Rosa's next words defended her son and gave Elizabeth more courage to hang on.

'Ben will be back. The police will be right behind. You have very little time left, Meredith. The police will piece things together, you'll see. They'll lock you away for good, in a place where you can't hurt another soul like you harmed this beautiful child here. You'd have killed me in a vicious burst of anger, except

Billy got in the way. You could have killed your own son! And you accuse *me* of neglecting *my* son! You are one twisted old lady.' Meredith sneered and kept her head shaking contemptuously.

'You are right about the police, I'll give you that. But it is Benny boy they'll be locking up. As soon as they identify *her* ring'—she pointed the gun at Elizabeth—'*and* the baby's nappy, in a certain garbage bin.'

'*What are you saying?*'

'I'll tell you what I'm say-ing! I took a trip recently to your son's house. D'you know what I did? Go on, ask me? I removed your son's dustbin lid.' She let out a roar of laughter, a cackle so raucous Billy heard it in his sleep and wakened, and was frightened by it. His first and only thought was: 'what has my mother done now?' He made some attempt to move. Rosa was puzzled. Meredith carried on with her brand of humour.

'When Billy went back to the boat to tidy up after the storm, he found the child's nappy and panties on the deck. You follow that so far? Good! He brought it home to burn; you know, to get rid of the dirty thing, and of course, the ev-i-dence. Yes? Are you with me still? Lo and behold! When I was about to burn it, the ring fell out. So, guess what?'—she sounded and acted like a spoilt child—'I didn't burn it. I kept it in a safe place because…can you think why, Rosa? No?

'Because I had a plan to switch the blame from my Billy to your Ben. Clever, eh? Billy wasn't too happy when I told him where I put them but he got over it. Do you see what the police will decide about Mr Ben Smarty-pants Tavistock? They'll have *his wife's ring* inside *his child's nappy* in a stranger's dustbin, with *his fingerprints* on the dustbin lid. Case closed, as they say. What everyone thought was an unfortunate accident will look a lot different with the new evidence. It will look very bad for your son!'

Convinced that the woman's heart was diseased with malice, Rosa saw this new information, straight from the woman's own lips, as corroborative proof of evil.

'When…when did you do this awful thing?'

'*Yesterday*, my dear,' Meredith offered smugly, 'I drove by his house and scooped up the lid, went straight to old mother Thornley's garden and exchanged lids. I was in the phone box on the corner about to make an anonymous call to the police when who passed by with her yappy mutt but that wretched woman, Angela Perkes. It couldn't have worked out better. There she was, handing the ring over to a female flatfoot. Her nosy-parker timing was perfect, Mrs T, she interfered perfectly. I expect Benny-Boy will be called in to explain his actions any day now.'

Rosa said nothing but she knew she had handled the dustbin lid yesterday. She gave the sinewy woman an amusing grin. It stirred Meredith's curiosity no end.

'As cunning as you are, as malicious as you are, Meredith, your scheme is full of flaws. It will fall apart once *intelligent* people put it under the microscope.' The old woman stepped back and lifted the weapon.

'Be careful with your tongue, girl, you might say something you'll regret.'

Rosa responded in a flash, 'Look at you, Meredith! Here I am tied up, unable to move, and you threaten to assault me! Did you bully your son with a gun, too, or did you get away with using your tongue to manipulate and imprison the young boy with fear? Is he stunted because of you? I certainly think so!' Meredith moved forward and raised the butt and hovered. Rosa didn't blink. The two women stared for supremacy. Rosa kept up her verbal attack.

'Why would anyone leave their fingerprints for the police to find? And why, why, why, would a man who has killed his wife and child take her wedding ring and the child's panties and hide them in a stranger's rubbish container? That's just plain stupid! Even *Billy* was going to *destroy* the items.'

Meredith raised the gun. Her eyes were penetratingly fixed, having vowed to strike Rosa but undecided about where to strike, as though she struggled internally. Rosa raised her voice in the hope to provoke the old woman and get Billy into the fray.

'And how will you explain this chaos, this anarchy in your house? Billy has been shot and seriously injured. I'm bruised and battered all over my body. My daughter-in-law lies…dying. Yes, dying, as a result of your *treatment.* How will you explain the mess when the police come knocking on your door? Because, knock, knock, knockety knock, they will! My son will work out that I'm here in your house. He will find the envelope on my kitchen table. He will connect it to Billy and he'll come back with the entire staff of King Street police station. Be assured he will.'

Meredith struck her sharply on the shoulder. Rosa screamed, then moaned and hoped the sting subsided enough to continue her verbal assault. She found Meredith's eyes again. The old hag glared back at the mutinous Rosa and then yielded to her immovable insurgence. She began walking in circles, spitting out obscenities and threats onto the floor and into the air. Billy came out of his room.

He halted by the door and leaned on the wall. Rosa interrupted Meredith's tantrums. The old woman turned to face her, with raging eyes, lips distorted. Rosa talked softer this time but she didn't let up on the attack.

'You could plead insanity, Meredith. After all, you *really* are mad. You wouldn't be telling fibs, either. You could explain you've been this way for a long time. The police will understand. They'd provide you with a very good psychiatrist and in time they'd let you out of the straitjacket on weekends, and maybe, if you behaved yourself, they may also reduce the medicine that keeps you drowsy. What do you think? Would you choose that option?'

Rosa knew she was walking on thin ice. She figured Billy would step in. Either way, she didn't care about being hurt. The only weapon she had now was her voice. There was no strength left, her body ached; all her intuition was exhausted. The tactics she used on the matriarch were designed to get her angry *and* get Billy into the same space. At this point in time, Billy was her only saviour. Hopes that Ben would return in time were slim. Why he left so easily perplexed her. The little chat she had with Billy earlier flickered into optimism, and her provocative words and raised voice now, might stir him to confront his mother and fight for *his* freedom from her clutches. And in doing so he might even get the courage to take the gun from her, and *this time,* physically restrain her.

Meredith rushed at her and shrieked in her face. 'Shall I crack your skull? Is that what you want, Mrs Tavistock?' Billy moved closer. It was painful for him to move. Now he was passing through the doorway. Meredith raised the gun.

Rosa taunted her once more. 'Meredith, you've hurt me many times. You can't hurt me anymore. So do... your... worst,' she goaded, stretching out the words in a mocking fashion.

Meredith brought the gun above her head and started the downward swing. Billy reached forward with his good arm, took hold of the barrel with his left fist and held on. Rosa had closed her eyes to accept the blow. Meredith felt the sudden jolt on her wiry body and spun to see Billy's large frame tower above her. She came up as far as his diaphragm. He steadily eased the gun from her bony fingers and weakly said, 'That's enough, mother. You've come as far as I am prepared to let you go. It stops now.'

His mother placed her hands around his waist and tenderly kissed his injured arm slung across his chest. Rosa saw at close quarters the old woman's manipulative skills go into operation, as she apologised in mock profusion for shooting him, blaming 'that Tavistock woman for trying to escape' and then made an affectionate plea not to heed the Tavistock woman, but listen to his mother instead. Meredith spoke as though Rosa was not present. Billy repeated his statement, only with more force. His mother reminded him of their little secret. She sweet-talked him but the threat behind her words was obvious.

'You don't want others to know of our little secret, do you?'

Rosa observed the reaction on Billy's face. He got angry then worried then displayed the features of a helpless child. The 'little secret' was a mystery to Rosa but powerful enough to rein in the boy-man once more. She made it her business to push a few buttons before Meredith got possession of the weapon.

'Billy! Your mother is dangerous with that gun in her hands. Look at what she's done already. *Everyone* in this house is hurt; everyone except your mother! She hurts people, Billy. You. Me. And look at poor Elizabeth? She needs medical attention, proper attention. If she dies, you'll go to jail. You'll be an accomplice—'

Meredith's fiery temper raged. She swung her hand at Rosa's face. Unable to duck the blow, Rosa took the back of the old woman's hand squarely on the temple. The force nearly sent the chair over. Rosa moaned and right away felt dizzy. With her head bent, her eyes closed, she made a silent, personal vow not to succumb to the spiteful viper that was ready to pounce again. Her speech faltered but her meaning was clear. 'You'll be… an accomplice… Billy. Or else she'll… find a way… to blame *you.* She's been… like that… all your life, you *know* that.'

Meredith struck her again. Billy was in a daze, stuck in indecision mode, vacillating between believing Rosa and not believing, between wanting to believe and afraid of the truth and not wanting to believe out of fear of his mother. Rosa grimaced again, taking the sharp slap on her cheek. 'Can't you see, Billy? That's all she knows. If she… doesn't get her way she *hurts* people. See her…for what she is. To save herself, she'll harm you too. She's been destroying you for the best part of your life, and if it means saving her own skin, she'll say *you* kept us prisoners, including her. Be careful she doesn't say she shot you to save Elizabeth and me. Keep the gun away from her! If you do nothing else, keep the gun away—'

Meredith raised her hand to strike again, her face deformed with rage. Billy spoke faintly, 'Mother, don't hit her again.' Meredith faced him squarely and began to pound his arm and chest.

'*That* wicked woman is trying to come between us, son,' she panted out her defence, 'she's a liar who is trying to break up our family. She doesn't know how to help *her* son, not like I love you, Billy. You need to help me stop her!' He watched her features change from unbridled anger to sweet persuasion. How quickly she could switch her personality to suit the new situation, he thought. He had not *realised* that before; he had not *seen* the concealed weapon she used to manoeuvre things to suit her schemes. Someone needed to point that out to him; he silently thanked Rosa for that.

The pain in his shoulder kicked in. The flailing punches his mother inflicted on him started to register. She had done to him exactly what Rosa predicted. He stared hard into her face, telling her and asking her in the same sentence.

'Mother, you are saying that if I don't stop Rosa, *I'll* be… responsible for breaking up our family. Is that right? You have turned it right around to *me*! Just like you did on the night of the school dance…when Dad came to see me…and you refused to let him. And you refused to let *me* see *him*. And then you made…you made me—'

'Billy! Be careful! That's our secret. No one else needs to know! They wouldn't understand, now would they, son?'

Billy began to shake. Elizabeth turned her eyes to mother and son. Rosa could not see Meredith's eyes but she watched fear enter into Billy's. Whatever threat he reflected, came from his mother. The atmosphere was tainted with alarm; Rosa reasoned that *this* was it. Whatever happened on the night of the school dance was the source of the ongoing hold Meredith had on Billy.

Rosa thought back to the story Ben told about that night. William Turner came to see Billy. After four years he came to see his son. Meredith said no. There were words. Strong words. Loud words. He left without seeing the boy. That's odd, Rosa contemplated. All he had to do was look for the boy, call out his name; find him. His strength alone would have assured he saw the boy! Why didn't he just move her out of the way and do what he came for? He came this far! Just to turn around and go back to Scotland? She examined the fear in Billy's face again and decided to probe.

'Billy, what happened that night?' The question hit him like a hammer on the forehead. He was mesmerised by the question as if he heard it for the first time and yet he knew that he had provoked it by making public something *did* happen that evening. Mother and son turned to face Rosa. Meredith wanted to shut her meddling mouth. Billy did not want her to repeat the question because he was afraid to answer it, afraid of the consequences. The other part of him wanted to scream the truth for all to hear. His head spun; his legs staggered backwards a few steps, the rifle dropped.

Rosa shouted, 'Billy! Keep focused!' The rifle butt hit the carpet, bounced and toppled to the floor. Meredith was upon it in a flash. Billy stamped his foot hard on the barrel, trapping Meredith's fingers. She yelped and instinctively pulled her fingers out and, still in autopilot, she rushed at Billy, stabbing her nails into his injured arm. He moved backwards awkwardly and fell through the open doorway, striking his shoulder on the way through and crashing onto the floor outside. He lay groaning, muttering Elizabeth's name over and over.

Meredith picked up the weapon. A victory grin broadened her thin lips. Her mouth emptied a barrage of mocking rhetoric upon Rosa, who raised her chin in defiance.

'You, Meredith, are neither in the throes of senility, nor do you suffer from Alzheimer's disease. You are, simply, quite mad. You are an actress, yes, and you've been acting for years performing the same role. You use whatever tools you can conjure up to get the sympathy and attention you crave. You must have given your parents an unspeakably dreadful time!'

Meredith danced up to the chair. Billy groaned again. She spun around at him and said, 'Be quiet, Billy. You've done enough damage.'

He grunted a few words: 'Elizabeth…stairs…'

She growled at him, 'What are you saying, boy?'

He moved his eyes to the stairs and said 'Elizabeth'.

Meredith darted to the bed and ripped off the blankets and screamed, '*She's gone!*' Shouting wildly, the hag rushed to the top of the stairs and screamed Elizabeth's name, only to see the hall door ajar. Seething with anger, she shuffled down the stairs and flung the door open wide. The driveway showed no sign of the girl. Meredith swung her head left and right. Nothing. Not a sign of her.

Out of breath and panting heavily, she pushed her body to the side of the house to start up the car. She blamed Billy for hiding the keys, screaming her anger at the windscreen. The thought of having to waste time running back to the key rack in the hallway angered her more. She cursed all men for their incompetence all the way back to Billy's fallen torso and demanded to know where the car keys were. He mumbled 'the visor'. She went to the car again and ripped at the sun visor. The keys fell to the floor.

Elizabeth, barefoot and wearing only a petticoat, hobbled across the road. Hardly able to see and ravaged by her illness, she staggered into the path of a speeding truck. The driver pulled at the wheel with a frenzied swerve and slammed on the brakes instinctively, missing her slight figure by a hairsbreadth. The rushing wind and the screaming, screeching noises of bedlam tore into her brain. The driver brought the ten-ton vehicle to a howling stop inches from the fence and, shaking uncontrollably out of fear he'd killed the girl, he studied the results in his mirror.

In the middle of the road, she stood, frozen like a sculpted statue. He heaved a part-sigh to see her still standing; and jumped out of the cabin to check further. The middle-aged man called out was she alright? Elizabeth turned to face where the voice came from and made a weak attempt to answer; words wouldn't come, *couldn't* come. She raised her hand and made the slightest wave to the man. Her vision was blurred; the landscape of trees and fields revolved in a slow arc.

The driver interpreted the girl's wave as 'I'm alright' but what she really meant was that he come and help her find her husband. *Ben* would take her to a safe place and then come back before mad Meredith killed his mother. The driver checked his watch; he had a tight schedule. Still shaking, he jumped aboard and pressed down on the accelerator.

A horn blasted somewhere in her head; she took it as a signal to push her frail body forward. A first car whizzed by as she reached the grass verge. The fleeting *whoosh* disoriented her; she swooned and fell to her knees, reaching for her stomach to protect her baby. Another car shot by with a group of teenagers blowing wolf-whistles through opened windows. Her sick-wearied frame was difficult to get off the tarmac. The ordeal to get from the bedroom to where she now was, had used up all her energy.

Two things filled her thoughts; the fear that Meredith would come and take her back, and the hope that Ben was coming to save her. Urged to her feet with renewed hope, she cupped her stomach with both hands as if to reassure the child inside that 'mummy will take care of you, baby', and made the effort to stand. She moved one pace forward and felt a thump on her arm; the impact knocked her to the ground, the momentum sent her tumbling down the slope. She came to a stop in the empty ditch; her body took on an awkward twist.

The shattered remains of the wing mirror of the little car lay a few feet away from her. The driver jumped out and, with her hand to her mouth and tears streaming, stood looking down at the thin, misshapen woman, having no idea what state the woman was in, nor that she was pregnant. Traffic began to pile up behind the Mini. More people reacted. Already a man was next to Elizabeth checking for signs of life. He yelled to another driver to call for an ambulance.

Elizabeth's eyes rolled, her head spun, but all she thought about was her child. 'My baby, my baby,' she kept repeating.

The man said over and over, 'It's alright, dear. Help is coming. The ambulance is coming. The ambulance is coming.' He stopped when she went unconscious. He put a handkerchief to the blood spot on her head.

Meredith Turner pulled out of the long driveway. Up ahead she faced the line of cars. Her face was stretched with exasperation, as she joined the waiting queue. *The girl can't get away*, she mentally ordered. She got out and spoke to the driver in front. The siren got louder by the second. The female driver in a business suit believed a woman had been knocked down.

'I think the woman was killed; isn't it awful.' Meredith ignored the woman and moved along the line of cars. The ambulance swung in; two paramedics were quickly into their routine. Meredith got close enough to see one of the paramedics shake his head; she stayed until they placed Elizabeth onto a stretcher. The ambulance roared away. Meredith returned to her vehicle. When she passed the businesswoman, she said, 'No, there was no baby. Just the girl.' Making a dangerous U-turn, Meredith drove back to the house and stood before Rosa, gun at the ready.

'I hope you are happy now, Mrs Tavistock. He never *could* look after his precious wife. Your son has finally killed her.' Rosa turned her eyes away from her eyes, to avoid the image of a highly venomous snake, but no, the image of the snake handler overwhelmed her senses. Meredith Turner was the handler, the gun was the snake, ready to strike.

She wept bitterly for Elizabeth and her baby.

Seventeen

Ben pulled into the driveway. A picture was forming in his head, like a jigsaw puzzle he had been working on and a definite shape was taking place. Except it wasn't like the picture on the box. There were odd pieces that wouldn't fit. Some things, peculiar things, about Meredith Turner, what she saw, what she said. The unusual behaviour she displayed. And Tommy Blake's evidence! The picture grew but the puzzle remained. Vital pieces were missing.

'Where is Plinter?' he questioned the rear-view mirror. 'He said he'd be right behind me! I need his quick police brain to help me.' And what about Billy? His attitude towards Elizabeth? He *had* changed since we met and got married. What was it he said? Something about…crossroads. That was it! *Crossroads*. He said their friendship was at a crossroads. An ultimatum?

'Surely Billy wouldn't harm Elizabeth, harm Stephie, because our friendship was on the wane? That's not how normal people react, is it?' He realised he had an extra strong grip on the steering wheel. His reflection in the rear-view stared back at him; he warned it not to give him a lecture on the vicissitudes of life. 'And if you are thinking of giving me an argument, then don't!' Ben didn't want an attack or a defence on Billy's character. He stared at his reflection. Both sets of eyes were locked in stubbornness. Neither of them would back down. Slowly the eyes in the mirror changed in colour, in shape, in intensity. The face became more round, the nose longer, the mouth angry.

Billy's face filled the mirror.

Ben's mental camera zoomed in to show the back of Elizabeth's head, her sandy hair darkened by the hurtling rain. Stephie's anxious little face showed signs of distress. Ben imagined his child crying out to her mother to take her in her arms. He replayed the memory of her sweet voice, with a hint of panic; 'Mama, Mama. Billy hurt.' Billy held her tightly against his chest, his hands clasped around her stomach. He had a glazed, unyielding stain on his face.

For the very first time, Ben noticed Billy had his mother's eyes. Or was he imagining it? Elizabeth clung to Stephie's hips, fighting to take her child back. There were no words; only synchronised lips in conflict, each one demanding the right to hold on to the baby. There was no Solomon entity to divide the child and neither party surrendered ownership. Ben's thoughts imagined Billy's big hands chafing along Stephie's delicate skin, and Elizabeth's fingernails combing her daughter's thighs and legs in a desperate bid to keep hold of her baby.

Stephie's nappy came away in her hands and fell onto the deck where turbulent rivulets ran. The struggle to keep hold of her child was all but lost. Bruises appeared on the little tot in front of Ben's eyes; he recalled the same ones when he identified her body. He cried for Stephie. He didn't know how she ended up in the water. The mirror gave him no answers. Only more questions. He felt rather strange, suddenly. Why didn't he cry for Elizabeth? Her pain was horrendous. Was it because Plinter had restored her to life with a hunch of his? A paradoxical clue-infested instinct that she was still alive and therefore no tears were necessary?

A flash of lightning gave Ben a unique view of Elizabeth's eternity ring nestling in the folds of the nappy; the gold band glistened in his eyes and made him blink.

Plinter pulled in behind the Rover. His windscreen flashed the afternoon sun's reflection in Ben's eyes. The imagery in Ben's head stopped; the mirror shut down.

The policeman tapped on the glass. Ben was lost between worlds. Slowly, he arrived in the present, and demanded: 'What kept you, man? I've been waiting for you.'

'I've been checking into a few things,' Plinter replied. In the kitchen, Ben settled down at the table with a jotter and biro. Plinter explained the results of the forensic examination on Rosa's hairdryer; they matched those on the dustbin lid. Ben said he had more important items on his mind.

The policeman carried on nonetheless. 'The blood left on the sliver of glass, Ben, did not belong to you or your mother.'

Ben stared hard at him. 'You had me checked, too. May I ask what you used?' Plinter casually said he found a hair on his shoulder and decided to clear his name. Ben smirked at him and called him a rogue.

'It had to be done, Ben. And now that it's done, what's the harm in it? It still points to the burglar; we just have to find a match,' he vowed, taking out a thin notebook with a hard cover. Ben was amused as the man put a small pencil to his tongue as if to 'ink' the graphite, as though the Inspector couldn't begin in earnest until he performed his quirky ritual.

'A few things trouble me,' Ben began. 'First, let's consider Tommy Blake's testimony. Let's assume that he heard a *baby* cry. That was his first instinct, his gut instinct. That is a reasonable assumption since we know there was a young child in the vicinity. Right?'

Plinter nodded his approval and added, 'The timing was a bit early, though. Still, a mother and baby were walking near the Marina before the storm struck, if we take Mrs Oughter's evidence. Remember, she said she *thought* it was Elizabeth she saw pushing the pram.'

Ben moved on to the boat in question. It struck him that Plinter was talking about his wife and child in the third person, like they were strangers to him, that he was indifferent to *who* was being investigated and concerned only with the *facts* of the case. Is this the way all policemen go about their duties, interested only in statistics, motives, opportunities? He reprimanded himself. Not all are calculatingly clinical, are they? He glanced at Plinter scratching something on his notepad and studied his face for clues, unsure whether or not the man had a heart inside that logical chest of his.

One thing he *was* sure about was: Plinter was *here*, helping him find the answers when he could be basking under a Spanish sun, perhaps lazing in the blue swimming pool of a five-star hotel in Madrid. Ben tried to imagine Plinter laying on his back floating on a cushioned pontoon with his white oversized belly aimed at the sun; a *Pina Colada* tilted and trapped in one hand, the fingers of his other hand caressing his neat but extended moustache. Ben decided Plinter was different; the man had *some* feelings.

'The *Fish Tale*, Corish! It was the *nearest* boat to Blake's. What are your thoughts? And…try to avoid hunches.'

'Your rules make it hard for a man to do his job, Ben boy'—he chuckled—'but I'll run this past you. The wind was blowing from the south—I checked with the weathermen. The pier runs north-south; therefore, Tommy was in the perfect position to hear any sounds coming from *The Fish Tale*. I believe his first story, i.e., that he heard *people* arguing and a *child* crying, all carried by the wind. Muffled perhaps, by the wailing wind and the pouring rain, but enough to decipher the sounds were human. That's a deduction, my son, not a hunch.'

Ben congratulated his colleague but pressed on. 'Did it have to come from *that* boat? There were two other crafts beyond…beyond Billy's cruiser.'

Plinter understood Ben didn't want to believe it was his friend on the boat. The policeman went by the only route he knew; establish the truth. The truth would place his friend on the boat that day or it wouldn't. Ben would have to admit to that principle.

'The exercise, Ben, is to ascertain *what* happened to your family! *Who* caused the tragedy will be revealed in the course of time through examination and discovery. The fact is that when Tommy Blake lifted the hatch to see what the rumpus was about, he saw human shapes through the rain. *He specified your friend's boat.* Combine that with the voices he heard, it leads to one conclusion. Until we are shown evidence different to these things, we have to believe that Billy Turner, your wife and little Stephie were on that boat together.

'They were fighting over something. To me, that is also clear. And why do I say that? Amid a windstorm, and with rain creating its own noise, *Tommy Blake was still able to discern their voices, angry voices, a woman's screams and a child's cry.* The disturbance was *loud.* I rest my case. *Now* we can talk to Billy. *Now* we can search his home for your wife, Elizabeth, and your mother, Rosa.'

'You…you think he has…has them both? Like prisoners?' Ben threw his body back, hard against the Windsor chair. His mouth stayed open while Plinter nodded aggressively.

'After I left you, Ben, I did some checking on the Turners. Maybe you can fill in a few details?'

'What did you learn? How can *I* help?'

'Firstly, there was the accident with the tractor. It appears Harold Palson got too close to the edge of a slope on his property, the land gave way and the machine toppled over, pinning him under it. His daughter, Meredith, was a witness to the tragedy. I read her statement; she described how she found him; also told him to be careful on that slope. A few things took my notice.'

Ben said they usually do. 'It happened a long time ago. Billy told me the story his mother told him. She was only seventeen at the time. It was an unfortunate accident, wasn't it?'

'Well, that's what the coroner concluded. However, let me put a few thoughts your way.' Ben nodded OK, suspecting another of Plinter's eccentric notions.

'The young woman said she brought sandwiches for her father, gave them to him and was returning to the house when she heard him cry out. I now quote her words'—he slid a sheet of paper from the file and found the line—'"I was about fifty feet from the tractor. I turned and saw it slip down the hill. I ran frantically to my father. He was trapped by the machine. Only his head was visible. The rest of his body was under the tractor. He wasn't breathing and there was blood trickling from his mouth. I ran back to the house and called for help." End of statement.'

'Ok, so what's the problem, Corish? She reported what she saw.'

'That's true, she did. It's the sandwich that is the problem. In her statement, she suggests that he lost control of the machine momentarily while he ate the beef and pickle sandwich. She said she warned him about the steep incline, that he should keep well away from it. Says here, "I worried about him but he always laughed when I reminded him not to go near it. There was plenty of land without going so close to the edge."'

'Maybe he *did* lose control. People are warned about using mobiles phones while driving. We do stupid things sometimes. Wouldn't be the first time someone was distracted,' Ben said in defence.

'Yes. However, the sandwich was found near his head. It was complete, uneaten, not a bite out of it.'

'Sooo…he put it to his mouth…and…took his eyes off for a second…the wheels went over the edge…he tried to control the thing…and…it tipped over.'

'And I suppose the two slices of wholemeal bread packed with two thick pieces of beef and a dollop of chutney fell *neatly* beside the man's head? *Outside* the vehicle, and not on the floor or *underneath* the machine? And, get this! The side that faced up was *clean.* No dirt or grime on it. None!'

'Is that all in the report, Corish, or are you inserting a little speculation here?'

'The detective who filed his report was a man after my own heart; he was thorough, Ben boy, thorough!'

'Ok. So the bread landed unscathed near the man's head. It's not *im*possible, Corish, now is it?'

'No….it's not impossible. But is it…likely…when you consider the tractor leaned over, emptied the man onto the ground and then rolled on top of him? When the tractor was lifted off Palson, a box of spanners was discovered…

pressed into the soil. The steel container was damaged and opened; tools were scattered also. So, my question is, what miracle saved the humble beef sarnie? I ask you?'

'Why, tell me why, why did the…police chap…take so much interest in the sandwich?' Ben queried.

'It's fundamental, Ben. The sandwich was given as *the culprit* in the accident. It was *specifically* named as the reason for the man's death. Meredith made two sandwiches, according to her statement *and* her mother's. DI Brantley explored it as far as he could. Only one sandwich was found. Birds were blamed for the missing sandwich, and please remember that point.'

'Go on then, Inspector, what do you think happened? I can't wait!'

'*It was placed there.*'

'I give up, Corish. Must say, you are starting to impress me with your skills. You said there was something else. Please go on.'

'Yes, and I believe, even more intriguing. But before I go on there's something else about the sandwich. DI Brantley quizzed both the wife and the girl separately. Each of them said they prepared the food for Mr Palson. Mrs Palson changed her mind later, blaming her distraught state for the error. So, Meredith both prepared it and delivered it to her father. Maybe something in that. Maybe nothing.

'Finally, it took the girl three minutes to run back to the house and another minute to tell her mother what had happened and then make the phone call to the Ambulance Service. The ambulance came to the scene in under twenty minutes. I think, and this is a personal idea, but I think in twenty-five minutes that sandwich would have been well and truly eaten by the local crows. To me, that is a contradiction. Since the birds were used to dispose of one sandwich, then why not the other? That may seem trivial—'

Ben finished his sentence, 'But you revel in trivia, Corish.' Plinter winked humorously and carried on.

'Now for the next point of interest. The coroner found various injuries on the man's body, all accounted for by the nature of the accident; heavy bruising, scratches, legs crushed, one arm crushed, ribs broken; his skull was cracked where he landed on a rock, and internal injuries. The coroner took note of four lines on the back of his left hand, scratched into his skin, each line bloodied and congealed. In keeping with the shape and the size he identified them as the nails of a small hand, a woman's hand.

'When questioned, Meredith said her father and mother had argued earlier. The argument got into rough stuff and Meredith came to the rescue by grabbing her father's hand to separate them. That's how he came to be scratched, she said. She agreed to a check under her fingernails and yes, the skin matched that of her father, thanks to Crick and Watson. Her mother also stated these were the facts. DI Brantley makes a note that Mrs Palson was nervous throughout the inquiry. This aspect of the investigation makes me sit up and ask questions, questions that were not asked at the time, however.'

'Before I ask why, Corish, who on earth is Crick and Watson?'

'They jointly discovered DNA; got a Nobel Prize for it. I thought everybody knew that. What was your question?'

'Why were these questions not asked at the time?' Ben said impatiently.

'Haven't a clue. Wasn't there myself. But it's not too late to ask,' Plinter countered.

'You are starting to bug me again, Corish. Just tell me what you *think*!'

'I *told* you what I think. The right questions weren't asked back then, which gives us added incentive to talk with Mrs Turner and Son now.'

'Oh.'

'One *other* side point. About a year before the accident the police received a complaint from a Swedish au pair. She claims Palson raped her. He said *she* came to him but he sent her away. The next day he fired her. The girl's parents flew to England and took her home. No charges were made. The allegation was dismissed.'

'Are you about to tell me the au pair came back, asked Palson to lie on the ground and she tipped the tractor on him?'

'Don't be ridiculous. She had no farming experience. Use your head, Tavistock!'

'Oh, I see! And Meredith Turner did. Is that where you are heading with this?'

'I'll turn you into an investigator one of these days, Ben. You too can be smart like me. I also dug into the history of Mr William Turner. I rang a friend of mine in Scotland—'

'Not another forensic man?'

'No. A police colleague. The odd thing is…he cannot trace the ex-husband of Meredith Turner. It seems the man has had no history for the past fifteen years. When did you say he came by to see his son and she wouldn't let him?'

'Eh...Billy was nineteen...he's thirty-four now...that makes it—'

'—fifteen years ago, Ben!' Plinter made a weird shape with his face and carried on. 'I haven't heard you mention *Mister* Turner, Ben. What do you know of him?'

Ben told him he what he knew. 'Billy said his mother drove his father out. He didn't go into details of arguments between them. Just that he was convinced his mother was the jealous type. More than once he told me she had *people* problems. His father came back once. To see Billy. Didn't happen. There was an argument, shouting and stuff. I was there that night; we were off to a school dance.

'I remember Billy bemoaning the fact that his father came all the way from Scotland to see him and he just turned around and went back home without a word. After that night, Billy didn't mention his father again. He blamed his mother for it; he said she got rid of him and that was the end of the matter. He was stuck with her until he got older and independent. Frankly, I've seen his mother in action. She's a weird one, is Meredith Turner.

Even as he spoke, Ben imagined his precious Elizabeth held captive by Meredith, tied to a bed, strapped by the wrists, unable to move. He tried to imagine how she might look after six months into her illness, and pregnant as well. The image that immediately came to him, the one that easily came to him, was the sparkling, cheery, beautiful girl he had married and loved. When she was pregnant with Stephie, she had absolutely blossomed. Her skin was clear, clean and rich. She was healthy; she was happy. She was thrilled with the prospect of motherhood. His mind refused to show her sickly, weak and dying, as Dr Ames had described. And yet...what else could be expected with...a creeping cancer roaming among her organs?

'Will you call in the troops?' Ben squeezed the obvious question out.

'No! No, Ben, no. What we started together we'll finish together. I...I didn't want to mention this...just yet...but when you...when you agreed to me helping you, I decided this would be my last case. You are the first to know of my future plans. In three weeks' time, that is, when my holiday is over, HQ will receive my resignation. Ben was flabbergasted.

'I'm flabbergasted! Gob-smacked! What...what brought this on? It's so sudden!'

'Yeah! So sudden it surprised even me!'

'Ok, I hear you, but, how, what and WHY?'

'Well, to be frank with you, Ben, I haven't been attracted to a woman since my wife died…until I met your mother. My cards are on the table,' he submitted and awaited the verdict.

'My mother told you she'd never marry a policeman? Is *that* what you are telling me?'

'No, no, no. I don't want anything to interfere…that is, if she, eh, accepts my proposal…I would devote all my time to her. That's what I would do. I have sufficient means to care for her.'

Ben swallowed and quietly said that if his mother made a commitment to someone, it wouldn't matter what job the man did. He tried to say it casually but it came out awkwardly. His secret thoughts demanded the man get to know her better, and in any case, why tell *me* these things, he thought. *Am I her father that you should ask me for her hand in marriage? Better not say that!* At least the man was upfront with his feelings.

'How…how long have you known my mother?' Ben asked possessively.

'Since the…the accident,' the other said, pleading his case.

Ben moved on. Having listened to Plinter's reservations about the Turner Clan, Ben returned to the items that bothered him (as though the subjects of resignation and marriage hadn't been mentioned). All the while he was languishing in depression—he commiserated with his ego—his mother was out philandering. And with a copper!

'Here's something that really gives me to reason to pause. Meredith Turner wanted to dance with Elizabeth, but Billy, she said, wouldn't let her. She told me so on the phone yesterday. Now, the woman is missing a few links in the chain, I know, *but she has never danced with my wife.* There was…there was an incident at our wedding reception—now I'm talking five years ago—when the old lady wanted to dance with the new bride. Elizabeth was distressed by the woman's antics, both then and prior to our wedding. I came to her rescue. She and Elizabeth did not get on. Elizabeth always felt uncomfortable in her presence, in fact, she avoided the old woman.'

Plinter broke in to assess the situation a little better. 'It's possible, that is, if the woman is not a hundred percent…it's possible the woman recalled an old memory. On the other hand, if Billy…and, we'll hypothesise here…*if* Billy took Elizabeth to his house after the…incident on the boat…then *that's when Mrs Turner saw Elizabeth*!'

'There's more, Inspector. On the day of the accident, Billy said his mother was dancing in the rain. He told my mother he had to sort out Meredith before he came to see me. The weird thing is the old lady intimated that Elizabeth *did not* have a ring on her finger. How could she possibly know that? Unless… *unless she saw Elizabeth on the day of the accident.*'

Plinter agreed. 'That accounts for the missing ring. Perhaps Elizabeth dropped it in a scuffle with Billy?' Plinter paused before going on, 'It suggests to me that Billy got your wife into his vehicle without opposition, probably…she was unconscious. Then…he had to collect the stroller and any accessories, i.e., blanket, pillow, toys, and of course, the nappy and panties and possibly the ring; she either dropped it and he retrieved it or he removed it from her hand. Perhaps he panicked, I don't know that, yet. But…placing the items in the dustbin was clearly done to incriminate you, Ben. We still have more to learn.'

These allegations caused Ben's head to spin. Could Billy be so jealous, so vindictive to do such a thing? He wasn't like that! At school he used to fight for him, Ben recalled, when kids would pick on him. Billy was never nasty. Certainly not to him, not to Elizabeth, and not to his mother, Rosa. Ben's thoughts switched to Billy's mother.

'Corish, there's something else Meredith said. When I spoke to her on the phone—I wanted to contact Billy to help with my car—she said he was out. What upset me, besides the references she made about Elizabeth, was the stuff she said about my mother. Things like…her hair was untidy, her wrists were bleeding. Is the woman totally mad? Why does she make up these…these horrible things?'

The Inspector shrugged his shoulders in an obvious gesture. 'Ben, we have already concluded that Elizabeth and Rosa are prisoners in the Turner house. And it is clear to me the Turners are dangerous people. The next step is to try and interview Billy. He has some questions to answer. Are we agreed?' Ben let the awful truth sink in.

'Ok. We are…agreed…but I think we should go at nightfall.'

'Why?'

'I don't trust the old lady anymore. I believe she deliberately stopped me seeing Billy earlier. If we are correct, then there is no way she'll let us through the front door. We can snoop around the house in the dark. We can find out what we want to know without asking a single question.'

Plinter wasn't sure about this line of attack. This wasn't his style, nor was it the way the police operated. He read Ben the riot act. Ben insisted he was not a policeman and as far as their agreement went, neither was Plinter. This was a private affair and they were *private* investigators. Stealth was the way to go and that's how he wanted to proceed. He wasn't taking any more chances and if Plinter wanted to argue then he could do so with Rosa Tavistock. 'You can take it up with my mother *after we have released Elizabeth and my mother*, Corish. After!'

Plinter relinquished his authority. Humble pie wasn't too hard to eat knowing that Rosa would be there when the plate was empty.

Eighteen

'Who is she, Sally?'

'The paramedics said there was no ID on her,' the nurse replied.

'She looks anorexic, deathly. What tests have been done?'

'None so far. She came in unconscious only minutes ago, so we put her straight on a drip. We were waiting for you.'

The doctor gazed at the thin figure. She shook her head, disappointed by the way people treat their bodies. 'Did she fall down the stairs or something? Look at those bruises. I don't believe this woman's mother would recognise her.'

'Hit by a car, Doctor.'

Millicent Castillo shone a light into Elizabeth's blank eyes. She moved a stethoscope across her chest then onto the roundness of her stomach. 'Get her straight up to ICU. This person is seriously ill. I want pictures, I want blood samples, and I want action NOW. If this girl survives the night…we may be able to save the baby…move quickly on this, Sally.'

'I'm on it, Doc!'

Nineteen

'Billy! You have to listen to your mother! Get yourself together now! The girl is gone. She's out of our lives for good. She'd *never* have made a good wife for you. So unfaithful! When you think of all the medical attention I gave her—such an ingrate! Now she's gone. We have to think of the Tavistock woman. We *have* to get rid of her, Billy, now don't we?'

Billy had managed to haul his body onto the bed. His shoulder throbbed; his head ached, his belly churned. But worse, his mind fought to keep control of his thoughts, to push her words away. He wasn't a *boy* anymore; a gullible, naïve, vulnerable adolescent, easily manoeuvred to do things against his will. He was a *man* now; Rosa told him so. Rosa gave him the courage to face his mother, to face her fierce temper, and when that didn't work, to face her soft, put-on querulous appeal to do what *she* wanted. But it was still hard to fight her.

The small boy in him, inflicted with fear, cajoled by a false mother-love, kept surfacing each time she applied her version of reality. To have his mother love him, *really love him,* like Rosa loved Ben, *that's* what he wished for. That's what he *needed.* It was strikingly obvious now. *She* never really gave him that sort of love. All he ever got was pseudo-affection, a mocking attempt by a woman who was not capable of loving for love's sake.

And now, it was happening all over again.

She was pleading with him to get him to do her bidding. *Now,* she wanted to get rid of another person. *Rosa Tavistock, his friend's mother.*

How easy she made it sound.

We have to get rid of her.

How cruelly she spoke of Elizabeth's death.

She's out of our lives for good…such an ingrate.

You are the ingrate, Mother!

Without feelings.

Without love.

From her position fastened to the chair and her mouth taped, Rosa went in and out of sleep. Her body felt like it had been tied to a car by a heavy rope and hauled over the hard and merciless tarmac. The assault on her body wouldn't let her sleep, her biological clock was having its own battle to persuade her to rest. The duct tape forced her to breathe through her nose and until she learned to do it, she gasped in panic. It was the raised voice of Meredith that caused her to perk up a little; the loud mention of her name that brought her to fuller awareness.

'Don't give me that, Billy! We *have* to get rid of her!'

'*No! Not Rosa! She's a good person. She's done nothing wrong, mother.*'

'Are you crazy, Billy? Once they identify Elizabeth's body, *they'll* come looking. Believe me, Billy boy; *they'll* come knock, knock, knocking, boy! I'll try to help you but a mother can only do so much for her son. You know that, Billy. The police will ask me questions about that day; I'll have to explain how you brought the girl here and…and…you knew she was sick. But you didn't…you wouldn't…let her go because you wanted her for yourself. Isn't that right?

'I'll have to tell them you were smitten with the girl; that she was married to your best friend, and you kidnapped her…yes, and you made me cooperate. You were too strong for me, I'll tell them…you were…too strong… for me, a weak old woman, seventy-two years old. So, you see, Billy, you can't let the Tavistock woman leave, can you?'

Rosa wished she could scream out to Billy, to provide him a bulwark against the cunning, hateful woman who masqueraded as a mother. She started to rock her chair.

'*No, Mother!*' Billy yelled out, still afraid of her power yet striving to loosen the emotional bonds she tied him with from his youth onwards. He heard muffled sounds in his head, which confused him for a second. His mother looked to where the sounds came from and glared at Rosa. Rosa found Billy's eyes through misty contact lenses and continued to growl throaty warnings for him to be a man and stand up to her.

He interpreted her meaning clearly and drew strength from her warnings. Meredith looked from one to the other, then made a decisive move towards Rosa and ripped the tape off her face, then dragged the chair into Billy's room.

'Now,' she boomed, 'you can have your say. Turn my son away from me, will you? But be warned! I'll have my say too! I don't think you'll last the distance, Mrs Know-it-all Tavistock.'

Rosa panicked for the umpteenth time since her incarceration. Her lips stung. Her thoughts were scrambled. She felt like she was in the witness box and had to make the best defence of her life. And *for* her life. For this mad woman standing over her was now the causal threat to her continued existence. In dreamlike images, she saw herself in a courtroom defending her client against the insanity of his mother; that she had to convince Billy she was crazy, that he now had to disown her completely before she destroyed him.

Rosa realised she needed to prove that his mother's mind was aberrant and for him to see that beyond doubt, but also that *his* mind had been systematically deceived because *she* fed him with oppressive fear and cruel domination. She had to show him that while his mother was incurable, he wasn't. *He* could come out of this with scars but no permanent damage.

In the oddest way, Rosa concluded cogently, saving Billy from his mother was her salvation also. And probably, win or lose, Meredith would not agree to the court's ruling. Win or lose, Meredith Turner would sacrifice her own son to maintain her insatiable lust for maternal power. As long as she had her wily ways, she had power over Billy. As long as she had the weapon, Rosa established, she had power over her. And if the old woman lost the hold she had on Billy…she still had the gun. An injured shoulder put Billy at a huge disadvantage. He couldn't fight her; her feral instinct for survival had sent him crashing to the floor earlier.

And *I'm* helpless to stop her, Rosa thought and stared into her uselessness, her futile position, tied to a chair, and even if she was free to move, the old woman would still have the ascendancy.

The gun rested against the end of Billy's bed.

What to say? Where to start? Rosa panicked. Her insides shook, she hoped it wasn't visible. Not the way for a defence lawyer to be seen. Must be forthright, chin up, confident, unassailable! That's it! That's the way to go, Rosa. Fight for your reputation! Fight for your life! Fight for Billy and fight for your life! Someone once said—she couldn't remember who or when—that attack is the best form of defence. So, Rosa Harriet Tavistock, attack!

'What happened that day, Billy?'

Meredith interrupted, 'You know *what* happened. Or are you deaf *and* stupid? Billy brought the girl home because *your son was not right for her!*'

'I don't mean *that* day. Billy, what happened the day your father came to see you?'

Meredith switched her gaze to him, a caveat that said: be careful how you answer, Billy. The boy-man became quiet, wide-eyed and fearful, which turned into searching glances at his mother, but darting ones at Rosa. With eyes now closed tightly, he started to speak. Meredith barked a stern rebuke. He continued, talking behind his eyelids.

'*She hid my letters.*' Meredith stamped her foot, a second warning.

'What letters, Billy? From your father?'

'I have them, you know, I still have them,' he nodded excitedly and victoriously, 'and I'll *never* give them up. Never!'

Meredith said, 'That's all in the past, Billy. Leave it where it belongs, son, for both our sakes!'

Rosa pressed for an answer. 'I'm glad you have your letters, Billy. What happened when your dad came to see you? Was it a pleasant visit?'

Billy's eyes shot open. Rosa knew she struck a nerve. Meredith moved to the door and shut it. Rosa saw that as body language that spelled defence mode; *nobody* was leaving this room. Rosa kept her eyes on Billy, waiting for him to answer, feigning indifference to Meredith's menace.

'Pleasant wouldn't exactly describe the occasion, would it, Mother?'

Rosa studied the by-play between them. Rosa kept the incursion going. 'Was there an argument, Billy?' Meredith stepped up and slapped Rosa.

'That's enough of you!' she screeched.

Billy reacted and said, 'Move away, Mother. Move away from Rosa. You will not hit her again! Do you *hear* me?'

His mother stepped back; her tongue was laced with malice for Rosa but sugared for Billy. 'She is conniving to split us up, son, but I know you are smart enough to see through her scheme. Aren't you, my son?'

'You gave her the chance to speak, remember? She hasn't finished yet'—he turned to Rosa—'have you?' Rosa saw a glimmer of light. Maybe she was getting through to Billy. She ran with the advantage.

'What happened before you and Ben went to the dance that evening? What happened, Billy?'

My mother was shouting, my father was…softer, eh, almost…well, begging. I should have gone in to see him, to tell him I was angry with him for leaving, to tell him I loved him and wanted him to stay…but I didn't. I hid instead…

Meredith reached for the gun. Rosa ignored her. 'Then what happened, Billy?' she coached.

There were more words, angrier this time, from both of them. I felt so ashamed… my parents fighting in front of Ben. A door slammed…then more noises. I remember… picking up a billiard cue… and asking Ben did he want to play. He took the stick from me but… he knew I was only trying to…to distract him from the… my parents.

'Then what?'

Then…my mother came out and said… my father decided to leave. She fixed my bowtie and we left for the dance. Meredith relaxed her grip on the trigger.

'Is that *it*? Billy, is that *all*?' The boy-man blinked a number of times, his lips quivered. Credible words wouldn't form on his tongue; he stuttered compulsively. He took a deep breath and reinvented his thoughts. They came out in lucid tones, coherent and brave.

We buried him in the storeroom.

The answer stunned Rosa. It didn't affect Meredith. There was a long pause. No one spoke. Rosa forgot she was tied to the chair; she attempted to bring her hands to her face in horror. The muscles in her upper arms stung. Billy continued his confession in a rehearsed and confident monotone, casually, sedately, as though this was his orange box, that no one could remove him, that his mother was a figment.

When I came home from the dance, my mother asked did I enjoy it. I replied, not much, since thoughts of my father filled my head all evening. She said she had something to show me. I asked, was it a gift from my father, did he leave something for me? I got a little excited that he would leave a gift for me. My mother told me to prepare myself. I could never have prepared myself for the sight of my father lying on the floor… a pool of blood by his head.

Meredith sat on the edge of the bed and resigned herself to hearing the rest of the details. Rosa saw the smirk on her face. And wondered about this woman, as to *what* she was capable of? Just *how far* would she go?

What I didn't know at the time was, my mother had gone outside, paid the taxi driver and said her guest was staying for the night. As far as Ben was concerned, my father came to our house briefly, and went. Only my mother and

I knew what had happened. She begged me to protect her so I agreed to bury the body. In the garage.

The memory of the stench of the room she had been tied up in revisited Rosa's nostrils. Again she tasted the foul, rancid odour that seemed to ooze from every dank, musty corner, from every crack in the floor. The imagined, awful, expected stench of decaying flesh of William Turner seeping up from the cracks in the concrete joined the putrescent queue. Her stomach heaved a dry retch. Billy kept talking.

I worked for hours digging the hole. It was quite deep...a metre or more. We wrapped him in thick plastic, two, three layers. Mother said it would keep the smell down. I flattened the earth and put the excess dirt in the garden. We cleaned up the living room and burned the carpet. Mother said nothing must be left. Later I saw mother clean the blood off the brass elephant in the sink. Before I went to sleep, I emptied my stomach down the toilet bowl.

Rosa wanted him to stop. She'd heard enough. Had to reason with him, to show him he must call the police, that there was still time to correct matters. He could plead diminished responsibility, that *she* manipulated his thinking, his behaviour, all his life. Rosa wanted to beg him to testify that *his mother* actually struck the blow that caused his father's death, *not him*. He was *used*; his mother used him, his own mother.

The boy-man spoke as if he was in a trance. Rosa gazed at him as he told of the crime and the crime scene in a steady flow of honest admission, as though he was already convicted and had accepted his punishment. At that moment, Rosa believed she had lost him. Reasoning with him in his present state of mind was futile. A furtive glance at Meredith was met with a knowing look of success.

The old hag was right, Rosa argued internally, *she had given me the chance to convert his thinking, but I failed.* Too long under her influence, Billy remained a child. He *learned* to rely on her, to trust her judgement, to believe her lies, to do her bidding, to stay a victim under her control. And he wasn't aware that his dependency had lasted fifteen years. The man was told he needed to break free from her, and as much as he desired it, he didn't have the skills to walk away.

The next day my mother ordered sand and cement and gravel from the DIY store. I spent the rest of the day mixing and making a concrete floor while mother kept watch for callers. No one called that day. I worked into the evening, until it was finished. I wanted to cry, Rosa, but I didn't know who to cry for. Me: for the awful thing I did? My mother: for the awful thing she had me do? My father: that he should die like this?

Mother said that if he hadn't come back to torment us, then this would not have happened. I suppose there is some truth in that. I wish he'd stayed in Scotland. I'm not sure who the victim is anymore. Do you know, Rosa? Do you know? Really know? I don't think anybody knows. Maybe Ben knows? He's clever at math and that. He tried to teach me once. About numbers and things. I told him I was hopeless, that he was wasting his time, but he was kind.

He said anyone can learn math, and then he said a strange thing, Rosa. Do you know what he said? Well, I'll tell you. He said, "Billy, you are already doing math in your head". I said, no way! Then he said every time I bought something and handed money over, I was calculating. When I ordered parts for motors, when I fixed electrical appliances, when I replaced the wiring in the vehicle's electrics, I had to know the sizes and shapes and part numbers. He said I was doing math.

He said when he was young, he was absolutely useless at numbers, but I told him I couldn't believe that. I thought he was always good with numbers and I told him so. But he said that all he needed was a good teacher, a patient teacher, and after that he got the hang of it. He said all I needed was a good teacher, too. I really liked him for that. Ben's a good friend.

As if to signal an end to his speech, Meredith moved to stand up. Rosa abhorred the smug expression on her face, the conceited look of I-told-you-so, the victory flag she waved. Rosa knew she was down on the canvas but the referee hadn't counted her out. One final charge for the jugular might, she wished with all her heart, just *might* win Billy over, just *might* shatter the shackles Meredith used to imprison him.

'Whose idea was it to bring Elizabeth here, Billy?' Contempt shot into his eyes. But not for Rosa. Meredith reminded him Elizabeth wouldn't cooperate.

I had to, Rosa. She…fell. She was unconscious…fainted…getting soaked on the deck. I brought the truck around and…put her in. The stroller…the baby things…I had nowhere else to bring her…the baby was…gone. No one would have believed me, Rosa. You…understand that, don't…don't you?

'I understand it was difficult for you, but why didn't you call for help, the police…anyone? You should have taken her to the hospital, Billy.'

I…I panicked, Mrs Tavistock. I…I called Mother up…she said to bring her home…home where she belongs…that's…that's what she…she said.

'And now, Billy? Where is Elizabeth NOW?'

He looked to his mother for support, for answers. Meredith addressed Rosa but screamed at her son, 'Tell her she's dead! Dead! Dead because *her* son killed her. Ran her over with his car! On that road right outside our house! He thought he could make it look like *we* did it by killing her right on our doorstep! He's a villain, that boy! Tell her, Billy. Tell her!'

Elizabeth is…dead, Mother?

'Yes, I told you before, son, before this…this busybody came in here to upset you with foolish questions.'

Rosa jumped in again. 'Is that what *you* wanted, Billy? To have Elizabeth die? Have her baby drown?'

No, no, it was an accident…I never meant to hurt anyone. Not Elizabeth, not her baby…

'Your mother went after Elizabeth, Billy. How do we know *she* didn't use her car to run her down? She said it was a *car* that killed her, didn't she?'

Mother?

'Tavistock is only trying to confuse you, son! It was *her* boy who did it. Don't listen to her!'

Rosa felt she had Meredith on the run. 'Listen, Billy. Ben was here earlier to see you. Your mother wouldn't let him see you, just like she wouldn't let your father see you that night—'

Mother, is this—?

'Lies! All lies!'

'Billy! Ben thinks Elizabeth died in the ocean. If he knew Elizabeth was here, alive, in your house, do you think he would have left without her?'

I'm confused, Mother…help me…

Meredith took his hand in hers and promised she would. Rosa resigned her ears to listening to the charisma that poured syrupy sweet from the well-practiced manipulator. Meredith convinced him that it would be dark soon and night time was a good time to get rid of vermin like Rosa Tavistock.

'We'll dig a hole down the end field, near the oak tree, son, and then we'll be soon back to a normal life. Just the two of us.' Rosa gently spoke to Billy in an effort to re-establish rapport with him but he seemed mesmerised by the tactics Meredith used on him, the tactics that worked when he was young and continued to keep him in subjection to her as a grown-up. Rosa used one last plea.

'What would Ben think, Billy? Haven't you been friends for such a long time? Is that how friends behave? Do friends, *real* friends, betray each other by hurting their loved ones? Billy, your mother wants you to bury me in a field. I am Ben's mother! Why would you *do* that? Why would you obey that kind of madness? Why, *why* do you listen to your mother, Billy? Why?'

I…I… never wanted anyone…to be hurt…

Meredith continued to fondle his hand. She kept up the charm without words. The mask she used to slip on and take off at will, the machinations she employed to draw the boy in like a magnet lures the steel filings; the manufactured pretence that worked so successfully in the past; the wounded features, the look that appealed for pity; pity for the hard life her father gave her, the terrible times her husband gave her, all the cruelty the *world* had given her throughout her life.

'She'll blame *you* for my death when the police dig up my body, Billy. She'll blame *you* for your father's death when they find his remains. Break away from her, Billy. Break free *now*! Don't wait another second.'

Meredith got his interest again. 'They'll never find her! They won't find your father, either. Trust me, son. Trust *me*, not *her*!' He swung his gaze to Rosa again, expecting a rebuttal but not wanting one.

'Billy,' Rosa appealed, 'even if nobody finds me, or your dad, how will you continue to live with yourself and what you've done? How will you face Ben tomorrow? Can you look him in the eye and lie to him, pretending that everything is fine. How long do you think you can keep up the lies? Every time you see him, you'll be lying to him. Is that what you want from a friendship with him?'

Billy stared at Rosa. He couldn't give an answer.

Twenty

'She woke up, said something and...and went out again. It was so quick, Lucy. I heard her mutter something...it sounded like... *Pen*. I asked her name, you know, like you said, if she woke up. She rolled her eyes and repeated *Pen*. Maybe she was trying to say Penny? She looks awful, doesn't she? *What* could have happened to her, the poor thing?'

'Yeah, she does, too. At least there is some good news; there are no bones broken and no internal injuries. She hit her head; it was nasty cut...hope it's not serious. The baby seems to be strong. The lab should have the results from the blood we sent them. Doctor Castillo wants them ASAP—here she is now!'

Castillo marched up to the two nurses. She was well known for her business-like bedside manner. As with the patients, so it was with the nursing staff, the cleaners and the big boys who ran the hospital. With Millicent Castillo, what you saw is what you got. A hard-working intern, a brilliant mind for medicine and a deep concern for the well-being of people who came under her care; the now fifty-something shared her time between St Luke's and a dwindling practice she took over from her father.

She had been short-listed for a place on the Hospital Board but the paediatrician outspokenly excluded herself for the job because she knew how rigid the patriarchs were, how tight they were with money. That kind of leadership in the serious business of people's health did not gel with her perception of health care. Someone once asked her why she chose to concentrate on paediatrics. The surgeon quietly replied, 'I love children.'

With a bad marriage and a worse divorce behind her (some whispered she had become more demanding, sterner in her approach, didn't mix socially with her peers and mainly kept to herself), Millicent Castillo became reclusive somewhat. And she'd be the first to admit to that, but *only* to her father. Much of her time of late was spent visiting her ailing father in the nursing home. Regularly, she would book into the hotel nearby for a week, and every day give personal attention to the man who taught her everything he knew about medicine. It was her turn now to tell him of new procedures, new techniques, and new drugs and some practices and treatments that weren't so welcome.

Although he didn't always comprehend, she told him anyway. He seemed to perk up a bit when medicine was discussed. Besides, she knew he was near to dying. A *loving* father is how she described him to others; always there for her, always gentle, never pushy. Millicent didn't inherit his mild-mannered approach to people. How *different* she was to him. Yet, sparks never flew between them; rarely did they disagree. The subject of her mother was kept to a minimum.

Eight years dead and he still missed her. When he cried, his daughter cried. In between tears, he would tell her the same story of how they met, he an intern, she a young nurse, and how between them they borrowed money from their respective parents to start the practice which grew, they believed, because they were a husband-and-wife team who cared for the community, and who were, in turn, adopted by the community.

The staff looked forward to Millicent's visits, because, one, she didn't hold back from offering advice, which was always respected, and two, she wasn't above getting her hands dirty when the blood gushed. The other doctors didn't like her 'helping hand' but she largely ignored them. They argued she had no right to interfere with their patients. She argued that caring is a heart thing, that power is a head thing. They figured since her father had only a little time left, she'd be out of their hair soon, so they tolerated her input in the interim.

'Good morning, Lucy. Those results back yet?'

'No, Doctor…I asked them to ring me.'

'That's fine, Lucy. I'll pay them a visit myself.' Ten minutes later, she returned to Elizabeth's bed clutching a printout of the woman's life, a medical history in abbreviated statistics, followed by a corresponding number.

Lucy Bensart greeted her with some excitement. 'She's awake, Doctor.' Castillo went straight to Elizabeth's side and took her hand in hers, as was her norm.

'Hello. My name is Millicent Castillo. I'm a doctor. What's your name, dear?' Elizabeth tried to fix her eyes on the woman above her. She was groggy, incoherent, but she knew what she wanted to say. It just didn't come out very well.

'Ben,' she breathed.

'Is that Pen? Is your name Penny? Penny what, dear?'

'Rosa…'

'Okay. So you are Rosa. Rosa what? Can you remember your name?' Elizabeth shook her head. It hardly moved. The effort was great. She whispered *Tavistock*. Lucy and the other nurse leaned forward. Castillo got closer to the woman's mouth. Elizabeth repeated her name. 'Is that *Tavistock*? Did you say Tavistock? *Rosa* Tavistock?' Elizabeth closed her eyes and moved her head a little. The doctor could see the frustrated strain on her face.

The younger nurse gasped. The others looked at her with questions. 'That can't be!' She uttered in disbelief. They let her get closer to Elizabeth.

'That…that is Elizabeth…my God! She went missing! They said she drowned with her baby. That's…*Elizabeth Tavistock!* She's married to Ben. I knew Elizabeth at school! This is awful….' Lucy settled Helena into a chair.

Castillo spoke again, '*Are* you Elizabeth Tavistock?' Elizabeth nodded. 'Who is your doctor, Elizabeth?'

'Ames…' she tried to form the name, Jeremy.

'Did you say *Ames*? Is that Jeremy Ames? In King Street?' Elizabeth struggled to say yes. Her eyelids fell, hiding her blue eyes. Castillo shone her torch in. 'She's slipped into a coma. Lucy, get Doctor Gillome in. I'll contact Ames and find out more.'

The receptionist answered, 'This is Doctor Castillo from St Luke's. Put Doctor Ames on the phone. It's an emergency.'

'The doctor is with a patient,' the girl said in her rehearsed and monotonous keep-you-waiting voice.

Castillo responded with more urgency, 'Is the patient he's with *dying*?'

'Well, no. The lady injured her hand.'

'In that case put the doctor on. My patient *is* dying.'

'Just…just a sec, Doctor.'

Jeremy Ames was a little irked that he was interrupted as he studied Mrs Plantham's X-ray picture.

'What is it, Olivia?' he said, attempting not to show his irritation in front of his patient.

'There's a Doctor Castillo on the phone. She says it's urgent…I'm sorry.'

Ames muttered under his breath, 'What does *she* want?'

'Ah, Milly!' he deliberately provoked, knowing full well she didn't respond to the nickname. She ignored his liberty-taking tactics this time in view of the patient's condition; they had crossed swords in the past and neither of them gave any leeway. She kept her temper in balance.

'Doctor Ames, I think you can help me. I have a patient of yours in a bad condition here at the Hospital. Her name is Elizabeth Tavistock. What can you tell me about her? She is very ill.'

Ames spurted out an incredulous 'What!'

Castillo yanked the phone from her ear. Irritated by the bad manners, she continued calmly, 'Is this the same woman who was supposed to have drowned along with her child?' Castillo continued.

Ames stuttered into the phone. It made his patient uneasy. 'I can't imagine…I'd have to see this for myself! Listen, eh, Doctor…I'll be right over.'

Castillo waited with Steve Gillome at the entrance to the Intensive Care Unit. Ames waved apologetically as he went to meet them. They took him straight to the girl's bed. She was unconscious. Ames checked her over and admitted he hardly recognised her. He was white as a freshly laundered hospital sheet.

'Mrs Tavistock was diagnosed with ovarian cancer; James Sandlier gave her three, maybe six months. I can't believe this. Just *can't…*'

Castillo showed a little sympathy for the man. 'Doctor Ames, we need to contact relatives. Decisions have to be made. There is a slim chance we can save the baby. I'd guess the little thing is about six months.' Ames probed his memory, did a mental calculation and nodded in agreement.

'The Tavistocks attend my surgery. Elizabeth came more often than Ben did; I rarely saw him. Stephie had the usual childhood illnesses and immunisations. Elizabeth, though, complained of stomach pains. She came more frequently. In September, she provided a sample that tested positive for pregnancy. I ordered blood tests as a result of her ongoing complaints; cancer was diagnosed. Then she was faced with the frightful choice of losing her child to radical surgery, with no certainty for her own survival. James sought another opinion. The diagnosis was indisputable.—and now this! How she hung on…and in *this* condition…only heaven knows…'

Castillo became more assertive. 'Come into my office. You can get your staff to ring through her husband's phone number. I want to bring him in here *now*.' Ames continued; he was visibly upset by the new development. Castillo was quick to discern his plight. 'We see sickness and death often, Doctor. Is there something that bothers you particularly?'

'Ben Tavistock came into my office this morning. He was on a mission… wanted to know about Elizabeth's state of mind, her health. No one told him she was pregnant and she…disappeared before she could tell him she had cancer. *Angry* would describe him…angry with me, really. Inspector Plinter was with him… although he…he waited outside while Ben and I talked…'

'Don't be too hard on yourself, Jeremy. When it comes to commiserating with relatives…well, ours is not the pleasantest vocation in the world! The Police will have to be called in, of course. I know Corish Plinter. I'll call him first. It's strange that he should be with the girl's husband today…or maybe it isn't?' Castillo had begun tapping the numbers in.

'Hello, may I speak with Inspector Plinter, please? Tell him it's Millicent Castillo.'

'The inspector is away at present. I'll put you on to Sergeant Brighton. Hold on.'

'Hello.'

'Sue! It's Millicent Castillo…from the hospital.'

'Hello, Millicent, how are you? Not in trouble, are you?'

'Not personally, Sue, but a problem *has* arisen. Can you get a message to Corish?'

'Yes, I can. Officially, he is on leave but he's still in town. I can get him to ring you or give you his mobile number, whichever you prefer?'

'No, no. Give him this message! Tell him that Elizabeth Tavistock has turned up in St Luke's Hospital. The woman has been identified by her doctor, Jeremy Ames, and Nurse Helena MacDonald, who went to school with her.'

Castillo heard Sue whistle down the wire. Sue said that Corish was never happy with that case; he'll be very keen to hear this information. She asked that Castillo cooperate by keeping the information from the media. Castillo agreed and promptly called the two attending nurses to her office, where she repeated the request to them and Ames to keep quiet while the police pursued their inquiries.

Eleven minutes later, Castillo was talking to Plinter, who said he'd be there before she had put the phone down. Plinter took Ben by the upper arms and squeezed hope, and support, into the man's being. 'Ben, listen carefully. Your wife, Elizabeth, is alive. She is in St Luke's. Shall we go and see her?'

Ben fainted.

Twenty-One

'It will be dark soon, Billy. Let's have some food together and we'll discuss what to do. I'll make your favourite ham and pickle sandwich…and…and a glass of beer to wash it down, boy. You'll like that, won't you? Of course, you will, son. We'll leave her tied up until we are ready to go down to the bottom field. Nice and dark, then. Get rid of her near the oak tree…where I…where *he* died.'

She checked the knots on Rosa's wrists. Billy was in a stupor. None of what he heard made sense. Only the last few words registered on his brain. Rosa picked up on Billy's surprised look.

'Mother, you mean where my grandfather died…when the tractor…?'

'Yes!' She snapped at him and pulled on the cord. Rosa winced, her wrists responded to the tourniquet.

'I thought…the tractor rolled down the incline…near the grey shed? The old oak tree is on the other side, by the old cowsheds.'

Meredith barked, 'Did it matter *where* he died,' and began to parade around the room, talking to a phantom audience. Intermittently, she remembered where she was and came back to addressing her son.

'He's dead these past fifty years. Who cares now, son? He deserved it! Any man who did what he did well and truly deserved what he got. *I* had to live with it. Me! I had to face him night after night. And all I wanted to be was a nurse. I wanted to get out of that house. Do you understand? My mother put an end to that, didn't she? She had the gall to tell me she missed him. Didn't want to *live* anymore, she whined.

'I told her we were better off without him. Both of us were. I told her if she didn't stop whining for the rat, I'd tell the world what he was like. *She* knew what he was doing to me. She *knew*! I began to hate her for it when I got older, when I realised she had *said* nothing to stop him, *did* nothing to stop him…' Meredith turned to Rosa and slapped her. 'You! You *knew* what he was doing to me and you did *nothing*, Mother! Nothing!' Her voice reached a screaming crescendo.

Rosa saw the hateful look in her eyes and reckoned that was the same look she had given her mother those fifty long years ago. Meredith had not forgotten. The old woman had mentally gone back to pour her rage on the mother who gave birth to her but apparently nothing else.

Shocked, Rosa now understood *she* had been substituted for Meredith's *mother*. A rush of pity for the young child Meredith described surged into her chest. She could only imagine the awful terror. Meredith turned to Billy and spat in his face. She grabbed his hand and drew her nails across it. Blood flowed freely from the veins on the back of his hand. 'And you!' she shrieked up at him. 'You were no father to me! No father does those things to his little girl…'

She stopped speaking and looked strangely at her son. 'Oh, Billy, he used to call me his *little girl,* his *favourite* little girl.' Billy stared at her, speechless and quivering. Rosa watched intensely as the old woman climbed onto the bed and, adopting the embryonic position, she lifted her dress to show her bare skin. She looked so small, Rosa thought. All curled up like a lost little child, gazing into nothingness with the blankest eyes Rosa ever saw.

Can this be happening? Is the woman reliving the past? How easily she got onto the bed. What awful things did that monster do to her? Is this the history behind Meredith Turner? Is this why the old woman does what she does? Is this why she hates all men? Has what her father done to her twisted her mind? Rosa felt her heart go out to the child inside the old woman, now seeing her in a strange new light. She wanted to reach inside and draw the child out and tell her that it was going to be alright, that her father was bad and he was gone now and there was no need to worry anymore. She began to communicate with the young child, to get her to talk her little heart out, for comfort's sake.

'Meredith, I'd like to talk to you. Will you tell me what happened? Once you talk about it, you will feel better. Won't you try to tell me? It'll be our secret; no one else needs to know what happened.'

Meredith became timid, scared. 'I can't tell you while *he* is standing there'—she gave Billy a quick, fearful glance—'he will hear us. He told me not to tell anyone, not even Mama!'

'If I send him away, do you think you'll be able to talk when he's gone?'

'He said he'd hurt my Mama if I told anyone.'

Rosa groaned inside. 'Meredith, how old are you?'

'I'm five now. Mama says I'll be six next birthday.'

Rosa groaned again, only from deeper within this time. Billy stood mesmerised, not understanding any of what was going on. Rosa got his attention. He blinked at the mention of his name. She had to raise her voice to bring him out of his stupor. 'Billy, I want you to go outside the room. Go to the kitchen and make yourself a sandwich, your favourite.'

Robot-like, the man moved to the door and closed it behind him. He leaned his back against the door and gazed through to where Elizabeth had once lay. The top sheet and the duvet were strewn on the floor where his mother had savagely ripped them off the bed earlier. The pillow stayed in the same spot where Elizabeth had lain for months; the indentation her head made on the soft cushion remained. He knew she was getting sicker and sicker by the week and all he could do was watch, watch her slowly die.

And worse, he knew his mother would let her die, which meant she was also *killing* her. It amounted to the same thing. He knew that. Just as surely as she killed his father with a brass paperweight, she was killing Elizabeth by doing nothing to help her. And was *he* any different? Was *he* not also responsible, by keeping quiet about his father, and now, being quiet about Elizabeth? Maybe it was better for Elizabeth.

The car that hit her did her a favour, he whispered. She has no more pain; no more does she feel afraid of what the next day will bring; no mother to incite her to do things she doesn't want to do. No more *little secrets*; no more hidden fears, no more dreams that come uninvited at night, dreams that remind of bloodied brass elephants and deep, crude holes and plastic bags, and concrete floors to hide the vulgarity of death.

He trembled against the door. He felt he was glued to it, that he needed help to unfasten himself but there was nobody to help him. He grasped that while he thought of Elizabeth's death as *freedom* for her, he now understood that is what he wanted for *him*. Freedom. In all of this, the only person who *really* tried to help him to come to terms with the real villain in his life was tied up and helpless. He'd wished he'd had a mother like Rosa. Her soft, soothing voice seemed to penetrate the wooden panels of the door and linger in his ears.

'Is that better now? He's gone. Are you able to tell me *now*?'

'No. He said it was our little secret.'

'And have you told anyone, Meredith?'

'Only Sally.'

'Who is Sally?'
'She's my friend.'
'From school?'
'No-oo!'
'From next door? Are her mother and your mother friends?'
'No, I said!'
'Where does Sally live?'
'In my wardrobe. I bring her out when my dad is not here and we talk.'
'About your secret?'
'Yes.'
'Is that because she won't tell anyone else?'
'Yes. I *trust* her.'
'What else did your father say?'
'He said he would leave us and we'd have no one to take care of us…'
'That's a horrid thing to say!'
'…and he would not feed us or take care of us anymore.'
'How old are you now, Meredith?'
'I'm ten, mama. Will you help me, please? Please!'
'Yes, I'll help you, child. What happened when you were ten?'
'He came into me.'

Billy forced his body away from the door. He didn't want to hear any more. It wasn't his mother in there, curled up on the bed like a little girl and talking like one, too. That was someone else, someone impersonating her, telling Rosa all those lies about his grandfather. She's making it all up, just to fool Rosa into believing that she knows too much and has to be buried near the oak tree to stop her telling the police, Ben, the daily newspaper.

Then they'd come and lock him up in a lonely prison cell and his mother would come to visit every two weeks for a while and then once a year because she was getting too old to travel. And after a few years, she'd never come at all because she was dead and the warden said he could go to her funeral but he would decline because she betrayed him by blaming him for the death of his father.

Billy raced down to the kitchen, jumping several steps at a time, forgetting his injury, forgetting his pain. He was panting heavily when he reached for the ham in the fridge, his heart palpitating feverishly from an attack that panicked his mind and reverberated throughout his whole body. The knife in his good hand hung poised, the knife laced with sauce to spread over the bread. It looked like thick, moist blood. Unable to hold the blade still, he let it drop to his side. The syrupy pickle slid off the knife and splashed onto the floor's shiny tiled surface.

He let the knife fall and watched the tip of the blade strike the hard floor and bounce, in slow motion; it did an awkward, rattling dance. He waited for the noise to stop; it seemed to go on and on. When it finally stopped, he stood in the absolute and tangible quiet and then sunk into the chair; he sheltered his face with his big left hand and wept like a little boy…

'How old are you now, Meredith?'

'I'm fourteen. I look like a woman now, mama, don't I?'

'And your father…where is he now?'

'Oh, he's fine. He loves me. I love him.'

'So, things have changed since you were ten?'

'Oh yes! Things have got a lot better since then. We really enjoy the time we spend together. He buys me *anything* I want. Mama gets jealous sometimes but Dad says she'll get over it.'

'And what about your little secret…did you ever tell your mother?'

'You don't tell secrets! Not to anyone! Especially not to *Mama*. Dad says it's better that way because she will only get more jealous than she is, and angrier, too.'

'Is Sally still around? *She* knew your secret.'

'Oh, I sent her away. She wanted to tell *Mama*. I pulled her head off and threw her into the fire. She *had* to go. A real troublemaker, that one!'

'Meredith, why would your mother be *jealous*?'

'Because! Don't you understand anything? My dad and I had something special between us. He told me so. She was jealous of that.'

'Did *she* ever tell you she was jealous?'

'Now who, *who* is going to admit that? Of course she didn't!'

'So, why do *you* think she was jealous?'

'Because he spends more *time* with me. I have *explained* that already?'

'Does he…does he still visit your room at night?'

'Of course he does!'

'Meredith! I thought you said things had *changed*!'

'And they have changed! When he comes to my room, I close my eyes and think of being a nurse.'

Rosa repulsed at the thought that the man had thoroughly won the child over to his vile ways. And the child had learned to blank out the atrocities. Rosa wanted to scream her anger at the dead man, and punish him with her fists; to scream at the little girl's mother for being so weak minded, so cowardly. A *real* mother would have been prepared to sacrifice her *life* to protect her daughter. Yet, she did nothing. Nothing at all.

Rosa stared at the old woman, whose eyes were glazed over, waiting for the next question.

'How old are you now, Meredith?'

'I'm fifteen, and I'm angry with him!'

'What has he done to make you angry?'

'He's making eyes at the au pair.'

'The *au pair?* When did she arrive?'

'Two weeks ago. From Sweden. She's seventeen, with long blonde hair. Dad says she is staying for six months.'

'Why do you need help at home? Is your mother ill?'

'She fell and broke her leg. She *said* Dad pushed her down the stairs. Dad said she'd do anything to get attention. I believe him.'

'Couldn't you have helped at home?'

'I started my nursing.'

'Do you think your mother is lying? Is that what you believe?' There was a long pause. Meredith turned away from Rosa and towards the window but kept the same curved posture. She pulled her dress down to cover her legs. Rosa wasn't sure about this gesture but she did think the child had a new conviction.

'How old are you now, Meredith?'

'I'm nearly seventeen. The police came the other day. The au pair is gone and he wants back in my room.'

'What do you want, Meredith?'

'I told him to get out, and never come near me again. He said he'd buy me a new car when I turned seventeen.'

'Did you accept that offer?'

'No! He persisted for a week, offering me other gifts. I said get away or I'll tell mother. He wouldn't believe me. He kept pestering me. So I told Mama. I told Mama what he did when I was five. She hugged me and said we have to get away from him. "He's a beast," Mama cried. Then she showed me the bruises on her back and arms. Mama always wore a long dress; it covered the bruises, she said. I never noticed that before. He had beaten her for most of their married life. I believed her about falling down the stairs. He did it. I hated him from then on. I hated all men from then on.'

'How old are you now, Meredith?'

'Turned seventeen. I'm behind the oak tree. He lured me down to the bottom field. Said he wanted water. He started it on with me. I'm running from him. I tripped. He pounced on me and said he knew what I wanted. I'm screaming for Mama to help me. She can't hear me. I break free from him. I feel my fingers on his hand… and now there's blood on them. I'm behind the oak tree. I have a stone in my hand…he's on the ground. His head is bleeding. I think…I think he's dead, Mama.'

Meredith turned back again to face Rosa and searched for her eyes and repeated softer, reconciled, 'I think he's dead, Mama.'

Rosa didn't know who she was staring at, the old woman or a teenager.

'Are you sure *you* killed him, Meredith? He was found *underneath the tractor*.' Meredith got off the bed. The young woman hid behind the old woman. Rosa asked again, 'You are getting things mixed up, Meredith. Your father *fell* off the tractor. It rolled over on him.' Still no answer. Rosa probed again.

'Meredith, how old are you now?'

'I'm eighteen now and that's all I can remember, Mama. Don't forget our pact…you must promise, Mama…'

Twenty-Two

Millicent Castillo took Ben by the elbow and prepared him. Jeremy Ames stood by her side; Ben chose not to find his eyes.

'Before you see her, Mister Tavistock, I must warn you that your wife is seriously ill. We can't guarantee she will survive the ordeal she has been through. We are also concerned for the baby. Do you understand? Elizabeth does not look like the woman you knew when you last saw her. You need to take on board what I'm saying to you. Be prepared for the worst.'

She opened the door for him. He was tense. Castillo's words resounded in his head. And kept resounding when the doctor asked him would he like the Inspector to go with him. Ben didn't hear that. Everything was surreal, like he was floating just above the floor. He felt a soft push on the small of his back and began to glide across the rubberised tiles. Someone must have slipped the machine into retro mode because he came to a cushioned stop as he brushed lightly against the bed.

Nurse Helena MacDonald stood worriedly on the other side. She had her hand on a drip bottle, seemingly adjusting the flow of syrupy fluid. Ben didn't notice the apprehension traversing her face. A tube ran in or out of Elizabeth's nostril; he couldn't tell which. It took him a minute of staring before he decided he didn't recognise her face. There were features that didn't belong, lines that did not gel with his memory of her. He turned to the doctors who stood in the doorway and beseeched them with a plaintive appeal to take this mask off his wife so he could see the real Elizabeth.

The philanthropy in Castillo moved her to his side. Her compassionate eyes told him she could not remove the sickness that swapped his wife's beauty for the hideous façade he was forced to witness. He looked deeply into Elizabeth's face in a frantic search for his lover. The nurse dropped a stainless-steel dish; it struck the floor with the patent peal of a lonely bell. Elizabeth opened her eyes as if by request.

'There she is,' Ben heard a voice call out. It was his own, and immediately he saw the blue but diminished sparkling eyes that could only belong to Elizabeth. She, in turn, studied the strange faces above her until finally she let a sound of a joyous discovery. 'Ben!' she cried. He reached down to her and they cried together. Castillo waved the *out* sign to Nurse MacDonald. She closed the door and gave them the privacy they deserved.

They talked of cool evenings under autumn skies, when stars were bright and easily counted; of tree-lined avenues dressed in rust-red beech and maple; of orange leaves falling, twisting, tumbling, floating, to soft-land on grass-green carpets. In whispered sorrow they cried for Stephie and for the joy she had given them. They cried for each other. They cried for the health and the life of the child in her womb; and talked of a name for their unborn.

And how often, during the fifteen minutes they spent together, Ben repeated how he could not believe she was alive. He told her of his isolation, his deep depression, his near renouncement of life itself. She told him of hers, laying on her death-bed waiting to die, wanting to die…

In the foyer, Castillo exchanged hopeful ideas with Plinter on treatment for Elizabeth when they were interrupted by Ben. His face was wet, his eyes red but he was happier. The two men spoke privately for several minutes. Ben gave Plinter the short version of what he learned from Elizabeth. The gist of their conversation pivoted on the rescue of Rosa Tavistock. Ben was restless to get to the Turner farm and begin their clandestine survey. Plinter demanded of the medical staff their silence until police inquiries were complete.

James Sandlier arrived, and along with Ames, Castillo, and Gillome, entered into the discussion of the pros and cons of appropriate treatment for Elizabeth's illness, and for the baby's welfare. The medico's plan was to begin heat treatment directly to the tumour, monitor the baby's progress and perform a C-section when it was deemed necessary. Sandlier and Castillo agreed to hold off removing the baby for as long as possible, to give it a fighting chance. They would start the treatment the next day.

Millicent Castillo sat close to Elizabeth and spoke caringly to her patient. Elizabeth's eyes shone. Castillo felt privately her patient received a good dose of hope and happiness on seeing her husband and while it would not cure her illness it had certainly perked up her spirits. The last thing she said to Ben was 'I want to get well, Ben, for you, for our baby, for us.' Her determination for life was different now, and stronger, unlike the numbness she experienced on Meredith Turner's old bed.

'The treatment we have in mind is not radical, Elizabeth. In other words, it's not chemo or radiotherapy. That is the other option, but in view of your pregnancy, we'd like to try the "heat" procedure first. You won't lose your hair; you'll feel virtually no pain from the procedure and it won't harm the baby. Chemotherapy is an aggressive form of fighting cancer cells. If it comes to that we'd have to take the baby away from you before we begin. Full term, naturally, is ideal, but we honestly think it prudent to perform a section—'

'Is…heat treatment… a new approach? I haven't heard of it.'

'When I was a young doctor, I learned about it from my father, a very caring doctor. Let me briefly explain the principle behind it. In cancerous tissue, blood flows much slower than in healthy tissue. Researchers used this knowledge to apply heat—similar to that produced by your microwave oven—to kill certain tumours. The surrounding healthy tissue stays cooler because of its greater blood flow.

'It's similar to a car engine kept cool by the continuous flow of water from the radiator. The harm to the normal tissue is minimal because it can cope with the heat. The cancerous tissue does not have that ability because it has a sluggish blood flow; therefore, the sustained heat kills the tumour. That's the theory, anyway. But you must keep in mind, Elizabeth, there is no guarantee it will cure you, just as the more aggressive therapy is not a guarantee either.'

'I…I only want the best for…my baby, Doctor. I can make it up to Ben, at least, for losing…Stephie.'

'I'm sure your husband does not blame you for what happened. However your baby died, this awful thing is not your fault. It was a terrible storm, I remember it vividly. Just try to be positive for what lies ahead. I'm a great believer in having the right mental attitude. Along with proper treatment, it can prove very useful in overcoming illnesses. I just need to know which way you wish to go. Do we try to eradicate the tumour with heat, or do we start chemotherapy?'

'For my child's sake…let's try the…first option. If that fails, I'm prepared to have my baby by…by Caesarean section. After that…I suppose…well, I'll leave it to you.'

'Fine, Elizabeth. I'll organise things for tomorrow morning. You rest now…and try not to worry.' Elizabeth closed her eyes and began to think about Ben. She had told him everything she could about the Turner house and its occupants; that Meredith had a gun and Rosa was in danger. Ben had told her the police were involved.

He did not tell her he and Plinter were off to spy on the Turners in the dark hours.

Plinter parked the car a hundred metres from the Turner driveway. The two men cautiously made their way up the winding dirt track under a neon moon. Occasionally it hid behind retreating clouds. They stuck close to the trees on either side of the laneway, wide enough for single traffic, and were prepared to duck into the bushes should a vehicle come from either the house or the main road.

A tawny owl gave out its tremulous *hoo*, followed by the longer *huuu-hu-huhuhu*. Ben jumped; then relaxed. Plinter tramped on a twig that made a loud *crack*. Both men stopped in their tracks as if *that* might muffle the sound. To them it sounded louder than it really was and, anyway, they were far away from the house not to be heard. Ben joined Plinter on the left-hand side of the path as they continued for the final fifty metres, when the house loomed before them. They paused under a verdant tree, where the grassy track turned to concrete; they scanned the windows for signs of life.

On the upper level, the light from a low-wattage bulb tried to get past the heavy curtains. A thin line ran down the centre where the curtains weren't fully drawn. Ben whispered to Plinter: 'That's Billy's room. Elizabeth said she was kept in a room directly opposite his, and Rosa in the room next to hers. We need to make our way around to the back of the house.' Plinter nodded agreement.

'Set your mobile phone to *vibrate* mode. We don't want any surprises.' Ben copied that and set his phone. They decided to split up and go from opposite directions; Ben took the left side, continually scanning the main door and all the windows as he stole along the privets in front of the house, until he came to the end of the building. The road swung in a circle behind the house and came out to re-join the track on the other side.

Clouds formed over the moon once more to give him a bit more cover, and a bit more bravado. This kind of activity was all new to him. Sneaking around the grounds of his friend's house was not exactly his choice or desire, but under the ominous circumstances, it was the thing to do. According to Elizabeth, Billy was the mule, Meredith cracked the whip. She was the ogre with the gun; she the real threat to Rosa.

Ben crept along the wall stopping now and then to listen for activities inside the house. Everything was quiet. The layout of the house he knew well; he came to a double door, behind which garaged Billy's truck and boat. It was locked. He carried on around to the rear of the house to find the roller-door was down but the timber door next to it was ajar. A gentle push and the wooden frame swayed inwards; he'd forgotten the hinges were rusty; they creaked like an out-of-tune violin.

With his breath held tightly, he waited for the confrontational reaction from inside the house. None came. Except for a thin spray of light under the door that opened into a large hallway, the musty room he was about to enter was on the good side of black. Ben waited for his eyes to adjust. The light under the door suggested one or both of them might be downstairs. Not in the kitchen, he murmured, since there was no light coming from the kitchen window. Could be in the living room or maybe the games room?

The smell suddenly impacted on his senses and his first thought was to flee the room and get fresh air into his lungs. He had forgotten about the smell. Billy still hadn't cleaned up. The table he used for cleaning his catch of fish gave off that nauseating odour and the damp, musty conditions surely brought its fair share of rodents. With his handkerchief to his nose, he braved the stench and aimed for the beam of light. Something struck his toe and immediately he saw the outline of a chair. He put his hand out to steady it and touched the ropes that once tied his mother's wrist and arms. All he could do was wonder about the chair.

Something touched his shoulder and he spun around in fright and quickly stepped back in defence mode. Plinter shone a small torch on his face and whispered Ben's name. 'Shhh! It's me!' Ben let his breath out impatiently.

'Don't creep up like that! Man alive, my heart is already weak!' Plinter ignored his complaint and shone the torch around the room, slowly, purposefully, examining the accumulation of tins and bottles on crooked shelves. The light showed up the tower of used car tyres that partly blocked a narrow window; a torn and dirty curtain hung loosely from a length of wire strung between two nails.

Plinter peered behind the stack and bent down. He produced a dustbin lid and handed it to Ben to inspect, as if to say, I told you. Ben quizzed his brain for a reason why Billy would try to frame him for Elizabeth and Stephie's disappearance. The answer to that will come soon, before the evening gets any older, he promised his fiery ego. Ben put the lid aside while Plinter continued his search. He stopped the light on the chair and examined the rope that dangled from it.

'That's a bloodstain, Ben. Someone was tied here, very likely your mother.' What a horrible smell! Plinter whispered even louder in disgust, as though his sense of smell suddenly woke up. 'We've seen enough here. Let's go in.'

Ben opened the door the barest crack and peered into the foyer. Plinter nudged him and said, 'Wait! Did you hear that?' Ben said *what?* The policeman concentrated hard on the noise he heard. 'It sounded like an engine starting up, a growling sort of noise. Gone now.'

Ben listened. 'Can't hear a thing, Corish. An animal, I daresay. Let's move quietly.' Plinter said Ben's guess was probably right, although he couldn't think of a local animal that made *that* sound. It was definitely some sort of engine. Maybe a generator or a pump? It *wasn't* near, however. Perhaps the noise carried from the adjoining farm. Farmers *do* odd things at odd hours, he concluded but kept the sound in a pending file. Switching off his torch, he followed Ben into the hallway.

Using sign language, Ben pointed to several doors while he tried the kitchen and the walk-in pantry and the downstairs WC. They carefully challenged each room for signs of life and finding them all in darkness, they advanced up the stairs. Ben saw that the door to the front entrance was bolted and thought maybe seven-thirty wasn't an *altogether* outrageous time to retire to bed, even under normal circumstances. But there was nothing normal here. If they were asleep, then his mother had to be tied up, likely to the bed posts. His fear for her safety took the foremost slot in his thinking. The light aglow at the foot of the stairs was either a practice Meredith had or else an oversight, but the door left open at the back of the house was not good security sense.

At the top of the stairs, the corridor went left and right. Plinter took the right wing which housed two bedrooms, a hot press, and a bathroom. The bathroom was empty. One door was partly open; no light came from it. The other one was closed. No light showed from under the door. He eased his way into the opened one and flashed the torch around.

Stepping lightly on the carpeted floor, Ben used the light that came from Billy's bedroom to avoid the splintered timber. He registered the broken panel and the dark stain on the cream carpet but didn't question it. Evidence of a struggle of some sort was apparent. Meredith, he remembered from earlier, had said that Billy was hurt. Ben's chief wish was that the blood on the carpet wasn't his mother's. Was he too late? Should he have waited *so long* to come for his mother? But he *had to go to* Elizabeth, see that she was truly alive.

The door with the broken panels was wide open. The room was dark. He turned to Billy's door and pushed it inwards. Plinter was moving towards him; Ben put his hand up like a traffic cop, to halt the man. Plinter obeyed and stopped past the stairs. Ben put his head into the room and gazed around, first to the bed and then in an arc. The room was empty. But it was a mess. The blankets were strewn across the bed and touched the floor.

He moved closer to the bed to examine the dark stain on the edge of the pillow and the sheet under it. It smelled of blood. In fact, the atmosphere smelled of blood. The bloodied rags lying against the skirting board caught his eye, as did the partly hidden knife. It was then he noticed the overturned chair, a déjà vu of the chair downstairs; ropes, partly knotted, dangling and touching the floor, and stained with black blood.

What has gone on in this house? He called out, 'Where *is* everyone? Corish, come and see this!' Corish didn't answer. Ben went to the door and beckoned him to come. 'There's no one in the house. Where's my mother? Where have they taken her?'

Plinter heard the panic in the young man's voice. He stood helpless. 'Did you not hear me, man?' Ben repeated. With only a modest light coming from the hall below, from Ben's perspective, Plinter appeared rigid; his back was certainly arched as though in pain. Ben threw a switch near his elbow and flooded the corridor with fresh light. 'Are you alright, Corish? You look pale. Are you sick, man? We need to search for my mother!'

Plinter quietly said he had something in his ribs. 'Mrs Turner, I believe, is behind me. I think she has a gun to my back.' The wiry woman stepped from behind the policeman and spoke her mind.

'You again! Talk about bad pennies!'

'What's going on, Meredith? Where is my mother?'

'Remember where you are, boy! This is *my* house, *my* rules. Get down the stairs!' She showed him the barrel. Ben made to challenge her. Plinter's eyes cautioned otherwise. The woman repeated her demand.

Ben tried a bluff. 'You couldn't use that thing. It's prehistoric, for crying out loud.'

'It's been fired today, boy. You want to see it again?' She smirked at him. Her grey eyes were set in their hollows. Ben backed off from belittling her any further; he tried diplomacy instead.

'You need to let us go, Meredith. This man is a high-ranking police officer. He has a lot of pull with the judge. Give over the weapon and tell me where my mother is.'

'You are not in any position to make demands, wife-killer! Confess now! You might just get a light jail sentence, but *I* doubt it.'

Plinter winked at Ben and said accusatively, 'I always thought it was you, Tavistock! How you fooled even me.' Ben took this as a ploy to sustain the 'dead wife' theory.

'How do you know she's dead, Meredith? Who told *you*?'

'I saw her with my own eyes, didn't I?'

'Yeah, and how did I do it? How did I finish her off?'

'With your car, you jackass! After you left here today you waited for her to leave the house—she was free to go at any time—and when she crossed the road you *ran her down*. I saw the ambulance men put her dead body on a stretcher. She was dead as a dodo…and *you… you* did it!'

'And tell me, if you will, Mrs Turner, what was Elizabeth Tavistock doing in *your* house all this time? How come she was here since the accident on the boat until today?'

'*My* Billy did nothing wrong! You planned it all…you made it look like Billy was the culprit when the entire time it was *you*!' she finished with a scream and bellowed, 'Get down the stairs!'

Plinter nodded towards the stairs indicating it was better to obey the woman. He spoke sternly that Ben was dealing with a very smart and perceptive woman and he really should listen to her. Plinter moved first. Ben followed. Meredith prodded him with the rifle. When they had descended the stairs, Plinter politely asked the old lady which way she would like them to go.

Meredith was abrupt and replied, 'The same way you came in, Mr so-called police officer. And no fancy stuff. I've killed many a fox with this rifle and there's a few more left; trust me, I am not finished yet!' Ben wasn't sure exactly what she meant and he wasn't game to ask.

Plinter was. Facing the old woman, he pointed out that he really was a policeman and he was on her side. He said, 'May I?' and took out ID and showed it to her.

She didn't look at it but kept her eyes focused on his. 'It doesn't matter who you are, mister, you know too much! The Tavistock woman knows too much. You *all* know too much,' she growled, 'now move into the garage!'

Meredith aimed the gun at a big torch on a hook. She ordered Plinter to take it and start walking. Ben stayed close to Plinter while the old woman shone another lamp at their backs. They picked their way along a narrow track made doubly visible by the moon. It led to an empty shed big enough to garage three cars and plenty of storage space as well. The doors were wide open and as they passed by Plinter took note of an old tractor in one corner, and a Volvo, partly covered with a tarpaulin. The car he recognised as Rosa's. He wondered if that was *the* tractor; he imagined a freshly cut sandwich by the driver's seat.

The full moon had the sky all to itself, now that the clouds had dispersed; its light was beautiful and if it wasn't for the madness under its placid rays, it would have been a very pleasant spring evening, Plinter mused, while keeping a rational approach towards the loose cannon with a weapon at her hip. The beam from his torch created eerie shadows as it danced from the grassy track to a stone wall here, a bush there, an old post leaning at an awkward angle, once bound with barbed wire to keep cows in or out.

Ben tried to work out how far they'd walked, counting the number of paces and making the calculation as he went; anything to stop his mind from thinking the worst about his mother. It wasn't working. He reckoned he counted two hundred and fifty paces of various lengths and estimated the distance to be one hundred and seventy metres. The worst possible scenario was the old witch had killed his mother, and that he and Plinter were next.

Or else, they were being taken to where his mother was tied up, for surely she had been prevented from leaving the house or using her phone. The chairs with bloodied ropes were proof of that. Elizabeth had said she was restricted to the bed and only in the beginning was she tied to the bedposts. 'So, my mother must have been tied to both chairs, at different times.' He imagined her being dragged from room to room; Elizabeth confirmed Rosa was sore from the beatings and the tight knots, and worn out through lack of sleep.

'How could *Billy* be a part of this?' He ached at his own question, even though Elizabeth explained Billy's obsession with her. 'Where was I all this time? How did I miss seeing it for myself? What has happened to the man?'

Meredith Turner was a different matter. Ben could see the crazy gleam she got in her eyes… but Billy? Why didn't Billy *stop* her? What kind of power did the old lady have over him? Maybe that's what Elizabeth meant when she said Meredith ruled the roost. He *should have* spent more time with Elizabeth to glean more information, but she was tired; she needed to rest.

A tree root caused him to stumble and he got a jab in the ribs for his clumsiness. The oak tree was straight ahead now. Plinter's torch picked up the white bandage on Billy's shoulder first, and the sling strapping his bent arm. Billy's large frame standing next to a small trenching machine sent shivers up the policeman's spine. Billy kept his gaze on the ground at his feet.

Ben could not see his mother; he thought the worst, imagining they had already killed and buried her. Billy's face was pained, Ben could see, but it wasn't the kind of pain his injury brought him; it was more like guilt. Plinter shone his torch around. A rectangle mimicking a grave, part excavated, lay at the front of the mechanical digger. Plinter made the connection now. The noise he heard earlier was this little machine starting up. He spoke politely to the woman.

'What have you done with Mrs Tavistock? You people are up no good here, aren't you?' Ben waited anxiously for a reply; he wanted to tear at the woman's face and demand she turn his mother over to him. The reply came slowly, mischievously.

'Wrong question, Mr Busybody!' She strung the words out. 'Maybe we are burying a dead animal. It is a *farm*, after all. Or hadn't you noticed? My father buried cows that the vet put down or ones he found dead in the field. Quite a normal pastoral practice, isn't that right, Billy?'

Billy didn't respond. Ben was about to make a charge at the woman. Plinter beat him to it with his next question. 'I don't see a dead cow, Mrs Turner. Where is it?' he said, casually shining his torch around in the darkness.

She said, '*Give me that light!*'—Plinter handed it over—'Not yet you don't! Bring her out, Billy! Bring out the cow!'

Billy said nothing until she repeated the order. Then, without lifting his eyes, he said, 'No, mother. We can't do this. It's wrong.' His voice quivered but his slow, deliberate response was emphatic.

Meredith threw her body at him, pushing him to one side. Her surprisingly lithe frame strode to the oak tree and hauled Rosa to her feet and presented her to them. Rosa, her hands tied behind her back, staggered on her feet but managed to stay upright. Ben went to help her, to hold her. Meredith waved the gun.

'There's your cow! The mother who didn't protect her son from a wretch of a wife, who let him steal what belonged to *my* son. *You*!'—she pointed the gun at Ben—'*You* found out the truth about your precious Elizabeth and saw how unfaithful she was, and then you *killed* her.' The words came out knife-like.

Ben prepared his tongue to protest but thought otherwise; the woman was not listening to anyone but herself. Plinter weighed up the situation; the old woman *was* mad. Whatever history she had borne, whatever tragedy, whatever dark side made her what she was now, had led to *this*. This *showdown*; where paranoia has left no room for reason, where rampant hatred left pity abandoned, where blind rage expels justice and leads to reckless revenge for perceived wrongs done.

Plinter had seen this scenario so many times in his long career and never gotten used to it. Whatever happened in Meredith Turner's past, all the classic symptoms of unbridled anger had taken its only course; like a river overflows from torrential rain and finally bursts its banks and wreaks havoc to all in its path. Plinter wondered if Meredith's banks hadn't burst fifty years ago, in this very place, and she'd been causing untold damage ever since. Tact was necessary. He'd try to convey that to the others.

Rosa looked sympathetically at Ben. Her eyes filled with elation when he told her Elizabeth was in the hospital, that she was in good care now. He turned to Meredith.

'Yes, Elizabeth *was* hit by a car, right outside your property. But she is *not* dead.'

Billy's eyes widened. He said 'Thank God' out loud and poured out his regret to Ben. 'It was an accident, Ben. Little Stephie…I didn't…mean to…' Meredith told him to be quiet. 'It doesn't matter now. It's too late for all of you!' She spat the words out.

Plinter asked, 'Since it doesn't matter, Madam, would you tell us, before you shoot all of us, why you are doing this? What started it?'

Meredith aimed her venom at Rosa. 'She knows! Don't you, Mrs Nosey Parker? I wanted to forget all that stuff, but you *just had to stick your beak in,* didn't you!'

Rosa said, 'It would be better coming from you, Meredith.' The old woman said she had said enough on the subject. Plinter said he knew about the sandwiches she had brought her father the day he died. She spun around to him.'

Meredith: Who told you about that?

Plinter: It was all in the police report. I read it, Madam.

Meredith: My Mama told the detective about that. She backed up my story.

Billy: What story, Mother?

Meredith: Be quiet, son!

Rosa: Tell him, Meredith. He should know about his grandfather.

Meredith: He needs to know nothing. He's only a boy.

Billy: What was the secret, Mother, between…you and your father?

Meredith: Who told you that, boy? Did she?

Billy: No, not Rosa…I was outside the door. You sounded…different.

Meredith: It must have been *her*! *She* keeps reminding me!

Plinter: It might help if you confront her, Madam.

Billy: Who? *Who* are you all talking about?

Rosa: A little girl. That's who. Who was wickedly…mistreated.

Meredith: By her father! Yes! She *was*! For ten years…

Rosa: …and she couldn't tell her mother…

Meredith: …*afraid* to tell her Mama. He told me he would *hurt Mama*…

Rosa: If you told your little secret to anyone, *especially* your Mama.

Billy: What did he *do* to you, Mother? *What* did he do? *Tell me*!

Meredith: Not for a little boy's ears…*too* young…*much* too young.

Ben: *Not* a little boy. He's a year older than me, Meredith. *Tell* him!

Billy: Yeah, I'm thirty-four, Mother. Not *a boy* anymore.

Meredith yelled out her frustration into the darkness, pacing in small circles, backing away from her antagonists, waving the rifle about. It would have been fairly easy to charge the pitiable wretch while her back was momentarily turned. No one thought of taking the gun away from her. Not Plinter; because the woman was unpredictable. Not Ben; because he wanted to hear vital answers from the woman. Both Rosa and Billy were in no physical condition to do much. They also wanted answers, and in an uncharacteristic switch, there was a trace of sorrow for the old woman.

'All these questions! Too *many* questions. No one would understand what he was like. Only *I* do.' Meredith moaned. She looked at each one in turn, examining their faces for a sympathetic response, searching their eyes and hoping to find a kindly face. She beckoned Rosa to turn her face to the moon for a better look at her. Rosa obeyed. A mother's face, the old woman said softly, the kind she wished for herself but never enjoyed the emotion of belonging like she enjoyed at this moment. Then it was gone.

Meredith touched Billy's arm and stroked the bandage. 'My Mama knew, Billy. She knew but didn't help me. She was afraid of him, very much afraid. I don't blame her for being *afraid,* Billy, you understand, you know what I mean, don't you? I blame her *for not doing something, anything,* to stop him. To stop him touching me…at night when… Mama was asleep. A mother should protect her children, like I tried to protect you, boy, and didn't I do a good job on you, Billy boy, didn't I save you from hard knocks in life. From a father who cheated on us, who abandoned us, and, from that *Elizabeth* vixen. Didn't I, Billy? Didn't I, boy?'

'Mother, I need to know…did you deal with your father the same way you dealt with my dad?'

'No! *She* did it. *She* took over and picked up the paperweight. *She* did it! It wasn't *me.* You *must* believe me, son. I warned her not to but she said it would be a secret between us and no one would find out as long as we kept our little secret.'

Billy looked to Rosa for support, for an explanation. Rosa thought she understood the old woman's dilemma when the little child in Meredith's body lay on the bed and related her ordeal beginning at five years. Now it seemed a third party had entered the scene, had become more prominent and now dominated. She was confused by the new arrival also but quickly reached the conclusion that Meredith Turner had been plagued with multiple personalities most of her life.

Rosa was no expert but she imagined the child *before* the ordeal was the real Meredith, the pleasant child; the child *after* the abuse emerged damaged and later enjoyed the incestuous relationship, her father having convinced her she was 'special'. Perhaps at seventeen years of age, she struck her father down in self-defense, an act that said she would no longer tolerate the abuse on her person.

No more would she see her mother beaten by a monster. The third character, she believed, was invented to support the actions of the damaged area of Meredith's persona.

Rosa didn't know how to answer Billy. How would he understand the awful struggle his mother had, every day, with raging hatred for what happened to her as a child, trying to be the mother to her son that her own mother wasn't to her; trying to cover up the crimes against her by making pacts, by little secrets, by hiding the truth, by reinventing the truth when things got suspicious. And now, by blatantly denying personal responsibility she let the other person, the vengeful side to her personality, take the blame.

Rosa stuttered out the horrible truth in simple terms. 'I think…I think your mother has… an inner struggle, Billy.' Meredith dropped her eyes to the ground and turned away ashamedly, like the child caught taking the chocolate biscuits without approval. Plinter took note of her body language and Rosa's insinuations. He admired how the mind of Rosa Tavistock worked, the care with which she went about her answer. She spoke to Billy but she aimed at Meredith.

'I think your mother feels guilty about what happened in this field…but it's hard for her to break free. Her father…he came after her…again. She fought him…and to protect herself…she…she found she had a stone in her hand. Would you…would you like to tell Billy… what happened next, Meredith?'

There was an extended pause. The sound of an animal rushing through the long grass broke the silence and made the pause a longer one. Piercing squeals from a feral cat tore into their ears. The thrashing came to an abrupt halt; the last guttural noises from the predator subsided, replaced by the faint rustling of leaves as the cat disappeared into the night with his supper between his teeth.

Billy said 'feral' out loud, with contempt; he was fond of Cassandra in the early days. They'd had her from a kitten but he believed the once lovely creature left because it was more bearable to live and manage survival outdoors than to stay near his mother. His one-word outburst became a cue for his mother to respond. Meredith volunteered to reply, taking Rosa into her confidence.

'He fell down, Mama. He didn't move. There was blood on his head…running down his face. So I bent over him and checked his breathing. He was face down so I rolled him over. His eyes were open. They were dead, dead and still *staring* at me. I couldn't bear to see his eyes…so I rolled him back over and went behind the oak tree. I think I must have cried for…for an hour. But when I checked my watch, it was only ten minutes.

'Then Sally came by. She was waiting in the bushes close by. She advised me what to do. I was *so glad* she came back. How she ever survived the fire I don't know. I told her I was sorry I treated her so badly when we were younger. We used to swap secrets in my bedroom, but she said I was doing things that were wrong. I told her she was interfering in my happiness. She said she cared for me. But I threw her into the fire. She forgave me instantly and said I should bring the tractor around. I was always a strong girl and so was Sally.

'Together, we lifted him onto the seat. I drove the tractor along the slope near the grey shed and pushed and dragged him down the slope. It was easy for me to turn the wheels and touch the throttle. I jumped out and watched it topple over. Sally and I waited until it completely stopped. It landed squarely on his body; only his head was visible. She gave me the stone I hit him with and told me to put dirt all over it and rub it well in, except where the bloodstain was. She told me later it was to erase my fingerprints. I lifted his head and put the bloodied side up and let his head press the stone into the soil...'

Plinter couldn't help being a policeman, Ben thought privately, at a time when he should have *just listened.* Ben tugged at his sleeve but the question was already out. Rosa gave him a scornful look; Plinter didn't see it, however.

'Was that when you went back to make the sandwiches and place them next to his head?'

Meredith looked at him, puzzled. Rosa regained her attention when she said, 'Pay no heed to *him*; he's a *man*, he wouldn't understand. Men just never seem to know when to be quiet. Just when a hurt woman is *spilling her guts* and offloading years of pent-up anger and remorse and guilt, she needs a *kindly* ear.' Rosa's spiel gave the policeman the warning. He bowed to it and apologised to Meredith.

The old woman fidgeted for a minute. Rosa didn't know which party would emerge. She hoped it was the little five-year-old, the real victim of her father. The other parties were by-products of a fragile mind, defenders of the psyche of a young child tortured by abuse, deceived by exploitation, and betrayed by the very ones who fashioned love into crass selfishness and affection into lust. Her parents had turned her into a copy of themselves.

'Meredith, did Sally come back again? Did she come to help you on the night of the school dance?'

'William came back to take Billy away from me. Sally said I mustn't let that happen. Mothers should protect their children, she said. He pretended he only wanted to see his son, but he was lying. *All men are liars, Mama.* He was heading for the door. Sally handed me the paperweight and...Sally took my arm and brought it down on his head. I'm tired now. Sally wants to go now.'

Ben rushed to catch Billy. His friend swayed, his eyes rolled. Ben was unable to get there in time. The bandages soaked up more blood; Ben didn't know this until his hand felt soggy. Rosa appealed to Meredith to call an ambulance for her son. The woman gave out an emphatic No! She pulled her wiry frame up onto the digger and switched on the engine. It growled in angry response. She pointed the gun at them and warned them that running would be fatal.

In several sweeps of the blade, she had scooped up the soft loam and deepened the hole by another foot. Feverishly she swung the machine back and forth until she was satisfied with the depth, and having climbed down she ordered the two men closer to the pit. She looked disappointingly at Billy and said out loud, 'You'll live', and to Rosa, she said: 'You will have to live with us, Mama, and share our little secret one more time.'

Plinter and Ben moved tentatively, each determined to take the first chance to grab the old woman. Meredith backed along the hole as they came forward. She poked Plinter in the stomach and slowly swung in an arc until the two men had their backs to the long pit. Ben glanced into the black hole and steadied himself on the brink. Rosa kept her voice soft and spoke like the mother Meredith really wanted. She yearned for the hurt little girl to step forward and dominate.

'Meredith, you can't go on like this anymore. Sally doesn't care about you. She is looking after her *own* interests. You can trust *me* now. I'm back to help this time. Give me the gun and we'll talk. We'll tell people who care, people who can sort out this whole mess—'

'—don't you dare make promises you can't keep, Mama! I wanted to be a nurse but you had to get sick after father died, didn't you? First, *he* wouldn't let me go nursing, and when he was dead YOU stopped me before I had completed my first year! I had to stop to nurse YOU for years, and then you decided you'd had enough of life! You missed the man you married, didn't you, you whiner! It was too late for me then, wasn't it?

'You were fifty years old, in the prime of your life and you wanted out! I was twenty-seven, living in a big house, on a huge property and the only company I had was that whingeing, five-year-old brat who couldn't, who *wouldn't* say NO to her father. I had to keep calling Sally back to help me deal with her! Sally made me promise not to throw her out again. Do you know what it's like trying to reason with a five-year-old, day in day out; complaining about what her father had supposedly done to her? Year after year?

'And when she was ten, she decided she started to li-ike it. She was *special* now, while I was taking the brunt of complaints from my mother, who said her husband wasn't tre-eating her very well, saying she had bruises to pro-oove it. Trouble was—my mother was *jealous*! Then at fourteen, the little vixen claimed she was a woman! I ask you! At sixteen, she was bellyaching because her father fancied the au pair.

'I asked Sally to help me deal with that drama, too. At seventeen, the poor dejected teenager said she had had enough of him and told mother what was going on. For the first time in a long time, we were a team. Sally suggested revenge. It was unanimous. Afterwards, I had to threaten my mother to say exactly what I wanted her to say in order to fool the policeman who came with his trivial questions. Questions about sandwiches! How *stupid* do men get! I told him the crows must have eaten it. I was hardly going to tell him what Sally did, now was I?' She finished with a harsh, throaty growl; a fixed gaze filled her wild eyes.

Rosa knew she had lost her. She had tried to appeal to the wounded child trapped between two powerful characters, and failed.

Billy gave out a low groan. Meredith looked down at him. Plinter made a sudden move. 'You stay where you are,' the hag bellowed and raised the rifle. He kept coming at her. Billy brought his shoe hard against his mother's ankle; a round was fired. Plinter grabbed his arm, staggered and fell to his knees. Ben got in front of Plinter to protect him and reached for the rifle in Meredith's flailing hands. Rosa screamed sharply. Billy struck again, only harder, bringing his foot sharply against her legs. Meredith shot forward like a stone from a catapult. The gun went off again; the bullet got lost in the branches of the oak tree. Ben went to grab her but the old woman continued on past him and, unable to control the momentum, she plunged into the hole. She didn't move.

No one breathed. Plinter and Ben gazed into the grave. Rosa picked up the torch and shone it into the blackness. They heard Billy ask, 'Is she dead?' Rosa shone the light onto the old woman's face. She thought she glimpsed a suggestion of serenity in the wrinkled skin. Did her mouth have a new shape to it, she queried.

Then she saw a slight movement from the old fingers. 'No Billy, she's…not dead.'

Ben jumped into the hole and raised her to ground level. Rosa touched his jacket. He quickly pulled it off his torso and laid it across Meredith's petite figure. She murmured something. No one knew what. The policeman panted. Billy sobbed quietly. Rosa was unable to hold her emotions in anymore. She leaned on her son's shoulder and wept out all of the pain the last two days had brought. Thoroughly sapped of mental and physical energy, she slid onto her knees.

Ben gazed around and surveyed the aftermath. It struck him that he was the last man standing. Plinter was down injured. Billy was…well, he was injured in more ways than one. And Meredith? How could her injuries be described? Someone more qualified than he could assess the old woman. And Rosa, his dear mother? She was down, drained emotionally and exhausted physically. His thoughts went to Elizabeth. 'My *poor, poor* Elizabeth.' She, too, was down. On a hospital bed, her life on a knife-edge. And Stephie? She was gone. Gone forever. And the little person in Elizabeth's womb? What would *its* fate be?

The doctor had promised he and his team would do their very best. But he could read between the lines. The mouth spoke but the eyes did the translation. Sandlier said, in the softest way he could muster, that Elizabeth was alive only for the baby, that she was the bravest fighter he had ever encountered. 'Against a horrible disease that ravages her body, Ben, I haven't seen such a stand…as she has taken. She has more grit than the toughest strongman! I have to prepare you…you have to prepare yourself for the outcome…

For a moment, Ben was back in his isolation, his chosen seclusion, locked away from all outsiders. He felt it was happening all over again. Instead of Stephie drowning in an angry ocean and Elizabeth presumed dead, now it was their unborn child drowning in amniotic fluid and Elizabeth sentenced to death by a deadly disease, confirmed by professional healers. Nothing had changed. He wanted to shout into the night and pour out all his dissatisfaction with the justices, to anyone who cared to listen.

For the second time, he silently agreed that nothing had changed. He drew his mother to her feet and together they leaned on each other exactly like this less than two days ago, in his kitchen. He softly cried along with her.

In the background, Plinter said, 'Yes, I need two ambulances here yesterday! And get Sue Brighton on the line…'

Twenty-Three

Ben didn't quite know why he was in this building. With all he went through over the past months, it was difficult to come to terms with his new relationship with Billy. He agreed with his mother that it was the proper thing to do. One last time.

A tall, strong male nurse built like a wrestler unlocked the door and let Ben in. He stood by the door with his arms folded across his chest much like a bouncer does outside a night club, on the lookout for *unwelcome* characters. Now here's a man who takes his job seriously, Ben thought, the consummate bodyguard protecting the public against dangerous inmates and the inmates against themselves. He swung the door to shut it behind him but a firm stare from the big man with bulging biceps made it plain the door must be left open.

The inmate sat in a chair facing the window. The heavy bars did little to block the view of the colourful summer garden beds, garlanded with pansies of every hue. His eyes were fixed as if in a trance. Nor did he see the cherry blossom tree flaunt its beauty of pink against a clear blue sky, nor the old man in the wheelchair being pushed by his youngest daughter who stopped briefly to wipe the spittle off his chin.

All his visions were in his head, his thoughts jumping frantically from one scene to the next in the hope of settling on a happy memory. The earliest memory he could recall was when he was six, or was it seven? It was with his father…he was quite sure it was his father…but he couldn't remember why it was pleasant. There were no memories now, none, not now. There were none after he left for Scotland. And none since then. None since he dug that hole. None since he sealed the grave with concrete…

He heard his name. It sounded like the voice of someone familiar, a friendly sound.

'Hey, Billy! It's me. Ben.'

The patient shook his head as if to clear it of misery and take in this new sound. Ben stood between him and the scenery framed in the window.

'Hello Billy, how are you doing?' Billy perked up on recognising his pal. Then the guilt set in. He kept his head low when responding.

'How can you come here knowing the trouble I caused you? *I'd* be the last person I'd want to see.'

'I know your mother treated you badly, Billy, it's not all your fault. Did you have a session today?'

'Yeah. It was hard going.'

'Was it helpful, though?'

'Doc said I have to…to learn to take…responsibility for myself.'

'He'll teach you how to, Billy. You'll come through, I'm sure you will.'

Billy worked hard to look at Ben. 'I'm…I'm really sorry about…about your baby. The deck was…was slippery…and…and Elizabeth was screaming at me, just like my mother screams at me. I can't handle that. Do…do you…do you think Elizabeth might…might come into…to…to visit me? I wouldn't blame her if she didn't want to see me again. I'm…I'm not responsible anymore. Doc said he'd help me, though.'

'I'm sure he will, Billy, I *know* he will'

There was an extended pause. Ben used the time to look around the room. It was sparsely furnished; a single bed with iron ends, prison style, blankets tucked in, hospital style, and one pillow for minimum comfort. A tall, but narrow, grey metal cupboard with one shelf up high and no door, stood stark against the white wall, a cabinet with enough space to accommodate the least amount of clothing required. A pair of slippers sat neatly on the bottom, waiting for their owner to cover his bare feet.

Certainly, a huge change from Billy's former lifestyle. It was strange to see him and not be surrounded by bits of machinery, nuts and bolts, spanners and screwdrivers and cordless tools. His hands were clean, too. No oil stains on his shirt, no dirty fingernails and definitely no smudges where he rubbed his nose and cheeks. His hair was neatly combed. Ben wondered if he missed fixing things; he certainly didn't give any signs of regret.

'I hope I didn't cause… too much damage to your…eh, bathroom window, Ben?'

'No, no, that's OK. It was easily fixed. I'm glad you didn't cut your hand too badly.'

'I was looking for…for the letter. I…suppose you know that…?'

'Oh, you mean the letter your father wrote. The love letter?'

'My dad loved her but she…she went crazy. He *had* to leave… you know that, Ben, don't you?'

'Oh yes! She was a nightmare. Any man would have left.'

Another pause, a short one, then Billy continued as though he had thought hard to organise another question.

'Was…was there much…much left when they…dug him up?'

Ben thought about the thick plastic William Turner was wrapped in and gave a half answer.

'Well, let me put it this way, Billy, there was an awful smell afterwards.'

Billy seemed indifferent to the information and offered his opinion in the clearest of terms.

'You know, Ben, I always thought that one day the floor would sag where I laid him, even as I spread the cement above him. Dead bodies break down and sooner or later the ground would sink, and there they were. The cracks appeared; the room reeked like I killed a cow and left it to rot!'

'You can say that again. It stank to the high heavens.'

'Did you know it was my idea to hide the smell by putting all sorts of chemicals in the storeroom? I had a ball, I tell you! Diesel and old paint, weed killer, even cow manure. I…I *think* it was my idea. Mother said the ether helped as well. And the fish heads. ' He laughed out loud and went quiet. Ben felt Billy had gone somewhere else. He didn't expect him to come back. He did, with a little more animation and feeling.

'I took care of the stroller for Elizabeth. She can use it again if she wants to. And the little blanket, too. And, *of course*, the pillow. You can't expect a baby to lie down without a soft pillow, now can you?'

'Yeah, Billy, we found them in the wardrobe…in Elizabeth's room…where you kept her.'

'I suppose you found the dustbin lid too. *That* was a dirty trick mother played on you…switching the lids, I mean. She could have got you into a lot of trouble, Ben. Don't tell anyone, but I went back and set fire to the garbage bin. A cup of petrol and whoosh! Up it went! I didn't tell mother so what she doesn't know won't hurt her. Don't you agree, Ben, don't you?'

'You might have something there, Billy. Hey, I've got to go now. Things to do, places to go!'

Billy went quiet again. Ben put his hand out but Billy ignored it. The patient didn't lift his eyes as Ben turned towards the door. Partway, Billy said, 'I have something for you.' Ben returned to his side. Without looking up Billy pointed to the narrow cupboard and said, 'There, on the top shelf. They are for you, if you want them. They mean nothing to me; they never have.'

Ben picked up the four pages, typed on A4 paper and somewhat yellowed. He strode down the corridor and through to the reception area. A flashback of Billy stepping in between him and the school bully to protect him lingered for a moment. He savoured the memory and quickly discarded it.

Ben carried on into the sunshine. Memories of Billy trying to get his head around the relationship between the diameter of a circle and the circumference brought a smile, and then a little sadness. He recalled the first time they met in the schoolyard and how quickly they became solid friends.

Ben climbed into his car and aimed for the steel gates that took him away from the mental institution. As he flicked the right indicator it hit him for the first time that Billy didn't ask about his mother or her well-being. Not once. He didn't ask what she said to the judge or what the judge said to her. Nor did he want to know where she was or what she did.

It may have not even registered on his emotional gauge that she might be unhappy in her new home or that she pined for her son in the night. It may not have crossed his mind that she danced around in small circles chanting songs of her own composition in a high-pitch voice, in a small room where the sharpest object was a dome-shaped door handle. Maybe, Ben decided, *maybe* Billy had finally eradicated her influence from his psyche.

He never spoke to Billy again.

Epilogue

On his way home, he could think of nothing else but the sparkling blue awaited him. It was almost two weeks since the doctors gave the go-her to come home. Rosa said she'd look after her while he went to see knew she was in good hands in his mother's care. She was always the For as long as he could remember, his mother was rock solid.

Elizabeth was the joy of his existence. Her attitude, her appro wonder of life had given him a different view of matters outside ar While he appreciated the design in things living, she opened his beauty of wildlife; the magic of the seasons, exhibiting their co openly; the ongoing cycle of rain and rivers and oceans and sun to basic needs of water and food, to prolong life. She helped him come c side of what he thought was an interminable winter; that part of hi hopelessness was king and survival seemed remote.

Rosa kissed her son to welcome him back. She pointed upsta quietly, 'She's asleep. I've just settled her down.' Ben said he' anyway. He said he had missed her; he'd be like a mouse. affectionately.

Ben entered the room to find her wide awake examining the l the ceiling light. He leaned over her and kissed her eyes. 'Yo *beautiful*, Elle. You would have given your mother *so much* pleasu